Praise for the Work of Patricia Harman

The Runaway Midwife

"In *The Runaway Midwife,* Patricia Harman delivers a fast-paced, engrossing tale of a woman on the run from a bad marriage and an estranged daughter. . . . The characters are convincing, the plot tight, and the conclusion convincing."

—Roberta Rich, author of *The Midwife of Venice*

"From the mountains of West Virginia to a remote island in Lake Erie, *The Runaway Midwife* takes us on a journey from loss, grief, and guilt to one of love, forgiveness, and redemption. Patricia Harman deftly tells the story of midwife Clara Perry, who discovers that she, too, can soar like the island's wild swans."

—*New York Times* bestselling author Mary McNear

The Reluctant Midwife

"An entrancing saga of birth and rebirth, of people you come to love as they confront loss and guilt, poverty and fear, silence and doubt. In caring for a devastated land and community, Nurse Becky Myers and the emotionally shattered Dr. Isaac Blum discover the unexpected, nearly inexplicable healing power of West Virginia's ancient mountains."

—Pamela Schoenewaldt, author of *Swimming in the Moon*

"Who better to write of midwifery, the powerful bond between birthing women and their midwives, and the bond between those providing care to birthing families, than Patricia Harman? [. . .] Laced with drama, accurate detail, and imagination, *The Reluctant Midwife* will educate and engage readers eager to further explore Hope River."

—Penny Armstrong, author of the classic *A Midwife's Story*

"This title is sure to appeal to fans of American historical fiction or anyone else looking ⸻⸻⸻⸻⸻⸻⸻⸻⸻⸻⸻n, spunk, and community spirit." *Library Journal*

The Runaway Midwife

Also by Patricia Harman

Lost on Hope Island: The Amazing Tale
of the Little Goat Midwives
The Reluctant Midwife
The Midwife of Hope River
Arms Wide Open: A Midwife's Journey
The Blue Cotton Gown: A Midwife's Memoir

The Runaway Midwife

Patricia Harman

wm

WILLIAM MORROW
An Imprint of HarperCollins*Publishers*

HarperCollins
P U B L I S H E R S
——— Since 1817 ———

HarperCollins books may be purchased for educational, business, or sales promotional use. For information, please email the Special Markets Department at SPsales@harpercollins.com.

FIRST EDITION

Designed by Diahann Sturge

Library of Congress Cataloging-in-Publication Data has been applied for.

ISBN 978-0-06-246730-0
ISBN 978-0-06-265961-3 (library edition)

17 18 19 20 21   RRD   10 9 8 7 6 5 4 3 2

Dedicated to R.P.
(my beautiful, brilliant, beloved friend)
Wherever She Flies

Acknowledgments

First, I thank my family (especially my husband, Tom) for their
continuing support of my writing.
Next, I thank my early readers, midwives and friends,
for their appreciation and insight.
Poor Angus, the Canadian Celtic/Folk band, allowed me to use
some of their lyrics and I thank them for their inspiring music.
Finally, I thank my editor, Lucia Macro, and her staff
for their support and guidance,
and my agent, Elisabeth Weed,
for her faith in the book.

And now, a note to my dear readers:
Life is not easy.
What we need to remember is that no matter how dark the
night,
the sun will rise in the morning
. . . and there is joy.

Prologue

Next to the dead man lying on the beach, mostly covered with snow, is a dead swan, its neck twisted at a strange angle.

A woman stands staring, not sure who she feels sadder for, the man or the bird. Then she turns for the cottage, hoping the waves of Lake Erie will take them away.

It's not that she's an unfeeling woman; she's just felt too much.

Winter

CHAPTER 1

Flying

The sun, a red eye, is just going down as we speed across the frozen waters of Lake Erie. Even with the ski mask on, my face is freezing and my eyes run with tears, but whether from the cold or my damaged heart, I don't know.

I think about my daughter. I think about my patient Robyn who died just days ago. I think about my friend Karen whose unexplained suicide has left me crippled. I think about the sudden turn my life has taken.

"This is safe, right?" I yell up to my driver as we bump over rough ice. "The cabbie said some men on snowmobiles went through and drowned around Middle Island last week." Lenny stops, turns on the Ski-Doo headlights and puts on a pair of clear goggles.

"Those guys were yahoos—didn't watch where they were going. You can tell by the surface where the ice is weak . . . You have someone meeting you on Seagull Island? I can't stay around."

"Yes," I lie. "Just leave me on the west side of Gull Point. You know where that is? There's supposed to be a little cove there. They'll pick me up on the road."

In truth there are no friends. It's just me and the ice and the snow and the now darkening sky. Big cumulous clouds sweep past the stars and for a minute I stretch out my arms just to feel like I'm flying.

"Hold on now!" Lenny suddenly warns before he makes a sharp turn around a pyramid of ice that juts up from surface.

"Yikes!" is all I can say.

Finally the half moon rises and illuminates the sky. The words to an old song Karen used to sing come to me . . . *I see the bad moon arising, I see trouble on the way.* But trouble has already found me.

We hit a tilted sheet of silver at an angle and take air as we crash. "Whoa!" yells my driver, and when I grab him around the waist, I find that Lenny's broad back in his black snowmobile suit shelters me from the wind. (He might be an outlaw, but he's a warm outlaw.)

"Is that the island?" I shout to my escort as a low dark shape rises up on the horizon.

"Yeah."

"How much further?" We hit ripples and bounce up and down.

"Another twenty minutes."

A half mile from shore, Lenny cuts the lights and moves in slowly.

"This is Gull Point," he says in a whisper. "Because of ice slabs that have blown in, I can't get any closer, so you'll have to walk, but tread lightly.

"Once you're on the beach, if you go along that path through the woods, you'll come to the road." He indicates an open place in the shadows a short distance away. "I hate to leave you like this, but I can't afford to get caught by Customs or seen by any of the locals." He helps me off and I'm embarrassed to say I have to hold on to him until my legs get their strength.

"Thank you, Lenny. I don't want you to get in any trouble.

I really appreciate your help and I'll be fine. I really will. I'll be fine."

It's colder here than in Ohio and I shiver as Lenny gets back on the snowmobile. "Call me if you need anything," he says. Then I'm alone, but I'm not fine. Not fine at all.

Canada

I pause on the beach, watching until the light on the snowmobile fades into darkness, then I shake myself to get moving. The sooner I get to shelter, the sooner I'll be warm, but it's hard going.

Lenny had said there were cakes of ice, but these are blocks of frozen lake water the size of doghouses and bathtubs. Twice I slip and fall and one time my backpack comes off, but I hold on to my tears.

When I finally get to land, I mentally celebrate. I'm in Canada without a passport. I made it! But the celebration doesn't last long. Once off the beach, I'm surprised to find the snow is twelve inches deep, and even with my flashlight I lose the trail and have to retrace my path; then I end up in the brush, snag my snowmobile suit and cut up my face. Finally I make it to the unplowed road and throw down my heavy pack.

There are no sounds of human habitation, no car noises, no barking dogs. There are no lights in the distance. Why would any sane woman do this?

MOST PEOPLE WON'T understand why I ran, though some will, the ones who have been there. You're going about your life, coping as well as you can, dangling from a silk thread in the wind, and then one day the line snaps. The breaking point for me was my patient's death.

But it wasn't just that. The line was already fraying. My best friend, Karen, had committed suicide six months earlier. My husband, Richard, was screwing around. My nineteen-year-old daughter, living on the other side of the globe, wasn't answering my phone calls or texts. And then my patient Robyn called out my name as she died. "Clara!" she called.

She called for me and I wasn't there.

CHAPTER 2

Grenade

It was nine o'clock Monday morning, three days ago, when I dropped into hell . . .

"Sorry I'm late," I tell my nurse-midwife partner, Linda, as I slip in the back door of Mountain-Laurel Women's Health Clinic in Torrington, West Virginia, and throw my briefcase on a chair in my office.

"You'll wish you were even later when you hear the news." She closes the door. "Sit down."

I take off my jacket and do what she says.

"A patient died at a home birth last night." She cuts right to the chase. "They've taken her body to Pittsburgh for an autopsy. The baby is fine . . . but the woman was Robyn . . . your patient Robyn Layton. She hemorrhaged and died before the emergency squad could get to her."

Her mouth is still moving, but I can't hear a word. A grenade has gone off and I'm deaf from the impact.

"Are you listening? A sheriff's detective has contacted the hospital and Dr. Agata, the administrator, wants to see you . . . Are you listening? Are you getting this?"

My head is in my hands and I feel sick to my stomach. I pull the wastebasket over but nothing comes up.

"Robyn is dead?" I hear my voice come out of a tunnel. "She can't be. She was fine when I left her. I didn't stay for the delivery. I was only there for a short while to give labor support. She knew from her first OB visit that the hospital doesn't allow us to do home births anymore. I left her with the doula Sasha Tucker. Robyn is dead?"

WORKING ON AUTOMATIC pilot, I stumble into the exam room to see my first patient, but it's no good. I go through the motions, asking how she feels, is she eating well, any contractions? I measure the uterus, listen to the fetal heartbeat, tell her to return in two weeks and hurry out.

"Linda, I can't do this. I have to go home. Tell Agata I'll call him tomorrow. Tell the secretaries to cancel my patients. Say I'm sick. Say it's a terrible migraine."

"But Agata wants to see you today! *He insisted.* This is serious. They're talking about charging you with medical negligence."

"I'm sorry, I have to go home." She stands in my way, but I grab my coat and briefcase and push past her, tears running down my face.

I need to call Sasha, find out what happened. *Poor Mike! Poor little kids! Poor Robyn!*

But Robyn is dead . . .

Sasha

In the parking lot, I sit in my cold Volvo for a moment, drying my tears, and then find the doula's number on my cell and arrange to meet her at a café in Oneida, halfway between Torrington and her home near Liberty.

As I drive into the mountains, I recall the last prenatal visit I had with Robyn less than a week ago. Everything was fine; baby head down and ready to go. Cervix already four centimeters dilated. Blood pressure and all other vital signs normal.

Mike was at the visit as well as the kids. They brought me a quart jar of honey from their honeybees and drawings the little girls had made of what they thought the new baby would look like.

Robyn and Mike had always been two of my favorite patients. Six years ago, before the hospital got the new CEO, I'd delivered baby Wren at their farm near Hog Back Mountain and three years later, their second daughter, Sparrow. Now Robyn is dead? It didn't seem possible.

Since Karen's suicide, I'll admit, I haven't been myself. There's a hole in my heart and my brain's fallen into it. Now I wonder if Robyn died because of something I missed.

SASHA TUCKER, MOTHER of five, all born at home, gets to the Sunflower Café before me. The doula, with disheveled long blond hair and dark circles under her eyes, is a mess and I can tell she's been crying.

We both order tea. The waiter, a longhaired guy wearing jeans and a T-shirt that says CELEBRATE LIFE, offers us lunch, but neither of us can eat. I can barely swallow.

"So, what happened?" I whisper when he walks away. "Robyn was low risk. I helped her have two babies at home before. She was as healthy as they get, an organic farmer for God's sake! Everything was fine when I left her last night."

Sasha's hands tremble as she chews on her fingernail. "Before you were out of the driveway, Robyn had an urge to push . . . Just like you told me, she was entering second stage."

Then the doula describes the birth so dramatically I feel like I'm there . . .

"A FEW MINUTES after you pulled out of the drive, Robyn wanted to squat and Mike and I assisted her into position. Her water still hadn't broken and I was excited that the baby might be born in the caul . . ." Sasha takes a sip of her peppermint tea then puts the mug down.

"'Push, Robyn,' I say. 'Push gently, your baby's almost here.' Everything was so peaceful with the votive candles on the dresser, the grandmother and the two little girls sitting in the rocking chair . . . but all of a sudden Robyn clutches her chest. 'I can't breathe,' she says.

"Then all hell breaks loose. The amniotic sac bursts and there's blood everywhere. All I can think is . . . maybe she wasn't fully dilated and her cervix ripped, but there's nothing I can do until the baby is out.

"I hear the grandmother gasp. Mike is pacing back and forth, flapping his arms like a stork, but Robyn has her eyes closed. She hasn't looked down. She thinks it's just her water pouring out of her. I swipe some oil around the perineum and order her to keep pushing. 'It's coming now, Robyn. Your baby is about to be born.'"

To get Sasha to stop her rush of words, I hold up my hand like a traffic cop. "Was the baby okay?"

"Yeah, fit as a fiddle, thank God . . . I cut the cord and hand him to the grandma, but I can't get the blood to stop and Robyn keeps saying, 'I can't breathe! I can't breathe!'

"Oh, Clara. I wish you'd been there. I was so scared. All that red all over the floor . . . I've never seen anything like it.

"I get Robyn up on the bed and do everything I can think of," the doula continues. "I massage the uterus and give her a swig of black cohosh to drink. 'Call 911!' I shout and the grandmother runs out of the room with the baby and the two little girls.

"My mind is jumping around like a squirrel. *Maybe she has a fibroid uterus. Maybe she has a clotting disorder. Why is she bleeding?* I deliver the placenta and the uterus is rock hard. . . . Then all of a sudden, Robyn pushes herself up on her elbows. She sees all the blood. *'Clara!'* she cries. I guess she got confused and thought I was you."

"She called my name?"

"Yes, *'Clara! I can't breathe! The pain! The pain!'* She holds her chest. Her face is gray, blue around the lips.

" 'I can't breathe!' she says again. Then Robyn's eyes roll back in her head. *Damn!* I think. *Is she seizing? Is she going into shock? Is she having a heart attack?*

" 'Stay with us, Robyn. Stay with us . . . Mike, talk to her!'

"*Blood is still pouring out of her. I have to get it to stop!* I reglove and look for a vaginal or cervical tear, but there's nothing and the blood keeps coming. Finally we hear the ambulance siren in the distance.

"*God help us. God help us!* I pray, but either God doesn't hear or he has other plans, because as I watch the red coming out of Robyn, it slows to a trickle and then stops."

The doula tells me how she did CPR. She describes the look on the paramedics' faces when they came into the room and saw all the blood. She explains how the medics started two IV lines, ran them wide open and continued cardio-pulmonary resuscitation on the way to the hospital, despite the fact that it was clear *Robyn was gone.*

SASHA AND I hug in the parking lot. "It will be okay," I tell her. "You did everything you could." But in fact, I don't think it will be okay at all.

For sure, the death will get in the papers. Possibly we'll be arrested. Most likely I'll get sued and lose my nurse-midwife license. The lawyers won't go after Sasha because she doesn't carry malpractice insurance and she doesn't have a state license to take away. She's just a mom helping other moms.

Before we part, I'd ask the doula if she thinks I should go by Robyn's house, try to clean up the mess and give Mike some support, but she says no.

She'd stayed for three hours with the little girls until he and his mother-in-law got back from the hospital, and she'd already scrubbed the floor and changed the linen. Mike was still in shock and family and friends were already arriving from Charleston. She said I should go tomorrow.

Breakdown

Driving slowly, I end up in the county park out by Crocker's Creek and try to call my daughter, Jessie, a sophomore at Torrington State University, who's studying with the sociology department in Australia. It's been three weeks since I talked to her. Once the two of us were close, but this last year a sinkhole has opened between us.

Today I really need to hear her voice, and when her cell is answered on the other side of the globe I get excited. "Jessie. Jessie. It's Mom . . ." Then the line goes dead. Tears come to my eyes again.

I stare at the low gray clouds, now spitting snow while I finger the silver medallion on a silver chain my friend Karen gave me. MIDWIVES HELP PEOPLE OUT, it says, above the imprint of two tiny feet. *I didn't do much to help Robyn.*

I suppose I should call my husband, before he reads about the home-birth death in the paper, but when I dial Richard's number he doesn't answer and, suddenly exhausted, I don't leave a message. It isn't just the patient's death and fear of getting blamed for it . . . it's Robyn's death *and* everything else.

OKAY, SO LET'S imagine this for one moment. Your best friend and ob-gyn physician colleague commits suicide by jumping off the side of a cruise ship and no one knows why. You feel responsible. You talked to Dr. Karen Cross every day. You're a sensitive person, for God's sake. Shouldn't you have known the pain she was in?

Then three months later you find out your husband is cheating on you *again*. You've been to couple's counseling before and the counselor determined it's a form of addiction. This time, still grieving your friend and walking around like a ghost of yourself, you don't have the strength to deal with it.

And then your OB patient dies and you're blamed?

Imagine all this for a minute. Sound impossible? I can tell you it isn't.

IN THE OLD days, they called it a nervous breakdown. I don't know what it's called now . . . but the challenges before me— confront my bastard of a husband, argue with the hospital CEO about my role in my patient's death, face a possible arrest for medical negligence all the while grieving both Karen and Robyn—overwhelm me.

I'm at the point where ordinary sensible solutions like counseling, antidepressants and divorce, things I would recommend to my patients, seem like climbing Mount Everest with two broken legs.

Sitting in the Volvo, staring out at the creek where a solitary mallard circles in the rushing brown water, I see only two choices: get on a cruise ship and follow my friend Dr. Karen Cross into the dark Atlantic . . . or flee.

CHAPTER 3

Liar

The first lie I tell is at the Mountain State Federal Bank and my boldness shocks me.

"My husband and I are buying a fixer-upper over by the university and we can get it cheap if we bring the down payment to the owners in cash," I explain in a hushed voice to the young teller behind the counter. His name tag says Matt and he has one gold earring.

"The sellers *insist on cash*. They're old and don't trust anyone," I rattle on, elaborating more than I need to. "Do you have $10,000 on hand?"

"Can I see some ID, Mrs. Perry? We don't usually get requests for cash in this amount and I'll have to ask my manager."

"That's fine. It's Doug Frazier, isn't it? I was his wife's nurse-midwife when she had her second baby." Matt leaves and shows the withdrawal slip and my driver's license to a tall man with a little goatee. The man studies the slip and comes over.

"How about a bank check, Clara?" Doug asks pleasantly. "That would be safer."

"No, I need cash. I don't want to lose this house. My husband is over there waiting." Hot sweat trickles down between my breasts. (This is a joint account and I'm worried they'll want Richard's signature.)

"How's the baby?" I ask just to be friendly, but I can't remember if it's a boy or a girl.

"Growing like a weed." He smiles and initials the withdrawal slip. "It's almost closing time. We can replace what you're taking with more cash from the main branch tomorrow." Then he goes back to his desk and Matt takes me into a glass enclosure next to the vault. "Wait here."

I glance at my watch. It's already four and I want to get out of town before Richard gets home. He's interviewing a new candidate for the biology department today and we're supposed to take her out for dinner. When the teller returns, he hands me a manila envelope.

"Is this ten thousand? I thought it would be bigger."

"Yes. There are a hundred hundred-dollar bills in a pack," the young man explains as if it ought to be obvious, so without counting, I put the money in my green L.L.Bean canvas briefcase and ask to be shown to our safety deposit box.

Matt takes a ring of keys out of his pocket and I give him my little key in the tiny red envelope. Then he allows me some privacy while I carry the family safe box to a table and unlock it.

Like Silas Marner, my philandering professor husband has been hiding his money away since he heard on NPR, back in 2008, how the whole banking system could crash in one day. He also just received a small inheritance from his aunt Ida. I don't know how much. He said it was none of my business.

There was a time Richard and I shared everything and made decisions together, but it's been years since that happened. More and more we lead separate lives, and to be honest I can't remember what it felt like to be close. All the things I loved about Richard have turned against me. His calm has been substituted with detachment. His skill in worldly matters and his ability to manage money have become a means of control. His affection for my sensitive nature has been replaced by cold scorn.

I used to be amazed by my patients who stayed in loveless marriages for convenience, but now I understand. In my case it's not the nice house or the combined income or even the children (Jessie's almost an adult). I just don't have the strength to face a contentious divorce.

And there's something else. If I use Richard's infidelity against him in court, it will come out that he's been cheating off and on for years and I knew about it. That will make me look like a fool. A small point to some, perhaps, but despite how it looks, I have my pride.

WHEN I OPEN the safety deposit box, I'm surprised to find two more bundles of hundred-dollar bills with red rubber bands around them. This could be another twenty thousand in cash, possibly more. I put them in my briefcase along with the other money. There's nothing much else in the metal container, but our daughter's birth certificate, our passports and the titles to our vehicles.

I grab the paperwork for the Volvo, then open my passport and study my photo . . . shoulder-length dark hair with a strand of gray at the temple, blue eyes, a nice enough smile with straight white teeth, a wholesome-looking person, not beautiful, but friendly-looking and kind.

The passport expires in less than a month. Too bad I didn't renew it, but then, I won't need it where I'm going and besides, it would be too easy to trace. I drop the little blue book back in the box; touch my daughter Jessie's birth certificate, saying goodbye; and snap the lid to the metal box.

Snow is blowing in sideways when I leave the bank. At the

stoplight before the entrance to the I-79, a blond woman in a blue parka stands in the median, not six feet away, holding a cardboard sign that says EVERYONE NEEDS HELP SOMETIMES.

Ordinarily Richard and I, on principle, don't give money to panhandlers. "They'll just use it for drugs or alcohol," my husband insists, but it's four in the afternoon and twenty-seven degrees out, so instead of averting my eyes, I roll down my window and hand her a twenty.

"God bless you, ma'am," the woman says, tears in her eyes. "God bless you!" It's the tears that get me. I am truly touched and think of reaching into my briefcase and giving her one of my hundred-dollar bills, but the light changes and I drive north alone.

Runaway

*A*ll night I flee through the sleet and snow, my hands like claws on the steering wheel. The blacktop is as slippery as shampoo, so I can only go about fifty miles an hour and once I see flares, flashing lights and three ambulances. A semitruck and an SUV are folded like cardboard over the guardrail and I pass at a crawl, sucking in my air. I'm not good on ice.

Around one in the morning, I pull in at a truck stop, lock the doors and sleep a few hours. Afterward, wondering if they are already looking for me, I buy coffee, drive around back, run over my laptop, stomp on my cell and throw them both in the Dumpster. Clara Perry is disappearing little by little, but it's not without cost. Every thirty miles, I break down in tears. Once I even have to stop, I'm sobbing so hard.

Pittsburgh . . . Cranberry . . . Kent . . . Akron . . . Cleveland . . . I pass the exit signs on the freeway. It crosses my mind

I should stop again to rest, maybe check in to a motel, but I keep pushing north as if a pack of gray wolves is hot on my tail.

By DAWN I pull into Sandusky, Ohio, and find a Target. It takes me a minute to unbend my body, but I slosh through the snow and into the bright white lights, where I purchase a new laptop, a prepaid cell and, because I'd left home with only what I had on, a red parka, two pairs of jeans, two pairs of black knit slacks, two sweaters, hiking boots, four colorful tees, underwear, a backpack and a soft flannel nightgown, things I'll need in the north country.

Just before checkout, I remember to buy toothpaste, shampoo and other toiletries . . . and in an effort to conceal my identity, a tube of bright red lipstick, a multicolored silk rainbow scarf, a black beret and a pair of weak off-the-rack glasses that I don't need for reading.

IT'S NOT LIKE this is the first time I'd thought of disappearing. Three years ago, when Richard had his first affair, I'd had repetitive fantasies of escaping my life, but I loved my patients and my work as a midwife, and Jessie was still in high school, so instead of leaving I went to counseling, enrolled in a yoga class and devoted myself to my family. Always responsible, it was my job to stick it out, be the good mom, hardworking midwife and loyal spouse.

What I'm doing is crazy, risking my life running like this through a near blizzard. It's the act of a madwoman, but that's who I am—a person who, wild with grief and fear, has lost her foundation and is flying like a lone swallow in front of the storm.

CHAPTER 4

Blocked

*S*andusky, Ohio, home to Cedar Point amusement park on the southern shore of Lake Erie, is a ghost town in the winter, so the rooms at the Lakeland Motel are dirt cheap and the out-of-the-way run-down establishment, with free breakfast and Wi-Fi, suits me just fine. Best of all, when I gave the night desk clerk a story about losing my pocketbook, she let me check in without ID. I used my dead friend's name. Karen Cross.

Unfortunately, Seagull Island, my destination thirty miles out in the middle of Lake Erie and just over the Canadian border, is proving harder to get to than I'd imagined. For one thing, in my fantasies it never occurred to me that the ferry wouldn't run in the winter. For another, even if it normally did, the lake's frozen over.

YEARS AGO, A lifetime ago, when I lived in Michigan, the nuns at Little Sisters of the Cross took us on an outing to Seagull Island. It was only a weekend, not a big deal, and I've never mentioned the trip to anyone, not even to Richard, so it seemed, in my day-dreams, a good place to hide.

There were six of us girls and two nuns who came into Canada across the bridge from Detroit. It was the first time I'd ever been to a foreign country. Not that Canada is very *foreign*.

The people look like us, speak the same language and watch the same TV shows. The only obvious differences are that they have strange money, there's rarely any gun violence and they cheer for unfamiliar sports teams.

We little band of nuns and female students drove in the convent van from Windsor, Ontario, to Leamington, with Sister Jean, my guardian, at the wheel, then took the ferry across to the island. I remember we had a choice, Pelee Island or Seagull, but the sisters chose Seagull because it was less well-known. I can still see the blue sky, the sparkling water and in the distance the green island getting closer.

I was fifteen, had only been at the boarding school for a year and it was my first outing since my parents died. Maybe that's why the place made such an impression. Sometimes, I think, as a person emerges from great pain, the world seems brighter, the flowers more colorful, the sound of the wind in the trees more intense.

"WHY DO YOU want to go to Seagull? There's nothing up there this time of year but ice and snow," the motel desk clerk asks. Her name is Ivy. She has jet-black short hair, a nose ring and a tattoo of a rose above her left wrist. The nose ring makes my heart sore. Jessie has a little stud in the side of her nose. I was furious when she got it, but I'd like to kiss that nose now.

Not wanting to seem too mysterious, I use the cover story I'd come up with on the drive north through the storm. "I'm a writer. I'm going there for the peace and quiet and to finish my novel."

"What's it called? Your novel . . ." Ivy asks, staring at a rerun of *M*A*S*H* on the lobby TV.

"*Alone*," I respond slowly as I try to come up with a title and plot. "It's the tale of a woman who's marooned on an island back in the 1870s."

"Huh," Ivy says, still staring at the screen. "Seagull is dead this time of year, but there are two ways to get there, Cullen Airlines in Sandusky or the new outfit, Red Hawk, in Lorain. Cullen is reliable and has been around for a long time, but Red Hawk is cheaper." She gives me a map and marks the small airports. "Don't forget you'll need your passport." That brings me up short.

"Just to get into Canada? I didn't bring one." (I picture that little blue book back in the safety deposit box. *Damn!*)

"No one used to need one, but that's changed. You know, terrorism and all . . ."

The phone rings. "Lakeland Motel, how can I help you?" Ivy answers with false sweetness. "No, ma'am, we *don't* allow pets. You can try Super 8." She hangs up, rolls her eyes as if that was the dumbest question she ever got and turns back to the TV.

"Be sure to take food. Cost you an arm and a leg if you don't," she says when a commercial comes on. "It's been years since I've been there, but I remember that much. The islanders have to bring in everything by ferry or air. You staying at one of the B and Bs?"

"No, I'm renting a cottage that I found on the Internet last night. The family that owns it lives only twenty miles away, so I drove over this morning and paid in advance. Thanks for your help, Ivy. I guess I'll try these airlines. See what they say."

I wave goodbye, but then return to the desk. "Can I ask you who cuts your hair?"

"Melissa, a few blocks east at Hair Palace. Tell her Ivy sent you. She'll give you a deal."

BACK IN MY room, I fall on the bed and bury my face in the pillow. Up until now I was running on adrenaline. Now I'm running on empty.

I open my new laptop. The photos of Seagull Haven, the little house I'd found, pop up on the vacation website. One bedroom, a kitchen, a living room with a fireplace and a two-level deck with a gazebo overlooking Lake Erie. What else could I want? Things were going so well until this hitch with the passport and I've already given three months' rent to Mrs. Nelson.

"I'LL GIVE YOU a discount, five hundred a month, because the house has been empty for almost a year," the woman told me when I talked to her in the living room of her two-story cedar house near Findlay, Ohio. A white Honda parked out front had a logo in blue that said, HOPE HOSPICE, WE CARE.

"No one has been there since my husband, Lloyd, was diagnosed with cancer. You'll have to do a little cleaning, but there's a washer and a dryer and linens in the bathroom cupboard. I can't remember if we made the bed. He'll never see the island again," she whispered. "It's pancreatic cancer. Very bad."

Mrs. Nelson was so upset, she didn't even write down my name or have me sign a contract, just took the money and gave me a hand-drawn map. It was like I was doing her a favor just to go there and check on their place.

"Wanda!" the hospice nurse called from deep in the house. "I need some help!" And the lady showed me the door.

OUTSIDE THE WIND roars in from the west again, slams against the motel and shakes the window glass. I put the pillow over my head. *Seagull Island. Seagull Island. There just has to be a way to get there!*

White Rock

*I*n the dream, Karen and I are flying, two hawks rising into a cloudless blue sky. I see her yellow beak, the ends of her wide flat wings and her beady black eyes, ringed in gold, and my heart swells. I am in love. Then we dive straight down toward the Hope River, rejoicing as the air rushes past our faces. "Kreeeee," we cry as we descend. "Kreeeeeeeeeeee! Kreeeeeeeeeeee!"

I wake, wipe my eyes and stare at the motel's popcorn ceiling. It's been almost six months since Karen's suicide. Six months of talking about her death to patients every day. There's no way around it. She was so beloved by the women she cared for that when I meet them in the exam room, I can't ignore Karen's absence, can't pretend that we aren't all still grieving.

"My name's Clara Perry, nurse-midwife," I introduce myself if the patient and I have never met. (If we know each other I just give her a hug.) "I'm sure you've heard that Dr. Karen is no longer with us." The woman's eyes get wet and I hand her a tissue, then I take one too.

"Is it true? What they said in the newspaper, that she committed suicide?"

"Yes, it appears to be. I didn't see the actual security video of her jumping from the cruise ship, but her husband did. It was awful, but he had to look to be sure. She didn't leave a note. . . . I talked to her myself that very morning by cell phone. There was no indication she was sad or distressed. She seemed completely normal. We planned to go to a concert at the university when she returned . . ."

The conversation goes on for another few minutes. The patient, like the rest of us, is still in shock, wanting to know what happened to this seemingly normal happy physician. "Could she have had cancer?" the woman asks. "Was she having an affair and something went wrong? Was her marriage breaking up?"

"I don't think so," I answer. "I don't believe so. She was my friend. She would have told me. I think she would anyway."

I REMEMBER THE dream about the hawks diving together . . . Last fall, a month or so before she left on her cruise, Karen and I hiked the trails of the White Rock State Park, built by the Civilian Conservation Corp over half a century ago and only an hour from Torrington.

We stood on the rock lookout next to the fire tower and stared out across the West Virginia mountains, row after row of ridges on fire, oak and maple at their autumn peak. At the bottom we could see the river, a ribbon of silver they call the Hope, winding down to the lake. There was no wind, not a leaf moved in the blanket of trees.

"Don't you wish we could fly?" Karen asked, as she stepped on the bottom rung of the split-rail fence that protects visitors from falling off the high cliff. She opened her arms wide and looked so joyous standing there!

"*Fly!*" she yelled, and her voice came back as an echo. "Fly . . . Fly . . . Fly . . ."

I hear it still, "Fly . . . Fly . . . Fly . . ."

Oh, Karen . . . Why did you do it?

CHAPTER 5

Red Hawk

The small airport, located along the railway tracks on Route 2, just east of Lorain, is about thirty-five miles from Sandusky. There's a low brick building that looks like a diner and a huge open metal hangar that holds two small planes. A Piper Cub, with the image of a red hawk on its tail, is strapped down on the runway and the orange windsock is stiff in the wind.

I park the Volvo next to three other vehicles, pull my beret down over my forehead, wrap the rainbow scarf around my neck and put on the glasses I bought at Target. Then, in case they're already looking for me, I lean down to wipe more mud on my license plate.

"Can I help you?" a man at the desk inside asks. He wears a blue sweater with a red hawk embroidered on the front, a handsome guy with auburn hair and a two-day growth of beard, probably an air force vet from Iraq or Afghanistan. "My name's Ben Walker, I'm one of the pilots."

"Hi. I'm trying to get to Seagull Island. Can you tell me how much it costs?"

"Seventy-five. One-forty round trip. When did you want to go?"

"How about tomorrow?"

"Sure. We're only making one flight a day in the off-season. How about three o'clock? I have to notify Canadian Customs and be sure the runway on the island is clear. They've been having some trouble keeping it plowed."

"A lady told me that I have to have a passport, but my purse was stolen at a gas station in Pittsburgh." (Lies come easier every day.) "Is there any way around this passport thing?"

The man takes a deep breath. "Not with us. Not with Cullen Airlines in Sandusky either. The Customs guys are real strict. One man, last summer, got on the flight to Seagull without a passport and the Canadian team sent him back. He was kind of a jerk, but he ended up paying round trip for nothing and was mad as hell."

"So there's no way?" My eyes tear up and I'm not faking. "I've already put down rent on a little cottage over there."

The man leans across the desk, looking first out the window toward the ice-covered lake, then around the empty waiting room. "I didn't say there's *no* way . . . there's just no way to fly."

I tilt my head, not understanding, and he hands me a little yellow piece of paper with a phone number written on it. "My brother-in-law," he whispers.

Lenny Knight. Snowmobile. 440-555-9123.

Blue Robin's Egg

*B*ack in the car, I slump down in the driver's seat, staring at the printed message on the little yellow paper and wonder what I've gotten myself into. When I left Torrington, it seemed so easy to disappear into Canada. It was a separate sovereign country, but still felt like the backyard of Michigan. I could drive to Ohio, then get on the ferry! No international flights or airline reservations. Just get in a car and disappear.

I picture my passport, still in the safety deposit box, wishing I had it but at the same time knowing I'm right not to use it. Once it was scanned, my whereabouts would be available to law enforcement everywhere.

At home, I imagine, the noose is already tightening. Richard has contacted the police after realizing I've cleaned out his pile of cash and our joint checking account. The sheriff and the hospital are convinced my disappearance proves I was at fault for the death of Robyn Layton. It's only my friends and colleagues at the clinic who will be worried sick. They will have heard about the home-birth death and, since I've disappeared and our friend Dr. Karen killed herself, they'll be thinking the worst.

KAREN AND I worked out in the gym, talked every day about our interesting patients, our kids and what was going on in the world. I told her my doubts about Richard. She told me she felt blessed that her marriage with her cardiologist husband was as "solid as a rock." Sometimes we'd bitch about politics or the new health care regulations, but I never thought of her as depressed.

Then one day she left for a cruise to Belize. She did this sometimes, just went off by herself on a white-water excursion in Colorado, a week at an ashram in India, a bike trip around Scotland. I admired her for it.

On the second day of the cruise during rough weather, she jumped off the sixth-floor balcony of the ship and her body was never found. No suicide note, *nothing*, and so we still don't know what drove her (literally) over the edge.

After Karen's death, it was like I could only hobble through my days. I never knew suicide would affect those left behind like that. Never understood that the *sin* of suicide is not that you took the life God gave you, but that you left those who loved you with a piece of their heart torn out and still bleeding.

As was my way, a few months after her death I researched suicide on the Internet, just to see how common it was. According to the World Health Organization one million people commit suicide each year, *one death every 40 seconds or 3,000 per day.* One million people dragging their loved ones into their graves behind them.

Only 20 percent leave a suicide note. This surprised me. In the movies and on TV, everyone does.

THE TROUBLE WITH Richard started a few months after Karen jumped, but I couldn't deal with it and, like an ostrich, just stuck my head in the sand.

What gets me is that I always thought of myself as so strong. I practically raised myself since I was fourteen, but when trouble was piled on top of me, I cracked like a blue robin's egg, a fragile blue egg.

I stare at the little yellow sticky note and the cryptic words in the pilot's neat hand. I can't go back and I can't go forward, unless I call Lenny, the pilot's brother-in-law, who apparently has been known to take people *without passports* across the frozen lake into Canada.

Lenny

The corner rib place called Marty's, in downtown Lorain, smells like beer and cigarettes and the music's so loud you can't hear yourself think. A TV is mounted high up on the wall and black-and-white 1920s photos of the once proud Lake Erie fishing industry cover the walls.

In the mirror behind the curved bar, I see a familiar woman in her late forties, wearing dark red lipstick, a black beret and heavy rimmed glasses. She sports a rainbow scarf and I realize with a shock that the woman is me!

A tall man approaches. Lenny Knight has gray-blue eyes, a long silver and gold ponytail, straight white teeth, a nice smile, a clean-shaven face with a cleft in his chin and tattoos up his arms—a biker, I think, or an aging hippie.

He greets me pleasantly, sits down, orders a beer for both of us and gets right to the point. "Mid-February is a little late to cross the lake, but the surface is still 90 percent frozen and this has been a hell of a cold week. You ever ride a snowmobile?"

I shake my head no, adjusting the reading glasses that I don't need for reading and watching his face, wondering if he's a man I can trust. (I really don't want to die on the cold dark bottom of Lake Erie!)

"You'll need a snowmobile suit, head gear and a ski mask. You can get all that for around ninety dollars at Walmart, but bring only forty pound of supplies in a backpack. How much do you weigh?"

I'm embarrassed, so I fudge a little. "A hundred and fifty." By this time lies come so easily.

"Yeah, forty or fifty pounds of luggage, not a bit more. Why do you want to go to Seagull Island so bad anyway? You in some kind of trouble?" He puts it like that, probably thinking I am.

"No trouble. I just need some time alone. I'm a writer and I want to finish my book."

"Novel or memoir?" Lenny asks, like he's interested in literature.

"Novel." (Once you lie, you have to keep going.)

"What about?"

"A woman abandoned on an island . . . Look, Lenny, when could we go and what do you charge?"

"Five hundred dollars."

"Whew! That's a lot! The plane only costs seventy-five dollars one way."

"I'm taking a risk, avoiding customs and crossing on the ice."

"It's dangerous then?"

"Babe, life is dangerous. You in or not? We could leave late tomorrow."

CHAPTER 6

A Plan

I have a little over twenty-four hours to prepare. Lenny already has my money and I just hope he's honest. I've paid him in cash and all I have is his word and his phone number.

My first stop, after leaving the café, is a twenty-four-hour Walmart in Lorain, where I purchase a snowmobile suit, snow boots, thick mittens and a ski mask. Just to be safe, I also throw in sunglasses, two pairs of long underwear, some wool socks, matches, candles and a flashlight.

Food is a problem and I have no idea what to take, so I decide to get things that are light; crackers, tuna in a vacuum pack, pasta, dried lentils, brown rice, powdered milk, granola bars, raisins and cheese; nothing liquid or canned.

It's when I'm passing through the dairy section that a wild idea comes to me. An exasperated mother and her two whining kids have their heads in the open door of the ice cream freezer. Her purse is still in the cart's fold-down child seat, the same place I keep mine. While she's not looking, I could easily swipe the pocketbook and have a new ID! The trouble is, the woman I'm watching is about six inches taller than me, has red hair and outweighs me by fifty pounds.

For the next hour, I cruise the store, checking out potential victims. Everywhere I look, women are leaving their handbags in the cart while they scurry around. I find at least five I could take with ease . . . *if I have the nerve.*

The trouble will be finding a woman who looks like me. I decide hair color doesn't matter; I can change mine to match hers and her weight isn't critical either. If questioned, I can always say I've lost or gained a few pounds. How tall my target is, her age and her eye color are most critical. Still mulling it over, I decide I'd better try a different store. Since I've been here so long, security may be watching me.

My next stop is an identical Walmart back in Sandusky and my heart thumps so hard, I'm afraid it must show. *Am I really going to do this?* I'm usually so honest Richard calls me a Girl Scout.

I HAVE IT all planned. I head for the linen section and toss a few towels in the cart as if I'm going to purchase them. Then I begin to troll the store, trying not to look like a thief. The trouble is, I've never done anything like this before.

In the clothes section I find my prey. There's a blue quilted pocketbook resting in the shopping cart's child seat and a little girl, around seven, is begging her mom to buy her a sparkly superstar T-shirt. I circle around her, touching a pink dress on the rack, then holding it up to the light, like I'm thinking of buying it.

"Please!" the girl pleads. "You said if I was good you'd get me something!"

The mother looks tired and she's about my height, five foot four, but she's probably ten years my junior. Too young? I push my cart nearer to get a better look. A short chin and round nose like mine, but what about the eyes?

"Okay. Okay." The woman squats down, trying to find the

right shirt on a lower shelf and the girl kneels down too. I decide to go for it. If her eyes are the wrong color, I can always just leave her purse and ID in the restroom and find another victim down the road.

Casually I pass her cart. I survey the immediate surroundings. No one else is around. Without missing a beat, I grab the handbag, stuff it under the towels and move calmly into another aisle. *Oh my God! I did it!*

Thief

$\mathcal{F}$ive minutes later, I'm sitting on the john in the Walmart women's bathroom. It took all my nerve to walk calmly through aisles of the store. Step by step, I pushed my cart through girls' clothes, boys' clothes, women's clothes, school supplies, jewelry and finally made it to the front.

Clara Perry stole a purse! I sit in the last stall of the women's restroom clutching the quilted handbag to my chest, feeling triumphant and horrible at the same time. My cart with the blue and green towels is parked just outside the restroom door by the drinking fountain and my hands shake so hard, I can't get the zipper of the stolen bag open.

Slow down, I tell myself. Breathe. I bite my lower lip to get calm. The hard part is over.

But what if someone saw me? What if they're calling security right now? Slow down. No one saw you.

Inside the handbag is a red leather wallet and I slip out the Ohio driver's license and then look through the cards. The owner of the purse, Sara Livingston, is an RN and has an Ohio nursing license and a CPR card. That's a bit of good fortune. I pocket these cards too. Then I hang the purse on the hook on the stall door as planned, but at the last moment, I have second thoughts.

If the next person who comes into the stall takes all Sara's credit cards and cash, I'd feel terrible, so I decide to do the right thing, even if I'm risking my neck . . . Bold as anything, I walk out of the lavatory and hand the purse to the nearest cashier, a very large pale woman of about thirty who reminds me of one of my patients.

"Excuse me," I say, trying to look pleasant and normal. "I found this in the ladies' room."

The clerk looks surprised and thanks me. "God bless you, honey. There aren't many honest people anymore." *If she only knew!*

BACK AT THE Lakeland Motel, still trembling, I close the drapes, bolt the door and take out the ID to look at the cards again.

Yes, if you squint, the photo looks a little like me. Luckily, Sara Livingston has blue eyes too. If I get my hair cut short like hers and wear the fake specs, I might just pass, and the fact that she's an RN is a stroke of luck, though there *are* more than three million of us in the United States.

Resting back on the pillows, I click through the forty cable TV stations, but there's nothing about a stolen purse and ID. It probably isn't considered newsworthy, then I see something that is . . . and it takes my breath away.

"THIS JUST IN . . ." a Toledo newscaster with straight blond hair and wide brown eyes announces. "Clara Perry, a West Virginia nurse-midwife, is being sought for medical negligence and second-degree manslaughter for allegedly leaving the scene of a home birth where her patient, a mother of three, died of hemorrhage two nights ago. The midwife, believed to be driving a 2012 dark green Volvo, was last seen in Torrington, West Virginia, at the Mountain Federal Bank. (A short silent clip of the bank security video plays, showing me talking to the teller, and then cuts off.)

"Any information on her whereabouts should be given to local police . . . And now we turn to Michael for the latest on the refugee crisis in Europe . . ." My heart skips a beat as I stare at the black-and-white photo of myself on the screen, then my face fades into a video of chanting angry protestors.

I TRY TO remember who in Sandusky has heard my real name and who's seen me without the heavy glasses and my hair up in the beret . . . Ivy saw me when I first checked in to the motel at five in the morning, but she was half-asleep. Mrs. Nelson saw me, but she was so distracted, she wouldn't recognize me if we met at a church social.

When I ran away I never imagined that the news of Robyn's death would reach this far or this fast. What was the name of that hair salon the desk clerk told me about? The Hair Palace? I've seen enough movies to know that when running the first thing to do is assume a disguise.

Exodus

*T*his morning, after my walk around the outside of the motel and a free breakfast of instant oatmeal and yogurt, I stand at the mirror and fluff up my new haircut. I'd asked for a short blond pixie or shag (like the real Sara Livingston was wearing when she had her driver's license photo taken), and this is what Melissa at the Hair Palace came up with.

For one hundred and fifty dollars and a good tip, she cut and colored my hair and threw in some shampoo and eight bottles of hair dye. I worried that she might have caught the news about Clara Perry of West Virginia who is wanted for manslaughter, but if she did, she kept her mouth shut.

"You'll have to recolor every month," she told me, putting the grooming products in a pink plastic bag. "If you go longer, you'll look like a mess."

Still staring at the motel mirror, I put on the thick glasses and the bright red lipstick but forget the beret since my new hair color and style have dramatically changed my look. Then I throw the rainbow scarf around my neck, sit down on my hard motel bed and call Lenny. "Hi. It's me. Are we still on for tonight?"

"Planning on it. You having second thoughts?"

"No, not at all. I just called to find out where we should meet."

"I was thinking Miller Road Park out highway 6. There's a lot of guys snowmobiling out there. I'll meet you at five in the parking lot, just before dark. I'm driving a black 4Runner and I'll be pulling a green Ski-Doo snowmobile on the trailer. Did you get all your gear?"

"Yeah, I'm set. But there's one other thing. I want to get rid of my Volvo. I don't have anywhere safe to park it in Lorain and I won't need it on the island. When I come back, I can buy something newer." (Hopefully never.) "Do you know a used-car place where I can sell it for cash?"

"Most dealers will want to write you a check."

"I figured, but there must be someone. I'll give them a good deal."

"It's not hot, is it?" He laughs.

"No! I have the title and everything."

"Try Bill's Used Cars on Lake Street in Sandusky. He's been known to take risks."

"Should I tell him Lenny sent me?"

"I wouldn't. We're on the outs."

TWO HOURS LATER, a rail-thin used-car salesman named Chester, with a chipped tooth in front, offers me $8,000 for the Volvo, no questions asked. It's only when I get out the Volvo's title that I realize I've made a mistake. I've already destroyed Clara Perry's ID. I have no way to prove who I am and that I actually own this vehicle, but he doesn't ask any questions, just gives me the cash and I'm out the door.

I grab a cab back to the motel and by evening I'm packed and ready. To save on the weight of the backpack, I wear as many of my new clothes under the snowmobile suit as I can, and when the yellow taxi shows up, the driver does a double take because I'm the same woman he just brought back from the auto dealer, only now I'm dressed in a puffy snowsuit with three layers of clothes underneath and look twice my size.

He puts my backpack in the trunk. "Where you headed?"

"Miller Road Park outside of Lorain."

"Whew! It's gonna cost you."

"That's okay. We're going out snowmobiling on the lake, my fiancé and I." (I don't know why I keep embroidering my lies.)

"Kind of late. It will be dark soon."

"It's fun to snowmobile on the lake at night. You ever try it?"

"Not me. Those guys are crazy," the cabbie says. "Two guys went through the ice last week around Middle Island."

The rest of the way, we are silent. Already the sun is low in the sky and the gray-white Lake Erie stretches out to the horizon. Once I see a broad-winged hawk on a fence post and think of telling Karen, but that's never again going to happen.

As we drive, I run through my mental checklist to be sure I haven't forgotten anything. Food, clothing, flashlight, matches and the briefcase with my stash of money . . . All I have in my wallet now is enough for the taxi fare along with Sara Livingston's driver's license, her cards and a photo of Jessie, taken last Christmas. Clara Perry has been terminated, deleted. She's gone.

THE CABBIE GETS me to the snow-covered park in about one hour, but Lenny isn't there.

This is not good. I'm so trusting I just gave the man my money, how do I know this hasn't all been a scam set up by Ben the pilot from Red Hawk? It would be easy to do and they already have my $500.

"Do you mind waiting a few minutes?" I ask the driver, getting out four twenties. "I'll pay for your time."

"I can give you ten minutes," the cabbie mumbles, and then he opens a copy of *Sports Illustrated*. I look at my watch, then stare at the lake. White drifts swirl up the stone breakwall and the rippled ice stretches as far as I can see.

"You think your boyfriend's going to show?" the taxi driver asks at eight minutes. "It will be cold tonight, fifteen degrees they said on the weather channel."

"Yeah. Sure. He's always late." I shiver, wondering if Lenny really will come and what I'll do if he doesn't.

Finally, the black 4Runner pulls into the parking lot. I jump out and give Lenny a hug, whispering into his ear, "I told the driver you're my fiancé." Just to be smart he gives me a big smooch on the mouth. "Hey!" I hiss, half-offended, half-amused.

The cabbie gets out my backpack then toots his horn and skids out of the lot. "You like that?" Lenny grins. "I was trying to keep it real."

CHAPTER 7

Dark Path

So here I am . . . on an island in Ontario, in the cold and the dark, with just a backpack and a new name. Lenny called this path a road, but it's really just a wide white trail through the forest with a few animal tracks like dark pebbles in the snow . . . It's so quiet I feel like I'm in a Robert Frost poem because I have definitely taken the road less traveled!

Eager to find the cottage, I load up and push on, but the hike takes longer than I expected. Even with my mittens and warm boots, my hands and feet are freezing. Visions of frostbitten digits begin to intrude, blackened toes and fingers like I've seen in photos of Richard's friends from the Arctic.

From the map of Seagull Island that I'd found online, I had estimated a quarter of a mile from the cove to Mrs. Nelson's cottage, but I'm beginning to wonder. There are no signs of civilization, except the untraveled trail. I begin to shiver inside. What if Lenny dropped me off at the wrong place? What if he left me on the wrong island? But that's a stupid thought. Why would he do that?

Finally a square shape appears in the moonlight, a squat little cottage set off from the road with a white picket fence, three big pine trees in front and a shed or garage to one side. What I see of the house with my flashlight is white peeling paint, two small windows flanking a wooden door, a porch and a carved white seagull nailed to the railing.

This doesn't look much like the cute little Seagull Haven I saw on the vacation home website, but then, I remind myself, the photos with the blue sky above and geraniums blooming in pots on the porch were probably taken five years ago.

Desperate to get out of the cold, I approach the dwelling and kneel down at the bottom of the steps. Mrs. Nelson said I'd find a key under a heart-shaped rock in the flowerbed, but I didn't imagine the depth of the snow. For five minutes I dig through the crusted ice, first on the left and then on the right. My mittens are getting wet and it's imperative that I find warmth. Finally I hit something hard, the rock with the key duct taped to the bottom. Things are looking up. I take a big breath and put the key in the deadbolt, but the key won't turn!

Damn, where is Richard when I need him? He was the handy one in the family. Whenever something didn't work he would fix it, but I paid for my dependence on him. Little by little I gave my power away, and as the years went by I began to feel more and more clumsy and inadequate.

I'm starting to wonder if I can find an unlocked window, but before I go searching I drop my backpack on the porch and try the door one more time. With my small flashlight in my mouth, I flip the key over, but it doesn't fit. I try three more times, jiggling the key harder, while I desperately pull the handle up and down . . . up and down . . . up and down . . . and . . . at last I'm successful! But as the door squeaks open, the smell of something awful assaults me. "What the hell?" I say out loud, and then I slam it shut again.

Home Sweet Home

ive minutes of cursing and I dry my eyes with the back of my mittens. There's no bed-and-breakfast establishment nearby. It's not like I can go somewhere else in the middle of the night. If I don't want to die out in the snow from hypothermia, I'll have to figure this out.

Shivering, from both cold and dread, I pull my scarf over my mouth and nose, open the door again, shine my flashlight inside a dark hall and reach for the light switch next to the door. I'd been afraid there might be problems with the electricity, but for a change I get lucky. It comes on as it should, illuminating a small entryway with a coat rack and a tall bookcase lined with books. The wooden floors groan as I drop my heavy backpack near the door.

The kitchen, I think. *I'll start my search there.* And I don't have far to go. The hall leads to a small dark room where the fetid odor is stronger and where I can make out a sink, a tile counter, wooden cupboards strangely left open and in the corner a round wooden table with five wooden chairs.

It takes me a while, but I finally find a dangling metal cord and when the kitchen light comes on, the source of the smell is obvious. Somehow, a raccoon has found his way into the house and destroyed the place.

Empty packages of cereal, rice, pasta and spoiled condiments are open on the counter and there's animal feces and urine in the sink and all over the floor. I stand six feet away, covering my nose, wondering what to do next. All I want is to fall into bed and pull a pillow over my head, but finally, despite my exhaustion, I start opening windows. I'll sleep better if I clean the mess up.

Behind me there's the open door to the bathroom and inside the small linen closet, like Mrs. Nelson promised, are neatly folded towels and sheets as well as a broom, a mop and a bottle of Clorox, so I get to work. First with a towel, I scoop up the dead raccoon and the poop, then dump it out in the yard.

In thirty minutes, the odor is already receding and I inspect my new domicile as I go about closing the windows. In the living room there's a worn blue sofa, a gold recliner and two maple rocking chairs, a pleasant space in a 1980s sort of way.

A huge stone fireplace dominates the room and the mantel is crowded with dozens of ceramic, glass and carved wood seagulls covered in dust and cobwebs. There's a picture window facing Lake Erie and a colorful braided rug that gives warmth to the room.

The one bedroom is dusty but spacious, with an iron bedstead, a relatively new bare mattress, a dresser and a closet. To the side is an alcove with a bureau, more shelves and a stacked washer and dryer. The alcove is odd, I think, but perhaps it once held bunk beds. Probably the Nelsons had kids.

Back in the living room, I find the thermostat and crank the electric heater up; then I build a fire in the fireplace. When the flames begin to catch, I throw in the cardboard from the kitchen, then I make my bed with clean flannel sheets and return to the living room to sit down by the blaze.

On the back of the sofa there's a green-and-white quilt in the flying-goose pattern and I shake it out and pull it around my shoulders. I know this design because my friend Karen was a quilter, a happy quilter and crafter, we all thought . . . until she jumped into the Atlantic.

Karen

*T*he first time I met Karen she was sitting in the conference room of Labor and Delivery at the University of Michigan Medical Center. Her long wild golden hair hung around her face as she bent over a quilt square she was working on. "Hiya!" she said, and when I saw the name embroidered on the left side of her rumpled long white lab coat, I knew who she was—one of the new ob-gyn residents.

Dr. Karen Naylor's reputation as a rebel preceded her and the midwives at the hospital were always happy when she was on duty because she would work with us to achieve a normal vaginal delivery. Unlike some of her fellow ob-gyn residents who preferred to wield the knife, she'd stay up all night just to assist us.

She was even present at my home delivery of Jessie, along with my favorite nurse-midwife, Sandy. You bond when you go through labor together, but after a while I lost track of Karen. She graduated and moved out West. This was back in the 1990s.

Then just six years ago, I met her again. I'd been up all night in Labor and Delivery at Torrington Community Hospital and needed a break. After twenty hours of back labor, my patient decided to get an epidural, which was fine with me because I was beginning to think she'd need a Cesarean.

When I walked into the doctors' lounge at 2:00 A.M., expecting the room to be empty, I was surprised to find another woman there, dressed like me, in blue scrubs. She was working on something that looked like a quilt.

I'd heard a new female physician was joining the practice but didn't realize she'd already started. There were four ob-gyns and two midwives in our group and since we nurse-midwives were employees, not partners, we weren't always kept in the loop when it came to hiring and firing.

THE WOMAN TOOK a few pins out of her mouth. "Hiya," she said. "I'm your ob-gyn consult tonight, Dr. Cross. The nurses told me your patient, Mrs. Ward, has been in labor for a long time. How's she holding up? How's the baby?" I was impressed that the new physician first asked about the patient's *feelings*, not how many centimeters dilated she was or whether I'd ordered a Pitocin drip.

"She's pretty discouraged." I flopped into a chair across from her. "We've walked and squatted. I had her on hands and knees and she's been in the shower and Jacuzzi. I thought after she got the epidural, I'd let her rest for an hour, then have her push again. The baby's tracing is fine, reactive with no decels. I'm Clara Perry, nurse-midwife, by the way."

"Clara! Clara Perry?" the woman shouted, jumping up and spilling her pins on the floor. "University of Michigan? Holy cow! I haven't seen you in what? Twenty years? It's me. Karen Naylor. Now Karen Cross. *Quilting Karen*." We fell into each other's arms laughing.

"Look at us. We both have some gray hair!" I said, running my fingers through her short, silver and gold curls. She was wearing round tortoiseshell glasses. No wonder I didn't recognize her!

"We've just moved out to Hope Lake from New Mexico. I have two grown boys living in New England. One is a medical student at Yale and one is a chef in Boston. My husband is the new cardiologist at Torrington Med Center." After she caught me up, I told her that Jessie, who she once helped deliver, was a soccer-playing junior-high-school student and that Richard was working his way up the ladder in the biology department.

Karen folded the quilt she was working on, picked up the pins and looked at me with a smile. "Let's go see your patient."

Two hours later, with gentle traction from the vacuum extractor, we assisted the mother to deliver an eight-pound baby girl, and the best part was, Karen didn't cut an episiotomy or make the woman feel like a failure. She brought the infant's head to crowning and then let her push her own baby out.

"Come on, Mom!" we both cried. "You can do it!" And she did.

CHAPTER 8

Open Water

*L*ying in Wanda and Lloyd Nelson's bed, facing the window, I remember again the events that drove me to this place: Karen's suicide, Richard's infidelity and finally Robyn's tragic death, a perfect troika dragging me under the wheels of a heavy runaway cart.

Outside big drifts of snow rise, like twisted sculptures, up the granite breakwall that protects the house from the waves of Lake Erie. Beyond is the frozen water and the gray-white sky of predawn. *I need a breakwall*, I think, a breakwall from life!

The wind roars around the little cottage and when I look out I see the leafless cottonwood trees near the shore, dancing with their bare arms raised. I've lost track of how many days I've been here because all I can do is sleep and think of Robyn and Karen and my daughter, who I worry may be thinking I made the choice to end it all.

Guilt and remorse, like black stones in my throat, keep me from swallowing, but there's nothing I can do to remedy my situation. I can't go back to the home birth and save Robyn. There's no way to turn back the clock and save Karen. No way I can think of, without Richard finding out, to contact our daughter and tell her I'm still alive and love her. This unsettles me most.

All this fall and winter with Jessie in Australia, the ties that bound us were strained to the breaking point. Sometimes, many times, I've been angry, told her in my head that I was through with her. Over and over I would try to reach her, but she rarely answered my phone calls or texts. I danced a strange dance, alternating between fear for her safety and being pissed off. Why did I bother?

I am such a bad mother. If I were a *good* mother, I wouldn't just run away in the middle of a snowstorm without trying harder to reach her. If I were a *good* mother, Jessie would have cared more and answered her phone calls and texts in the first place. If I were a *good* mother, I wouldn't give up on her ever.

How can a midwife be a bad mother? We're supposed to be the defenders of motherhood. We encourage women in labor. We tell them they are beautiful and strong. We mother the mothers. In some countries we are called the wise women.

I lie on my back, hands folded over my chest. "Forgive me," I whisper. "Forgive me." But I don't know who I'm praying to, Jessie or God.

PULLING THE GREEN-AND-WHITE flying-goose quilt over my head, I turn over and fall back to sleep. This time I dream that I'm with both Karen and Jessie at Robyn Layton's home birth. There's red all over the bedroom floor. Jessie and I are scooping it up with silver spoons and somehow returning it to the limp patient. "Hurry," I say. "Hurry! She's dying!"

"It's alright," Karen tells me in her calm way. "We have time." As I watch, the color comes back into Robyn's face and she sits up and recognizes me. "Clara," she says. "You came back!"

I wake, my heart pounding. It was only a dream. Just a dream! And when I pull back the curtain next to my bed, I'm shocked to see that toward the south, about a quarter mile from shore, the ice has parted. Only a few days ago Lenny and I raced across that frozen sea. Now the white has torn apart as if it were a sheet of parchment. Reeling in the sunlight over the open blue water are hundreds of seagulls, diving, catching fish, rejoicing. *Klee-ew. Klee-ew. Hahaha,* they cry.

CHAPTER 9

Timberland Boot

It's the first of March, or somewhere near there. (I'm estimating since I have no calendar.) The sun shines and the air is full of birdsong, so I bundle up and go out on the deck. There are two levels, one just outside the back door and one up higher on the breakwall. I find a seat in the gazebo where I can see huge cakes of ice bobbing in the blue sparkling water and I almost expect to see a seal riding along on top of one.

The effect of climate change on animals in the northland is one of my husband's main obsessions. Actually, I think Richard cares more about the Arctic polar bears than me. It's been his life's passion, and for the last five years he's spent four months of every year in Alaska, studying the consequences of global warming, four months out of twelve as we grew apart.

Apparently, polar bears are going hungry because the polar ice is melting at a rate of twenty thousand square miles a year and the bears can't travel and find food like they used to. Twenty thousand square miles a year! Can you believe that?

To survive, the males eat each other's cubs or die of starvation. This image, of course, greatly affects the midwife in me. There's nothing so appealing as a fuzzy white baby polar bear, or any kind of baby, really.

SINCE I'VE BEEN to the island, I've gone no further than the porch and the deck, but seeing the water nearly free of ice inspires me. Bundling up, I prepare for a cold hike and step off the porch into the remaining two-foot drift with caution. A broken leg might be the end of me. No one here knows that I'm here. I'd freeze or I'd starve before anyone would happen by.

Carefully I test the snow and find that it's now frozen solid, so I follow my trail across the yard. When I get to the road, I understand now why there's no traffic. Except for my footprints coming in from the lake, and the footprints of a few small animals, it appears that nothing has passed all winter.

The snow is softer under the evergreens and, stomping down the unplowed trail in white up to my knees, I head through the woods to another smaller trail that I follow down to the beach. Here I can see all the way along the curved spit to Gull Point.

Sparkling ice chunks are piled up on the shore, but the bare sand is frozen so it's easy to walk. I'm so entranced by these winter sculptures that I almost trip over a dead swan. I study the form. Yellow and black bill bleached by the sun. Long neck bent in a curious way. White wing feathers half-covered with snow. Did it die during the last Arctic blast? Did it starve because it couldn't get food through the ice? Did someone shoot it?

A tan leather Timberland boot, with the familiar tree logo on the side, lies next to the fallen bird. Then I realize the boot is connected to a half-buried leg and the leg to a man in a black hooded jacket, and I almost fall to the ground.

For a minute, I think of running for help, but where would I go? I take a few deep breaths and calm myself to better assess the situation. The body is frozen so there's no smell and the man's face is buried in the sand, so he seems less like a dead person and more like a manikin.

I take another deep breath. I have seen dead people before as a nurse. I have even done dissections on human cadavers in nursing school, so I'm not as horrified by the corpse as some might be. My main thought is *What to do now?*

I have a cell phone in my briefcase, but I haven't tried it yet and anyway who would I call? Not the police, assuming they have some kind of law enforcement on the island. How would I explain my presence here? A woman without a passport, who didn't come through Customs, just dropped down like a dead swan out of the sky?

I'm sure, like the guy at Red Hawk said, I would be instantly deported as an illegal alien. This would start a chain of events that would draw me back to West Virginia and the county jail. They wouldn't even allow me the opportunity to be bailed out. I've already proven I'm a flight risk.

No, it's best to leave sleeping humans where they lie. "Rest in peace, stranger," I say out loud. "When the next storm comes, the waves will take you away."

Expedition

For three days the rain and wind pound the shore. The waves crash up on the breakwall and the cakes of ice boom as they collide.

To entertain myself, I do a thorough cleaning of the cottage and then I go through the books in the bookcase and discover a binder with lined paper that I can keep for a journal instead of the old appointment book that I found in my briefcase. I also find a three-year-old tourist brochure titled *Welcome to Seagull Island.*

In the back is a detailed map and I'm surprised to see that the island is roughly shaped like a gull and is about three miles across and seven miles long, smaller than I remembered, though everything is smaller now than when I was a kid.

In 1781, the pamphlet explains, the first European settler, an Irishman named Simon Gaul, purchased the island from the two indigenous people camped here for the equivalent of a hundred dollars. The natives thought it was a joke because, first of all, they didn't own the land, and second, it was mostly swamp and rocks. Over the years "Simon Gaul's Island" became "Gull Island," then Seagull Island, and in 1893 the Canadian government made the name official.

Studying the map, I make note that the names of the main roads are easy to remember. Sunset Road runs up the west shore, where presumably one can watch the sun drop into the blue water. Sunrise Road runs up the east shore. Down the middle, north to south is Middle Way, and across, east to west, is Middle Loop. At the top, North Wing Road runs from Light House Park to the island cemetery with many short roads running into the interior. Not far from my cottage, which I learn is on the un-plowed Grays Road, is the town of Gull and a grocery store.

FINALLY, IT STOPS raining. I fear meeting people, but my provisions are low and I have to get food. I have no idea what the store's hours are, but despite the risk, I've got to shop, so I charge up my cell phone and attempt to get the store's number from information.

What the . . . ? When I stare at the screen the little circle goes around and around. When I power up my laptop there aren't any Wi-Fi networks to connect to. Damn! I should have thought that I might not have service, but I'm so used to being plugged in, it never entered my mind. I stare at the useless phone and realize

the date is displayed right under the time. It's already March 5.
I've been here two weeks.

There's nothing else to do, I just have to walk to the store and
hope it's open. Ten o'clock seems like a good guess, so midmorn-
ing, dressed like an Arctic explorer, with a pocket full of money
and an empty backpack, I leave the cottage and head into the
unknown.

CHAPTER 10

Molly Lou

$\mathcal{S}$truggling through wet snow halfway up to my knees. I push on for an hour, until I see a white farmhouse about one hundred yards ahead. There's smoke coming out of the chimney and I stop in my tracks. *Should I go up to the door?* What would I say? What if the people aren't friendly? What if they ask a lot of questions? What if they've seen my mug on TV? Do Canadians even get the US TV stations?

Still uncertain what I'll do, I plow forward until I'm almost in front of the two-story dwelling. Here the road has been cleared and there's a tractor with a snowplow blade in the yard, along with a fishing boat in front of a barn. A little boy of about six is playing on the boat and he yells, "Mom! There's someone in the road."

Apparently, the woman hears him because a lace curtain moves in the front window and the door opens. "Hello," she calls from the porch. "Need some help? Come on in." Still unsure what I'm going to say, I decide to improvise. "I'll be right with you," she continues. "I have something on the stove."

On the porch, I step out of my boots and enter a large warm living room. The first thing that strikes me is the big-screen TV, a shock compared to the relative simplicity of the rest of the home, furnished with an overstuffed sectional sofa, an easy chair and a recliner in front of a fireplace. The volume on the TV is muted while a commercial plays, then the news comes on and I freeze. It's the blond newscaster again, with Clara Perry's photo, bigger than life, behind her. The woman's mouth moves and words run in a line along the bottom of the screen. "West Virginia midwife still sought for manslaughter."

I swallow hard, cross the living room and stand in front of the screen to block it from the woman's view. Now I know the answer to my question. Yes, Canadians in Southern Ontario do watch US television, a danger I hadn't counted on.

"You have car trouble?" my host asks, coming into the room from the kitchen, wiping her hands on a white dish towel. "I'm Molly Lou Erickson by the way. Worst winter we've had in years. Supposed to be almost spring, not that you can tell. The roads are a mess. Township doesn't have the money to keep them up, so they just plow Sunset Road through the village, Middle Loop, Middle Way and Sunrise. The rest of us have to fend for ourselves, except the people on North Wing because of the school."

She stops for a breath and I'm glad I studied the map, because I have a vague idea what she's talking about. Molly Lou is a big natural blond who looks to be of northern European extraction. She wears a blue turtleneck that matches her eyes and her skin is perfect and pale pink.

"My husband, Chris, has a new snow blade on his tractor, so he's got us plowed from here to the township office. You didn't try to go down Grays Road, did you?" She rolls her eyes as if that would be crazy.

"I'm Sara. I'm staying at the Nelson place, Seagull Haven," I introduce myself.

"You aren't one of the hippies, are you?" She narrows her eyes.

"Ahh, no," I say, unsure what she's talking about. "I'm a writer."

"Good. We've had some problems with a group of hippies on the north end. I was hoping they weren't spreading like weeds."

"I understand," I comment (though I don't understand at all). "You may have heard, Lloyd Nelson's very ill, so I'm taking care of the cottage. They have the hospice nurse at their home in Findlay now. That's why they haven't been back this year." Without planning it, I make it sound like I know the family. "Wanda is pretty broken up."

"So you're a relation? Here, take off your things."

"No, just a friend. I'm a writer and wanted to stay somewhere quiet to finish my book. The Nelsons needed someone to take care of the cottage. Wanda was worried about the pipes."

"So do you need your vehicle pulled out? Christian will be home later for lunch. He's on the township road crew and a handyman for some of the cottages. Had to tow the mailman out yesterday. I'll get him to plow down to Seagull Haven. We didn't know anyone was living there. You by yourself?"

"Yes, but I don't have a car. I thought I could just walk to the store. Would it be open this morning?"

"Oh, honey, that place hasn't been open for years. We have to go to the north end for supplies. Since the population's dropped, there isn't enough business for two stores."

My face must have shown my disappointment. In truth, I feel like crying. By the map, the north end is almost seven miles away. What have I gotten myself into?

Island Tour

Tell you what. Little Chris and I need to get out of the house. Why don't I give you a ride up to Burke's Country Store? That's where we all shop. You can get almost anything you need."

"I hate to trouble you."

"No trouble at all. It's just a hop and a skip. I need some milk and eggs anyway and there should be fresh fruit."

Twenty minutes later we're bouncing along a rutted, partly snow-covered road in Molly Lou's gray Subaru. A pickup comes toward us and the driver toots his horn and salutes with two fingers. Molly toots back and gives him the peace sign.

"Friend?" I ask.

"Not really. It's a tradition. A toot and a wave is what Mayor Ambroy asked us to do when we pass someone. Good PR for the island. The salute just gradually turned into a peace sign. Even the tourists and the summer cottagers are into it." Now and then, where waves have splashed over the breakwall, we hit an icy patch, but my driver handles them easily.

"That's Seagull Island Cider Farm and the dorms for the migrant workers," she says as she turns onto Middle Loop, sliding sideways, almost into a ditch. She points out a large rustic wooden building with a glassed-in wraparound porch, surrounded by an extensive orchard of midsized bare fruit trees. In back, away from the road, are three white metal outbuildings and a long cement block structure that looks like a motel.

"The cider farm is a big deal in the summer. Lots of people from the Canadian mainland and the US come over on the ferry to watch them press fruit and make cider and wine, then they stay for lunch or dinner. Those are the apple orchards. They'll bloom late this year because of the hard winter.

"Earl Prentiss, the owner, has hundreds of acres of apple trees all over the island. He's started to grow peach and apricot trees too. Makes beautiful wine. During the summer, they have live music at the Cider Mill and also at the two taverns. The orchards, the sheep and the tourists are about all that keeps the island alive."

Then she's silent as we pass fields flat as a pancake, but covered in snow with black rocks sticking up like jagged teeth. Here and there I catch sight of a farmhouse with a barn and white and brown sheep dotting the white fields. For long stretches there are the rows of apple trees she'd mentioned, a semi-dwarf variety with their gray pruned limbs reaching up for the blue sky.

Alongside the well-tended orchards and upscale beach cottages are homes with multiple vehicles in the yards, some of which are up on cement blocks just like you'd see in West Virginia. Rusty farm equipment is parked next to old boats that haven't seen water for years. Some of the houses are abandoned, surrounded by brush and about to fall down. There are FOR SALE signs everywhere.

"No school today?" I ask the little boy in the back, just to make conversation.

"Teacher's sick," he responds.

"We've had so much time off this year, what with the snow, and we only have one teacher. She's from Toronto and doesn't like the island life," Molly Lou informs me. "When I was a kid we had two teachers, but enrollment is down. The new people, the hippies, do home schooling. It isn't fair."

"Why not? Lots of families prefer home schooling for religious reasons or maybe they just think they can do a better job than the public schools."

Molly Lou doesn't respond at first and I think I've offended her, but she finally answers in a low voice. "It's just different here than in the States. There are only about 250 people living on Seagull Island year round. Actually, more like 275 since the hippies came in. They live on a farm on the northeast shore. If their kids came to the township school, we could have two teachers and the island children wouldn't be missing so much."

We stop to let a red squirrel cross the road. It halts in the middle to stare at us, munching something in its chubby cheeks, then continues into the ditch.

"To the right is the Nature Conservancy's Park." My driver indicates a sign and a parking lot. "The tree huggers and land speculators are gobbling up every piece of empty land that goes up for sale . . ."

A few minutes later, we pass a small airport where two officers in dark uniforms with dark glasses lean against a white van that says CANADIAN BORDER SERVICES AGENCY on the side. I shrink down in my seat. Presumably, they're the ones who would have registered me if I'd come on the plane.

Molly Lou stops in the middle of the road and rolls down her window. "Hear that? It's the eleven o'clock flight from Ohio. After a while you can keep time by the planes." We both shade our eyes as a single-prop aircraft with a red hawk on the tail circles and lands. SEAGULL ISLAND INTERNATIONAL AIRPORT the sign says on the side of a tiny brick terminal.

I watch, holding my breath, as the two unsmiling customs officers approach the plane with their clipboards and begin to ask the five arriving passengers questions. "Where are you from? How long will you be here? Where are you staying? Do you carry any firearms, weapons or alcohol?" They intently scrutinize the passports and hand them back. One guy tries to make a joke about the bumpy flight, but the officers don't smile. There's no kidding around. No friendly greetings. No "Welcome to Canada!"

My driver pulls back onto the road and I let out my breath, glad to leave the Customs agents in the rearview mirror.

Hippies

H ere we are!" Molly Lou points to a two-story green building with a sloping red roof. Beyond is the lake, with big chunks of ice floating in the water, a rocky snow-covered beach and seagulls crying in the wind. I'm surprised when a shiny white convertible speeds into the lot, throwing gravel. What's the hurry? A woman in tight designer jeans, a fitted leather jacket and knee-high alligator boots runs up the steps in front of us without saying hello.

Over the double glass doors, there's an old fashioned sign that says BURKE'S COUNTRY STORE and underneath in the center a seagull in flight. A little bell rings when we enter.

"Thanks so much for bringing me here, Molly Lou. I really appreciate it. This was a lot more than a skip and a hop." (In fact I'm so grateful, I feel like hugging the woman. Except for her remarks about the hippies, she seems so generous and kind.)

"Nothing to it. Now Little Chris, don't go begging for everything in the store. You know money's tight until the township pays your daddy."

As we enter the establishment, I take a few minutes to look around. There are six aisles in the middle that hold dry goods and canned food, coolers in the rear with dairy and pop, a section for hardware and an L-shaped coffee bar with six stools in the corner. On the right is an area called The Beer Store, apparently a separate outfit run by the province, like a state liquor store in the United States.

Molly Lou pulls me aside while I'm picking out apples, asks my name again then leads me up to the counter where two clerks, a male and a female, are waiting on the woman in alligator boots. "Anything else, Charlene?" the female cashier asks with deference. "Just got some nice cheesecake flown in from the mainland."

"No thanks, all I need is the beer and the sandwich stuff. I wish you would get some IPAs like we asked, though, like Hop

Circle out of Victoria or Imperial Beer made in Halifax. My brothers, Jake and Will, prefer them and they're flying in tomorrow to look at some real estate." She grabs her bags and two six-packs of beer and without saying goodbye, lets the door slam behind her. No one even blinks.

"Who's she?" I ask under my breath, but my companion doesn't answer.

"Hi, Molly," the woman at the checkout says. "Surprised to see you back. Forget something? We just saw you yesterday."

"Oh, I needed a few more things and I wanted to show our new neighbor the store. This is Sara Livingston. She's staying at Lloyd and Wanda Nelson's place down on Gull Point. Sara, meet Helen and Eugene Burke. If you need anything special they can try to get it for you from the mainland."

"Nice to meet you," the woman answers. She's about my age with short curly black hair. "I didn't know anyone was staying down there. Where you from?"

I swallow hard. I've told so many lies I'm getting confused. "Oklahoma," I try, hoping she doesn't ask me what town. I don't know a single city or person in the whole state.

"How'd you happen to come to Seagull, of all places?" Helen asks.

"Sara is a writer. She's working on a book," Molly puts in.

"Really, what kind?" That's Helen again. (I never knew people would be so curious!)

I'm just getting ready to explain *"It's a story about . . ."* when the glass door opens again and four hippies enter. The conversation stops, abruptly. A cold fog has rolled in.

"Howdy, Mr. Burke. Miss Helen," says the bigger of the two men, who looks like someone out of a documentary about the 1970s: long hair, short beard, fringed leather jacket. The smaller of the males is clean shaven, has a buzz cut and wears a green down jacket over a plaid flannel shirt and jeans.

It's the women who interest me, probably because my work has always been with women. One is blond and round and carries a baby in a sling on her hip and the other has a long brown braid down her back and is thin and almost as tall as the men. Outside on the porch I see two hippie kids about Little Chris's age. Molly Lou's son stares at them like he would like to go out and say hello, but his mom pulls him away.

"Hi, I haven't seen you around before," the tall woman greets me in a friendly way. At first I don't answer, wishing she'd go away. (Since I'm new on the island I don't want to get involved until I know more about the social scene.) Out of the corner of my eye I watch as Helen turns her back and picks up the telephone.

"Yeah," I hear the storekeeper say into the receiver, "same ones back again. You better get over." Molly Lou and Helen continue to gossip in hushed voices, but neither takes her eyes off the newcomers.

"What's your name?" the hippie woman persists.

"Sara," I answer in a low voice. "I just moved here a few weeks ago from Oklahoma, but I've lived all over. I'm a writer." (I don't know why I offer this information. It's like I'm beginning to believe it.)

"I'm Rainbow. I write too, short stories." She has a pleasant face, tanned without many wrinkles, late thirties, maybe forty, and I realize Rainbow may think I'm another hippie since I'm wearing heavy boots, have the messed-up short spiky hair and am still walking around the store with my backpack on.

All this friendliness is making me uncomfortable and then out the front window, I see a black-and-white squad car pull into the lot. *Now I'm really uncomfortable.*

Long Arm of the Law

*D*ressed in a navy blue uniform parka and the regulation mirrored sunglasses all cops seem to favor, the officer gets out of his vehicle and comes into the store. He glances at me and then at the hippies, tips his baseball-type hat that says Seagull Island Police on it and asks Molly Lou how her husband is.

"Watch the expiration dates," my new hippie pal whispers, apparently unaware we're under surveillance. "If you're nice about it Helen will reduce the price. Not Eugene though. He never does."

"Sara!" Molly Lou calls. "About done? It's noon and I have to get home and make Big Chris his lunch. He's been out in the cold all day."

I nod to Rainbow. "Nice meeting you."

"Hey," she says as I turn away. "We have a little writers' group at the farm. You're welcome to come. It's the first Wednesday of the month."

"Thanks," I say. "I'll think about it."

THE SIGN BEHIND the cashier says US CURRENCY ACCEPTED, and my bill is $49.01. "Don't you use a bank card?" Helen asks as I hold out a hundred-dollar bill. "I don't have change for a hundred." Everyone in the store turns to listen, even the cop, especially the cop, and it's the last thing I wanted to happen, to call attention to myself.

"I don't have a card with me. Could I just give you the hundred and you write down that I have credit?"

Helen looks at her husband and Eugene shrugs. "Fine then. You have $50.99 in credit."

"I'll try to get smaller bills or a credit card for next time. Is there a bank on Seagull Island?"

"There's a credit union at the ferry dock the first and third Monday of the month," Eugene offers. "They come over from Leamington."

"We need to go, soon," Molly Lou says. She's pulling me by the sleeve now and I wonder if something else is going on, or if her husband, Chris, just demands his hot lunch on time.

Eugene hands me my two plastic bags of groceries and puts in a complimentary Burke's Country Store calendar that features scenic photographs of the island and the store's phone number and I thank him for his thoughtfulness.

"Officer Dolman, this is our new neighbor, Sara," my driver says as we prepare to exit. The cop tips his hat and his big silver ring flashes in the light. It's the kind made by Navajo artists with a turquoise stone and an image of an eagle carved into it.

"Nice to meet you, Sara," he says in a low voice, deceptive and soothing. He's a pleasant-looking man with short salt-and-pepper hair, but still dangerous. "So you're Molly's neighbor. I wondered. Thought maybe you were one of the organic farmers." He tilts his head toward the men in the hardware section sorting through plumbing fixtures and for a second I see myself reflected in his mirrored glasses: white face without makeup, big eyes, wild spiked hair, a scared rabbit.

I nod hello but don't say anything and it's good he doesn't offer to shake hands because mine would give me away. They're as cold as ice.

"Sara's house-sitting Seagull Haven on Gull Point. She's a friend of Wanda and Lloyd Nelson," my companion explains.

I see now what Molly Lou is up to. She wants to get me away from the hippie chick and make sure the police officer knows I'm not one of them, which since they seem so disliked, is probably a good thing.

"How *is* Lloyd, anyway?" Dolman asks, shaking his head in a sad way.

"Not so good," I answer, taking a breath and trying to sound normal. "Wanda is taking it hard. They have the hospice nurse now. It might not be much longer."

"Damn shame," the cop says. "Nice to meet you, Sara. I didn't get your last name."

"Livingston," I mumble, wondering why he wants to know. Do I look like a thief and a runaway? Do I look like someone wanted for manslaughter?

Middle of the Road

Bouncing over the rutted roads on the way home, Molly Lou and I are both quiet. I want to ask more about the hippies, but it's so clear she doesn't like them that I keep my mouth shut.

I've never been a free spirit, but many of my patients were new age hippies, organic farmers, artists and yoga teachers. Lots of people think midwives by definition are granola crunchers, but it's not true. Though our inclination is toward natural child-birth and we believe in a patient's right to choose her birthing attendants and birthing environment, that's about where our similarities end.

Some midwives deliver naked women in the warm salt water of the Pacific Ocean. Others attend high-risk OB patients in tertiary-care hospitals. Some own their own freestanding birth-ing centers. Others work overseas in international health.

On reflection, I'm what you might call a *middle-of-the-road* midwife. University educated as a registered nurse with a master's degree, I belong to the American College of Nurse-Midwives, go to medical conferences, have a West Virginia nurse-midwife license and attend deliveries in the hospital . . . or I used to, I remind myself. Those days are gone.

My one radical notion is that home birth is wonderful, and nineteen years ago I delivered Jessie in my own bed.

I HAVE BEEN pregnant two times. The first baby miscarried. This was in the early days before Richard and I were married. He was a graduate student teaching freshman biology, and I was a freshman.

I don't tell everyone about losing my baby, just women who are going through the same thing because I want them to know that I understand the terrible empty feeling when the embryo leaves you.

Looking back I can see that even then Richard had a penchant for younger women, females he could protect and eventually smother, but I didn't know about that then and loved being taken care of.

YEARS LATER, AFTER we were married, we conceived again, this time on purpose, and I carried the pregnancy full term. Richard was thirty-two; I was twenty-seven and we still loved each other.

The decision to give birth at home was an easy one for me; I instinctively knew that I would be most relaxed in my own environment. The labor was short and intense, only six hours, which surprised me. I was expecting it to last for a couple of days. Sandy, my favorite midwife from the hospital, was there and Dr. Karen and Richard, of course.

When Jessie came out of me, I swear I could feel each part of her body. The head, with a burning pain, then the shoulders, then whoosh, the whole body. Sandy and Karen were laughing. Richard was weeping. I was in shock. It had all happened so fast. Jessie opened her eyes, looked right at me and howled.

CHAPTER 11

Harbinger

For six days it rains and the waves crash up on the break-wall dragging the chunks of ice in and then out. On the fourth day, in the afternoon, the clouds, like battleships, pass over the horizon. Spring is coming. I can feel it, but there's no joy in my heart.

I've been here almost four weeks and there's a change in the light and the sky is bright blue, but I've slipped into the gray waters and I'm floating back and forth with the ice. Clara Perry is dead but Sara Livingston of Seagull Island has not quite been born.

Besides leaving my home, my job, my patients and my daughter, I think I know why I'm in the doldrums. I haven't delivered a baby in over five weeks and I hadn't realized how much being a midwife carried me on wings.

Birth is a miracle, not just for the patient and her family, but for me. When I was with a woman in labor, I wasn't thinking about what to have for dinner or who Richard was screwing. My full attention was on the patient and there was peace in that.

It's like meditation, there's only one thing that matters; getting the mother and the baby safely through the passage with love and grace. I miss it . . .

NOW THAT I'VE identified that the *absence of* midwifery and caring for patients is partly what's wrong with me, I take in a full breath of air and blow it out through my nose, like a cleansing breath, then from the back of the sofa I grab the quilt, wrap it around me and go out in the sunshine.

"Brrrrrrrr!"

It looked like spring from the big front window, but stepping *outside* is like entering a walk-in freezer. Before me the sculptured drift that was eight-feet-tall is shrinking, but it radiates cold and there's not a crocus in sight.

Sitting with my face to the setting sun, something catches my eye, movement in the rocks on the breakwall. A raccoon? A fox? A cat? It's the first wildlife, except the red squirrel in the middle of the road and the birds, that I've seen since I arrived. It's been so still and white and cold . . . but whatever I saw is already gone, like a ghost. Maybe it was only my imagination.

JUST IN CASE, after dinner, I bring out a saucer of milk. By this time it's so dark I can hardly see my feet, but above me is a sky filled with little ice chips. There's the Milky Way. There's Orion's Belt. There's the Big Dipper.

The stars are so bright because there are no street lamps on Seagull Island. As far as I can tell there's not even one billboard or neon sign. As I put the old blue-and-white saucer by the door, my fingers linger on the chipped plate. Is this something Lloyd put his toast on?

In the morning the saucer is empty, the milk is gone.

THE FOLLOWING DAY, the sun rises again into a clear blue sky and I remember that though I can't call on my cell phone or connect to the Internet, it still works as a camera, so I charge it up again and go down to the beach to take photographs. The first thing I look for is the dead man wearing the Timberland boot, but the man and the swan are gone, washed away by the breakers.

Happy that the beach is now free of that darkness, I take photos of everything—the curved snowdrifts, the sparkling icebergs floating in the water. I even get a shot of a white seagull soaring over the house.

As I return to the cottage, I notice that the snow is now only a few inches deep in front of the shed door and this gets me excited. I don't know what I expect. The small garage is probably just full of garden tools, but I kick the ice and snow out of the way and jerk on the handle until I can finally slip through. It's a little creepy, sneaking around looking through other people's stuff, but I don't intend to steal anything.

Inside, by the dim light coming through the one dirty window, I discover a neat workbench with hammers, clippers and screwdrivers mounted on the wall. There's a box of old newspapers and cans of old paint. There's also a rack that holds saws, shovels and rakes, but the real reward for my snooping is an old Raleigh bicycle.

Struggling the bike out and up onto the porch, I inspect its condition. It's not great. Both tires are flat and the treads are worn thin. The chain is off and the back fender is bent. The gears appear to work, although they probably need oil. There's a basket on the front and cute little tassels on the ends of the handlebars. The body is bright purple. Perfect! (Well, it will be perfect when I get it fixed up.) It's so retro it's cool.

Richard and I used to bike together, when we were at the university and lived in Ann Arbor. Those were the good days . . . when we were still in love. Then later we would bike on the trails around Torrington with Jessie in a child seat behind me. I think of those times and wonder about our marriage. Fifty percent of all marriages in the US end in divorce. Why did I think we would be immune?

Propping the bike against the porch rail, I take the steps to the upper deck looking out at the huge expanse of blue water and sky. A few last ice floes bob up and down and far in the distance, I can hear geese, one small V heading north, a harbinger of spring.

WHEN I GET back inside, I get out *Birds of Lake Erie*, a book that I found in the Nelsons' small library, and settle myself on the sofa to read about geese. Seagull Island, the book says, along with the other islands of the Lake Erie Basin, is a stopping place for migrating birds. Thousands will come here in spring and fall.

This is my opportunity to learn more about them, I decide. The Nelsons have left a pair of binoculars. I was always a good student and what else do I have to do? I'll keep notes in my journal using the bird book. I'll be the Sara Audubon of Seagull Island! I pick up a pen and begin.

CANADA GOOSE
The most widespread goose in North America
Black head and neck with a marked white "chin strap"
Dark gray upper body, light gray underneath
Voice: a deep musical honk or bark
Migrates Alaska to Mexico, (overwinters in some places in the USA)
Wingspan: 4–6 feet
Alaska to Mexico . . . amazing!

CHAPTER 12

Angels

Pale blue sky without a cloud, dark blue water of the inland sea with small ice blocks bobbing up and down.

There's something romantic about calling Lake Erie a *sea*, as if I live on the shores of the Baltic or the Mediterranean, and I try to imagine how this place will look in the summer. It should be beautiful. I've paid rent for March, April and May. I'll have to figure out how to call Mrs. Nelson and see what the rent will be for June, July and August. Probably lots more because it's the tourist season, but it will be worth it. Also, money isn't my problem. *My* problem is getting a bank card and checks.

Eugene Burke said the credit union came to the ferry dock every other Monday, so I get out one pack of hundred-dollar bills and hike into the village. As I plod along the now muddy road, I sing to give myself courage. I'm really going to stick my neck out today and the mood of the bank teller may be my undoing.

"This old man. He played one. He played knick-knack on his thumb." Since I came to Seagull Island, my voice has grown stronger. I even make the hand motions for the song, like we did when Jessie was little.

Suddenly, from a distance, I hear dogs barking, a high-pitched *whooof. Whooof. . . . Whooof. Whooof.*

I turn, but nothing stirs. I look toward the woods, still nothing. The noise stops, so I shrug and head on.

A few minutes later . . . *Whooof, whooof* again. High and clear. Then . . . I see them! Twelve white birds, flying low in a V just over the tops of the bare trees. I've never seen swans in the air before, have only seen them swimming in a city park (or lying broken on the beach next to a dead man), but what else can these be? Their black beaks stretch out in front; their black legs trail behind. What I heard a few moments before was not *whooof whooof*, but *whooo whooo*.

I think of my friend Karen and how she would have loved this. The huge white birds are like angels against the blue sky and if it were not so cold, I would kneel down. White swans like angels passing over me!

Nature is a healer, I think. It brings us peace. It opens our hearts. It gives us wings.

Village

An hour later, I finally enter the Village of Gull. This is said tongue in cheek because there isn't much of a town. No stoplight, no sidewalks, not even a red stop sign. There's a new concrete ferry dock with a ferry, but it's still locked in by ice. There's a white clapboard ferry terminal on the lakeshore along with a matching office that says CANADA BORDER SERVICES AGENCY: IMMIGRATION AND INSPECTION. The two men I saw at the airport, wearing sunglasses and their black uniforms with gold patches on the shoulder, come out of the building and get in the white van.

I keep my head low and my face turned away. The one thing I didn't anticipate when I came to the island was how tiny the population would be and how noticeable a new person is. When the men pull out of the lot and drive off, I take a big breath and continue to look around.

On the other side of the road, facing the water, there's a place called the Black Sheep Pub, the Island Family Health Clinic, Seagull Island's Ontario Provincial Police headquarters, Mike's Garage and finally a boarded-up grocery store with a sign in the window that says FOR SALE.

The ferry terminal that doubles as a bank is my destination and I'm relieved when I see a wooden placard out front announcing it's open for business . . .

ESSEX COUNTY COMMUNITY CREDIT UNION
OPEN THE FIRST AND THIRD MONDAY OF EACH MONTH,
9:00 A.M.–3:00 P.M.

Here goes nothing. One slipup and I could be deported, arrested and extradited to West Virginia. I put on my heavy plastic-rimmed specs and black beret, pull open the red front door and find myself in a large sunny room with wooden benches for travelers and a folding table set up on one side.

At the table sits a young man, dressed in a white shirt and tie with short blond hair and a silver nameplate in front of him that says Girard. He has no vault or money box, just a laptop computer and an aluminum briefcase, the kind a courier would chain to his wrist in a spy movie.

"How can I help you?" he asks in a precise tenor.

"I'd like to open an account."

"Certainly. What kind of an account?"

"Both actually, checking and savings."

Girard gets out several forms and I sit across from him at his table. Sara Livingston, I write at the top of the form in loopy feminine cursive like the Livingston woman used on her driver's license. Address: 402 Grays Road, Seagull Island, Ontario.

He looks over what I have done so far. "Is there a Mr. Livingston? Did you want a joint account?"

"Not anymore," I answer, making a sad face. "He died in Iraq." (Another lie slips out like a weasel!)

"I'm so sorry," Girard says without sounding like it. He opens the aluminum case, which is set up like a teller's tray, and hands me a deposit slip after he writes my account number on it. "How much did you want to put in?"

"Five thousand dollars US."

The man's eyebrows shoot up. "That's a lot of cash. What did you do, rob a bank?" He thinks this is funny.

"No." I join in with false laughter. "I sold my car . . . The money has to last me awhile. I'm here writing a book. Can you put half in savings and half in the checking account?"

"Sure. I just hope no one robs me on my way back to the airport. I'll have to get Officer Dolman to guard me!" he continues, still snickering.

I pull out the pack of bills and watch while Girard counts them and carefully places the bills in his case, along with the deposit slips and my forms. (I purposely didn't bring my whole stash. It's hard enough to explain the five thousand, let alone thirty-eight thousand.)

"What kind of checks would you like to order?" Girard asks, handing me a brochure titled *Personalized Checks*. I've never had fancy checks before (Richard thought they were a waste) so, just to be contrary, I choose a pale blue design with white clouds and seagulls.

The teller explains that it may be a few weeks, but he'll mail the bank card and checks from the main branch in Leamington to the post office at the country store. "There's just one more thing," he says. "I need to make a copy of your driver's license. We don't have a Xerox machine, but I can use my cell to take a photo."

This was what I was afraid of.

Test

This is the big test. Will Girard look at the real Sara's picture and challenge me? Will I pass? My heart is beating so hard, I fear he may hear it, but with shaking hands I pull out my wallet and hand him the stolen ID. Jessie's photo and some change falls on the floor and I lean down to retrieve it. *Oh, Jess! What would you think of your mother now?*

"What are you writing about?" Girard asks, while he lays the plastic card on the table and adjusts the image on his iPhone. I purposely drop some more change and kneel down to find it, keeping my face turned away.

"A woman, abandoned on an island by her husband, in the 1800s. She survives alone for a year and then some French traders find her, but things go from bad to worse and she's abused, almost a slave . . ." I go on and on, embroidering the story, hoping to draw his attention away from the real Sara's picture.

He picks up the Ohio driver's license, squints at it and glances over. "And a passport? If you're a US citizen a passport is usually required."

"You just said two forms of ID. Can't you accept my driver's license and social security card? I left my passport at the cottage."

Girard looks at the pile of money in his till. "I'd hate for you to have this cash sitting around at home. Give me your social security card. I'll take it for now and you bring the passport the next time you come in. It's only for your file, anyway." He smiles, takes another photo with his cell and hands the cards back. "That's one of the things that's different with a credit union. You're actually a member now and especially on a small island, our service is more personal. We're always happy to serve you."

"Thanks a lot." I stand, in a hurry to leave before he asks to see my photo again. Just then the door opens and Rainbow comes in.

"Sara! I'm so glad I ran into you!" she says, giving me a big hug as if we're long-lost friends. "I want you to come visit the farm someday or maybe I'll visit you."

"Fine. Fine." (I just want to get away before the teller realizes I'm not really who I say I am.) "See you later, Rainbow." I take a deep breath and hurry outside.

Halfway home, I stop in the road and look out at the lake. What will the credit union do with the copy of my driver's license and social security card, anyway? It had never occurred to me. In the US when you open an account, the banks do the same thing, make a copy of your driver's license. Does it just go in your file or is the license number and name run through an international database? Will it show up as stolen?

I was feeling so happy that Girard didn't say anything about the photo, but now I have a new worry. By tomorrow, will the Mounties be at my door?

TUNDRA SWAN
White with a long graceful neck
Black beak and black legs
Swans migrate over the Great Lakes from Florida to the Arctic
Diet: Mostly vegetation on shore or underwater
Voice: a *kwooo, kwooo* often mistaken for hounds in the distance!
Size: 4 feet
Wingspan: 5 feet 6 inches
Magnificent!

CHAPTER 13

Intruder

In the night, cozy and warm wrapped in the green-and-white quilt in front of the fire, I fall asleep and I dream again.

With a flock of swans, I fly through the night sky, the cool wind against my face, my neck stretched out. *Whoo-Woo. Whoo-Woo.* Below, Seagull Island, like a black cloth against the gray water, looks like a seagull with its wings outstretched. Then I begin to fall. I whirl through the air, trying to right myself. Frantically, I flap my wings, but they won't work. I flap and flap, but the earth rushes toward me and then with a thump, I land next to the dead man half-covered in sand. *Whoo-woo. Whoo-woo* call the swans in the distance.

CRASH! A LOUD noise nearby shatters my sleep and I sit straight up, my eyes wide open in the dark room. The fire has gone out and the air is as cold as the dark waters of Lake Erie. I hold my breath, don't move a muscle . . . just listen . . . There's no sound but the waves.

Slowly I throw back the quilt. Slowly I put my bare feet on the chilly floor. I strain my ears for footsteps and move silently toward Lloyd's walking stick where it leans in the corner. I grab the stout oak pole and creep through the house to check that the doors are locked, and then I pad into the bathroom where I can peek out the window that looks out on the porch.

For five minutes I stand there. There's no movement, no footsteps, no shadow slinking away across the yard, and a chill ripples down my back. *And what would I do if I saw someone? I have no phone, no way to call for help.*

Finally, still gripping the walking stick, I sit back on the sofa. What made the noise? An animal? A person? What was I thinking when I moved to this remote cottage on an island in Canada all by myself? Who do I think I am? Sacajawea? Some brave woman explorer? Not hardly.

The fact is, I went from living with my parents to living with the nuns at the Little Sisters of the Cross Convent to living in a women's dorm at the University of Michigan to living with Richard after we married. I have never been alone in my life.

AT DAWN, I pull myself up, back stiff, wondering how I ended up on the sofa. Then I remember the crash in the night! This calls for an investigation, so I put on a kettle of water and dress for the cold.

I leave by the deck door and, seeing nothing amiss, circle the house looking for footprints. I peek in the shed; nothing is out of order.

Was the sound only part of the dream about the white angel swans and the dead body? I return to the cottage and find the kitchen door still locked. "Darn! I'll have to go around back."

It's when I'm cutting through the front porch that I notice the rusted bike. It's tipped over and lies on its side. That was the crash in the night! I thought I was losing my mind, imagining phantoms or thieves, but what made the bicycle fall? The wind? An animal? A Peeping Tom trying to look in the window?

Still puzzled, I return to the back deck to let myself in. That's when I notice the blue and white saucer is empty again. The milk that I've been putting out is gone. Someone is visiting me, but he may not be human.

Jessie

All day it rains and the sound on the tin roof is driving me crazy. I think of Jessie when she was little. We were a happy family then, weren't we? Richard's infidelity didn't start until three years ago. (That was the first I *knew* about it anyway.)

Often I wonder how Jessie is doing on the other side of the globe in the outback of Australia. Is she immersing herself in the cultural experience, living with her fellow students and professors in an aboriginal village? Is she studying or is she just screwing around? Does she worry about me? Does she miss me?

I think of writing or calling, but if she knew where I was, I fear Richard would find me. (Knowing him, he's probably already hired a private detective.)

MY HEART BLEEDS for Jessie and to survive I place my fist over the ragged wound and hold the red in. I tighten my jaw. Jessie will survive without a mother, the same as I did. She didn't seem to need me much the last few months! Someday I may reach out to her, but I won't go home again, won't go back to my old life. Not only did I steal all the money in our joint account and all of Richard's private stash, there's something else and it takes my breath away every time I think of it—*Robyn*.

Over and over, I've run through the doula's description of the patient's sudden chest pain and difficulty breathing. The only medical diagnosis I can come up with that involves both chest pain and hemorrhage is an amniotic fluid embolism, a rare obstetrical complication that starts with the introduction of minute particles of amniotic fluid into the woman's bloodstream and results in an immediate shutdown of the lungs, shock and then uncontrollable hemorrhage. It is so rare I've never seen it in over twenty years of practice.

My own birth was wonderful and I understand how home-birth families think . . . With the C-section rate at 34 percent in the US, women who believe birth is a normal part of life feel safer *out* of the hospital and away from a surgeon's knife.

THE RAIN HAS stopped and the sun has come out, so I put on my parka and take the wooden steps to the upper deck. Robyn's death is in the past. Clara Perry, nurse-midwife, has disappeared and she didn't do anything wrong. I say that last part again. *She didn't do anything wrong.*

As I take a seat in the gazebo, something catches my eye. Soaring high overhead in the sunlight is a huge black bird with a white head, white tail and yellow bill. It circles three times, out over the last few ice caps, flapping its huge wings once or twice, then moves on.

I have never seen one before, but I know instantly what it is. A bald eagle.

BALD EAGLE
The national bird of the United States
Lives from Mexico to Alaska
Dark with white head and tail
Yellow talons, yellow beak
Diet: Fish, mammals or waterfowl
Voice: a harsh cackle, *kleek-kik-ik-ik-ik*
Size: 31 inches
Wingspan: 7–8 feet!

Spring

CHAPTER 14

The Eagle Lands

It's March 30, by the Burke's Country Store calendar, and I'm surprised when Rainbow bumps her truck into my driveway. (I'd hoped she'd forget about visiting me and trying to make friends.)

She hops out of an old red-and-white Chevy and bounces up the steps to the porch with her long braid swinging. "Can I see your house? Sometimes I wish I had a little place of my own." Gliding from room to room, she touches the books on the shelves and the wooden cupboards, the quilt on the sofa and the stone fireplace.

"You really love seagulls!" She laughs when she sees the collection of gulls on the mantel.

I smile. "They aren't mine. The owners of the cottage collected them. The place is called Seagull Haven. It's kind of a haven for me too."

"Hey, I brought some apple wine. Want to go out on your deck and drink a glass?" Though I'm not much of a drinker, it would be rude to refuse.

Up in the gazebo we watch as a prop airplane circles the island getting ready to land and then another and another.

"Is that the plane that comes in from mainland Canada three times a day?" I ask. "Molly Lou told me about it."

"No. You can set your clock by the Windsor flights," Rainbow informs me, shading her eyes and looking up. "Eight, noon and five. The ones we can see are the planes coming in for the Ninety-Nines event this weekend."

"The Ninety-Nines?"

"It's an international organization of women pilots having a rally on Seagull. Nell Ambroy, the mayor, is really involved. Wouldn't it be wonderful to be a pilot? To wing your way through the clouds? Did you fly over from the States in that little prop plane?"

"I came by snowmobile. My boyfriend brought me."

"No way! Across the ice? I wouldn't have the nerve." (*Ha*, I think. You might if you were as desperate as I was.)

She pours us each a glass of wine then holds the amber liquid up to the sun. "Apple wine is about all Seagull Island has going for it. Wine and the sheep and the bird count . . . but we love it here."

"Molly Lou told me the same thing. What's up with the sheep anyway?" I ask. "I've seen pictures of them on several buildings and when I walked down to the credit union I counted thirty-five in a field. Are sheep like the island mascot or something?"

"You don't know about the sheep-shearing festival and the sheepdog trials?"

"No." I shrug.

"They're a big deal, bring in a lot of tourists and a lot of money. I've only been here a year, but when they have the events, all the B and Bs are full. Anyone with a spare room rents it out. The bars and restaurants are hopping. Gives people on the island enough cash to get through the winter. So what are you writing about?" *Oh great! I should have known the conversation would get around to this.*

"It's a novel about a woman abandoned on an island for years and how she survives. Finally she's rescued by some French traders, but then she's treated like a slave."

"Sounds interesting. So is that why you came here? To get the feel for island life?"

I think that she's joking, but I can't be sure. "Yes, I thought it might help."

"Do you already have a publisher?"

Now she's making me nervous. Should I have a publisher? Do you get one before or after you write a book? I don't even know a real author.

"I don't mean to be elusive but I don't really like talking about my writing that much." I evade the question. "I don't have any particular training and I'm new to the whole business. I used to be a nurse." This is only a half lie; I was a *nurse*-midwife.

"So you quit your day job to be a novelist and retired on your parents' fortune?" Rainbow teases me.

"No, my parents both died in an auto accident when I was fourteen." The truth just slips out.

"That must have been awful." Rainbow puts her warm hand over mine. "Did relatives raise you?"

"No. My parents were both only children and I was an only child too."

"So adoption, an orphanage or foster care?"

"No. I had a social worker and she got me a full scholarship to Little Sisters of the Cross Academy, a Catholic boarding school for girls. The nuns kept me until I was eighteen, then I used my parents' life insurance money to put myself through college."

"I grew up on the West Coast in Seattle," Rainbow shares. "Pretty conventional life with two parents and two brothers.

Moved to Ohio when I went to graduate school at Case Western Reserve University in Cleveland. That's where I met Dian from New Day and she brought me to the island for a visit.

"At first I thought the people on the commune were really out there trying to live off the grid. That's one of the things we're experimenting with at the farm—trying to find a level of technology that's healthy. People are *too connected*. Know what I mean? They can't get along without their cell phones or computers for an hour. They have to check their email and their Facebook accounts every few minutes. Have to tweet about everything and see if anyone's tweeted them."

"I guess I can agree with that. I've been without Internet or cell service since I got here and I seem to be doing okay."

We sit staring at the sky in the west as the sun falls into the flaming clouds and the sky turns purple, then Rainbow stands up to leave. "Red sails at night, sailor's delight. Red sails in the morning. Sailors take warning," Rainbow says as she hugs me goodbye. "I want you to visit the farm soon. We've invited so many local people, but no one ever comes."

"I guess . . . Maybe someday. I'm pretty busy with my writing just now."

I wave from the porch as she swings the red-and-white Chevy truck out of the drive, then I take the stairs back to the deck to watch the stars come out.

When I return to the gazebo, three tall gray water birds stand in the shallows hunting for fish. They're as still as stone. Then, one by one, they lift off the water, their great wings flapping slowly as they come down the beach. When they see me they turn and I follow them with my eyes as they round the point.

GREAT BLUE HERON
The largest heron in the Americas
Nests in dead trees
Feeds in shallow water for fish and small reptiles
Range: Summers in the northern US and Canada;
winters in the southern US
Voice: Very deep hoarse trumpet sound: *Franaahk!*
Size: 3 feet 6 inches to 4 feet
Wingspan: 6 feet!

CHAPTER 15

Sentry

Every night for two weeks I've put out my tempting milk and in the morning it's gone, so this evening, eager to find out who's drinking it, I decide to stay up and wait. First I lock all the doors and turn off the lights, and then I push a rocking chair up by the big front window. I'm determined to catch a glimpse of my night visitor even if I have to sit here till dawn.

IN THE QUIET, the *tick, tick, tick* of the clock on the mantel sounds too loud, and around one I begin to nod off. *What kind of lookout am I?* Just then, a shadow moves on the breakwall and I freeze. Did I imagine it? No! Slowly the animal slinks down. The dull glow from the fire illuminates the deck and I can see by its tail that my visitor is indeed a cat and a very skinny one too.

Silent as the stars, I watch the poor thing as it gobbles up the milk and lunchmeat, then licks its paws, then licks the bowl again. In the gloom I can't be sure, but the animal looks orange with white stripes. What do you call that, a tiger cat?

Weary of my perch at the window, I decide to try something daring. In my bare feet, I tiptoe over to the door, unlock it quietly and open it a crack, hoping maybe the warmth will tempt the kitty in, but it's still very wary and, smooth as mist, it slinks away under the rocks.

"So you want to play that way, do you?" I whisper. "You know you were tempted . . . I'm a patient person. If I can stay with a woman for twenty-four hours while she labors, I can out-wait you!"

Mountaineers

In the morning, I decide to take a walk up to the ferry dock. Rainbow had mentioned that people can get cell reception there and I remember seeing cars parked in the lot a couple of times when Molly took me up to the country store.

Halfway there, I begin to doubt my plan. Whitecaps top the waves, the surf is roaring and the wind is so fierce the big gray-and-black gulls are blown backward as they fly. Who will I call, anyway? Maybe the Nelsons to let them know that the cottage is fine and I'd like to rent it a few more months?

I'm surprised when I see in the distance an auto approaching along Sunset Road. As the vehicle gets closer, I realize it's the island police car and for a minute I contemplate slipping into the bushes, but that would look suspicious, so I hold up my hand in a half wave and put on a smile that seems pleasant but not very sociable.

"Hi," the cop says, stopping and rolling down his window. "I was just heading your way. Need a lift?" (I really don't want to have anything to do with the law, but to refuse a ride would seem peculiar in this weather, so I have to accept.)

"Sure, I guess. Thanks." He reaches over, throws open the passenger door and I get in but position myself as far away from him as I can.

"Where you headed?" he asks, looking toward me, and again I get a glimpse of myself in his mirrored sunglasses, short wild hair whipped by the wind, no makeup, a strange-looking character.

"I'm headed for the ferry dock. I don't get cell reception or Internet at the cottage and I was going to try to see if I have any emails . . ."

The officer expertly turns the auto around in the road. I've never been in a cop car before and surreptitiously I inspect the interior. There's a laptop computer mounted on the console, a CB radio, an instrument for tracking the speed of vehicles and a set of handcuffs, which I hope I never have to try on.

Officer Dolman doesn't seem to wear a gun, so if he has one, it must be locked in the glove compartment.

"Where you from, Sara?" Dolman breaks the silence.

"The States."

"I figured that much. What part?" I glance at the man out of the corner of my eye. *Is he just making conversation or does he suspect my presence in Canada is illegal?*

"I've lived all around but grew up in Oklahoma," I improvise.

"Oh yeah? What part? My grandmother lived in Oklahoma for a while."

Here I almost poop in my pants, but instead of compounding my error, I try a diversion.

"Is this what they call the Village of Gull?"

"This is it. Not much to see." He points to a few of the buildings. "That's my office, the Customs office, the health clinic, the Nature Conservancy, the Black Sheep Pub. Good food at the pub and it serves as a community center when we have meetings." He pulls the vehicle smoothly into the parking lot, decorated with big wooden containers of red geraniums, beautiful against the blue water and white waves. One sailboat skims the water, its sail tight with wind.

"Oh, I almost forgot. Helen at the country store sent me with a couple of letters from the credit union. I hope you don't mind. I signed for you. My cell phone number is on the back, if you need anything."

"Thanks. I'm doing fine. It's very quiet and private down there on the point . . . very isolated."

"That's what I worry about," the cop says. "Too isolated."

As soon as I get out of the cruiser and the cop takes off, I tear open the envelopes. I'm pretty sure that with special delivery I was supposed to sign for them myself, but apparently on the island things are informal. As expected, the thick envelope has my new bank card and checks, the smaller one my password. I'm as thrilled as a lottery winner. Sara Livingston of Seagull Island is becoming more legitimate every day! I just have to avoid Girard and the passport issue.

About a hundred feet ahead, I note that the white two-story ferry is now free of the ice. A few men are loading a cart, so apparently even in this wind the ferry is now running back and forth to the mainland. I'm surprised by the size of the boat because I thought it would be much bigger. It must hold only six autos and maybe three dozen people. With each wave it bounces nearly five feet in the air and then crashes down, and the huge yellow ropes that hold it are strained.

THERE ARE ONLY two vehicles parked in the lot, both facing the churning water. One is a white Toyota with a familiar yellow, blue and white license plate, and the hair on the back of my neck goes up. WEST VIRGINIA, it says. WILD, WONDERFUL. If I was beginning to feel safe in Canada, I was mistaken. It hadn't occurred to me that tourists from the Mountain State might someday visit Seagull Island.

I slink by, keeping my head down, but when I glance over, a redhead gets out of the car. "Clara!" she yells. "Clara Perry!"

I whip my head around. "Are you calling me?"

"It's Sally Heldreth from Snowshoe, West Virginia. You and your husband used to rent our cabin."

I pull back my parka hood, letting my blond spiked hair shine in the sunlight, then I shove on my false glasses as if I need them to see. "Sorry," I say, staring right at her. "Wrong person. I've never been to West Virginia."

The woman shakes her head, embarrassed. "Oh," she says. "You looked so much like someone I once knew, but it's been a long time."

"It's fine. Enjoy the island." I add this last touch, hoping I sound like a local, then scurry away, my heart still pounding.

Jed

The other vehicle in the small lot, a beat-up yellow Jeep, has Ontario plates. "Hey!" A man with a brown ponytail and a black knit cap rolls down his window and waves me over. He's long and lean with a nice smile. "You the woman staying at the point?"

"Yeah, how'd you know?" I lick my dry lips, wondering if he heard the interchange with the passenger in the white Toyota.

"Molly Lou described you. Said you had punk hair and walked everywhere because you didn't have a car. You checking your texts and emails? Want to get in? It's windy out there."

"Thanks, I'd appreciate it. I've seen people parked here and never knew why. You from the commune?"

"Nah. My name's Jed Williams. I live on the west side." He opens the door and sticks his hand out. "I'm the nurse practitioner at the clinic. Where you from?"

I stall for a moment as I crawl into the Jeep for the warmth (and to get away from the woman from Snowshoe). "I've lived all over, but I grew up in . . . Oklahoma. What about you, Jed?" He has very blue eyes, Lake Erie blue, and his face is tanned like you'd expect of a man who spends a lot of time outdoors.

"I grew up here, went to the University of Windsor and majored in writing, but then I realized I couldn't make a living at it and changed to nursing. Moved to Toronto, worked at Mount Sinai and then was lucky enough to get a job back home. What brought you here?"

I try to remember my story. "I was just looking for somewhere peaceful to finish my novel."

"You're another writer then. Cool. No family? No husband?"

"I have a daughter. She's studying abroad." (The truth forces its way out of my lying mouth, but I divert it with a more potent fabrication.) My husband died in Afghanistan."

"That's rough."

"What about you, Jed?" I try to turn the conversation. "Married?"

"Nah. I never found the right man." He gives me a sly grin, waiting to see if I'm shocked, which I am, but I try not to show it.

"You're scandalized!"

"No, not at all. Just a little surprised." (Jed looks and acts as straight as Richard, maybe more so.)

"Anyway, go on . . . Check your emails," the man says as he looks back at his own phone, a fancier one than mine and almost twice as big.

I take a big breath, still shaking inside after seeing the woman from West Virginia. I recall her ski slope condo well and the three or four spring vacations we took there when Jessie was in grade school. Those were the good days and if I weren't in this stranger's Jeep, I would break down and cry.

I take another big breath, get out my cell phone and blow away my sorrow. *This won't take long,* I think. Who knows my new email address? *Nobody!*

Connected

*W*hen I touch the search icon, the little circle goes around and around, then finally *AT&T* appears with four bars. Wow! I'm connected.

First I look for email and am surprised when I find two messages since no one knows my new email address, Runaway Bunny@outlook.com, conceived with bitter humor while sitting in the motel room in Sandusky. One email is from a senator in Ohio asking for a donation and another is from Target with a photo of their spring women's collection.

"Would you mind if I made a phone call?" I ask my silent companion.

"It's fine. I'm just playing Words with Friends on my phone."

I have only two contacts—Wanda Nelson and Lenny—so I tap Wanda's name and after four rings someone picks up the receiver.

"The Nelsons!" a man answers, his voice like sandpaper scraping over a carrot grater.

"This is Sara Livingston. Could I speak to Mrs. Nelson?"

"No. Sorry." He hangs up.

What the hell? I try again and this time the phone is answered in one ring.

"Nelsons! What is it?"

"Hi. This is Sara again. I'm on Seagull Island and I'm renting the Nelsons' cottage." I try a new approach. "It's really quite important. I don't usually have a phone connection. Can I speak to Wanda, please?"

"Well you *could*, but she's not here. She's at the hospital. What's so urgent?"

"I'm sorry to hear Lloyd had to be hospitalized. I think about him so often here at Seagull Haven. I just wanted to tell Wanda that the pipes didn't burst and the cottage has withstood the winter. I also wanted to see if I could rent the house for another six months. See if she had any plans for it."

"I'm sure she doesn't." The voice is still brusque. "Just send her a check for how long you want to stay. What does she charge you? Five hundred a month? Well, you'd better send seven hundred a month for the summer and into the fall. Also are you paying the electric?"

"You want me to? I will. How do I transfer the electricity bill into my name?"

"Listen, lady, just contact the company. I have another call coming in. Is that all?"

"Yes. Tell Wanda I love it here and I'll take care of all the bills."

"Look, I gotta go." And he hangs up again before I get a chance to ask his name.

"Problem?" asks Jed.

"No, not really. It was good. I got the cottage for another few months, but Lloyd Nelson must be getting worse. He has cancer and is back in the hospital. The man I talked to was understandably stressed and kind of rude. You probably heard I said I'd take over the electric. I wonder what other bills there would be."

"Well there's the hydroelectric, yard work and water . . . No, you probably have a well on the property. I cut lawns and trim trees in the summer if you ever need someone, but hey, I'm due at the clinic in thirty minutes. You want a ride home?"

"Sure," I say, surprised and grateful.

Outside it's still blowing and the bushes and tall grass along the shore bend in the wind.

"You know where I'm staying?"

"Everyone does."

BONAPARTE'S GULL
Gray with black head in spring
Pointy tail when in water
White in the summer with black on edge of wing
Common on lakes, rivers and the ocean in large flocks
Diet: small fish and crustaceans
Voice: a rasping grrrrr
Range: Alaska to Mexico
Smallest of all common gulls
Size: 13 inches
Wingspan: 3 feet

CHAPTER 16

Ambassador

*N*ow that the beach is no longer covered in snow and ice, I take a regular afternoon hike to Gull Point, always looking for a Timberland boot (and the body connected to it), but there's only sand, driftwood and the occasional plastic water bottle, which I carry home, planning to recycle them if I ever figure out how. This morning it's almost hot and the waves are as big as the Atlantic.

THE LAST TIME I was at the ocean was with Richard. We left Jessie with one of our friends and went away together, trying to save our marriage. (This was after his first affair.)

The romance with a biology department secretary only lasted a semester. It was Karen who told me. She'd seen them kissing at Jackson's, a local bar. Richard begged for my forgiveness and, because of our daughter, I gave him a chance.

His second affair was with a graduate student in geology and it lasted longer, but we went to counseling and I decided that at least some of our marital problems were my fault. I was working sixty hours a week as a nurse-midwife, teaching new midwifery students, taking doctoral courses and trying to be a mom. I was riding the fast train and the track was beginning to wobble. What time did I have left to nurture our marriage?

Hoping to heal our relationship, I gave up my aspirations of getting a PhD. (What did I need one for anyway? Delivering babies and caring for women was what I loved.) I stopped teaching midwifery students and lost fifteen pounds. It didn't work. Three months after Karen died, Richard was at it again, and this time my nurse-midwife partner, Linda, had to break the bad news.

While attending a medical conference, she'd seen him at a hotel in Charleston with a thirtysomething blond. Just to be sure it wasn't an innocent flirtation, she followed them to his room. No doubt about it. They went in together, arms around each other, and shut the door.

This last dalliance was the straw that broke the camel's back. I moved into a bedroom upstairs, took off my wedding ring and gained the weight back. I didn't bother to confront Richard or ask that we go back to counseling. My husband was a cheat. It didn't matter if the woman was a secretary, grad student or his dentist. It didn't matter if he said it was all a misunderstanding. He was guilty, I was sure, and I was through with him.

As I STROLL along the beach today, I scan the horizon from east to west, looking for people on the beach, boats in the bay or storm clouds threatening. During the night a log has floated in and, using it for a bench, I sit down and take off my shoes. I'm just going to do it, I decide. I'll go wading!

I'm not one who boldly dives into the water. I take it step by step, letting each inch of my body get used to the cold. Richard used to tell me I was torturing myself, that it was better to just jump in.

That's what is so unbelievable about my running away. You'd

think, if Clara was going to do something so extreme, she'd have come up with a detailed plan. Now, here I am, up to my knees in the freezing waters of Lake Erie, an illegal alien, living day to day, always checking the horizon for danger.

A SMALL FLOCK of ducks lands in the water in front of me. At first I think they're mallards, but I'm wrong. The males have smooth brown heads with black and white wing feathers. Both sexes have long necks and pointy tails.

There must be some courtship activity going on because the drakes keep stretching their necks in an erotic way and puffing their chests up and then shaking their tails. Over and over they do their water dance, while the speckled brown females innocently swim around watching the dancers out of the corners of their eyes. When I wade closer, the flock rises from the lake with a clattering of wings all around me and this brings me unexpected joy.

"Hello, ducks!" I cry like the official ambassador of Seagull Island. "You are beautiful!" I raise my hand in salute. "Welcome. Welcome! Welcome to Canada."

NORTHERN PINTAIL
Common on fresh water
Swims in pairs or small groups
Breeding male, long neck, white breast and long tail
Female looks like female mallard
Diet: eats seeds on shore and in water (that's interesting)
Range: Alaska to Mexico
Voice: Quacks like a mallard
Size: 21 inches
Wingspan: 3 feet

Trapped

On my way home from the beach, I hear a strange wail. *Eeeeeeeeee! Eeeeeeeeeeow!* It seems to come from the porch. Running, I circle the house, seeking the source, and for the first time get a good look at the feral cat. It's a pitiful sight—boney and covered with burrs, eyes caked with mucus and an infected torn ear.

The bike on the porch has fallen on top of the poor thing and the cat's tail is caught in the spokes. It probably wanted to play with the tassels on the handlebars and it occurs to me that maybe that's how the bike fell down that dark night.

As I approach, the cat begins to hiss. He bares his sharp teeth. I can see now that the animal is a *he* and I'd like to capture him and tend to his wounds, but there's no way I want to get scratched. (Cat scratch fever is a bad one. Some patients even have to be hospitalized for IV antibiotics.)

Running inside for my heavy mittens, I grab the cardboard carton that's used to hold kindling and dump what's left of the twigs on the hearth. Then I hurry back outside. Pussy is still there, cowering and hissing. This is going to be tricky!

First I lay a gloved hand on the cat's back. "Nice kitty. Nice kitty."

Hisssssssss. Meeeeeeoooooow!

"Okay, forget the *Nice kitty*. Listen up, feline, this is what's going to happen. First, I'm going to try to get your tail out of the spokes while holding you down with my other hand. If I can get your tail free, I'll flip the bike off, grab you by the back of the neck and stuff you in this box. You're going to be terrified, but trust me, I know what I'm doing." This makes me smile, but Pussy doesn't get the joke.

"Okay, here goes." Within seconds the tail is untangled and the hissing cat's in the bag (well, box).

Pleased with myself, I carry the shaking receptacle into the cottage and contemplate what to do next. I would like to wash the poor beast, cut the burrs from his fur and at least wipe out his infected eyes, but in the animal's current frenzied state, that seems impossible.

It would be nice if I'd purchased a first-aid kit back in the States with some antibiotic ointment and a few other things like Band-Aids and cortisone cream, but I didn't think of it and all I have here is a bottle of acetaminophen, some Rolaids and an old package of Dramamine I found in my briefcase.

Not knowing where to start, I decide to feed the poor thing, so I get out a piece of salami. "Here, Kitty," I say sweetly and shove the meat into the box.

If only there was some way to anesthetize the cat . . . a little barbital or Valium. Then, with a devious smile, I remember the Dramamine in the bottom of my briefcase. I used to carry it for Jessie, who would get carsick when we drove in the mountains, but what interests me is its side effect . . . drowsiness.

The old Dramamine box says each pill is fifty milligrams. I could crush a pill and put it in milk. The trouble is, I have no idea how much a small animal can take. I don't want to end up the Dr. Kevorkian of cats.

Deciding the small feline can probably handle a quarter of a tablet, I split the tab once and split it again. Then I crush the tiny quarter tab into powder. Just to make it really tempting I warm up the milk, then I slip the milk, in a teacup, into the box.

Meoooooow! goes the cat, and it tries to get out, but the flaps are already down. While I wait the thirty minutes I estimate it will take to sedate the animal, I collect my supplies: shampoo, a bar of soap and a pair of fingernail scissors that I find in a drawer in the bathroom. Having time to kill, I snoop around some more, just to see if I've missed anything.

There are four deep drawers and four shallow drawers under the bathroom counter. What I find is a razor, a half bottle of cough syrup, some safety pins and a condom still in its wrapper—some of them useful items. I can use the razor for sure. The hair on my legs is getting absurd. And the cough medicine might be useful someday. But the condom? No use for that!

In exactly thirty minutes, I go sit by the box to see if the cat seems sleepy. There's no hissing or scratching, not even a peep. I shake the box a little (still nothing). I just hope I haven't killed the poor thing!

Slowly I open one of the flaps. Slowly I put my one hand inside.

"Kitty? Kitty?" He's out cold.

SINCE I HAVE no idea how long the cat will be sedated, I have to work fast. First, I submerge the floppy animal in a sink full of warm water, up to his neck. I wash him all over with shampoo. Next, I cut off the burrs and clean his eyes with a soft cloth. Finally I attend to the torn ear, but there's not much I can do besides cleanse it with the bar of soap and remove the caked blood. Finally, I take the pitiful thing and lay him on a towel on the hearth.

Tiger, that's his new name, has short striped orange-and-white fur that is now clean and shiny. Except for his thinness and the torn ear, he looks almost normal. While I wait for him to come to, I curl up on the sofa with my dinner (a cheese sandwich, an apple and a glass of milk) and watch to see what will happen.

Within minutes he opens one eye and then closes it. What occurs next is completely unexpected. The woozy cat stands up and wobbles toward the sofa, still somewhat drunk from the

Dramamine. I pull my bare feet up, afraid he might claw me, but all the starving thing wants is some food. When I put a small piece of cheese on the knee of my jeans, he jumps up on the sofa and eats it, then he curls up next to me, closes his eyes and purrs.

RICHARD AND I never had pets. Jessie wanted a puppy, and she and I pored over the Petfinder website together, but Richard said dogs were a useless expense and also he was allergic. Now, staring down at the feline, I realize how lonely I've been and I softly pet him with one finger. "Are you going to be my buddy?" I say.

Outside the big picture window, a flock of small black birds lands on the highest branches of the still-bare cottonwoods. I strain my head to see them, careful not to disturb Tiger, and make out a slash of red on each wing.

RED-WINGED BLACK BIRD
Male has distinctive red epaulets with yellow margins
Female and young are brownish with pointed bill
The birds are very gregarious, traveling and roosting in large flocks
Most live near waterways
Voice: A loud metallic check or a gurgling o-ka-lay
Range: Canada to Costa Rica
Size: 7–9 inches long

CHAPTER 17

Band of Black

*W*armth! Finally! The sky is a pale blue with a row of white cotton-ball clouds along the southern horizon. Seagulls wheel overhead, geese honk, ducks quack and red-wing black birds twitter in their squeaky metallic voices. Today, only patches of snow linger along the breakwall. Even the grass is beginning to green. It's really spring now! I can feel it and I've opened all the windows to let in the air.

Sitting on the upper deck, one side of my face warm from the sun, I hold Tiger in my lap and stroke his soft fur. He's still a skinny thing and will probably always be small, but I think that I've tamed him. I've kept him in the house every day since his bath. I even brought up a bucket of sand from the beach and he's using it in an old dishpan I found in the shed.

I close my eyes and take a deep breath, letting all the sorrow and fear of the last few months flow out of me. I take another breath and another. If I start thinking about Karen or Jessie or the fate of poor Robyn, I drop into despair, but I'm shocked at how content I am the rest of the time, happier than I have been for years, as if I've dropped into a secret world of my own, a sanctuary, a place of peace.

When I open my eyes a few moments later, I notice a dark

cloud on the horizon, a thin black line. As I watch, it moves closer and the lake becomes agitated. Turquoise water turns gray and soon whitecaps are hurled up on the rocks. Spray even dampens my face. "Holy cow!" I laugh, jumping up and dropping Tiger.

When I glance toward the western horizon again, I see that the line of black is now a band of black and getting closer. "Looks like rain," I say to myself and decide I should close the windows and bring in some dry wood for the evening.

"Tiger," I call. "Tiger! Kitty . . . Kitty?" No answer. I just let go of him for a minute, but Tiger has run off under the rocks.

I'M ON MY way back from the woodpile, when the air temperature drops twenty degrees and it starts to snow. *What the hell?* I just make it up to the front porch as the wind slams the door behind me. The whole house shakes and I run around closing windows. Within minutes I can't even see outside.

This must be a blizzard, but I've never seen anything like it. Snow swirls madly. The sky, the deck and the gazebo are gone. When I go into the kitchen I can't see the pines out the window. I can't see the road! We're cut off from everything. I say we, meaning Tiger and I, but where's Tiger?

"Tiger!" I call, cracking open the front door. "Tiger!" But my voice can't penetrate the roar of the storm.

"Tiger!" I call more loudly, going to the deck door. When I pull my head in, my hair is caked with hard snow and already three inches covers everything. If the power goes off, it will really be cold. Maybe I should try to get some more wood . . .

Bundling up in my snowmobile outfit, complete with boots and heavy mittens, I stumble down the steps. This is risky, I know, and I've warned myself before not to do anything foolish, but if I can just get the logs onto the porch, I can bring them in one by one later . . . Pushing forward against the raging wind I stumble and fall, rise and fall again. The swirling whiteness is smothering me. The icy particles sting my eyes and the hood of my snowmobile suit blows back off my head.

With hands stretched out, I crawl forward until I finally hit something solid, the corner of Lloyd Nelson's work shed. A little to the left and I could have wandered into the woods and been lost. I don't even bother to bring back the wood. I just crawl through the snow, following my trail, until I get back to the porch, exhausted.

ALL AFTERNOON THE snow comes in sideways and beats on the windows, beats on the doors. The lights flicker and come on again and I find myself wishing Richard were here. Not that I miss him, but he's so competent and calm. In the Arctic this storm would probably be nothing.

I get out my candles and matches, glad I'd thought to purchase them. I get out my flashlight and extra batteries. By seven P.M. my bean soup is done and it's time for supper. At eight the lights flicker again and go off. I wait, but eventually conclude the lines have blown down. I can live without light, but can I live without heat?

As the electric baseboards cool and tick more slowly, the cottage grows colder, so I build up the fire but I'm careful not to waste wood. I close my bedroom door and the bathroom door to keep the heat centralized. I hang quilts over the arch that leads to the kitchen and over the big picture window.

Outside the wind shrieks, trying to get in. I think of the birds. Where do the seagulls go in a blizzard? Where are the geese and the red-winged black birds? I peek out the picture window. There's nothing to see, just white flying everywhere. White. White.

ALL NIGHT IT snows and all the next day. Every few hours I crack the door and call for Tiger, but he never comes in. It's hard to tell day and night anymore and I have no idea how deep the snow is, but when I go out on the porch for wood, I estimate two feet on the flat with drifts up to three.

IN THE NIGHT the wind sounds like wolves outside my door.

"Mommy!" someone calls. It's a child and I must get to her through the blizzard. "Mommy! Mom!" It's Jessie. I know I'm foolish and risking my life, but I bundle up in my snowmobile suit and prepare to go out in the blizzard to find her. In the yard, an army of honking Canada geese bars my way. They flap their wings and peck at me, but I fight through them as they tear my snowsuit to shreds. "I'm coming, Jessie . . ."

The wind is still howling when I jerk myself out of the dream. My covers have come off in the struggle with the geese and I can still hear the voice out in the storm. *Mommy! Mommy!*

Sun God

In the morning it's the silence that wakes me. The drift that once separated the upper and lower deck is back. Like a sculpture, the white mound is carved and swirled, but there's no way I can get the front door open.

Since the power is still off, I put the quilt back up over the big front window and stoke the coals. I hate to use the Nelsons' nice cooking pot over the open flame because it will be blackened, but I must have something hot to drink. And while the water heats, I put on my winter gear and go out on the porch. Here snow has drifted in too, but only a foot and I'm able to find a few remaining logs.

Everything is so quiet. No wind. No motors in the distance. There's only the whisper of snow falling from the pines. Then I hear a *cheep cheep.*

It's a bright red cardinal sitting on the porch rail that makes me smile. "You survived too, did you?" He cocks his head and looks up at me, asking if I have any food. I bring out some breadcrumbs.

The woodpile is only thirty feet from the porch and I can see it quite clearly now, but the depth of the snow intimidates me. Cautiously, I place my foot down where I think the steps must be and am surprised when I find the snow is as hard as cement. Carefully I move forward, walking across the surface as light as a fox. Only once I break through and I remind myself that a broken leg might be the end of me. In ten minutes I've brought in three armloads of logs, all the while keeping an eye on the horizon, afraid the blizzard will be back with a vengeance.

BY NOON THE sun shines in and warms more than the air. It warms my heart. I take down the quilt over the picture window. Lake Erie is calm and the seagulls are back.

Inspired, I stand in front of the glass, bend down to my toes in a yoga pose and then reach up and back in an arch, saluting the sun. I do this three times and when I open my eyes an orange cat is sitting on top of the snowbank, the Sun God himself. I am so happy to see him, I run out on the deck . . . and slip on my butt! Unfortunately, it's not my butt that I injure. A bruise wouldn't be so bad. It's my ankle. I have twisted my ankle!

Damn. Damn. Damn. The whole time I've been here I've reminded myself that an injury when I'm alone could be fatal. Now, in one moment of inattention, I've done it. I grab my cat, grimacing with pain and hobble back inside.

NORTHERN CARDINAL
Distinctive bright red bird with a marked crest
Female is orange-brown
Diet: Seeds
Does not migrate, lives in the eastern and Midwestern US
down to Texas and Mexico, and is gradually moving north
Voice: a piercing cheep cheep
Associated with open woodlands
Size: from 4 to 8 inches

CHAPTER 18

Thaw

For two days, I'm in tears. Every time I move my ankle throbs and I have only a few Tylenol left in my purse. I bind up my ankle with strips of old sheets. I use the walking stick for support, but keep my foot elevated and try to move around as little as possible. Under the bandages the ankle is purple, a sure sign of some kind of bleeding. At first I was worried that I'd broken a bone. Now I think it is probably just a bad sprain. I let out a long sigh. Dumb. Dumb. Dumb. How could I have been so stupid!

TWO DAYS AFTER the storm, the air is balmy and it's spring again. Snow is melting everywhere. It drips from the trees. It drips through the cracks in the deck. It pours down the gutter spout, but I am still hobbling around with the support of Lloyd's walking stick.

My biggest concern is food. I can't hike to the store or even to Molly Lou's, and I limp into the kitchen to make an assessment. I have three cans of beans, a can of tomatoes, a liter of milk, two pieces of bread and some cornmeal. Not much, but I guess I won't starve.

To comfort myself, I pick up my cat and go back to bed. It's two in the afternoon, but they say, when healing, "rest is best" and within a half hour I'm dreaming again.

IN THE DREAM, Karen is taking care of my ankle. Her soft hands remove the strips of sheeting and she looks at the injury. "Now you can go to the dance," she says.

"What dance?" I ask.

"The Cinderella Ball," she tells me. "Bring Jessie."

"I can't bring Jessie," I tell her. "She is lost to me." And here I'm filled with deep sorrow.

"HELLO!" A MAN's voice calls from the road. "Hello! Miss Livingston?"

I wake with a jerk, my pillow wet with tears.

Hopping into the kitchen, I peer out the window. It's Officer Dolman, plodding up the drive on snowshoes and looking like a Canadian Mountie in a red parka, a brown cowboy hat and the shiny sunglasses.

Before he gets to the porch, I throw water on my face at the kitchen sink, hoping I don't look like the mess I actually am.

"How you doing? Did you make it through the storm?" he asks when I open the door. "I'm calling on everyone who lives alone or seems vulnerable. You come under both categories."

This ticks me off. First of all, I don't like him sniffing around like a bloodhound. Second, I don't want to be seen as vulnerable. "Well, you can remove me from your list in the future," I respond coldly. "I had candles, a flashlight and plenty of firewood."

I have no intention of asking the man in, but he takes off his snowshoes and hands me a blue nylon knapsack. "Brought you some provisions, just in case you're getting low. It will be days before the plows get down here and maybe a week until the hydro company is able to repair the downed lines."

At this point, I have to ask him in (it would look more suspicious if I didn't), so to thank the cop for bringing me groceries, I limp over to the stove and make us some tea. Then the policeman carries two kitchen chairs out on the porch, so we can sit in the sunshine listening to the snow melt.

"What did you do to your ankle?" Officer Dolman asks, still wearing the intimidating shades, and I realize I've never actually seen his eyes. On such a bright snowy day, the glasses are needed, but on a lawman they're also intimidating. Probably that's why he wears them.

"I slipped. Just a few more days of rest and I should be fine."

"Want me to look at it? I've taken advanced first aid."

Now he's getting on my nerves, all three of them.

"No, I'll be fine!" To change the subject, I point out a little gray bird, eating the breadcrumbs I'd previously put out for the cardinal. Dolman tells me it's a junco and that I can get bird feed at the country store.

"You're more of a social worker than a law enforcement officer, aren't you?" I ask to keep the conversation away from me and my injury.

"I have my master's degree in social work. Most people don't know that."

"So how did you end up a cop?"

"I was working for social services with inner city youth in Toronto and got recruited to be a detective with a gang unit. Social work is noble, but frustrating as hell."

"So now you're a cop on Seagull Island. That's a switch. I've never seen any graffiti here. I doubt there are gangs."

"No graffiti. No gangs. Not much crime either."

"So why the turnaround?"

Dolman starts taking the groceries out of the backpack—a liter of milk, some cheese, a box of crackers and a sack of apples. "It's a long story." He runs his hands through his short brown hair, which is peppered with gray, and puts on his cowboy hat. "I got to go."

Abruptly, he slides his feet into the snowshoes, fastens them and tromps away down the drive.

"Wait, Officer Dolman. I should pay you for the supplies," I yell after him, not wanting to seem unappreciative or get on his bad side. "Thanks for bringing them!" I yell. But he doesn't turn. He doesn't answer.

SLATE COLORED JUNCO
Little sparrow that flits about the forest floors
Crisp gray markings
Bright white tail feathers that flash in flight. Often seen in flocks
Diet: Seeds
Range: Canada to the southern US
Voice: a trill
Size: 6–7 inches

Dance

Fog today. The sky is flat gray and the water's gray too so there's no horizon. Finally, little dark specks come into focus and I can see birds, hundreds of them, floating out in the lake about a hundred yards away. Ducks, I think. Some new kind of duck.

This is the first time I've experienced fog on the island. Outside, on what's left of the drifts of snow, steam rises and makes more fog. By eleven in the morning I want to go back to bed, but then I remember the dream about dancing.

Shake it up, Sara! Get up and dance.

Sorry, I have no heart for it, I answer. *And anyway my foot hurts!*

Oh, for God's sake! (That's Karen talking.) *Get your butt moving.*

Hearing her voice so loud in my head, I do what she says. On my cell, I find the icon for music, then locate a free song that came with the phone, a reggae tune—*"Stir It Up."* Soon I'm standing next to the sofa, holding on with one hand and waving the other above my head. Then I try hopping and singing along. *"Come on and stir it up, little darlin'! Stir it up; come on, baby! Come on and stir it up, yeah!"*

WHEN JESSIE WAS little we used to dance a lot. We'd put on the stereo, turn up the volume and do our wildest imitation of rock stars. Those were the good days! And I wonder if we'll ever dance together again. *We will. We will!* I promise myself.

I also encouraged my patients to dance in labor, not wild like Jessie, though if they wanted to, that would be fine. Mostly, the women slow danced, holding on to their partners, standing in the middle of the birthing room, swaying to the music on their cell phones or boom boxes or just the music in their head.

It was the nurse-midwives on the Labor and Delivery floor where I worked as a new RN in Ann Arbor who showed me how beautiful birth could be. Like mother birds, they took me under their wings. Sandy was my favorite.

The first time I saw her deliver a baby, the room was dim. Pachelbel's Canon was playing on a stereo. The patient was slow dancing with her partner. Then she was in the shower singing. Then she was on her hands and knees, no stirrups, no drapes, just a mom grunting her baby out.

Sandy, who later helped me have my baby at home, didn't even tell me to take the foot of the birthing bed down; she just took a seat on the edge of the mattress and asked for some warm compresses. "It's okay, Annie. It's okay," she said softly to the mother. "It will all be over in a few minutes." And I watched as

Sandy helped the father deliver his own baby, her gloved hands over his gloved hands, and the patient didn't have a single tear.

"I did it! I really did it!" the mother cried, reaching for her wet wailing infant. Sandy gently laid the newborn across the mother's bare chest and covered it with a baby blanket. "Oh, my sweet tiny girl!" the mother whispered with tears running down her face. The father was crying too and he bent over and kissed his wife, their tears running together.

THAT'S WHY I love helping women in labor. (*Loved,* I should say.) Not that all deliveries were as simple as that one. Case in point— Robyn Layton, my home-birth patient. What kind of a wimp am I, to run away after that? I did nothing wrong. I don't think I did, anyway.

Assuming she had an amniotic embolism, as I suspect, the complication was completely unpredictable. The only thing is . . . if she'd had her baby in the birthing center in the hospital one floor away from the intensive-care ward, we might have saved her . . . we might have . . .

UNTIL DR. AGATA WAS recruited to be the head of the hospital, we nurse-midwives were allowed to attend home births. It wasn't often, maybe two or three times a year, but we enjoyed it. The soft lighting, the music, the children helping their mother.

The birthing center was nice too. We could turn the lights low and have music playing and kids present, but there were always nurses coming in and out to get vital signs, chart on the computer and monitor the baby. There were dietary personnel and housekeepers too. Occasionally you'd hear a woman screaming in the next labor room. Sometimes, in the middle of everything, they'd announce a code blue over the intercom.

When Agata changed the rules about attending home births, we midwives protested. I brought the administrator a copy of the 2014 study of nearly seventeen thousand home births that said home delivery for the low-risk mother accompanied by a trained midwife was as safe as the hospital. I highlighted the findings that 97 percent of babies born at home were carried full term, weighed an average of eight pounds at birth and were only transferred to the hospital in 1 percent of cases, but the man wouldn't budge. I told him that the C-section rate for home births was only 5.2 percent compared to the hospital C-section rate of 34 percent, but still he held firm.

"It's the malpractice insurance company that sets the rules," he told us. "It's out of my hands. You can tell your patients you're no longer able to deliver their babies at home or you can resign."

I was so mad, I actually considered leaving and starting a home-birth practice, but in the end Richard said it wouldn't be worth it. I'd have to pay for my own medical liability insurance, my own assistant, my own office and equipment, so I kept my head down and went with the program, the obedient wife and midwife.

IN THE NIGHT I wake and find moonlight streaming in from every window. I just have to go out! Hobbling out onto the lower deck, I scoop moonlight over my half-naked body. The light from the three-quarter moon spreads out across the silver water. I take the stairs to the higher deck on top of the breakwall and a sound involuntarily comes out of my mouth. "Ahhhhh!"

In joyous salute, I reach for the moon, the eye into heaven. I can't help it. A big smile comes over my face. It's pure joy. I'm in as much trouble as I've ever been in my life, wanted by the law, estranged from my daughter, hiding out on an island in Canada without a real friend in sight and still the moon follows me, dances with me, calls me.

CHAPTER 19

Obstinate

$\mathcal{I}$t's been well over a month since I provided my driver's license to Girard at the credit union and so far no Mounties have knocked on my door asking about my passport. This makes me wonder if the teller didn't run the number through a database or if they only do that when someone seems suspicious. Perhaps he forgot. It's possible.

TODAY MOLLY LOU and I are bumping our way to Burke's Country Store. Molly expertly bounces around a muddy pothole as we drive past the cider farm where the apple trees are in bloom and ten or twelve men, dressed in matching tan coveralls with hoods, are out pruning trees.

"The migrant workers always come back this time of year," Molly announces. "They make good money working here, eleven dollars an hour plus room and board. In six months they can make enough to support themselves and their family for the year back in Mexico."

I wait for her to beep and give them the peace sign, but she looks away. (Is the woman prejudiced about the farm workers as well as the hippies?) Rolling down the window to wave to them myself, the smell of the sweet apple blossoms almost overwhelms me. "So beautiful!" I say. "Rows and rows of snowy trees."

"It's a late bloom this year. Further up, you'll see the peaches and apricots," Molly says when we're well past the men. "The blossoms are a little pinker. We don't know how the crop will be yet. It was a long hard winter. At least they didn't bloom too early like last year. That's the trouble with this climate-change thing . . . Freeze. Thaw. Sun. Snow. The poor trees are as confused as we are."

"I want to say again, how much I appreciate Chris plowing me out and you taking me to the store. Did Officer Dolman tell you I hurt my ankle?"

"Yeah. He left his patrol car at our house when he plodded on his snowshoes down Grays Road. He's a good guy. Tries to take care of everyone. Smart too. Not much gets past him."

That's the part I don't like, I say to myself, and then something catches my eye.

All along the shore, big birds of prey are catching the updraft from the water's edge and circling higher and higher. There must be twenty of them. "Look. Stop. It's a flock of eagles!"

Molly pulls over on the side of the road and we get out. "Those aren't eagles," she explains. "Those are vultures, migrating north to the mainland but a dozen or so will stay here all summer."

We watch as scores of the big birds circle over our heads like bombers from a World War II movie. Just about the time I think the show is over, another ten or twenty show up, soaring higher and higher. "How can you tell they aren't eagles?"

"First, eagles don't fly in flocks and, second, can you see how the feathers on the tips of their wings curl up? Eagle's wings are flat. When the vultures land to feed it's even more obvious. Turkey vultures have featherless bloodred heads and are as ugly as sin. Still, you know spring is here when the vultures come back."

FIVE MINUTES LATER, Molly Lou pulls into the lot at Burke's Country Store and parks next to five other vehicles, some old, some new, but all muddy. (There's apparently no car wash on the island.)

"Shoot," says Molly. "It's the day the shipment comes in on the ferry and look how many people are here already. I hope they still have bread and milk. Also, I want some ripe tomatoes."

When we enter, I see what she means. For a little store on a little island, this is probably as busy as it gets. First I pick up my electric bill and junk mail at the post office, reminding myself that Molly told me I could get home delivery . . . then I head right for the tomatoes and take the last four. They're grown in greenhouses across the lake in Leamington, bright red and still attached to the vine, the prettiest I've ever seen and I give two to my companion.

"That's the last of them, two for you and two for me. No, maybe you should get three! You have more people to feed." I hand over another of the jeweled fruits.

"Hi, Eugene. Hi, Helen," I greet the shopkeepers.

Because she knows where everything is, Molly finishes first and leans against the post-office desk, gossiping with Helen, while Eugene bags my groceries. "How you doing down on the point?" Eugene asks me.

"Fine," I answer, wondering about his sudden interest.

"You going to stay through the summer?" What's with the man? He's never said two words to me before.

"I hope to. I sent Lloyd and Wanda a check." I refer to them with familiarity.

"The reason I ask is . . ." Before he can finish his sentence, Rainbow and five other hippies burst through the door. Molly Lou gives them a look that would freeze hell, and Eugene turns away, but Helen goes to the coffee bar and makes a quiet call to the cop again.

What's with these people? They act like Rainbow and her friends are a band of thieves about to steal the whole store.

"Sara!" Rainbow calls when she sees me. "How *are* you? Can you come out to the farm next week? We have six new lambs and a baby goat. You told me you would."

All the eyes in the store are on me, turkey vultures watching from the limbs of dead trees.

"Next week? What day?" I ask, as if my social calendar might be full.

"How about Friday?"

I know the locals want me to say no, but I'm obstinate and they piss me off. The hippies might be weird, but they don't seem like bad people. "Sure, that would be fun."

"Great! I'll pick you up." She gives me a one-armed hug and all the locals look the other way.

Charity

As we leave, I notice someone has set up a yard sale in the parking lot. "Can we look?" I ask Molly Lou.

"Suit yourself, but hurry," Molly answers coldly. "I have to get home." She sits in the car, staring at the lake, watching the little white ferry bounce over the waves, while I limp over. It's not that I particularly like to shop, but all I have with me is winter clothes. Summer is coming and it's going to get hot. In five minutes I've picked up a worn bathing suit, some leather sandals, an orange knit shift, a summer nightgown, two short-sleeved faded tees and three pairs of shorts, a whole summer wardrobe, all for nine dollars.

The ride home is a quiet one, until I break the silence. "What's with you and Helen and Eugene?"

"What do you mean?"

"You know, with the hippies, the organic farmers. Your eyes were like ice when they came into the store and no one even said hello. I understand you resent them for not letting their kids go to the island school, but there must be more to it than that. I felt like I was shunned myself when I said I'd come visit them."

"We want those people off the island. If we give them the cold shoulder, maybe they'll go away."

"I don't understand. I thought you said you wished they'd send their children to your school so you could get more teachers. I thought that's why you were mad."

Molly hesitates. "That's true about the school, but it's not just that . . . It's complicated."

"So what's the scoop?" At first, I don't think she's going to answer, but then she begins.

"Two hippies raped and beat up Helen and Eugene's girl, Charity, twelve years ago. She'll never come back to the island again. Helen is my aunt. Charity is my younger cousin." She takes the turn from North Wing to Middle Way a little too fast . . .

"It was summer. Charity was nineteen. She was working at the Black Sheep Pub as a waitress, and she told Dolman and the detectives from the mainland that two hippie men waited until she got off duty and she was getting on her bike to ride home. They threw her in their van, took her down to the woods on Gull Point, beat her up and had their way with her for hours. When they were through, the men tied her up, left her for the mosquitoes to feast on and took the plane or the ferry back to wherever they came from, the States or mainland Canada.

"The rapists were never found or arrested, not that it would have changed the outcome for Helen and her family. After being in a mental hospital in Toronto for a year, Charity moved to Montreal."

"But that was years ago. The people from New Day Farm probably don't even know those assholes," I say.

"It doesn't matter. We don't like their type. We want them gone. The island has a long memory."

Molly Lou drops me at the house with my food and yard-sale bargains. "Can I give you something for gas?"

"Nah, I was going there anyway."

"I'm sorry, Molly. I'm sorry about our conflict. I do understand people's feelings about Charity. It was a terrible thing and I feel so bad for Helen and her family, but I can't judge a whole group of people when likely this bunch of hippies is completely different . . . You know?"

The woman lets out a long sigh and looks straight through the windshield at the lake. "I gotta go. We just don't like them. We want them gone and we won't give up until they leave."

Returning to the cottage, I feel very blue. Not Lake Erie blue, but the blue of Jessie's eyes when she's crying. Jessie is, like Charity was, just nineteen years old.

TURKEY VULTURE
A large scavenger, gray-brown with a blue or red naked head
When in flight, the wing tips curve up
Usually seen soaring in the sky, catching the updraft or perched on dead trees
Voice: low guttural hiss when irritated
Range: Southern Canada to South America
Size: 26 inches
Wingspan: 6 feet

CHAPTER 20

Lady in Black

It's the end of April and most of the snow is gone, except little piles of it in the shade under the pines. Just for fun, I've made a little collar and leash so that I can take Tiger for walks, and today, as I'm hiking down the beach, I notice a flock of long narrow ducks riding the waves.

The ducks aren't mallards, that's for sure. The males are white with dark green heads and the females are gray with auburn heads. They cry to each other in short croaks and they swim with their faces and bills in the water looking for fish. When they dive they stay down and then they pop up again, twenty or thirty feet away.

After watching with the Nelsons' binoculars, I move on and am startled when I catch sight of a lone figure walking toward me along the sand. I don't really feel like talking to anyone, but I'm curious. As I get closer, I make out a female, tiny in stature and all wrapped in black.

"Hello!" I call, waving a greeting, but the wind takes my voice away and I realize now that the woman is not as tiny as I'd thought, she's just bent over, searching for something.

We are within fifty feet of each other before she looks up and I see that she's not just *wearing* all black . . . she *is* black.

"Hello," I say. "What are you looking for, shells?"

The woman tilts her head to one side and adjusts her dark glasses, then says in a low voice, "I haven't seen you around here before. Nice cat. I had one like that years ago. Not all cats will tolerate a leash."

"My name's Sara Livingston. I'm staying at Seagull Haven, about a half mile up the beach." I expect the older lady to introduce herself but she doesn't. Instead she explains what she's up to.

"I'm looking for pieces of colored glass, pieces of pop bottles or beer bottles that are ground smooth by the water and sand. This is the only beach on the island where you can find them. In the 1930s there used to be a tavern in Lorain, Ohio, directly across from here, on the other side of the lake. They dumped a lot of broken beer and whiskey bottles off the docks. Almost one hundred years later, the shards arrive on Seagull Island. I call them glass beach stones and use them to make jewelry and sun catchers. You won't copy my idea, will you, honey? There's not enough for two of us."

"No, but if I find any, I'll save them for you."

"Well, that's very generous . . ."

"Have you lived on the island long, Mrs. . . ."

"You ask because I'm of African descent?" She chuckles. "Funny isn't it, to be the only person of color, except the Mexican boys, with all these white folk. Wait until the summer—you'll see people of all races then.

"I've lived here fifteen years. Came from Windsor with my husband, Lowell. It was our dream to retire on Seagull and we did, but he only lasted two years. Lowell's heart failed. He died in his own bed, right next to me."

"You didn't try to get him to the hospital? I saw they have a landing pad with a big H for helicopters behind the clinic."

"No. He wanted to stay home. Said he was at peace. Died looking out the window at Lake Erie." Her eyes are dry and she smiles fondly. "Died looking at the waves and the water and the seagulls. A big white one flew over just as his heart stopped."

"Were you all alone? Just you and him?"

"Just us. Oh look, you almost stepped on it." I stare down at the sand and right next to my boot is a round oval disk the size of a tablespoon. "That's a beauty. Blue is the rarest," the old lady tells me as she holds it up to the sun.

COMMON MERGANSER
Diving duck with long pointed bill
Male: White body, green head and black back
Female: Gray with a crested rufous head
Diet: Fish
Habitat: Rivers, ponds, lakes
Range: Northern Canada to Mexico
Voice: Harsh quack or wheezy yeow
Size: 22–27 inches
Wingspan: 34 inches

Cedar and Incense

The best time for observing birds in the cove is the very early morning. Then huge flocks are to be seen: Canada geese, ducks of all kinds, seagulls and some I can't identify. There's another new bird, smaller than a mallard, a black-and-white diving duck that I've identified as a lesser scaup. (There are also greater scaup, but the book says they're mostly found on the ocean.) Sitting on the upper deck, I'm so immersed in my bird book, looking at the photos of waterfowl, that I jump out of my chair at the sound of a vehicle.

"Hi, you ready to visit the farm?" It's Rainbow, standing on the lower deck. Damn, I think, and send out a sharp sigh. I don't really want to visit the commune. I just said yes because the locals irritated me with their prejudice. I'm perfectly happy right here, and not only that, I expect it to be weird. Still, there's no getting out of it now.

"Be a couple of minutes. I've got to lock my cat in the bathroom. If I don't, he'll tear something up or pee on the rug."

"I didn't know you had a cat."

"I just adopted him, a miserable, wild, malnourished stray with a lot of health problems. He definitely had infected eyes and also a torn ear where he got in a fight with something, maybe a dog or raccoon. Apparently, I needed a roommate."

For the next five minutes we search the house and finally find Tiger under the dresser. Rainbow is able to catch him and comes to me holding the animal up to her chest.

"Wow, he really likes you," I comment.

"I've always had cats. We have three at the farm."

"I've never had a cat or a dog. My husband is allergic." (Whoops!)

"I didn't know you're married." She sits down at the round wooden table in the kitchen holding Tiger, while I check the litter box in the bathroom.

"I'm not anymore. He died in Iraq. I don't like to talk about it."

"Gosh. When was that?"

I give her a very sad look, take a big breath and repeat my mantra. "I don't like to talk about it. Brings up too many feelings. It was a long time ago." That should shut her up.

"Sorry." She comes over and hands me the cat, then on the way out to her truck, she takes my hand and pulls me close. "I just have to give you a hug! John, one of the men on the farm, was in combat in the Middle East too. He lost his left hand in an explosion, but the wounds were deeper than that. It's been hard." She's a tall woman, taller than me and she smells of cedar incense. It's like being hugged by Mother Earth.

CHAPTER 21

New Day Farm

I'm not sure what I thought the hippie commune would be like, but I suppose I'd pictured tepees with longhaired dudes walking around half-naked and people smoking dope. Maybe there would be an open shed with a wood cookstove and a long picnic table, a couple of shaggy horses out in the field, a cow, chickens scratching, a few new lambs, babies sitting in the dirt. What I discover is totally unexpected.

New Day Farm is situated on the northeast part of the island, about a half mile south of Burke's Country Store. The main house is a big two-story log lodge, well back from the road, probably built in the 1950s by some wealthy family for a retreat. It must have seven or eight bedrooms.

"I thought you'd have a hand-painted sign at the entrance that said NEW DAY FARM, with multicolored streamers blowing in the wind," I kid Rainbow as we pull up to the house, but she doesn't get the humor.

"We talked about having a sign but decided, at this point, to keep a low profile. I don't know if you've picked up on it, but the locals don't seem to like us."

"I've noticed."

"Well, can I show you around? Then we can go in. Lunch will be soon."

For the next thirty minutes we walk around the buildings and into the fields. There's a blue metal barn, two big plastic greenhouses, two small ones and a white wooden structure they call the school up by the road with windows that face the lake. Most remarkable to me are the four huge solar panels, each with thirty-six window-sized sheets of glass, situated behind the barn, invisible from the road. (*Oh, how Richard would love this!* I think, and though I no longer love *him*, I do love the part of him that wants to find a way for people to live sustainably.)

"The big greenhouses are heated by solar power," my host explains. "The others have cold crops, like spinach and kale. Eventually we'll grow our own tomatoes too."

"How'd you get the big solar panels? They must cost a fortune."

"Terrance and Dian sold their house in Toronto. We're looking into getting a wind generator too. Canada is very supportive of alternative energy."

"What about the farm? Land on an island with a lake view has got to cost a bundle." (I'm afraid I'm asking too many questions, but Rainbow is so open, if I asked her bra size, she'd probably tell me.)

"Wade inherited the farm and another ten acres further north from his uncle who didn't have children. The lodge was in bad shape when we moved in. We only had an outhouse and we had to carry water, but we have three bathrooms now."

She takes my arm and leads me up on the back porch and into the kitchen where I smell onions and garlic and the sweet aroma of baking bread.

"Hello, everyone. This is Sara, my friend from Gull Point,"

Rainbow introduces me. Two women wearing long skirts are working at a wooden cookstove and they stop to give me a hug. A man at the sink is washing fresh greens. (It's the tall guy with the ponytail I saw at the country store, now wearing an apron that says YOU ARE WHAT YOU EAT, and he has to stop and hug me too.)

LUNCH IS A noisy affair with twelve adults, four children and a baby all eating and talking at once. I'm served split pea soup with bits of carrots, a fresh micro-green salad and corn muffins. There's also cold unpasteurized cow's milk, homemade butter and honey that comes from their bees.

At our table, I'm introduced to Wade and Dian, two of the people I saw at the store. Dian's baby is Annie and Rainbow seems like the infant's second mom. There's one other man named John, who I noticed at the country store, but I didn't realize he has only one hand. He eats in silence, looking down at his plate, a handsome guy in his early thirties with short brown hair, an aquiline nose and wire-rimmed glasses.

"I wish you could stay longer," Rainbow says as we stand in the drive, ready to get into the truck. "Tonight is the May Day drum circle. It's really cool. A few of the locals came last year. This is the first one this spring."

I give her a half smile. I know about drum circles. They had them in Torrington every Friday night in the summer at Maple Ridge Park, but my husband and I never went. "Those people are a bunch of crazies!" Richard said and I believed him.

People like us didn't go to drum circles. We went to silent auctions for the Sierra Club, biology faculty dinners, concerts at the civic center, or we went nowhere at all.

When I get home, I wave goodbye to Rainbow, then I go up to the gazebo to watch the sun set in a blaze of red and orange.

It's been a good day and I'm happy I went to the farm. Molly Lou may be prejudiced toward the hippies, but I was impressed with their dedication and all they've accomplished.

It makes me wonder about my old life, how much my parents, the nuns and Richard influenced my opinions. Here on Seagull Island, where no one knows me, my life is a clean slate and my mind is clearer too.

To the right of the gazebo are a flock of white gulls floating sedately, but there's another flock further out, whirling in a circle as if they've found a new school of fish. I have my bird book and binoculars and for the first time see an auburn-headed mother duck and two fuzzy yellow babies. I study the pictures in my guide and finally decide she must be a canvasback.

In the quiet, a thought comes to me. *This is pure happiness. When you stop trying to figure everything out, you find happiness.*

CANVASBACK DUCK
Male: Gray with a white chest and round chestnut-red head
Female: Paler with rust on the head, black bill, red eye
Diet: Dives and dabbles for seeds, buds and snails
Habitat: Lakes, estuaries, marshes
Voice: A low croak and a quack
Range: Canada to Mexico
Size: 20–24 inches
Wingspan: 3 feet

Trillium Flowers

Lately I've been taking my feline on longer and longer strolls on Gull Point and he's gained in strength and girth. His eyes have cleared and his torn ear has healed, though it will always have a V-shaped notch on the top.

The thing is, we are like friends. I talk to Tiger, explain things to him. I ask his opinion. I sit on the sofa with him and rub his orange fur while I read. And petting him is not just for *his* pleasure, though the cat's purr tells me he's happy. It's also for mine.

Each time we walk on the beach, I look for the old lady, the one who makes sun catchers out of glass beach stones, but I've never seen her again and it makes meeting her seem like one of my dreams. Maybe it was . . .

TODAY FOR THE first time I saw two robins out on the lawn, the first ones this spring. The bigger brighter one had a long juicy worm and the smaller one, the female, wanted a bite. I watched with the Nelsons' binoculars as she chased him and finally got a nibble. Good for her!

Later, for the first time, I took an inland walk, but left Tiger at home. With his leash, he'd get tangled in the undergrowth and without the leash he'd wander off.

Hiking into the forest, I see pockets of water everywhere and the bare twisted trees are thick with vines. This is truly a swamp and I have to scramble in and out of the thickets to make my way through.

Sick of the brambles, I head for the light at the edge of the woods and there in a pasture, well away from the road, I observe a strange sight.

A ewe is lying on the ground, straining silently, with a little water balloon coming out of her vagina, and I instantly know what it is. *"Baaaaaaaaaaa,"* the mother says. (It's the amniotic sac, her water bag.)

I have no business here in the farmer's field and know nothing about lambing, but the midwife in me must see the mother and baby safely through their passage, so I sit down on the grass and rest my back against a tree.

The sheep strains over and over, but with no great distress. Now and then she looks at me with big eyes and then goes back to her work. *"Baaaaaaaaaaaa!"* she says, and I know it hurts, so I say words of comfort, just like I would to one of my patients.

"It's going to be okay . . . You are almost there . . . Your baby will be born soon . . . You can do it . . . You are powerful and strong . . ."

Little by little, the transparent water bag emerges intact until I can see movement inside. First come two hooves! There's a nose! Then suddenly . . . swoosh . . . the whole slimy wet mass is lying on the grass.

I fight the urge to jump in and help, but the big white sheep doesn't need me. She rises and begins licking her newborn. Lick. Lick. Lick. Her long pink tongue comes in and goes out. Lick. Lick. She's removing the sac from the little animal's face and he gasps and shakes his head. *"Baaaaaa, baaaaaa,"* goes the lamb. *"BAAAAAA,"* answers the mother. One life coming out of another! Just a simple miracle, but all around us are miracles.

BESIDES SEEING THE birth of the little lamb, the amazing thing about my hike is the new bird sounds. I've been so fixated on the water birds that I haven't paid much attention to the songbirds. There are hundreds of red-winged black birds, robins, starlings, wrens and slate-colored juncos. There are so many twittering high in the treetops that it sounds like the Amazon jungle!

On the way back, deep in the woods, I come to a swampy place so wet I have to circle around it, and that's when I see them, hundreds of trillium flowers, white trumpets with three petals, looking up at the sun. They are so beautiful I have to kneel down.

We humans think we are so important because we build houses and we can transport ourselves on horses, in autos and airplanes. We think we're better than other animals and plants because we can talk and read and destroy the whole earth with the push of a button, but here in the woods I'm just one other life form, no better than a tree or a sheep or a trillium flower.

Praying is something I've done a lot of—at Little Sisters of the Cross Academy, of course, but also more recently when I asked God to take care of Karen and Robyn (wherever their souls may be) and asked Him to watch over my Jessie on the other side of the world. Today my prayer, kneeling in the circle of trilliums, has only two words.

Thank you.

STARLING
A short-tailed iridescent black bird
Very social, congregates in large flocks
Diet: Mostly insects
Introduced from Europe to NYC in 1890
Sometimes they crowd out native species
Voice: Squeaky, raspy, can imitate other birds
Size: 7.5 inches, smaller than a robin

CHAPTER 22

Crumpled

It's a cold windy Friday and Tiger and I are on our way to visit Jed, the nurse practitioner at the clinic, for the third time. If he's busy with patients, I'll try to help him wash instruments. If it's slow, I'll sit on a stool in his office, my cat in my lap, and listen to the latest chapter in his novel or a new poem he's written. (He still thinks I'm a fellow writer, so he likes to share, but knowing nothing about the art of writing, I don't offer a critique.)

Jed, I've come to realize, is a poet as well as a novelist. He reads like the narrator of a nature show on public TV and walks around gesturing. I smile, imagining my new friend. *My friend,* I think, quickening my pace. Jed doesn't know who I really am, but he's still my friend.

About halfway to the village, crouching, ears back, my cat stops in the middle of the road. "What is it, Tiger?" I squat down, expecting to see a dog up ahead, but there's something lying in the tall yellow grass.

I approach slowly, until I see what it is, and then run forward. It's a child, a boy of about eight crumpled like a wad of Kleenex under his bike. A large limestone rock is next to his head and he's bleeding at the temple. Is this a hit-and-run motor-vehicle accident or did the kid just wobble into the ditch, fall off and hit his head?

I check his pulse. It's 38 beats per minute. Too low. Respirations are 10. Also too low. Tiger is pulling on his leash, so I tie him to a nearby bush. I have nothing with me to staunch the bleeding but my own clothes, so I unzip my parka and take off my flannel shirt in broad daylight.

Quickly I get my coat back on and then use the soft shirt to make a bandage around the boy's head, but what to do now? It's not like I can flag a vehicle down. I might wait all day.

I look at the child's body. He probably weighs sixty or seventy pounds, too heavy for me to carry. I could run to the clinic and get Jed, but something about leaving the boy lying here distresses me. It's forty-six degrees by the seagull thermometer back at the house, and if *I'm* cold, the boy lying on the ground must be close to hypothermic . . . What if he died?

There's nothing else for it. I will *have* to carry him. Even if I only make it thirty feet at a time, I must do it, but Tiger will have to stay here. I kneel beside my cat and check the rope. "Sorry, Tiger. I'll be back soon." Then I scoop up the child and stumble along, counting the steps as I go, until I make it to thirty.

Gently I lay the boy down in the road. *Breathe. Breathe.* Then I'm off again, hoping a vehicle will come along, but no one passes. "It's going to be okay," I say to the boy over and over.

As I get close to the clinic, I begin to call out, "Help! Jed, help me! Jed, help."

Fracture

"Accident! Unconscious child. Head trauma, blood loss and probable concussion," I shout, when Jed finally hears me and opens the door. Within minutes he has the boy inside.

"Warm blankets." He points to a stack of white flannel hospital blankets on a shelf, while he assesses the boy. "Are you a nurse or something, Sara? You sound like one."

"I used to be," I say and quickly change the subject. "I found him along Sunset Road near the cider farm, lying in a ditch next to a bike. I have no idea how long he was there. Know who he is?"

"Might be the Kelly boy. I haven't seen him for a while. They live on Middle Loop and school's out again today. I better call Dolman; maybe he can find the parents, and I also have to call Windsor to get a helicopter here fast. He's got to be transported."

Jed goes to the phone, while I take the boy's vital signs again.

"Blood pressure 70/40. Pulse 42. Temp 96.5," I say, writing the stats on a scrap of paper. "Not good."

When we remove my makeshift dressing, I see that the gash on the child's head is worse than I remembered. It's a triangular flap about half an inch deep. "The skin would be easy to suture." I think out loud. "But there's a good chance there's a skull fracture underneath that will require surgery. Why don't we just pull it together with butterfly closure and apply a pressure dressing? I can do it if you want, while you start an IV."

Jed looks at me, his blue eyes thoughtful. "That's what I was thinking. Probably a compression fracture. There's a neurosurgeon in Windsor. The helicopter will be here in thirty minutes. I've got to call the hospital and have the surgeon and radiologist on standby, but I'll get Dolman to start looking for the parents, then I'll start the IV." He hurries to the front office to call the regional transport team and give the report. Five minutes later, the outside door opens and the cop comes in.

"That was quick," I say under my breath, wishing the guy wouldn't hover so close.

"My office is just down the way," Dolman answers looking at the boy's face. "Don't think I've seen him before. Jed says you found him in a ditch. Good thing you were walking by. I'm going to go back and get his bike. Maybe I'll recognize it or maybe it will have something on it that will help with identification."

"Can you get my cat too? He's tied to a bush next to the bike, back on Sunset just before the cider farm and his name is Tiger."

"You carried the boy all the way from down there?" Dolman asks, and I can tell he's impressed.

"It was hard."

What happened next was harder.

Seizure

While the clinic's nurse practitioner makes phone calls and Dolman is off getting my cat and the kid's bike, the injured boy begins to seize. His eyes, which were closed, suddenly open and roll back in his head so that only the whites show. His legs stiffen. His arms shake. He takes a deep gasp for air and stops breathing. *Shit.* My adrenaline shoots up to ten and I break out in a cold sweat.

"Jed!" I yell. "Seizure!" But he's still in the front office and must not be able to hear me. I bend over the child who's moaning and shaking all over. Foam comes from his mouth and his face turns blue. I know what to do for a seizure. Give a sedative, but I can't hold the kid down on the exam table, run for Jed, start an IV and find a vial of Valium all at the same time. "Jed," I scream louder.

"What the hell?" He runs into the room. "I should have been prepared for this. I should have started the IV right away!"

"That's okay, I can inject a sedative into the vein, just get me a vial of Valium. Do you have a pediatric airway and some oxygen?"

"Valium's in the lockbox. There's an airway in there too. I'll get the oxygen set up." He runs out of the room, returns with an orange container that looks like a fishing tackle box but is filled with meds and, when the boy stops jerking around for a second, I slip the small plastic device in his mouth.

"Do you know the pediatric dose for Valium?" Jed asks. "I think it goes by milligrams per kilogram of the child's weight. What do you figure he weighs? Thirty-six kilograms? I have the dosage and weights here somewhere . . ." He begins to search through a textbook.

"We can't wait, Jed." The boy on the exam table is still seizing and very blue. "We don't know how much he weighs in *pounds or kilograms*! I'll give a small dose starting with two milligrams and see how he does." With shaking hands, I pull the clear medication into a syringe. The fact is, I have no idea how much it takes to stop a seizure in a child.

At exactly that moment, just as I'm trying to find an accessible vein, the door bursts open and three hippies, followed by Dolman, burst into the room. The only one of three hippies I recognize is Wade.

"My baby!" the woman screams, seeing the child's blue face. She spies the syringe in my hand. "What are you doing to my baby?" She has a long skirt and boots, no makeup, a nose ring and a streak of blue hair, but despite her radical look, she's as concerned and frightened as any mom would be.

"It's a medication to stop the seizure," Jed says, while trying to hold the boy still. "Your son hit his head when he fell off his bike and has a concussion. We have to stop the seizure."

"Wade." I look him in the eye. "Please get them out of here. We're doing what we can to save the child's life."

"I'll handle it," Wade says. "Come on, guys. This is like the ER. They don't need us messing up what they are trying to do for Ziggy. I know Jed and Sara. They're okay. Good people." He and the cop guide the two frantic parents into the waiting room.

Within seconds I have the vein, withdraw a little blood to be sure and slowly inject the Valium. We watch as the boy's breathing returns to normal and the seizure stops. Then Jed begins to get vital signs again.

"Heart rate 60. Respiration 16. Blood pressure 80/60. Temp 97," he announces as he writes the numbers on the leg of his scrub pants. "What kind of a nurse were you, anyway?"

"ICU," I say as if it were true. (Lies come so effortlessly once you get started.)

In the distance we can hear the *chop, chop, chop* of the helicopter from Windsor. Jed is frantically trying to finish his notes, so I call the parents into the exam room and explain what happened. I give them reassurance that there's an excellent neurosurgeon in Windsor, if Ziggy should need one, then I step back while they go to their son.

Wade comes over and puts his hand on my shoulder. "Thanks," he says, and his hand stays there, warm and reassuring until the medics, a man and woman in full flight uniform arrive, competent and kind. At that point, I back out to the waiting room.

"I HAVE SOME bad news," Dolman says, standing to hand me Tiger's leash. "Your cat was gone when I got there. I'm sorry. I called and called for him, but I knew my priority was finding the boy's parents. Can I give you a ride home? We can look for Tiger as we drive."

"You couldn't find him?" I say numbly as I climb in the squad car and shrink into the passenger door. "It took me so long to tame him."

"Maybe he'll come back," the cop commiserates. "That often happens."

All the way home we drive slowly with the windows rolled down. "Tiger!" I call. "Kitty! Kitty!" But there's no answer.

Nightwatch

Tiger is gone and I am alone again. For five days I wait, hoping he will come home. As before, I put out lunchmeat and milk in a saucer each night, but when I get up it's still sitting there. I've walked up and down the beach. I've even gone into the swamp and my mood is as dark as the overgrown forest.

Then this morning the food is gone and I decide that tonight I'll sit up as I did weeks ago and watch at the picture window, but this time I'm going to do a Hansel and Gretel trick.

Around ten, I go out to say goodnight to the stars and am surprised to hear a night bird singing. What could this be? The song varies from the voice of one bird to another, first a cardinal, then a chickadee, then a wren. Could there be several birds up in the cottonwoods at this hour? But no, cardinals and wrens and chickadees never come out at night. It's some new nocturnal species.

I shake my head in wonder. What a world we live in where there can be stars and singing birds in the dark trees and the smell of grass and the cool air on our skin!

When the bird flies away, I put milk in the bowl, crack the door open and leave a trail of dime-sized salami treats on the wood floor that leads inside to another bowl of cat food.

Then, with Pachelbel's Canon, the second free tune on my

cell phone, playing softly, I turn off the lights and prepare for my vigil with a cup of strong tea. *As I sit there I call to Jessie in my mind. I am here. I am alive,* I tell her. *I love you.*

At exactly 3:00 A.M. by the clock on the mantel, I see what I'm waiting for, a silent shadow moving over the breakwall. It jumps from one giant slab of limestone to the next. It disappears and reappears a little closer and then in one leap lands on the deck. It's Tiger!

He approaches cautiously, sniffs the food, looks around and begins to lap up the milk. When he finishes, he steps into the crack of the open door. (Here I hold my breath.) Innocently, Tiger licks a dime-sized piece of lunchmeat with his rough kitty tongue. He takes another step forward and devours the next piece. So far he hasn't noticed my presence.

For ten minutes I watch as he moves further into my lair. I am the hunter and he is my prey! Two more pieces of meat and he's *Mine! Mine! Mine!* I cackle in my head, like the bad witch in *The Wizard of Oz.*

Finally I hear him munching the kitty food and I make my move, but when I stand the chair creaks. Damn! The cat looks up and heads for the door, but I move faster. I slide across the hardwood floor and bump the door closed with my butt. Ow! *Not a smart move!* I twisted my ankle again, but I smile anyway. It was worth it. Tiger is back.

NORTHERN MOCKINGBIRD
A medium-sized gray-brown songbird, more slender than a thrush
Thin bill with a hint of a downward curve and long legs
Sings over ten other species' bird songs at a time,
sometimes even at night!
Diet: Eats insects
Aggressive about its territory
Southern Canada to Central America

Landline

*E*ating my breakfast of oatmeal and local maple syrup at the kitchen table, I startle when I hear heavy footsteps on the porch. "Hello," calls a man.

What's this? When I open the door, I'm dismayed to find the cop again. *What's he doing here, snooping around? And where's his squad car? Did he come on foot so he could sneak up on me?* Then I notice a black ten-speed bike leaning against a pine.

"Yes?"

"I wonder if could come in?" *If he pulls out a little notebook and starts asking me questions, I'll know I'm in trouble.*

"I've been thinking about you, Miss Livingston." (*Miss Livingston!* That doesn't sound good. I feel like I'm in trouble back in Catholic school.)

I lead him into the kitchen, my limbs like branches covered with ice, waiting for him to start firing questions. "When did you land on Seagull Island? Where did you come from? How did you get here? Why doesn't Customs have a record of your arrival?" But if that's on his mind, it's not where he begins.

"I know you won't think it's my business, but every time I come out here I think about how isolated you are. I don't like you living all by yourself without a phone. Your nearest neighbor is a half a mile away and the next nearest a mile. You already sprained your ankle once. What if you were seriously injured or got ill? What if you had unwelcome visitors, how would you deal with those things here alone?"

This takes me aback and for a minute I just stare at him. He's wearing a warm-weather uniform, khaki cargo shorts, a navy T-shirt with a patch on the shoulder that says Seagull

Island Police and a navy baseball hat with the same insignia. He's a big guy, with a strong chin, someone you wouldn't want to mess with and he must suspect something because he keeps showing up.

"I'll get to the point. I'm in charge of public safety on the island. A telephone line runs right to this cottage. Wanda and Lloyd used to have a phone here and I'd like you to get one. The guy from Bell Canada is on the island today and could do the installation. If you don't have the money, I'll lend you the deposit."

"Okay . . . but I'll take care of the deposit."

Dolman raises his eyebrows. "I thought you'd be a harder sell. I thought you were trying to go off the grid like the hippies."

"No, not me. I'm not that radical. Actually, I'm not even a little bit radical, I just didn't think about getting a landline. Where I came from we all used our cells."

"Where *did* you come from? I mean lately. You said you grew up in Oklahoma, but I don't think you spent your whole life there. You have no accent." I feel my heart quicken.

"I thought I mentioned it. Last place was San Francisco."

"Were you a nurse there?"

"Yes."

"Which hospital?"

"I'm a traveling nurse, so I moved around. Or I was a traveling nurse."

"And now you're a writer."

This is starting to feel like I'm being interrogated under the lights, so to keep Dolman from observing the sweat under my arms, I stand up and move toward the door. "How do I find this phone man, anyway? I need to get back to my novel."

"I'll chase him down. I'd hate for anything to happen to you. Bad things have happened to women on Seagull Island before."

Reaching Out

*N*ow that I have a telephone here in the cottage, I'm excited to use it, but who can I call? Just for a lark, I decide to try Lenny. The phone rings three times and then I hang up. What was I going to say anyway?

I consider calling Jessie in Australia and close my eyes yearning to hear the sound of her voice, but there's too big a chance my number would be traced and my whereabouts revealed to the police back in Torrington.

Frustrated, I resolve to take a nap, but not even the nap works. Tiger wants to play, so I roll on my side with my hand under the quilt and move it around like a mouse. Over and over he pounces on it. This makes me laugh and I forget to be lonely.

An hour later, I jump when the phone rings.

"Hello," says a man when I pick up the receiver, and my first thought is, it's Dolman, but how could he get my new number?

"Hi," I answer cautiously.

"Who's this? I saw your number as a missed call on my cell."

I smile with relief, now recognizing the voice. "Who do you think?"

"Someone in Canada. I can tell by the area code. Is this Rainbow? What's up, girl?" This takes me aback. Lenny, from Lorain, Ohio, knows Rainbow?

"No, Lenny. It's Sara. Remember me? The night ride over to Seagull Island on the snowmobile last February? I just thought I'd call and let you know I'm still alive."

"Oh hey, Sara! Yeah, I wondered how you were doing. Pretty strange place over there, isn't it?"

"I don't know. I guess I kind of like it. A little lonely at times, but I'm meeting people like Rainbow. How do you know her?"

"I'm friends with Wade and I've done some work for their farm."

Now I feel awkward. "Well, I just wanted to say hi. Take care of yourself."

"Sure, whatever. If you need anything, just give me a ring." He laughs and the line goes dead.

I stare at the receiver. How could Rainbow and Lenny be associated? What work could the man do for New Day? He seems like an outlaw of sorts and apparently specializes in illegal transport . . . I can only think of one thing . . . drugs. Maybe the New Day Farm is growing marijuana in the greenhouse or maybe they deal heroin or cocaine. Picturing the wholesome group around the tables in the communal kitchen, it seems unlikely, but then I'm naïve. Richard has often told me that.

A Friend

A few days later the phone rings again. "Hey, Sara. It's Jed. Molly Lou gave me your new phone number. I have a patient coming in with vaginal bleeding this afternoon. I'm really bad at this stuff. Since you're an RN, want to be a friend and give me a hand?"

"You trying to butter me up with that 'friend' line?" I smile into the phone. "What's the story?"

"I'll tell you when I pick you up. If you want, I can take you to lunch and then we'll see the patient, but later if a lot of sick people come in, I can't take you home . . . Maybe Peter Dolman would do it. I heard you hurt your ankle. You doing okay?"

I tell him I'm fine, though, in truth, I'm still limping.

At five minutes to twelve, there's a beep in the drive. It's Jed in his yellow Jeep. We park at the clinic and walk over to the Black Sheep Pub, where I notice again the shiny white convertible backing out of the parking lot.

"Whose car is that?" I ask Jed. "I've seen it around before. It doesn't look dirty and dusty like the rest of the island cars."

"Couple of real estate agents from the US. They have a home in the fancy part of the island, the Estates. With the recession and the low property prices, they've been buying up houses like crazy. You might know them, they're related to the owners of your cottage."

"Nope. Never met 'em . . . What's up with the billboard?" I shift my gaze to a new sign on the side of the road.

Enjoy Seagull Island. It Gets Better and Better
10th Annual Seagull Island Birding Celebration, June 15
Canada Day Parade and Fireworks, July 1
5th Annual Wild and Wooly Sheep Festival, July 14
Blue Water Folk Concert, August 14
Annual Essex County Sheepdog Trials, Oct 22

"Yeah," Jed says. "The township is really working on getting more tourists to come here. Seagull Island is smaller and less well known than Pelee and the other Erie islands. Two of the big draws are the dog trials and the sheep-shearing contests. Brings in contestants from all over the Midwest and Ontario, some of them national winners.

"We used to have the Monarch Celebration when they still migrated en masse across Lake Erie. It was something to see when I was a kid. Seagull Island, Pelee Island and Point Pelee on the mainland were covered in butterflies, but about 900 million have vanished and now since they're practically on the endangered species list we had to drop the event. That's why we started the Folk Fest. To bring in more tourists. It was great last year. Had about ten bands. All the tickets sold out."

"What happened to the monarchs?" I'm surprised when, as we walk along, Jed takes my hand. It's big and warm and feels safe.

"No one knows. It could be this global-warming thing or loss of habitat. Factory farms in Ontario and the US have destroyed the monarchs' habitat and the only food they eat is the milkweed plant that grows in wild places."

"The waves are bigger on this side of the island," I note, looking out beyond the sign at the whitecaps, "but I see the ferry is still running." The little white boat is just coming in.

"Oh, it always runs. Well, almost always," Jed comments.

"The lake on my side of the island is as smooth as glass today," I share.

"That's always the way it is. If it's rough on the west side, it's smooth on the east. It depends on which way the wind is blowing."

"Kind of like life. Sometimes it's rough; sometimes it's smooth. It depends on how the wind is blowing."

CHAPTER 24

Border Patrol

*A*s we enter the pub, I'm alarmed to see two new Canadian Customs agents in uniform at the counter ordering food, a man and a woman. I quickly lose my appetite and would like to get out of the pub, but I have no excuse so I suggest a table as far away from them as possible.

"Let's sit over here. It's quieter." I lead Jed to the darkest corner and position myself with my back to the officers. Everyone in the pub, except the female Customs officer, the waitress and me, is male. "How come so many men?" I ask Jed in a whisper.

"There's a work crew from the mainland here this week, setting up a couple of solar panels on the north end."

"It takes this many construction workers?"

"It's a government project. Lots of people are getting into it. Money to be made."

When the door opens again, I duck my head down as two more Customs agents enter. *What is this? A convention?* These are the ones I saw at the airport and they take a table right next to ours.

"Hi, Stan . . . Hi, Elroy. Haven't seen you for a while," Jed greets them.

"We been around," the older of the two men jokes.

"Where's your sidekick from the winter, the red-haired kid?" Jed asks.

"Oh, they transferred him last month. You know the young agents don't like it here for long. Not enough action. They want to be at the big border checkpoints so they can catch a terrorist or drug dealer. Elroy and I will be transferring back to Windsor ourselves tomorrow. Those are our replacements up front getting lunch."

I lift my head. So that's why no one from the border patrol realizes Sara Livingston didn't enter Canada in the usual manner. The Customs officers are apparently transferred regularly. Since I arrived in late February but didn't start moving around until spring, there's a good chance the new officers never noticed me and, unless there was a reason, they would never look back on their records to see when and where I entered Canada. . . .

The waitress comes over to our table. She's a small woman, maybe twenty-eight, with an upturned freckled nose and a pink uniform top that says Kristie.

"What you having, Jed? The usual?" She stands very close to him, leaning on one hip and flashing her eyes. Is she flirting? (Jed gives me a half smile, letting me know he gets the irony, since he's not interested in women.)

The nurse practitioner is a good-looking man, tall with clear skin, strong arms and straight teeth. He's also competent and kind. I'd be attracted to him myself if he hadn't told me his sexual orientation. Then again, he's probably only in his late thirties and that would be like robbing the cradle.

"No, maybe something different, Kris. Any specials?" he asks.

"Corned beef and cabbage, your fave." She hands us a laminated menu that's curled at the edges with the lunch items printed on both sides.

"Get whatever you want—my treat," Jed says to me. He turns to Kristie. "I'll take the corned beef . . . Put us both on my tab."

"You want a beer, hon?" the waitress asks him.

"No, I'm working . . . Kristie, this is Sara Livingston. She's the nurse who helped with the little boy we had to transfer to Windsor Regional the other night. She's going to give me pointers, on occasion, with women's health. You know that's not my specialty."

"Oh, the cat woman. That's great!" Kristie sits down at our table, crossing her legs, her skirt hitched up to her thighs. "People have seen you walking that orange kitty. You gonna do paps and everything? Lots of us need paps and birth control pills, but Jed doesn't like to do gynecology."

"Kristie!" That's the cook calling, indicating that there are orders ready. The girl gives me a little squeeze on the arm and hurries off.

"I'll have fish and chips," I yell after her . . . "And a diet Pepsi if you have it."

Elsa

*B*ack at the clinic, wondering what I'm getting myself into, I put on a medium-sized gray scrub top that matches Jed's. "So how do you want to do this? Give me a rundown. Have you seen this woman before as a patient?"

"Yes, but only for her yearly physicals and blood pressure."

"Well, what's her story?"

"Elsa Aubrey is a sixty-one-year-old married woman with vaginal bleeding, ordinarily very healthy. That's all I know."

"Is she on hormones?"

He consults her yellow manila folder. "Not as far as I know."

"Does she have any history of cancer? Or family history of cancer?"

"No."

"Is she sexually active?"

"God, I don't know! I guess so. She's married, but maybe they don't do it anymore." His face turns beet red.

At 1:15 P.M., the door opens and a very short woman with gray curls and square rose-colored glasses comes in, looking tense.

"Hi, Elsa," Jed greets her. "This is Sara Livingston, RN. She's going to assist me with your visit."

"It's a pleasure," she says, clearly looking like it's *no pleasure* and she'd rather be going down with the *Titanic*.

"Come on back." Jed opens the door to the exam room and shows the patient to a guest chair. He takes the rolling stool and I stand in the corner.

"So can you tell us more about what's going on?" Jed asks. "When did the bleeding start and have you ever had anything like this before?"

"It happened the first time a week ago. Then it happened again today."

That's all she says and Jed just sits there staring at a poster about the importance of vitamin D, so I take over. "Mrs. Aubrey, are you having any cramps with the bleeding?"

Here she hesitates. "No . . ."

"Any problem with vaginal dryness? Any pain with intercourse?" Poor Elsa's face is now as red as the nurse practitioner's.

"Yes to both questions. Intercourse hurts because of the dryness. Then the bleeding starts."

I don't have the heart to ask this poor lady, in front of Jed, about any possible exposure to a sexually transmitted disease, so

I just proceed with the exam. "We're going to step out while you take off your bottoms and then, just as a precaution, I'm going to do a pap test and an infection check. But most likely the cause of the problem will be something simple and easy to take care of," I reassure her.

Five minutes later I'm done with the exam.

"That wasn't so bad," Elsa says, smiling for the first time. "I didn't sleep last night I was so nervous. I haven't been checked down there for ten years. Thank you for your gentleness. And thanks to you too, Jed, for your sensitivity. So what do you think the problem is?"

I explain about vaginal atrophy. "The vaginal mucosa gets very dry and thin. It's a normal part of aging, but it makes it difficult to have marital relations and many people, even after menopause, want to have sex. I'm pretty sure that's the cause of the bleeding because it seems to happen after intercourse. The good news is that there are medications that can reverse the problem." I smile. "Just as a precaution I'd advise an ultrasound. Can you arrange that on the mainland, Jed?"

In the end, Jed sets up an appointment for the ultrasound in radiology at Windsor Regional. He calls in a prescription to the hospital pharmacy for a vaginal estrogen preparation and we send Mrs. Aubrey on her way.

"That was definitely worth the fish and chips!" Jed exclaims as soon as the patient is out the door. "God! I could never talk to a woman like that. You were wonderful."

"Thanks." (I would like to tell him that it comes with years of practice, but I keep that to myself.)

"Here, let me give you a hug!" He takes me in his arms and gives a good squeeze while rubbing my back and he doesn't let go until two cars pull into the lot. "Shoot," he says. "Looks like the clinic is going to get busy. I'll call Pete Dolman to take you home."

"It's okay. I can walk," I protest, not wanting to be around the cop any more than I have to.

"No. No. I insist!"

Howling Dog

S orry it took so long to get here. I was on the opposite side of the island checking out a complaint about a howling dog." Dolman excuses himself when he arrives at the clinic thirty minutes later. Once in the squad car, moving toward Gull Point, we are quiet.

Finally the silence feels too creepy, so I speak. "Do you ever get bored here?"

"No. Do you?"

"Not really," I answer, staring out the window as we pass cottonwood, maple and oak trees that are just beginning to bud out, little flames of green, reaching for the sun. "I have a schedule. I exercise or walk on the beach every day. I do a little house or yard work. I play with my cat. I watch the birds. I read. I write." (This last part is a lie. There's really no writing going on, except this journal and my notes about birds.)

"But I meant your job as a police officer. Most people in law enforcement seem to enjoy the rush of danger and Seagull Island isn't exactly a hotbed of crime."

"We have a few emergencies a month, some of them serious, but most of them not. It suits me fine. Mostly, I just patrol the roads, keep an eye on the empty cottages, get involved if there's a domestic dispute, help people who run out of gas and occasionally drive drunks home.

"In the summer it's a lot busier, but still not too bad. I was shot in the arm in a gunfight when on duty a few years ago in Toronto." He pauses and then goes on. "I don't tell everyone this . . . I killed a kid, just a nineteen-year-old. That was the end of that. My wife left me and I quit the force." He turns to see my reaction, but with his sunglasses on I can't see his eyes so I can't tell how he's feeling. Killing a kid has got to be traumatic.

"Your wife left you? Right after all that happened?"

"I know it sounds harsh, but she'd begged me for years to give up law enforcement. She was so afraid something would happen. She'd threatened to leave and then when I actually got shot she said, 'That's it!' I wasn't critically injured or anything, just my arm. Killing the boy was the real wound. Not that I had much choice. It was him or me."

We pull into my drive. "Would you like to come in?" I ask to be polite, praying he'll refuse. (Every time I run into the cop, I end up sharing a little bit of information I'd rather keep to myself. He's friendly enough, but still a threat, and sooner or later he's going to get suspicious . . . if he's not already.)

"By the way, did you get your phone?" he asks, getting out of the squad car. "Can I have your new number? You know, just in case I want to warn you that a tornado is coming or to provide some other public service." He grins, knowing he seems over-protective.

I scratch it on a piece of paper and he copies it down in a little blue book. "What else do you have in there about me?"

He reads it off. "Sara Livingston, new winter resident. Lives alone at Seagull Haven. Writer, Registered Nurse. Blond, late forties, approximately five foot six, a hundred and forty-five pounds. No vehicle. No phone."

"Really? You have a whole profile on Sara Livingston?"

He flashes the notebook, but I can't see what's written except the phone number, so I don't know if he's kidding. "Do you keep notes on *everyone* on the island?"

"Actually, I keep notes on everyone who lives here year-round or who owns a cottage. Then, like I might have told you, once or twice a week I go around checking on a couple of disabled or vulnerable islanders who live alone."

"Now that I have a phone, I was thinking I could call the ones you worry about. Sometimes I feel I should do something for other people, not just for myself. I could call a few times a week on days that you aren't going to visit."

"You'd want to do that?"

"Well, I'm a nurse, I have the time and now I have the phone. Might as well give it a try."

"That's great. Nita Adams hurt her hip and can't get around. She and Terry Jacob, who's a paraplegic, have no family here and everyone else is so busy working two or three jobs just to make ends meet, they don't have time to visit . . . I'll get you their numbers."

The cop's cell phone whistles once. He looks at the text message then frowns. "Shit! Pardon my language. The dog that's been howling and driving the neighbors crazy just escaped from its kennel and bit someone. Now the victim's threatening to get out his gun."

CHAPTER 25

Tough Love

This morning, I lie in bed remembering a nightmare that woke me up around three. Peter Dolman and I are walking on the beach when he pulls a gun. "You're under arrest," he says. Terrified, I break and run, but he's right behind me. I stumble in the sand, but get up just as the cop grabs my arm . . . "No! No!" I yell as I struggle to free myself. "No! No! No!" Until the sound of my own cries wake me.

What was that about? I've never been much for premonitions and signs, but the dream was so real. I haven't seen the cop for over a week, but I must double my caution when I'm around him, be friendly in an ordinary way but keep up my guard. When I escaped to this island, it all seemed so simple. I would reinvent myself and blend in, but I never counted on the local people's curiosity or a cop with a mind for sniffing out trouble.

At noon, when the phone rings, I don't get such an adrenaline rush this time. It's getting to seem almost normal.

"Hi. Sara? This is Peter Dolman. I wonder if I could ask you a favor." (*Oh yeah,* I think, *just what I* didn't *want. More cop contact.* Maybe the dream *was* a premonition!)

"That depends. I'm really busy with my writing, kind of at a critical point. I just started a new chapter." *Liar. Liar. You are just playing with your cat!* "What is it you need?"

"Well, I got a complaint about the hippies and I need to go talk to them. Wade seems like a nice enough guy, but I've never been to their commune and I thought it might help if you came along since you're on friendly terms."

"What's the complaint? Anything serious?"

"No, that's what's so aggravating. I don't know if I told you, but people who leave their vehicles at the airport have to purchase a hangtag or get a fine. Well, the hippies didn't buy the parking pass, even after I left three notices on their van, so now the township wants me to go collect the fee, plus an extra fine for ignoring the warnings."

"Wow, that's kind of harsh."

"I know! It's stupid. I'll buy you dinner later, if you'll come."

"I could just pay the fine and purchase a sticker for them."

"You're kidding, right? That sounds like the opposite of tough love. Good thing you aren't a mom." *Whoa! That was a low blow and he doesn't even know he hurt me.*

I take a deep breath and consider my options. I could stick to my story and say I don't have time to assist him, or I could go along and stay on friendly terms. Somewhere I read about two groups of anthropologists exploring in cannibal country. One group moved into the village and became friendly with the natives. The other group kept their distance and camped outside the tribal compound. They got eaten. After all, it can't hurt to get on the police officer's good side by helping him out.

"Okay, I guess I'll come, but you don't have to buy me dinner. I understand the whole situation is weird."

"Could I pick you up around four?"

"That will work."

When I hang up, Tiger still wants to play, but my energy has been sucked out of me. The cop inadvertently stabbed a hole in my mother heart. He's right. Discipline was never my strong point. I was a pushover and inconsistent. Now I sit on the couch, thinking about Jessie. I tried to be a good mom. I thought I did anyway, but maybe I didn't try hard enough. I stare at my hands and then wipe away tears.

The Scenic Route

I'm reading a new book I found on the Nelsons' bookcase when the cop shows up . . . It's called *Jonathan Livingston Seagull*. Since I'm Sara Livingston, it seemed a good pick. "You have the freedom to be yourself, your true self, here and now, and nothing can stand in your way," the author writes. I put my bookmark in the page. Do I have the freedom to be my true self? I don't think so. Not with the secrets I hide.

"Hi," the cop says, coming up on the porch and knocking. "I really appreciate this. I'd rather face a gang of thugs than a peace-loving commune." He gives a small grin.

"You do look kind of nervous. Did you shine your badge?" He's sporting a full uniform with button-up shirt and tie, complete with the hat, the sunglasses and a heavy belt with a flashlight and a holster for Mace or some other deterrent.

This time we take the scenic route north, as if we are out for a Sunday drive, probably because Dolman is dreading his errand. Instead of heading inland on Middle Loop, where there's just flat agricultural land, rocks, orchards and pasture for sheep, we follow the lakeshore on the west side up Sunset, windows open, the wind in our faces.

Everywhere there are fruit trees, but most of the blossoms are gone. Two cars approach and Dolman does the island greeting. (Funny to see a cop giving the peace sign, but why not?)

We pass the ferry dock with the little white ferry. We pass the clinic and the pub. We pass the auto repair place and the ice cream stand, which now has a placard out front.

OPEN FOR THE SEASON: WE ALL SCREAM FOR ICE CREAM.

"You know it's June when they put out that sign," Dolman comments.

"That's the Estates, isn't it, where the richie rich live?" I ask as we pass a cedar-and-stone entrance sign.

"Yeah, but not everyone who lives there is rich. I live in the Estates, for example, in a four-bedroom stone ranch. Too nice of a place for a guy like me, but I got it for a song when the housing market crashed. A sporting-goods manufacturer from Toledo had to sell his second home. I use only one bedroom, the kitchen and the den where I have a gym and wood-working shop."

We drive on past small and large beach houses of all kinds: yellow, white, blue, green, mostly wood, but some made of stone.

"There are so many cottages on this side of the island!" I say, to make conversation.

"There are cottages all around the island, except where you live."

"How come? It's pretty where I live."

"Well, Gull Point and all the woods down there are too wet, except the little rise where your cottage sits and on the other side where Nita Adams lives."

"Yeah, I discovered the swamp a few weeks ago."

"This whole island was a bog when the indigenous people hunted here. The settlers drained most of it for farms, little by little. That's what all the ditches are about."

"I noticed the ditches. They didn't look natural, too straight and deep."

"There's some more wetland up by the lighthouse in the north end. Say, did you get that bike repaired?"

"You mean the deluxe Raleigh on the porch? Not yet, but I'm going to fix it up someday."

As we cruise along the curving shoreline, I'm startled to see a large flock of sheep standing in the middle of the road. There must be one hundred or more with twenty little lambs. "Oh, look," I whisper. "Aren't they cute?"

"Yeah . . ." says Dolman, not sounding as excited as I am. He pulls to a stop, turns off the motor and rolls down his window. "It's going to be a while . . . Look there . . ."

An orange-and-black bird is sitting in a honeysuckle bush growing at the edge of the roadside ditch. "An oriole. He's after a mate." We watch as the beautiful bird hops through the leaves in pursuit of a yellow female, all the while singing a courting song.

The sheep are still milling around in the road, as if unsure where to go, when a man with white hair and a red face closes a gate. Two other fellows with darker skin follow him. "Eay. Eay," the shepherd says to the animals. "Eay. Eay." Then he whistles and out of nowhere a white and gold border collie comes running across the field and leaps over the fence. The dog seems to fly.

"Oh my God. Did you see that?" I ask. The man whistles once more and the dog jumps back over the fence and circles around behind the remaining confused sheep.

"That's Austin Aubrey and his dog, Amber. The other men are his hired hands, Mexican workers, Roberto and his nephew Santiago, who's taking courses in mechanical engineering online. Austin built an apartment for them in the loft of his barn. The same two guys come to help him every spring and summer."

"Eay. Eay," the shepherd calls, and finally all but one lamb have crossed the road and passed through a second gate. He picks up the last little lamb by the scruff of its neck, the way you'd pick up a kitten, tucks it under his arm and approaches the cruiser. "Sorry for the delay," he says.

"Hi, Austin." Dolman greets him through his open window, lifting his sunglasses, but he's turned away so I can't see his eyes. "This is Sara Livingston from down on Gull Point. I'm showing her the sights." The shepherd gives me a nod and I smile.

"How you be, Pete?" Austin asks.

"Fair to middlin'," the cop answers with a shrug. (*Fair to middlin'* is an expression that in West Virginia means *Not swell*.)

Dolman must really be dreading his errand.

ORIOLE
Small robin-sized songbird
Bright orange males with black wings and head
Female is yellow with brown wings
Voice: Beautiful whistling song
Habitat: Open woods
Diet: Insects, berries and fruit
Range: Southern Canada to Mississippi Valley and Virginia
Winters in Mexico, Florida and Jamaica

CHAPTER 26

Copper on the Commune

We stop about a hundred yards before the mailbox that says NEW DAY and I try to give Dolman the picture.

"As we drive in you may be surprised. There are three or four buildings, a big barn, a little schoolhouse and a large log house, also a bunch of greenhouses in which they grow organic vegetables and, most amazing of all, behind the big barn are four huge solar panels. Really impressive. They sell the produce and have chickens and cows just like a regular farm.

"Some of the hippies are teachers on the mainland and only come home on weekends. I'm sure that's why their car is at the airport, and they probably won't mind buying a permit and paying the fine if you explain things."

Just as we turn into their road, another vehicle pulls in behind us. It's the communal truck, but Rainbow isn't driving. It's John, the guy with one hand, and four other men, two in the front and two in the truck bed. Suddenly, I'm aware that we're sitting in a squad car, complete with a CB radio, a computer screen, and probably a handgun in the dash compartment. I hadn't given much thought to the effect the cruiser would have on the communards, especially if they happen to be growing pot or dealing drugs.

Before we can get out, hippies surround us and these don't seem like the peace-loving type.

"Hey, what's happening? Somebody busted?" says a big fellow wearing a cowboy hat and a leather vest. He thinks this is funny and everyone laughs.

Dian comes out of the kitchen, but I don't see Rainbow or Wade.

"Maybe we should come back another time," I whisper.

"Like that's going to happen!" Peter grunts and opens the driver's door. I follow, thinking maybe I can defuse the situation.

"I'm Officer Dolman of the Seagull Island OPP." He looks around the group. "Can you tell me who's in charge?" The hippies all laugh.

"Can you tell *us* who's in charge?" The cowboy with the long blond hair laughs again. (I'm sure I smell pot and Dolman probably does too.) Finally, Dian comes down from the porch, holding baby Annie. She pushes up her round wire-rimmed glasses.

"I'm in charge today," she says with authority. For a little woman, she stands very tall and the testosterone in the driveway drops two notches.

"Won't you come in, Officer?" She looks at me. "Nice to see you again, Sara. We can sit at the table. Can I get you chamomile tea? We grow and dry it ourselves."

"Yes, please," I say before the cop can say no.

Dian hands me the baby and goes to the kitchen where I can hear her putting on the kettle and getting cups out. Peter stares at the infant. Being a midwife, I'm used to people plunking their babies down in my lap, but he probably doesn't understand that everyone takes care of the children on the commune.

"Sunglasses," I say, indicating that the cop should remove his shades. (I'm surprised at my boldness, telling the cop what to do, but I know the silver bug eyes can only make the hippie woman feel uncomfortable.) The cop swiftly removes his shades and gives me a sheepish smile.

"So is this visit a social call or professional?" Dian asks when she returns with three steaming mugs and some cookies on a tray. I like her style, right down to business, and reluctantly give back her baby.

Dolman clears his throat. "Professional, I'm afraid. Is someone here the owner of a white Ford usually parked at the airport?"

"That's our other vehicle. It's registered to the corporation, New Day Farm."

"I don't know if you're aware, but anyone who leaves a vehicle in the lot at the township airport or the ferry dock has to buy a pass every year."

There's a long pause. "I guess we were remiss. How much do these permits cost and where do we get one?"

I'm trying to figure out if this is the first Dian has heard of the passes or if she's just pretending to be unaware. (Richard had an irritating habit of acting like he didn't know the rules and then pleading for forgiveness if he got caught.)

"Well, here's the problem. Your vehicle has been tagged three times with a warning that you'd get a fine if you didn't buy a permit. I put each notice under the windshield wiper myself. It's been over a month. I'm here to notify you that you have to pay or your vehicle will be towed."

Dian looks at him through those round spectacles and I imagine she's thinking this is ridiculous and I agree.

"Okay, Officer Dolman." The woman stands to get her purse. "Can you cut to the chase? How much is the fine?"

Officer Dolman looks as uncomfortable as a prostitute in a Seventh-Day Adventist Church. "Five hundred dollars."

I gasp and almost choke on my cookie. "Five hundred

dollars!" Dian and I both say in unison. I'm stunned and the hippie woman's impressive composure is gone.

"That's ridiculous, Officer Dolman," I say. "A fine that large for ignoring your warnings? Did the printout you put on the windshield say how much the fine would be?"

"I don't believe it did." The cop shifts his gaze to the window and for the first time I see that his eyes are gray with little yellow flecks around the iris.

"Isn't the punishment supposed to fit the crime?" I go on. "It's not like the van did any harm!"

Finally, Dian finds her tongue and speaks. "Thank you for coming, Sergeant Dolman. I never go to the airport, nor have I ever heard about these notices. Is there a chance they blew off in the wind?"

"I don't think so." The policeman rises and puts his shades back on. "No one else has gone this long without paying."

"Well, I'll tell the rest of the commune about it. I know we don't have that much money on hand. How long do we have to pay?"

"I imagine the township office will give you a week, but you'll have to move the car."

"Can we just buy the parking pass now and pay the fine later?"

"No, I'm sorry. You have to pay the fine before you can get a pass." Outside we can hear the men coming up on the porch. The loud guy is obnoxious and I can tell Dolman is anxious to leave.

"I'm sorry, Dian," I apologize. "I just came to show Officer Dolman where you live." (This is another white lie. Everyone on the island knows where the hippies live.) "I had no idea the amount of the fine."

Back on the road, the officer is quiet.

"That went well," I say sarcastically.

"Shit," he says. "Sometimes I hate this job. You're right. The fine is way out of line. A speeding ticket is only seventy-five dollars."

"So what's going to happen?"

"The township will probably stand firm and have the car towed and impounded." Now we're both depressed.

"I'm sorry you didn't get to look around. Their place is beautiful. I was hoping Rainbow and Wade would be home."

"It's okay. I was glad to get out of there."

"You knew their reaction was going to be bad, didn't you?"

"Yeah, I felt stupid, telling them they'd have to cough up $500."

"And my being there was going to help?"

"Moral support . . . A rain check on dinner then?" Dolman says, taking the turn onto Grays Road.

"Nah, you don't owe me anything."

"I mean it. I'm just not in the mood this evening." When I get out of the cruiser, he hands me a folder. "You still want to call a couple of the shut-ins?" I stare at his hand holding the file, his long fingers and silver ring. The sunglasses are on again, part of his armor.

"Okay . . . What shall I say when I call them? How shall I introduce myself?"

"Just say you're a friend of Peter Dolman, the cop."

A friend *of Peter Dolman, the cop,* I think as I watch him make the turn onto Grays road.

I don't think so.

Gray

For two days the rain blows in from the south. "It's too nasty to go out, Tiger." I stand at the picture window observing the roiling lake and watch as a long V of waterfowl flies low over the water. These birds seem to be neither geese nor ducks, but I see them every day. Sometimes flock after flock pass over the cove, hundreds of birds in long Vs. In the morning they fly north and in the evening they return to wherever they came from.

Dolman's folder is lying next to the phone, and for the first time I look inside. The former social worker has given me two names and numbers along with a little history of the people themselves.

The first one is Nita Adams, whom he describes as an eighty-year-old diabetic who broke her hip, had surgery a few months ago and is hobbling around again. Eugene at the country store delivers her groceries, and Jed makes home visits once or twice a month. Lately she has become terrified about falling again. Mentally, he tells me, she's sharp as a tack.

I take a big breath and dial her number. "Hello, Mrs. Adams?"

"Yes?" This is said with hesitation.

"This is Sara Livingston, RN. I'm a friend of Officer Dolman and I thought I'd call and make your acquaintance."

"Sara who?"

"Sara Livingston," I say louder. "I'm new on Seagull Island and I'm trying to make some friends."

That seems to open the door. "Oh, a newcomer. From the mainland or the States?" Here I hesitate, wishing I could say I'm from Canada, but it doesn't seem to bother her when I tell her I'm from the States.

"You're a nurse, eh? Wish you'd been here last year. Did Peter tell you I fell?"

"Yes. How'd it happen?"

"Slipped on the damn kitchen rug. I was working on one of my projects, the same thing I'm doing today. I slipped and fell and heard the bone crack. Never felt so much pain."

I remember how it opens the door to ask about people's ailments. Just to have someone listen to our troubles means a lot, especially if they're someone new, someone who hasn't heard before about our aching back, our aching hip or our aching heart.

"Do you still have a lot of pain?"

"Not so bad, except when it rains, but I can't get around like I used to. I haven't been on the beach for months. You got a man here?"

This takes me aback and for the first time I wish I could tell her the truth . . . *I did have a man, Mrs. Adams, but he cheated on me and I left him . . . I ran away. I stole all his money and took someone's ID. I left my girl too . . .* But I stick with my lie.

"No. He died in the Iraq War."

"I'm sorry. Well, honey, I got to go. You come by and visit me, if you get lonely. And call me Nita."

"I will, Nita, and you be careful. No slipping on rugs!"

The old lady chuckles and I hang up happy.

It's a feeling I used to have every day when I worked as a nurse and a midwife, the joy of helping someone else. A song comes to me and I hum the chorus. *"And in the end, only kindness matters . . ."*

Is that true?

I think that it is.

DOUBLE CRESTED CORMORANT
Black waterfowl with a long neck
Lives in open water, ponds and rivers
Roosts in trees at the water's edge
Dives for fish
Often seen standing with wings outstretched to dry the feathers
Range: Southern Florida and Mexico to midlatitude Canada
Size: 33 inches
Wingspan: 52 inches (That's almost 5 feet!)

Summer

CHAPTER 27

Bird Fest

School in Ontario must finally be out because almost overnight the island changes. There are now frequent cars and bicycles on the roads and the ferry runs three times a day. People are waiting in line at the ice cream stand and I realize that what the old lady on the beach said is true. I'm seeing evidence of so many cultures: African, Haitian, Chinese, Japanese, men with turbans, women in veils, hipsters with multiple piercings, drivers in black SUVs wearing gold chains and even some Mennonites in black hats and suspenders, the women with little white bonnets.

I knew Seagull Island had been preparing for the Bird Festival as if it was a United Nations summit, but now that it's here I see its importance. Seagull Island, and Pelee Island twenty miles to the west, are the equivalents of health spas for migrating birds heading north.

Not only are the islanders proud of the habitat that provides a haven for songbirds, raptors and waterfowl, it's a money-making venture. The population has tripled for the celebration. All the B and Bs are booked. All the cottages are rented. All the restaurants are full.

Before six this morning there were strangers with binoculars out on my beach and later there were two women on bikes in my yard, looking at a redheaded flicker up in the cottonwoods.

"So, you're from Oklahoma," Helen says casually. "What part?"

I've been asked by the owners of Burke's Country Store to volunteer at the refreshment booth located at the entrance to Seagull Island Community Park. The proceeds will go to the school library, so it seemed a good cause.

Glad I had a chance to do research on Jed's computer at the clinic last week, I answer calmly. "I grew up in Ada. It's a small town in the southern part of the state; nothing much there but the head-quarters for the Chickasaw Indian Nation and the state university."

"A pelican! You've got to be kidding. We don't have peli-cans on Seagull Island!" A man with a huge pair of field glasses around his neck appears upset.

"I swear!" a little woman in shorts and a T-shirt argues. "I saw it and I want credit. I'm not backing down!"

It's here at the entrance to the park that the bird watchers give an account of their sightings and, as I prepare hot dogs and lemonade, I watch the participants arrive on foot or by bicycle to tell Eugene Burke what they've seen. He writes the species on a long homemade blackboard.

"I'm putting it down," says Eugene. "Two years ago the Nature Conservancy biologist spotted a pelican near the light-house, so it's possible."

During the bird fest, only seniors are allowed to use motor-ized vehicles, a recent change to the rules, I've learned. Accord-ing to Helen, three years ago two competitive birders had a car crash at the intersection of North Wing and Middle Loop . . . and also a lady from Toronto got run over because a driver had spotted a rare American Pipit and wasn't watching the road.

So far no one has been killed or permanently maimed, Helen says, but the township board now restricts automobiles, except for disabled birders or people over fifty-five and their grandkids under ten. Everyone else has to walk or bike. Also, according to Molly Lou, the count is all on the honor system, but there's a highly coveted award at the end of the weekend.

So far today, everything is calm, except for the disagreement about the pelicans, and I listen as I work to the names of the birds as they're called out. Some are familiar—great blue heron, American robin, Canada goose. Some I've just learned to identify—bufflehead, lesser scaup and merganser. And some I've never heard of before—brown creeper, American coot and northern shoveler.

It's a soft sunny day with big puffy white clouds sailing past on the breeze and the bright blue lake in the distance. After the birders turn in their lists, some grab a bite to eat and stand around talking. Others just hop on their bikes to look for more birds.

Apparently there are even bird-watching *teams* and some are sporting matching T-shirts like THE MERRY BAND OF BIRDERS, THE BLUE FOOTED BOOBIES and the CLEVELAND NIGHTHAWKS. This all-male group wears black baseball caps with white nighthawks on the front and wraparound black shades, very intimidating.

"Hey, babe!" A low voice interrupts my observations as a tall man leans over me. He has on shades, a faded green T-shirt that says I HUG TREES and his arms are tanned and tattooed. At first I think it's one of the hippies from New Day, but when I see his gray-blue quick eyes, I jump up and nearly knock over the table.

Lenny

Lenny! What are you doing here? I didn't know you were a birdwatcher. Where are your binoculars?"

He gives me a wide smile and a short laugh. "I enjoy nature, but I'm not a birder. Too much work to remember their names. I brought the Cleveland Nighthawks over in my boat early this morning." He indicates the men I'd been watching just minutes before. "I thought I could stay at New Day with Rainbow and Wade, but they have all their extra rooms rented and even some cots in the loft of their barn. Any chance I could invite myself over and use your couch?"

"I guess. Sure, why not?"

"You going to the Birder's Banquet at the Cider Mill tonight? It's pretty entertaining."

"I don't think so. I didn't buy a ticket and I heard it's sold out."

"Yeah. It sells out every year, but one of the Nighthawks broke his leg skiing at Vail and he gave me his tickets. I'll take you to the banquet if you'll lend me a bed. What do you say?"

I'm suddenly aware that Helen, sitting next to me at the hot dog table, is as still as one of the black rocks in the green pasture across the road. I glance over and the expression on her face would freeze hell. She's the mother of Charity, the girl who was viciously raped years ago, and hates hippies, I remind myself.

"Can you excuse me, Helen? I'll be right back." I stand and lead Lenny into the crowd where he gives me a big hug, almost lifts me off the ground.

"Hey!" I cry out.

"What? We're still engaged, aren't we? You look great! Got a tan. Look like a real islander."

"We were only engaged for five minutes and that was months ago, but it *is* nice to see you."

"I really appreciate your taking me in. My other choice was to sleep on the boat, but there's a wind coming up and it will be choppy."

"What time is the banquet?" I ask, glancing back at the refreshment table. Lenny gets out the tickets and looks them over.

"Seven o'clock."

"Is it fancy?"

"Nah. I'm just wearing jeans and a button-up shirt."

"Okay. Do you want to meet me at my cottage? I have a few more hours before I can leave. My neighbor Molly Lou is bringing me home. You don't have a vehicle, do you?"

"Brought my ten-speed bike over in the boat and I'm docked at the sailing club on the east side, not too far from Gull Point. I'll find you. Then we can walk back to the Cider Mill together."

Our refreshment stand, I notice, is now inundated with customers so I quickly give Lenny directions, then hurry back to our table.

"He's an old friend," I tell Helen as she watches Lenny get on his bicycle and ride away.

"You're a grown woman, Sara," she says. "But be careful."

Wine and Moonlight

That was fun. I didn't know birders could be so amusing," I comment as Lenny and I return from the Cider Mill. I hang up my sweater and take off my scarf. I wore my black knit slacks to the banquet, black flats, my blue Target T-shirt and the silk rainbow scarf, the best I could do for the occasion. Lenny has on black jeans with a checked black-and-white long-sleeved shirt with the sleeves rolled up. We'd walked home under an almost full moon and it's now after eleven. His ten-speed is parked on my porch along with the ancient rusted Raleigh.

"I know what you mean. The first time I went to one of these affairs, I was mildly shocked. That bit with the trio from Toronto dressed up as turkey vultures singing Bob Marley's 'Three Little Birds' cracked me up. How'd the song go?"

"Don't worry 'bout a thing," I answer, imitating the singers. *"'Cause every little thing gonna be alright."*

"Every little thing gonna be alright," we sing together.

"It's nice to have you here, Lenny."

He comes up from behind me as I'm putting our containers of banquet leftovers in the fridge and wraps his arms around me, but before I can squirm away, he lets go and then I think maybe I liked it.

"It's nice to be here," he says. "I had a good time. Want a glass of wine? Where's your bottle opener?"

"I guess I could have another small glass." I open the top drawer next to the sink. Lenny has purchased two bottles of apple wine from the gift store at the Cider Mill.

"Which one?" he asks.

"Apple Rosehip? We can sit out on the upper deck and look at the lake." It's possible I am already a little tipsy. Each banquet ticket had included two glasses of wine along with the meal of roast lamb, grilled portabella mushrooms, asparagus and wild rice with spinach. (The organic veggies all from New Day Farm.)

Five minutes later we're up in the gazebo, looking down at water as still as molten silver under the moon. "Nice place," Lenny observes, putting the uncorked bottle down by his feet. "I can see why you like it."

I take a deep breath and smell the pines and the lilacs out by the picket fence, a nice surprise. All winter, I just thought they were scraggly old bushes that needed to be cut back; now they're full of the fragrant purple blooms. Little waves lap gently against the sand below.

Something about Lenny relaxes me. Maybe it's because he knows I'm in Canada illegally and doesn't care. Maybe it's just the way he is, a person without expectations.

He reaches for my hand and covers it with his bigger hand, long fingers, big veins. For some reason, I don't pull away. It's probably the moonlight . . . or maybe the wine.

"So what have you been doing with yourself, Lenny?" I ask, just to fill the silence.

"I was in Mexico for a few weeks. Then I came back to help my mother move into a retirement home and then I went to Italy, but that was a short trip." (This was something I hadn't expected.)

"What were you doing there? I mean, what was the purpose of your trips, business or pleasure?"

"Business." That's all he says, then he puts one finger to his lips. "Listen . . ."

"What?" He puts his warm hand on the back of my neck and turns my head toward the sound.

"Listen," he says again. Then I hear it.

Whip-poor-will. Whip-poor-will. I smile and we look at each other.

"I haven't heard a whip-poor-will in ten years," I tell him.

I didn't mean it to happen. It's just that he was so kind and his hands so warm. After the whip-poor-will we walked on the beach, took off our shoes, rolled up our pants and waded into the water holding hands. It was cold and I was laughing. Then I tripped on a rock and he caught me. That turned into a long hug and I felt something I haven't felt for years . . . a pleasure like pain in my lower pelvis . . . and my knees almost gave out.

Lenny's nice shirt was up on the deck and his torso was bare. Oh, I know I shouldn't have, but we kissed so softly and it seemed at first rather innocent. "Sara," he said into my ear as if he was calling me.

In time, we finished the wine up in the gazebo and then he led me down to the cottage, singing, "Don't worry 'bout a thing. 'Cause every little thing's gonna be alright."

And it was . . . My past and my future disappeared and there was only Lenny's strong body over mine, like a quilt of moonlight.

WHIP-POOR-WILL
A medium-sized brown and gray spotted bird, seldom seen but occasionally heard
Range: Eastern US and southern Canada in summer
Winters in Florida
Nests on the ground in the woods
Is active at night. Seen in clearings
Diet: Insects
Voice: Whip-poor-will, whip-poor-will
Size: 9 inches
Wingspan: 19 inches

Morning Has Broken

Seagulls cry. Tiger is meowing for breakfast. I'm alone in my bed, but it's clear I wasn't always alone. Lenny's backpack is on the floor along with his loafers, his jeans and an empty condom wrapper on the dresser.

I smile to myself, my body at peace.

"Morning has broken like the first morning, Blackbird has spoken like the first bird." Lenny sings the old Cat Stevens song, and there's the smell of pancakes coming from the kitchen. "Breakfast," he calls.

I think of our lovemaking. It was the first time I'd had sex with anyone other than my husband in a very long time and it surprised me in its intensity . . . but now I'm embarrassed. This is a man I was naked with only a few hours ago, not just naked of clothes, but all the way naked, down to my soul . . . now I have to go have breakfast with him and act normal?

"Coming!" I pull on my blue T-shirt and a pair of shorts. I forget the bra but stop in the bathroom to wash my face and run a comb through my hair.

Lenny is turned away, still singing, *"Mine is the sunlight. Mine is the morning."* And I sneak up behind him and wrap my arms around him, press the side of my face against his warm back. He's wearing only his knit boxers and I feel a familiar stir, but step back. At 8:00 A.M. I'm no longer under the influence of apple wine and moonlight . . .

"So what do you have to do today?" Lenny asks reaching across the table for the maple syrup.

"Nothing special. I'm on my own. My days are pretty free. I've helped at the clinic a few times and I write. I do yard work and I'm going to start calling some of the older or disabled people around the island a few times a week to make sure they're okay. It's a pretty boring life, but I like it."

"No job you have to go to?"

"Nope."

"No social life? I thought you were friends with Rainbow."

"I was."

"Was?" He pauses with a two-inch square of pancake on his fork and holds my eye.

"Yeah. I *think* she's mad. It's kind of dumb really. There's this provincial cop, Peter Dolman—a nice enough guy, I guess, but he asked me to go with him to the commune to present them with a fine for parking illegally at the airport. He'd never been to New Day before and wanted moral support.

"Rainbow and Wade weren't even home and the fine was *five hundred dollars!* Outrageous! The commune folks were pissed and I felt like a fool for even being there. Five hundred! I shouldn't have gone. Now I think Rainbow sees me as the enemy."

"We could go over and visit. Maybe that would melt the ice." I make a face. "I don't know . . ."

"Come on. I don't have anything else to do until this evening when I take the guys back to Cleveland. I'll bike back to the marina, get my boat and pick you up out in the cove in an hour. Then we'll cruise up to the north end. There's a place we can anchor just across the road from the farm. I've done it before."

I take a big breath. "Nothing ventured, nothing gained, I guess."

Lenny takes my hand and kisses the palm.

Drum Circle

"I'm nervous," I tell Lenny as we secure his long white-and-yellow speedboat about twenty yards out and wade into the shore. "Maybe this isn't such a good idea."

"Shush," he answers, taking my hand. "We can't go back now."

We arrive at New Day just as the commune is setting out lunch on picnic tables under the shade trees. Wade greets Lenny with a big hug. "Hey, man! I was hoping you'd come."

"Wade and I went to school together years ago, at Bowling Green State University just south of Toledo," Lenny explains.

I sit next to him and Wade with a group of birders from London, Ontario, and try not to look at Rainbow, who is running back and forth to the kitchen. The food is delicious. Citrus chicken with walnut pesto as well as green salad with black beans, kale and rice casserole for the vegetarians—a special spread for the visitors.

After lunch, John, who I've never heard speak before, stands up and tells people how much the commune's support has meant to him this year.

"When I came back from the war in the Middle East, I was a lost soul. I got into some bad stuff on the streets of Detroit. I met Wade and Rainbow from New Day while hitchhiking across Canada and that changed my life. They accepted me as I was, a broken warrior . . ." Here he stops and wipes his eyes. "I guess I just want to say thank-you. Thank you, everyone." He glances around the circle and then looks down.

Wade lifts his glass of wine. "Amen, brother," he says, and there are tears in his eyes too.

"Enough of this," John shouts and lifts a wooden drum over his head with his one hand. "Let's hit the beach. Everyone's welcome!" With that, we all leave the tables and follow his lead. Rainbow is on the porch steps passing out all kinds of percussion instruments. Small and large drums, cymbals, rattles, tambourines, even pots and pans with spoons for banging. I grab a wooden block and a mallet, not meeting her eyes. As we head down to the beach, Rainbow catches up with me and puts her arm around my waist, a generous gesture.

"I'm sorry about the whole thing with Dolman." I broach the subject cautiously. "I had no idea what I was getting into when I agreed to come to the farm with him. He's not a bad guy, really, and he thought the township fine was as stupid as I did. I felt like one of the bad guys." I let out my air in a long sigh.

"Forget about it. It was partly my fault. I'm in charge of paying the bills and because we didn't have the money, I kept putting the parking pass warning on the bottom of the pile." She gives me a little squeeze. "Wade and Dian went to the township meeting. They're going to let us work it off by mowing the grass in the campground. It actually might turn into a paying job. John's really into it. He loves to drive the big tractor."

Rainbow's carrying a wooden drum with spirit animals painted on it. Cars are parked along the road and more people are assembling, some with trashcans, some with real bongos. One fellow I've never seen before has a steel drum, the kind they use in the Caribbean.

I'm surprised to see Jed here too, carrying a guitar and a wooden flute. Wade and Lenny are building a driftwood fire. I can't believe I am sitting here with a bunch of hippies, but they aren't all hippies, some of the people seem to be cottagers and there's Kristie from the pub and a couple of Mexican guys from the orchard.

Just as the sunset fades in a blaze of red, *Boom* goes a bass drum . . . *Boom* answers a bongo . . . *Bam* . . . *Bam* . . . *Bamity bam bam* come in the others, slowly at first and then picking up speed.

I can't help it. The music is infectious. I begin to tap my wooden block in rhythm with the others. The sky turns purple and the flames of the campfire rise. I forget everything but the drums . . .

I forget Rainbow and Wade and Lenny. I forget Jed and John. I forget the kids running around the circle. It's the music and the firelight that transfix me and the feeling of oneness with the other drummers. I have never experienced anything like it . . . except maybe sex . . .

CHAPTER 28

Dank and Sour

In the days that follow my brief affair with Lenny, loneliness stalks me. I was feeling almost happy, living a solitary life in Canada, but when Lenny entered me, he left a hole and it's now filled with rusted water, dank and sour.

"I am rock, I am an island." I sing the Simon & Garfunkel hit. "I have my books, and my poetry to protect me . . ."

As I sit on the deck, looking out at the water birds, I find myself comparing my husband with Lenny. Did I let my marriage go too easily? Maybe . . . Probably not . . . Maybe. (I go back and forth.)

Richard and I were married in a church, but not a Catholic one because I wasn't Catholic. We had a small wedding at the Unitarian Universalist Church in Ann Arbor with a few of the sisters from the Little Sisters of the Cross, our college friends from the University of Michigan and Richard's siblings and parents.

"Until death do us part," we had vowed. I try to remember the last time we were close. For sure when Jessie was a baby and when she was in grade school, but then Richard began to travel for his research.

It wasn't that I didn't care about the issues that compelled him. I understood that global warming was real and threatened the planet; it was just that we were living in two different worlds. My life revolved around Jessie and the mothers and babies I cared for. His life revolved around his colleagues, the polar bears . . . *and other women.*

Richard isn't a bad husband. He's good at saving money and pleasant to look at. He's six feet two inches, a hundred and seventy-five pounds with straight teeth and green eyes. He donates to the Nature Conservancy and the World Wildlife Fund. He went to his daughter's soccer games. He fixes things around the house and even occasionally cooks. He takes the cars to have their oil changed. He doesn't gamble or drink to excess. He's not evil or abusive, but how many chances do you give a man who's unfaithful?

Let's face it. The marriage vows were broken long before I left Torrington.

Shut-in

Surrounded by midsummer greenery, the cottage lately seems small and close. It's only when I go out to the upper deck and look at the sky that I find relief. I lie on the warm deck and study the clouds. They move so slowly, but are always changing. Sometimes I look for the shape of an animal, a duck or rabbit or horse. If you stare long enough, whatever sadness or worry you have will ease.

Seagull Island is not wilderness. There's nothing foreign or wild about it and yet the relentlessness of nature assaults me. Everything *grows so fast.* Cobwebs that I sweep off the house today reappear by tomorrow. Weeds that I pull are back in three days.

I'm sitting on the deck reading when I notice the whine of the first mosquito. It lands on my forearm and I study it dispassionately. Soon, unless there's a strong wind, I'll have to stay inside or use insecticidal spray.

Tiger doesn't care either way. His fur protects him and for the first time I wish I were covered with fur too, instead of being one giant vanilla ice cream cone for the bloodsucking insects.

Then the midges hatch out from larvae laid in the ditches last year. They look like large mosquitoes but don't bite, and at dusk they rise like smoke from the tops of the cottonwoods. The clouds of flying insects swirl in the wind, along with the tufts of cottonwood seeds that are shedding just now.

By morning the carcasses of the midges hang in the cobwebs that cover the clapboards along with new tufts of cotton from the cottonwood trees, making the cottage look dirty and forlorn. On the other hand, the fish eat the midges and mosquitoes. And the swallows that live in the shed swoop all over the yard with their beaks open, gulping them down.

To cheer me up, Jed shares the rest of the flat marigolds he didn't have room to plant in his window box and a packet of zinnia seeds, which will brighten my yard.

I go back to the list of shut-ins. I call Nita Adams again and this time she recognizes me. Her hip is hurting more today, but otherwise she's doing okay. She needs to find someone to fix her roof, because it leaks when it rains. I make a note to ask Jed if he could do it, and I'll offer to pay him.

The next name on the list is Terry Jacob, age forty-four. She has paraplegia and has used a wheelchair since a sailboat accident five years ago. According to Dolman's social-worker notes, she's an American, had always loved Seagull Island and returned to reside permanently in her parents' renovated cottage two years ago.

Terry apparently lives alone, doesn't drive, runs the Seagull Island Weavers' Guild, has a handyman who keeps up her yard and who also brings her groceries. Otherwise, she takes care of herself.

Here goes nothing, I think. For some reason, calling someone who's about my age feels awkward. "Hello, Terry?"

"Hiya," answers a youthful voice. "What's up?"

"Oh . . . This is Sara Livingston. I live on Seagull Point and I just thought I'd call and say hello. I'm a friend of Peter's."

There's a long pause. "Pete put you up to this? Tell him to mind his own business." She slams down the receiver. *Whoa! That was worse than awkward. So much for my do-gooder spirit.*

I stare at the phone, wondering what to do next. Maybe my idea of checking on people wasn't so great. Maybe they won't appreciate it . . .

The phone rings and I answer it hesitantly. "Hello . . ."

"I'm sorry. This is Terry. I got your number on caller ID. I shouldn't have been so rude. What's your name again?"

"Sara. Sara Livingston. I'm new on the island, and I thought I could help Peter by checking on some of the people he worries about."

There's a snort on the other end of the line. "That man! If he weren't a cop, I'd shoot him myself. I don't know how I got on his list. I'm doing fine."

"I know what you mean. I'm on his list too. I live alone and he told me I had to get a phone. He was even going to pay for it. I have a cell, but it doesn't get reception except up by the ferry dock."

"Tell me about it! Cell phone reception is spotty all over the island. It sounds crazy, but it depends on which way the wind is blowing."

"So you're a weaver . . . That must be nice on an island full of sheep."

"It's great. I've just started making my own yarn. What do you do?"

"Well, I'm a nurse or was. I got burned-out and now I'm writing a book."

"Sounds interesting." There's a commotion in the background. "One sec . . . Hey, I got to go. Austin Aubrey is delivering a load of raw wool. Why don't you come over sometime? I'd love to meet you and hear about your book. Give me a call." Then the line goes dead . . .

I look at Tiger. "Well . . . that was weird. What do you think, success or failure?"

Tiger shrugs.

"This is harder than I thought and I never even asked about Terry's health."

> BARN SWALLOW
> A blue-black songbird with white to orange underneath,
> a long forked tail and pointed wings
> Feeds exclusively on insects in swooping dives
> Voice: Lilting with a squeaky quality
> Range: All over US and much of Canada
> Size: 6–7 inches

No Woman No Cry

On Sunday, Molly Lou and her family pick me up for the July 1 Canada Day celebration. We eat our picnic at the island park on a blanket and watch the tractor parade, which includes John Deeres, Fords, Internationals, some new and some old, all decorated with red and white streamers and Canadian flags. There are even kids driving lawn tractors.

It was strange celebrating the birth of a nation that wasn't mine.

No lump in my throat when they played their national anthem. *O Canada! Our home and native land! True patriot love in all thy sons command.* No tears in my eyes when I looked around at the vets wearing their old Canadian military uniforms. *With glowing hearts we see thee rise, the True North strong and free!*

THEN YESTERDAY, I was convinced to go out to dinner with Dolman. I'd told Jed, when I was at the clinic, that the cop made me nervous, though I didn't divulge why. (Jed has become my closest companion, but we still don't share secrets. That's one thing I like about him. He's private and so am I.)

"He's not a bad guy," Jed said. "We've been friends for years, been in some tough spots together. He's solid. I count on him. We have a good time. You should go."

"He wants to take me out to dinner to repay me for going with him to the commune that time he had to present them with the big fine. It was a real mess."

"He was just doing his job. Give the guy a chance. You need some male companionship."

"That's what I have you for," I tease him.

"Not the same." He grins and gives me a fake swish of his hand.

Now here I am at the Cider Mill sitting at a cloth-covered table with Peter. (I've decided I'll try to call him Peter. Everyone else does, but that doesn't mean he's not *the cop* in my mind.)

The restaurant is a step up from the Black Sheep Pub. They actually have candles in small glass containers, flowers in vases and a three-piece band on a low platform playing a reggae tune, "No Woman, No Cry."

"Nice dress," Peter says. I'm wearing the orange knit shift and leather sandals that I picked up at the yard sale across from Burke's Country Store. He's wearing khaki pants and a white polo shirt, no cop clothes, no sunglasses, and it's nice to look in his gray eyes. They are kind, I decide. Maybe that's why he has to wear the silver glasses, to look like a tough guy.

While we wait to order, I look around the large room. About half the tables are full, but there's no one I recognize. There's a bar on the side where two women sit watching the musicians. In the rear, there's a party of seven, all men, a tough-looking crew who don't appear to be tourists. Wise guys, it comes to me, but I know that's ridiculous.

Peter and I even dance while we wait for our meals, first to another reggae number—*"I shot the sheriff, but I didn't shoot no deputy"*—which cracks us both up. Then just when I think I can get off the dance floor and out of the public eye, the band starts up again and Dolman pulls me into his arms. It's an old Cyndi Lauper song I used to sing with Jessie and tears come so fast I can't stop them.

"If you're lost you can look and you will find me, Time after time."

I wipe my eyes with the back of my hand and he holds me closer. *"If you fall I will catch you, I will be waiting, Time after time."*

On the way back to the table, I excuse myself quickly by saying I need to use the ladies' room and he squeezes my hand. Once in the stall, I let the tears come. *If you're lost you can look and you will find me.* Is Jessie looking for me? Does she think I've followed Karen into a watery grave? I hold my heart with both hands to steady the spear that pierces it.

Call for a Good Time

The door to the bar opens and a strong perfume wafts into the john. I take a deep breath and blow my nose on the toilet paper. When I step out to wash my hands and face, I discover a petite blond in tight black jeans and pointy high heels, a Marilyn Monroe–type, putting lipstick on in front of the mirror. She fluffs up her bleached hair with both hands. "Hi, honey," she greets me in the glass without turning. "You live on the island?"

"Yes." I let her assume I'm a native.

"You know the big guy at the corner table?"

"Yes," I answer again, drying my hands on a paper towel. On the front of the white enamel dispenser, a message has been carved with the point of a pocketknife: "Call Charity for a good time!"

(*What the hell! Charity is the girl who was raped years ago, and that's the most tasteless graffiti I've ever seen!*) Surely no one who knew the story could think it was funny. Maybe whoever scribbled the message was some crude tourist, referring to a different Charity, but still the words have to go!

The woman behind me is probably a little drunk because she's now in the second stall fumbling with the sliding lock. "He's kind of hot. Is he a swinger?" she calls out.

"You mean Peter Dolman? He's the island cop. Doesn't seem like it."

"I thought you islanders knew everything about everyone and were all having affairs with each other. That's your reputation on the mainland."

"Really?" I swallow hard, confused and a little defensive.

"Well anyway, hon, you must know this. Is there a pharmacy or a store around here that carries rubbers?"

"No, I don't think so. They might have prophylactics at the clinic, but it's not open at night." (I say *prophylactics* just to be snooty. She pisses me off . . . implying that Seagull Island is some kind of hotbed of libertines and nymphomaniacs!)

"You don't know much, do you?" She snorts.

"I guess not." Eager to get away from her, I open the door and head for the bar to see if they have a black Magic Marker.

The bartender is in deep conversation with one of his customers about the news on the flat-screen TV mounted above the shelves full of liquor bottles.

"Another shooting at a junior high school, this one in Utah, the Mormon state," announces the female blond newscaster with the wide eyes from the Toledo station against a backdrop of crying students. The headlines under the video rank the US states in numbers of guns. West Virginia, I notice, is number four, but that's no shock. Everyone in the state hunts deer. The schools in most West Virginia counties even close for deer season.

When I ask for a Magic Marker, the bartender rummages around in a drawer and hands me one without asking what I need it for. He turns back to the screen. "Goddamn Americans!" he says to his customer. "When will they ever learn?"

Back in the women's restroom, my semi-intoxicated companion is gone and I do my best to obliterate the crude message.

Covering the words with the black ink won't alter the island girl's past, but I feel like I'm doing something to protect her. That's the midwife's job, to comfort and protect.

"I'm sorry, Charity." I lay my hot forehead on the cool white towel dispenser, giving her a hug as if she were one of my patients.

DRIVING HOME ALONG the west shore I see two sailboats bobbing up and down in the waves, their sails open, and for the first time I don't feel wary around Dolman. I know he felt me crying when the band sang the Cyndi Lauper song. *If you're lost you can look and you will find me.* I wipe my eyes again and he looks over but doesn't say anything, just reaches across the console and touches my hand. *If you fall I will catch you, I will be waiting, Time after time.*

CHAPTER 29

Wild and Wooly

Today is July 14 and the Fifth Annual Wild and Wooly Sheep Festival at the community park on the west side of the island. I planned to walk the whole way for exercise, but Molly and Chris came by just as I was making the turn onto Middle Loop and I was glad when they stopped in their Subaru.

"You should have called. It's too far to walk and too hot," Molly Lou starts out. "And we're supposed to have a thunderstorm later."

"Thanks" is all I say, promising myself again that I'll get my bike fixed next week *for sure!*

All along the shore the cottages are open for the summer with both Canadian and US flags flying from the porches. Cars and SUVs are in every driveway and kids run around on the beach.

"Look at those trees. Funny they don't have any leaves yet. What kind are they?" I indicate a grove of tall shade trees that don't provide any shade.

"Those are dead ash trees," Molly explains. "They're everywhere. The emerald ash borers kill them. It's an epidemic in the States and Canada too. Very bad. Whole forests are gone."

As we drive north, I see another stand of bare trees and another. They are not late to leaf out as I had imagined. They are just dead.

Soon we're at the park and I'm surprised to see so many people. Vehicles are pulled onto the side of the gravel road and the parking lot is full. Across the entrance is a long banner that reads, WELCOME TO SEAGULL, THE WILDEST AND WOOLLIEST ISLAND IN CANADA. Luckily I brought a couple of twenties. It costs $10 to get in.

When we get out of the Subaru, Little Chris runs off with his friends and Chris and Molly Lou wander toward the bleachers, but I want to look around first. "Meet us at the car if you need a ride home, but don't try to hoof it. Okay?" Molly orders.

"Okay, boss," I joke, but really I'm grateful for her protectiveness.

As I follow the slow-moving crowd toward four big tents, I decide to investigate the first one. It's for livestock and I find that inside someone has built rows of wooden enclosures. The pens hold sheep of all kinds. I never knew there were so many breeds.

Just for the fun of it, I inspect them all as if I was planning to raise one. In the last stall are three merinos and I decide they're my favorites—a gray ewe with two little lambs whose wool is so thick I want to dig my hands into it.

Outside in the fresh air, I take a few deep breaths and head for the next tent, a large yellow one. WEAVERS' GUILD says a banner on the side. That looks cheery! A man and a woman are sitting in the corner on bales of hay, playing a guitar and banjo. Several other women and even a little girl are carding wool. There's also a tall guy dyeing yarn in a big pot of orange liquid and a couple of weavers sitting at looms.

This is the tent for me! Just being inside with these artisans makes me happy. *"Oh then dance around the spinning wheel, grab your partners for a reel,"* the musicians sing. I walk around touching all the woven and knitted goods for sale and looking for Terry, who I've now talked to several times on the phone. She should be easy to spot, but I don't see her.

Outside, a male voice comes over the loudspeaker . . . and the music stops.

"The sheep-shearing contest is starting in the main arena!" the voice says. "Take your seats now." Everyone in the tent, save the man tending the orange dye, puts down what they're doing and heads off to the bleachers, which surround a wooden stage.

On the platform are more enclosures with sheep in them. The announcer tells us that the contest will begin with the junior sheep shearers. They'll be judged not only on speed, but also on the quality of the wool that they shear. Any nicks to the animal will count against them.

Four young men and one young woman, all dressed in jeans, stand ready, one at each pen. Then the announcer rings a bell.

When the gates swing open the contestants grab their animal and begin to clip its wooly coat with electric shears. The poor sheep don't stand a chance. Before they know what's happened they're standing naked before a crowd of hundreds. The winner is the girl, a high school senior from West Virginia and I cheer louder than anyone.

Next there's a lull while more sheep are brought up and six burly fellows in tank tops that show their muscles take the stage. Some of them are apparently regional and national winners.

The whole time we're waiting for the second contest to begin, I scan the crowd for Lenny. It's not that he promised he'd come back or that there's any suggestion of commitment, I'm just hoping . . . And what will I say to him if I do see him? "Hi there. Want to go back to bed?" We've shared so little of our lives.

It isn't until hours later, after the sheep breeders parade, that I spot him leaning against a picnic table in the back parking lot, smoking a joint and talking to a couple of men I've never seen before. Luckily he doesn't see me and I hurry on by, darting behind a blue van.

"Take a deep breath, Sara," I silently admonish myself. "You aren't Clara Perry anymore, suburban mother, faculty wife and respected medical professional in a small college town. You don't have to worry about your *reputation*. Who cares if Lenny smokes a little grass now and then? Is it any worse than downing a beer?

"Hey." I feel a touch on my arm and jerk around. "Were you going to go by without saying hello?" He swings me around and presses his body against me. I'm just about to tell him in an irritated way to get off, when he kisses me softly.

"Sorry I didn't call. I'm kind of like the New Day people that way . . . off the grid," he apologizes.

I can't help but smile. "Are those your friends?" I indicate the men at the table.

"Naw, just guys from Ohio who are members of the sailing club. I brought them over in my speedboat this time. What are you doing tonight? Want to hang out? Go on a picnic?"

He's holding me close, kissing my forehead. Who can say no to a man who kisses your forehead? Who would want to?

Sunset, Red and Gold

I catch a ride home with Molly and Chris, and at seven I'm ready and waiting for Lenny on the upper deck, dressed in my orange stretch knit dress. A small bright yellow bird lands on the banister that surrounds the gazebo and looks at me. "Hello, Mr. Finch," I say. "You're the first of your kind I've seen since I left West Virginia." Tiger comes over and rubs my leg. He doesn't even notice the yellow bird.

"I must be feeding you too well," I tell my pussycat. "Once you were a wild hunter, now you're a softie." As I carry him back down to the cottage, I rub my face in his fur.

I'd like to rub him all over my naked body, he feels so good, but I know I am only thinking of Lenny. Such strange ideas have never come to me before. And then I hear the boat. Sun Dancer it says on the side, a sleek bright yellow-and-white powerboat with a roll bar and a metal railing around the front.

When I wade out to meet him, carrying my sandals with my orange knit dress hiked up to my thighs, Lenny has already dropped a short ladder and pulls me up into his arms. I hadn't necessarily thought about making out in the boat, but I can see that he's ready. Not only is a quilt spread on the floor, he even has pillows.

A few hours later, I prop myself up on my elbow and stare down at his face, brown from the sun and wrinkled around the eyes. He is naked, lying on his side with his hands tucked between his legs and I am naked too, my nipples still at attention. The boat rocks with the waves.

Maybe it's because he's mysterious. Maybe it's because he's a good lover—patient, generous and kind. Maybe it's just pheromones, hormones that help bees, bears and gorillas find mates. I sneeze and Lenny wakes up.

"Did you do that on purpose?"

"Yeah," I say, running one finger down his chest. "I want you to wake up and play with me."

"Say that again."

"I want you to wake up . . ." He puts one finger on my lips and grabs me by the back of the neck.

"Just the first part . . ."

"I want you."
"Say it again."
"I want you."

GOLDFINCH
Male, bright yellow in spring and summer
Female (and male in winter), speckled brown
Diet: Eats only seeds with its conical beak, complete vegetarian
Habitat: bushes and second-growth timber, backyards and parks
Call *Per-chick-ory* or some say *po-tat-to-chip*
Range: US and Canada year-round, but only where the
temperature stays above 0° F

CHAPTER 30

Message

*B*efore Lenny left, I told him the truth. Not all of it, just the part about being on the run and wanting to send word to my daughter that I'm still alive and I love her.

"The thing is, this letter has to be sent to Australia *without* a return address and from someplace far away from Seagull Island," I explain. "She's studying abroad. Could you mail it from Mexico or wherever you go next? I don't want anyone to find me."

"Is it the law?"

"Yes, and my husband and the ghosts who haunt me. Can you do this for me? Can you mail it?" I read the short letter to myself one more time.

Dear Jess,

    It's me. I know this sounds crazy, coming from your old-fashioned, conventional mom, but I can't tell you where I am because I'm wanted by the police for man-slaughter and for stealing a lot of money (all of it from your father, but you know how he is about money). I

*just wanted to tell you I'm alive and I love you. You're
in my heart and prayers every day . . . every hour. When
things calm down, I will find you.*

Be safe.
Mom

I fold the sheet of notebook paper and stuff it into an old
envelope I found on the Nelsons' bookshelf.

He takes the message and puts it in his shirt pocket and lays
his hand over his heart. "You can count on me . . . I knew there
was something . . ." Then he kisses my forehead again and then
my mouth and he leaves.

SENDING THE NOTE has taken a weight off my sorry heart. I might
be a liar, a runaway, a thief and wanted for manslaughter . . . but
at least Jessie will now know that her mom is still living and cares
for her.

From experience I know what it does to you when someone
you love just walks away, never says goodbye. Karen did that. She
was my friend and then she was gone. Poof! No note. No explanation. I was closer to her than I am to Richard. I can't imagine
what it was like for her husband and children to lose her.

I go over in my mind, for the hundredth time, the last day I
saw Karen. We were walking across the lawn from the hospital to
the clinic with our arms around each other's waists, both wearing scrubs. Her hair was pulled away from her face and stuffed
up in her puffy OR cap because we'd just finished a C-section
together. The baby was breech and everything had gone well. It
was the parents' first child and they named him Romeo. (We'd
had a private laugh about that.)

"So when you come back you want to go to the concert at the university with me? The Indigo Girls are back in town," I said.

"Sure," Karen answered. "Get the tickets. The cruise is only four days long. I just need some *me time* and to feel the wind in my hair." She laughed and I still hear that sound between dreams and waking.

Six days later I was at Shop 'n Save when I got a text from my fellow midwife Linda. "Call me," it said.

It could only mean one thing. I was off duty, but she wanted me to come to the hospital for a second patient in labor.

"What's up?" I asked Linda when she answered her cell phone.

"Are you sitting down?"

"No, I'm in the store grocery shopping."

"Go home and call me."

"I won't be home for an hour."

"No. Go home now."

"Oh, for God's sake, Linda. My cart's almost full. I'm not going to just park it and walk out. Call me back again in thirty minutes. I'll hurry." *What could be so important? Apparently, it wasn't a woman in labor.*

Thirty minutes later my cell rang again. "So what's up?" I asked when I heard Linda's voice.

"Are you sitting?"

"Yeah, I'm in the car, but I'm not home yet. Why so mysterious? Is Dr. Agata resigning or something?" I think this is funny, but Linda doesn't laugh.

"Pull over."

"Oh my God! If you insist." I take the next side street and park at the curb. "Okay. I'm stopped. What's so earthshaking that we can't talk while I'm driving?"

"Dr. Karen is gone."

"I know she's gone. She'll be back in two days."

"I mean she's dead. Her husband called Dr. Agata a few hours ago. It's all over the hospital. Apparently she jumped off the side of the cruise ship during a storm two nights ago. They've been searching, but they can't find her body."

She goes on for a few minutes but I can barely hear her. *Karen is dead. Karen is dead. Karen is dead . . . as in forever. It can't be . . .*

The next morning we closed the clinic and Dr. Agata called a meeting of the whole staff. "I know everyone has a lot of questions. All I can tell you is that our beloved Dr. Karen Cross was last seen on surveillance video on the cruise ship, on its way to Cozumel, climbing over a railing on a sixth-deck balcony. Her body has not been found and after three days the US Coast Guard has called off the search.

"I know there has been a lot of speculation about her death. According to Karen's husband, no suicide note has been found, but the cruise ship video clearly shows her alone on the deck and purposely jumping, not falling. A memorial service is being held next Saturday at St. Mark's Lutheran Church. Her family asks that, instead of flowers, we donate to the National Breast Cancer Foundation."

LINDA AND I went back to the clinic later that night and by flashlight, like a couple of Watergate burglars, went through Karen's files and then her computer, looking for some correspondence or email that would explain her desperate action, but there was nothing. No letter to indicate a secret love life gone wrong, or copy of an MRI showing an inoperable brain tumor . . . nothing to explain why a successful, apparently happy woman who seemed to have everything, just went off and killed herself.

I never went to the Indigo Girls' concert, just gave the tickets to some friends. Richard, wearing a dark suit and tie, accompanied me to the service as if we were actually husband and wife. I couldn't cry, just walked around giving hugs like Karen would do if it were my funeral.

THIS EVENING WHEN I go up on the deck to watch the sunset, I hear a strange quivery cry. I look down the shore expecting to see someone giving voice to great sorrow, but the beach is empty. The cry comes again and this time I realize it's from out on the lake. Two waterfowl are swimming together and as I adjust the Nelsons' binoculars, I realize that one of them has a baby bird on her back. How incredible! I have seen photos of this before. The mother allows her baby to ride along on top. The bird with the strange cry is a loon.

COMMON LOON
A large heavy-bodied, long-necked bird
Male, distinctive black head, white underbody with white spots on back
Female, Brown
Voice: melancholy yodeling
Diet: Dives for fish
Range: Summer: all over Canada and northern border of US
Winter: Both coasts and southeastern US
Size: 32 inches
Wingspan: 4 feet

Nita

It's a bright sunny day with a roaring wind and whitecaps as huge as those on the Atlantic, and Peter Dolman and I are on our way to visit one of the women that I've been talking to on the phone—Nita Adams. I wasn't excited about hanging out with Peter Dolman after my crying scene at the Cider Mill, but when he asked me to come, I couldn't say no. Nita seems like a nice old lady.

The cop turns the cruiser into a long gravel drive on the interior of the island. Here green fields are dotted with sheep and the long green grass lies flat in the wind. Two white lambs stare as we pass, their short tails wagging like dogs and their brown ears sticking out sideways.

"Do all sheep have short tails? I never noticed before. Are they born that way?" I ask.

"No, the owners dock them when they're young. If you let their tails stay long, they get shit all over themselves."

When we get to the little vine-covered cottage on the east side of Gull Point, no one answers. "Nita!" Dolman calls over and over until we just break the door open and find the old lady sitting on the sofa.

"Oh, Peter!" she whispers, tears streaming down her wrinkled brown face. "You're my angel. I've been sitting here for almost twenty-four hours just praying someone would come. My hip went out again and the telephone is in the other room, so I couldn't get to it . . . I can't stand or even crawl." She wipes her eyes with a faded blue apron. "And I've soiled myself . . . It's my hip. Can you help me?"

I'm surprised to see that Nita Adams is the elderly black woman I'd seen walking on the beach when I first came to Seagull Haven, the one who makes sun catchers out of beach glass. Dolman lifts her up and very gently carries her into the bedroom.

The old lady sounded so chipper on the phone when she told me about working on her *projects*. I had no idea she meant her artwork . . . or that she was the person I'd met before . . . or that she was so frail.

"Can you put some hot water on, Peter? And maybe make Mrs. Adams some tea and something to eat? Canned soup or something. I'll clean her up. Mrs. Adams, I'm—"

"Feed Mr. and Mrs. Doodle too," Nita interrupts me. *I have no idea what she's talking about, so I don't even comment.*

I try again. "I'm Sara. Sara the RN."

"You're the girl from Gull Point," Mrs. Adams comments as I wipe her bottom with a clean washcloth and warm water. "The one on the beach. I recognize you now. All this time, we've talked on the phone, I never realized."

"I'm not exactly a girl, but it's funny, isn't it? I didn't know it was you either . . . Do you have any medical conditions, Mrs. Adams? I mean besides your hip," I ask this like a nurse, which actually I am, a nurse-midwife.

"Just my sugar, honey. I haven't eaten anything since yesterday at four. Do you still think I need my insulin? It's in the refrigerator."

Three trips to the bathroom for water and clean washcloths and I have Nita cleaned up and comfortable, then I go out to consult with the cop where he's making canned chicken noodle soup.

When I enter the large sunny kitchen, I'm surprised to see that the room must also be the old lady's studio. It explodes with light and color. There are high workbenches and a wooden desk. There's a small vise, a big magnifying glass and all sorts of small tools. In the windows, on the walls and even hanging from the ceiling are necklaces, earrings, mobiles and sun catchers made of the green, gold, brown, clear and blue glass stones.

My hand goes to my throat as if to catch a shout of joy. "It's beautiful," I say to Peter. "Like standing in a room made of stained glass."

"She is a great artist and a great lady," he answers, stirring the soup and turning to me. His cop hat and sunglasses are on the counter and he has a dishcloth tucked into his pants for an apron.

"But she's in a bad way, isn't she? I can see why you include her in your rounds. If we hadn't come by, she could have sat there in her own pee and poop and starved to death or died of diabetes. She says she may require insulin. Do you think Jed would come over?"

"Already called him and he's on his way. He says she probably needs to go to the mainland for a few weeks to a long-term care facility. They can get her artificial hip back in the socket, her sugar regulated and her strength back."

Just then the cop's cell phone whistles. "Excuse me," he says and goes out of the room, but I can hear him talking in the back hall.

"Dolman . . . Yeah . . . I'll take the ferry tonight . . . Yeah . . . Okay." When he returns to Nita's bedroom, his face is dark, almost angry.

"Sorry, Nita. I've got business and we have to cut this short. Sara will be checking on you by phone and Jed's on the way. You just stay in bed."

"WHAT'S UP?" I ask when we're back in the squad car.

"Another missing-person case from Windsor. Third one this year. Probably gang related, but there's some indication the guy was last seen on Seagull Island. They have a man in custody for a related matter on the mainland and they want me to talk to him. No more rounds for today."

A missing person . . . I think to myself. *Would he wear Timberland boots?*

Discovery

*F*eeling slightly less weighted after sending the note to Jessie, I've turned over a new leaf and have instituted a self-improvement plan. Every morning I will do yoga and meditate. I will drink eight glasses of water, take a walk and swim . . . unless there's a storm . . . then I'll dance inside for exercise.

It's on my third afternoon of my *crusade for fitness* that I hear a vehicle coming down Grays Road. I'm on the beach, a good hundred yards from the cottage, but I hurry home, wondering who it could be. (Now that it's summer, traffic has picked up and often some tourist gets lost in the boonies.) I hear the vehicle pull into my drive, but by the time I get there, it's gone.

Thinking maybe someone left a note, I check the screen door, but there's nothing. It's then that I notice the old Raleigh is gone, and that sets off an alarm. It's not just that I was planning on getting the broken-down bike fixed, but the idea of people creeping around and stealing things right off my front porch is disturbing. I don't usually lock the house, but I guess I will now.

I look under the bed where I keep my briefcase to see if anything's missing. There's no point in counting my money. If someone discovered it, they would take the whole satchel and it appears to be undisturbed. Nevertheless, I decide to find a new hiding place.

I consider the shed, but it seems too distant and the bureau seems too obvious. Finally, I turn to the small bedroom closet. I don't have many clothes, but what I have nearly fills up the space. On the top shelf are Mrs. Nelson's handmade quilts along with an extra fan. I take the canvas briefcase, roll it into one of the quilts, then stand on a chair and push it way back. As I pull out my hand, I feel a flat folder, something I hadn't noticed before. *What's this?*

The brown packet with the elastic band around it doesn't look like anything special. It's the usual kind of file folder you can get at any office supply store. What intrigues me is its hiding place. It must have been something Lloyd or Wanda felt was special.

Feeling like a sneak, I take it into the living room to investigate. The packet includes the deed to Seagull Haven, a letter
about donations to the Nature Conservancy and a handwritten
will dated September 2014 and signed by Lloyd Nelson. Could
Lloyd have already known he was dying?

I sit down and read through the short document.

"I Lloyd Nelson, being of sound mind and body, do bequeath
my property, known as Seagull Haven, to the Ontario Nature
Conservancy, to be used in perpetuity as a place of peace."

There's more . . . the legal description of the five acres . . .
then it's signed.

Is this something I ought to give to Wanda? Did she know
about it? I look at the property title. The land and house are only
in Lloyd's name. As his widow, wouldn't she expect to inherit
it? I decide that this is not the time to bother her. Probably she
knew he wanted to preserve this special place for the use of all
who came to Seagull Island, but then why were the documents
hidden?

CHAPTER 31

Cleanup

So what do you want done first?" Jed asks, looking around. "Your yard is a total disaster!"

"Well, let's start with the lawn. The summer is half over and if those real estate agents from the Nelson family ever come over, I want them to see that I'm taking good care of the place. Any suggestions?"

Jed looks up at the cottage roof. "It would help if the gutters were cleaned. This is a good time to do it. See there, how the water has been collecting along the foundation. That's because the gutters are full of leaves and the rain isn't going down the drain spout.

"The place could use a paint job too, but that's not your concern. I'd probably straighten that shutter and repair the one weak step at the top of the porch." *This is more than I was thinking of doing, but it's not like I don't have the money.*

"How much will that be?"

"Say a hundred dollars?"

"What if I helped you? There's a ladder in the shed. I could clean the gutters."

"You don't mind heights?"

"Well it's only one story."

"Then it's seventy-five."

"And will you teach me how to repair a step?" (Back in West Virginia, my husband took care of the household repairs, but there's no Richard here, so I'd better start learning.)

"Sure, it'll be fun."

ALL DAY WE toil in the July heat. Jed takes off his shirt when he's cutting the weeds and I put on a pair of my baggy new shorts and a T-shirt. For lunch I make us peanut butter and banana sandwiches with cold milk and apples. We sit in the gazebo companionably, looking down at the lake.

"A bald eagle," Jed says, pointing out the huge dark bird with a white head and tail. "Look, it's got a fish in its claws." Suddenly, another eagle shows up. Initially I think they're friendly, but no, the second eagle is harassing the first.

It moves in and tries to grab the fish, but the owner won't let go. The attacker sweeps the other with his wings, circles and comes back. This time the fish drops from the owner's claws and we watch as the thief dives and catches it in midair, just above the water.

"Amazing," I say. "Have you ever seen that before?"

"Sure, lots of times. I grew up here, remember. I've seen eagles attack the osprey on the north end too. Funny that the bald eagle, your country's national symbol, is a scavenger." He cracks a smile.

"Yeah, funny," I return with sarcasm. "So you grew up here, went away and came back. Does your family know you're gay? Do other people on the island know?"

"My family knows for sure."

"So does everyone else know? I mean people like Molly Lou and Helen at the store?"

"Pretty much. Most of them are related to me in some way.

I came out in 2010 when I returned to the island. I had a lover then, Tony, a guy I went to university with in Windsor, but he was a flake. I'm kind of interested in John now. You know him, the vet from the States, but don't say anything, okay?"

I think back to the drum circle at New Day. Jed and John were on the other side of the drum circle, half-obscured by the light of the fire. I see again, their two bodies, close together. Jed is playing his guitar and John the harmonica.

It takes me longer than I expected to clean the gutters and by three in the afternoon, I'm sweating like a pig.

"Why don't you take your shirt off?" Jed asks.

"And work in my bra?"

"Or go without the bra."

"I don't think so!" I say, but I do pull off my T-shirt and pretend my bra is a halter top.

We fix the step on the porch together and straighten the shutter, then Jed gathers up his tools to go home. "Hey, wait. I'll get you your money!"

"Forget about it. What are friends for?"

"Come on! That's the deal."

"Save it," he says. "You're my girl!" And he gives me a long sweaty hug.

Summer Ice

On Tuesday, I lock the house, take Tiger and hike up to the village to visit Jed and see if he needs any help at the clinic. It's a slow day and he's filing medical charts.

"Want a hand?" I ask.

"Nah, it won't take long. I tell you what you *could* do though.

In a couple of weeks, I have to set up a medical tent at the Blue Water Folk Concert here on the island. Want to help me man it Friday night? John will help Saturday."

"Sure," I say. "You mean *woman* it?" Then we have coffee, he reads me a new short story he's written and I walk home, watching Lake Erie sparkle in the sunlight.

Five minutes after I get in the door, the island's squad car pulls up my drive. *What now?* I think.

Peter Dolman opens his trunk, pulls out my bike and rolls it up to the porch.

"Peter! It was you who took the Raleigh? And look at it! It's like a new bicycle! I was going to call and report it stolen, but it was such a piece of junk, I didn't think it would be worth your time to look for it. Why did you do this?"

He shrugs. "It's a surprise. I'm still paying you back for the visit to the commune. Also the bike's been lying around all summer and I didn't know when or how you'd get around to fixing it."

I laugh. "Well, thanks!"

We sit on the porch steps, admiring the bicycle and listening to the wind in the dry cottonwood leaves. The bike has new tires, new handgrips, even a new kickstand. "Want a glass of apricot wine?" I ask, trying to be hospitable and thank him somehow for the wonderful gift. "I bought some in case I ever had company."

"Nah, I'm on duty. I guess I should go." He stands and looks out toward the road where we can both see a cloud of dust boiling along behind a vehicle. It's the familiar white convertible I've seen around the island, and I'm surprised when it turns into my drive as if it knows where it's going. Two men and a woman get out and walk toward the house. Peter stands, pulls down the visor of his hat and adjusts his silver sunglasses.

"Hello. It's Sara, isn't it?" asks the woman, petite with dark hair, wearing a gray linen jacket and white linen pants. "I'm Charlene Nelson and these are my brothers, Jake and William." She dismisses the cop with a nod of her head and shifts her eyes back to me.

Standing next to her is a short blond fellow, balding in front, dressed in khaki shorts and a blue polo shirt that says SEAGULL ISLAND SAILING CLUB. The other man has longer dark hair and wears jeans and a black T-shirt. All three have a family resemblance, the same strong jaw and brown eyes, the same lean build and straight teeth; people of privilege. I recognize the type right away because most of the girls at the Little Sisters of the Cross Academy came from that social class.

"Nice to see you, Charlene. William, Jake," the cop says, stepping forward to greet them, but the evening has gone chill.

William, the older of the two men, snubs Dolman when he sticks out his hand, then he turns to me. "Sara, is it?" (I recognize that voice, sandpaper on a carrot grater. It's the man who was so rude when I called Wanda that time.) "We just came by to tell you that our father, Lloyd, died four weeks ago, passed in his sleep, and we buried him back home."

My heart goes cold, a lump of ice in my chest. I knew Lloyd's death was inevitable and coming soon, but it feels strange to learn that he's been gone all this time.

"You alright, Sara? I'm sorry if we shocked you," Charlene apologizes.

Officer Dolman interrupts us. "I was just leaving, but I express my sympathy."

"Thanks," says Charlene, not even looking at him, and the three take seats on the porch steps as if the place belongs to them, which, in a way, it does . . .

"You and the cop an item?" Jake, the dark-haired brother in jeans, asks, staring at Peter's back as he walks away. This seems an odd question, but I answer truthfully.

"No, not at all. He just had my bike repaired. Actually, it's the old bike I found in the shed. I hope you don't mind."

"It's fine . . . You're taking good care of the place and we appreciate it," Charlene says, looking around at the flowers I planted that bloom along the picket fence and the neatly mowed lawn.

"Have you given any thought to where you might move when your lease runs out?" asks William, staring up at the roof and jingling change in his pockets. Jake stands and walks around to the back of the house and up the stairs to the upper deck as if looking at the view.

"Will you stay on the island?" Charlene goes on. "Mother said you're a writer."

This pushes me up against a wall. "To be honest, I haven't really thought about it. I'm paid up until November. I was hoping to stay through the winter, but I suppose I'll try to look for another place if you need the cottage." (All this time, I'm thinking about Lloyd's handwritten will. The one they may not know about.)

"Well, you have some time. It's only August now. That gives you four months. The three of us are in real estate. We're planning to tear down the old cottage and put in a hotel and casino. It will be great, bring in lots of tourists and high rollers from Detroit, Toledo, Cleveland and Toronto. Provide lots of jobs for the people on the island."

Tear down Seagull Haven! The more they talk, the sadder I feel. "Do the people here want this?" I ask. "I thought they liked the peace and quiet."

"Well, you can't have it both ways." Jake has come out of the house, letting the screen door slam behind him. *The jerk must have been walking around inside!*

"The Seagull Island Township Board is always discussing the tax base," Charlene breaks in. "They go on and on at the meetings about how they hardly have enough money to grade the roads and run the school and that they need to diversify the economy, but they never want to try anything new. Luckily, there's enough people with common sense that they'll outvote them."

At this point I don't know what to say. *Who are the islanders and cottagers eager for hotels and casinos? I don't even know them!*

"The house looks nice." Jake stares at me. "Dad loved the old place. We had a lot of good times here too, right, Will?" He gives his brother a wink. "Learned to drive on the island. Had our first liquor here. Our first sex—"

His sister cuts him off. "Well, if you need a little time to make the transition, Sara, let me know. We won't start demolition until late November, but we'll be on the island often, meeting with builders and architects."

When I say goodbye, I'm surprised that Jake takes my hand. "Nice to meet you, Sara, and I look forward to seeing you again." He wears a bright gold wedding ring, so he's clearly married, but I have a feeling that neither the ring nor his vows would slow him down. It didn't slow Richard.

Tootsie Roll

*W*hat to do now? I thought I had time, but Lloyd is already dead and I need someone's advice on how to handle the will, but who would know something about probate law? I pull a chair into the bedroom from the kitchen and reach on my tiptoes into the back of the closet where I had replaced Lloyd's packet. While I'm up there I peek at my stash, which is still rolled into a quilt, and decide to get down a couple of hundred-dollar bills, just in case I need money.

"Hello again. Want some help?" It's Jake Nelson standing *in my bedroom*. I'm so startled I lose my balance and start to fall, but his hands catch me around the waist just before I crash-land in a cascade of money.

Recovering, I push the quilt out of sight, cover my briefcase and throw the documents back on top. *Did he see?*

"Sorry if I startled you. I knocked before I walked in. Thought maybe you were down on the beach. I just came back for a couple of the seagull carvings my mother asked me to bring home."

This really bugs me. I certainly *don't* want the man strolling into my cottage anytime he wants and I also feel there's something overly sensual about his touch. "Next time knock louder" is all I can say. Jake helps me jump off the chair, missing the edge to my voice.

"If you aren't busy tonight, I'd like to take you to dinner. Charlene and Will have other plans, but we could go to the Roadhouse near the sailing club. Just a little thanks for taking such good care of Seagull Haven for us."

"Actually, I have an appointment this evening," I lie. "And you really don't *owe* me anything. It just happened I needed a place to rent and Wanda appreciated someone watching over the property. It's a contractual arrangement."

Jake's cell rings and he fumbles in his jeans pocket to grab it. The ringtone is a hip-hop song Jessie used to listen to, "Tootsie Roll." The tune goes on and on while he tries to get the phone out of his tight jeans. *Yeah, tootsie roll—Let me see that tootsie roll. Yeah, tootsie roll—Let me . . .* He shrugs, embarrassed, and answers.

"What's up . . . ? Charlene . . . ?" His face goes white. "Stop blubbering! What do mean Mom's dead? She can't be dead. We just saw her three days ago . . ." He looks at me wildly, forgets the seagull carvings and runs out the door.

CHAPTER 32

Orphan

All night, I keep thinking about the Nelsons. What could have happened to Wanda? I try to imagine a car wreck, a stroke or a heart attack, or even suicide. It often happens that when one older spouse dies the other passes a year or so later, but not usually in a few weeks.

I don't know why, but I have a vague feeling that I shouldn't just hand Lloyd's handwritten will to the Nelsons. It would seem rather cruel to say, right after their mother died . . . "Oh, by the way. Lloyd doesn't want anyone in the family to have Seagull Haven. He gave it to the Nature Conservancy." Not only that, if I give them the handwritten document it might end up in the trash.

I remember it like it was yesterday, the day my parents died and my life shattered, like a window blown in by a twister.

"Mrs. Mallory!" The school counselor at Wilson Middle School, just outside of Ann Arbor, Michigan, calls from the door of my eighth-grade math class. "Mrs. Mallory!" The teacher steps out of the room, her face loses all color and she beckons me over.

"Honey, they need you in the office," she says.

I can't imagine what for. I'm a good student, haven't been in any fights and keep my locker clean, but I follow the counselor obediently.

When we enter Principal Monroe's office, a policeman is there along with a woman I've never seen before. "Sit down, Clara," the lady says. She's dressed in a dark blue suit, a white blouse and black heels and somehow looks official. Now I'm getting afraid.

Everyone takes a deep breath and lets it out slowly, and the lady slides her chair closer and takes my hand. "Honey," she says. "We have some bad news. Your parents died this morning in a terrible car wreck. We didn't know who to notify. Do you have any relatives, a grandparent or an aunt? The emergency number on the card in the secretary's office lists only your mother and father."

I never heard myself scream, but I was told later that I did. The grown-ups kept asking me over and over who to call and I couldn't answer. There was nothing else to do. The social worker took me home. She ran a warm bath, but I couldn't move and she had to take off my clothes.

I LOVED MY parents, both employees at the local Argus camera plant, but I don't think they loved each other. If they did, they didn't show it. At night in the dark, as I lay in my bed with a pillow over my head, I could hear cursing, plates shattering against the walls, doors slamming, doors opening again and . . . more cursing. In the morning their faces would be pale and peaceful, like Lake Erie after a storm.

That's why I didn't grieve for them the way other kids would. Part of me was just glad the war was over and I wondered if maybe my parents were too . . . Though I never said anything to anyone, I imagined that one of them had *caused* the accident, had pulled the steering wheel and plowed into the semi-truck on purpose.

THE GROUP HOME in Ann Arbor that I was sent to was short-term and then, because I had no other relatives, the social worker, Mrs. Dennis, found me a place at Little Sisters of the Cross Academy for Young Women in northern Michigan. I'm sure the nuns took pity on me when they learned that I was orphaned because I received a full scholarship for all four years of high school.

It was Sister Jean who mothered me. Compared to the hell I'd experienced before, the convent was heaven . . . and the sisters were angels protecting me with their wings.

Little Sisters of the Cross

*I*n the morning, I decide there's only one person I can talk to about the will, so I check the tires on my reconditioned bike and head for Nita's. Since she's come back from the hospital, I've visited her several times and I've come to respect her opinion. Not only that, she puts things in perspective. Because of her age, like the nuns, she has the long view.

As I pedal along, I find my mind wandering back to the convent and I remember my first image of the girl's parochial school and religious retreat for women. As Mrs. Dennis and I drove up the long spruce-lined drive, my mouth dropped open.

In the distance I saw what looked like a stone castle with two square turrets. A long stone wall ran around the grassy grounds and an adjoining stone building a few hundred yards away had a cross on the top. (This I learned later was the dorm that housed fifty girls aged fourteen to eighteen.)

A marble statue of Jesus being crucified on the cross with Mary kneeling below him was positioned in the turnaround in front of the castle, which was, in reality, an abbey for some twenty nuns, mostly widows.

As we approached, I pictured the sisters as small cheerful women with big white hats like *The Flying Nun* on TV or conversely as small mean women, dressed in black hoods and habits, who labored under heavy wooden crosses strapped to their backs. The reality was neither of my imaginings.

The fact that most of the nuns were widows gave the convent a unique atmosphere, though I didn't realize it at the time. The sisters, who had once been wives and mothers, were only "born-again virgins" and they often flirted with the priests who came to say mass, as well as the tradesmen, who did major repairs and landscaping.

There were usually three or four grieving widows staying at the retreat at any given time and I was impressed with the tenderness the nuns showed their visitors. The sisters weren't always so kind to the students. If your plaid skirt was too short, Sister Collette would whack you on the behind with a ruler. If you didn't know your lessons, she'd make you kneel for an hour in front of the class. This was back in the early eighties when you could get away with such nonsense. Myself, I didn't get tortured because I always had my homework done, but my friend Mary Kay wasn't so lucky. She was a cut-up and got whacked at least once a day.

At the academy, only Mary Kay and I were on scholarship. Old Sister Bernadine made our plaid uniforms, so they were always of regulation length. There were ninety or so girls at the school, fifty who boarded and forty locals who went home at night. All scholars had to be wealthy because the tuition was so high.

I believe Mother Angelica assigned Sister Jean as my special guardian because Sister Jean, a widow of ten years, had once lost a baby girl at birth and her husband had been killed in Vietnam. Sister Jean had had a hard life, but that only made her a more wonderful nun. Life is like that, I've noticed. Tragedy and misfortune can break a person or make her more compassionate and courageous.

It's now that I'm alone that I realize how much I learned from the sisters. Though I lived as Richard's wife for almost twenty years, I always knew that it was possible to be happy without a man. I didn't ever do anything remotely mechanical, but I still had a vision of Sister Clare under the convent's old school bus. I never balanced our checkbook, but I knew Mother Angelica kept the academy open through her creative financing.

Our school had the same curriculum as any Catholic high school, rigorous academics mixed with such courses as the Revelation of Jesus Christ in Scripture. These religious classes didn't make me more of a Christian, in fact maybe less, because by the time I got to college I found the Unitarian Universalists a breath of fresh air.

Mighty Jungle

After an hour's hard ride, I throw my bike against Nita's porch and run up the steps. I'm like a little girl coming home from school and the old woman's my granny.

"Knock, knock," I yell, not waiting for an answer, and when I take the turn into the living room, I'm surprised to see Nita dancing. She has a wheeled walker and a cool popular song from the early 1960s is playing on the stereo.

"A-wimoweh, a-wimoweh, a-wimoweh, a-wimoweh, In the jungle, the mighty jungle the lion sleeps tonight, In the jungle, the quiet jungle the lion sleeps tonight," Nita sings with the recording and I join in. "A-wimoweh, a-wimoweh!"

"What do you think?" she asks, indicating the wheeled walker. "Jed brought it to me. He changed my meds too." I plunk down in a chair.

My friend is wearing an African print dress with a scarf wrapped around her white curly hair and she seems, except for the walker, almost like her old self.

"You kill me, Nita. You're in the hospital for a couple of weeks and now you're home dancing. The next thing I know you'll be cruising the beach looking for beach glass. I looked the other day, by the way, after the storm, but didn't see any."

"You have to have the eye," she says, spinning around, and then she begins to cough. She coughs so hard she can't get her breath, and just about the time I think I'm going to have to call for the ambulance, she points to an inhaler on the end table near the couch and I hand it over. Three puffs and she's better, but I insist she sit down and I get her some tea.

When I come back from the kitchen with cups and a teapot on a tray, she's resting in a high-back wooden chair staring out the window at her bird feeder. "I love the birds on the island," she says. "I saw a falcon this morning and a V of geese going south. Look there! It's a chickadee. See its little black cap. They're my favorite. Do you mind putting out some more seeds in the feeder while you're here?"

"Sure, Nita, but I need to talk to you. Something's happened and I'm scared."

The old lady sets her cup down and folds her hands in her lap, waiting, giving me all her attention, her big brown eyes on alert. "So . . ."

"Well, a couple of weeks ago, I found a handwritten will by Lloyd Nelson giving the cottage and his five acres on Seagull Point to the Nature Conservancy. I didn't know what to do with it, so I just put it back in the closet. Yesterday, the Nelson brothers and sister visited and told me their father died a month ago. They want me out of the cottage and they intend to tear down Seagull Haven to build a casino and hotel.

"What's almost worse is that while they were at the cottage, they got a call from Ohio and it seems their mother just passed away too. Now, I don't know what to do with the will. Do you know anything about probate law?"

"First take a few deep breaths," the old lady says, reaching for my hand. "And you have to start locking your cottage. Possession is nine-tenths of the law. It takes a good two or three months to get evicted . . . Then you better take the will to Officer Dolman."

"You really think I need to get him involved? I'm not sure it's my place."

"Don't think about it. Just do it," she says.

CHICKADEE
A small gray bird with a black cap and a black bib
measuring 12 to 15 centimeters
Habitat: Lives in tree-covered areas
in southern Canada and northern US
and down into the Appalachian Mountains
Diet: insect eggs, larvae and pupae
Voice: chic-a-dee chic-a-dee

There Will Be Trouble

The next day, I lock the cottage, bundle up and get ready for a ride to the village, planning to show Peter Dolman the handwritten document and ask him what to do. I take a soft bath towel, make a bed in the bike's wicker basket for Tiger and tie him in with the leash so he can't jump out.

As I pass Molly Lou's, I drop my feet and straddle the Raleigh. Molly's out in front watering flowers. "Nice," she yells, indicating the passenger in my bike basket. "Like Toto in *The Wizard of Oz!*"

Riding on, I look out at Lake Erie. A light rain last night has cleared the air and visibility is good. Two sailboats bob up and down in the waves and all along the breakwall goldenrod nod in the breeze.

Despite Nita Adams's advice, the decision to give Lloyd's handwritten will to the cop was a hard one. I debated it from several points of view. Being wanted by the law and arriving on Seagull Island without a passport are my real problems. What if the handwritten will is contested and I have to go to the mainland to be a witness in court? What if it comes out that I'm here illegally? Would I be arrested? Would I be deported and sent back to West Virginia to face the mess I left behind? I have no way to find out, but becoming involved in a legal squabble can do me no good.

On the other hand, I can't just leave Lloyd's envelope sitting in the closet . . . so presenting it to the only official I know seems the best thing to do. I just hope I'm not shooting myself in the foot.

Gathering Tiger under my arm, I tap twice on the green wooden door of the Seagull Island OPP and wait for an answer. Since the squad car is here, I assume Dolman is too, though he could be down at the Black Sheep Pub or hanging out with Jed at the clinic.

"Enter. Welcome. Hi, Tiger. Hi, Sara."

The cop is sitting at a large gray metal desk wearing his usual khaki pants and a navy blue T-shirt, but not the shades and cap. I let my cat down to explore the small room.

"To what do I owe this visit?" Dolman asks, smiling. "Can I get you a cup of coffee?"

"Sure." While he washes a mug in a corner sink, I inspect the small room. Arranged on a counter is some kind of CB radio, a printer and some equipment that may have to do with the weather. On either side of the front window are two gray metal file cabinets that match the desk, and behind the door is a tall bookshelf full of books, mostly Ontario Provincial Police manuals with a few bestselling novels on top.

There are also two substantial oak chairs (the kind you might see in a courthouse), and I sit down in one, picturing someone handcuffed to the armrest . . . maybe me.

"So what's up?" Dolman holds out the mug and throws a packet of sugar and a packet of creamer across the desk.

"Well, I have a problem . . ." I begin. He leans forward on his arms listening, his gray eyes never leaving my face.

I explain how I found the will on the top shelf of the closet a few weeks ago but didn't know what to do with it and how afterward when I learned that Lloyd was dead, and now Wanda too, I knew I had to give it to someone.

"There's a feeling I get from the Nelson brothers and sister. I don't trust them," I go on. "Maybe it's just the type. Also, did you know this? They're preparing to tear down Seagull Haven to build a hotel and casino." As I talk, I fumble in my woven Mexican shoulder bag for Lloyd's will.

"There's always rumors of development on Seagull. Most of the schemes never come to anything. What have you got there?"

I open the folder, hand him the document and watch as he reads. Finally, he puts the paperwork down.

"It looks legit . . . The Nature Conservancy will be ecstatic about this, but a lot of other people won't be. Sorry about your house though. How long is your lease?"

"I've paid until the end of November. That gives me four months. I guess I have to start looking for another place."

The cop stands and I take that to mean he's busy and ready for me to leave, but he walks over to the printer, lifts up the top and begins to photocopy Lloyd's last will and testament along with the description of the property. While he waits, he leans down and picks Tiger up and rubs his face through the animal's fur, a familiar gesture. I do it myself, at least once a day.

"I'll take the original will for safekeeping to a lawyer I know in Windsor. I'm going over next week. And I'll make three copies, one for the Nature Conservancy. They'll want to have their attorney in Toronto take a look at it. One for the Nelsons and one for the township president.

"The Nelsons won't let go without a fight," he continues. "I know what you mean. I've never liked them much either. The Conservancy will be determined to preserve the land. And the community will be split down the middle. It doesn't sound like much, just five acres, but I can tell you now . . . there will be trouble."

CHAPTER 33

Shipwrecks and Squalls

On the way home, I stop at Molly Lou's because I want her to spread the word that I'm going to need somewhere to live by the end of November. Big Chris is out in the yard fooling with his John Deere tractor and he lifts his head in greeting, greasy hands still in the engine.

He's a strange man, I think. Not *unfriendly*, but not *friendly* either. Maybe Chris doesn't like me. Maybe he sees through my novelist mask, to the scared midwife I really am.

"Molly!" I yell from the front porch. "You home?"

"Come on in! I'm back in the kitchen. Want a homemade brownie? They just came out of the oven."

Despite my promise to myself to cut back on calories, I can't resist. "Sure."

"Milk too?"

"Might as well. It goes good with chocolate and I need the calcium." This is said with a smile, because I get plenty of calcium.

While she readies our snack I tell Molly Lou about the Nelsons' visit, how I have four months to move and that they want to build a casino right on Gull Point. I leave out the part about Lloyd's handwritten will, not sure I want that made public.

I expect Molly to be upset about the coming development, but she just hands me my brownie and calmly sits down. "Yeah, I heard rumors that something was in the works, but I didn't want to mention it because it was all kind of vague. Actually, having a casino on the island will increase all our property values. Most of the people I've talked to are excited about the idea, but not everyone . . . Excuse me," she says and stands to do something on the stove.

While Molly works, I glance around the kitchen, which is as neat as a pin. There's a calendar on the wall from the Leamington Fish Company and a map of the Lake Erie Basin.

Notations show the shoals and the reefs that aren't safe for boats. All the shipwrecks are marked with a bold dot, starting with a wooden schooner that went down in 1768.

My neighbor notices me reading the map. "The reason Lake Erie has so many shipwrecks," she tells me, "is because it's only 210 feet deep versus Lake Superior at 1300. The storms are worse here too, with the wind whipping the shallow waters into ocean-sized waves."

"I know. I've seen the big breakers on Gull Point."

"My brother Elliot and my pa were fishermen," Molly tells me as she hands me a good-sized brownie on a plate and pours the cold milk. "We owned the marina but sold it to the sailing club in 1995 after Elliot and Daddy drowned on the lake. A sudden squall came up and they were washed over. Both of them were gone in only seconds. The fish were about played out by then, anyway. We used to be able to make a good living."

She turns to the framed photo of a white-haired man wearing coveralls and a handsome young guy in shorts looking at a net full of fish on a boat, both with big smiles that remind me of Molly.

"I'm sorry about your brother and father."

"It was a long time ago. Mom lived with Chris and me until she died a few years ago."

"Why can't people make a living fishing now—why do they need casinos? Is Lake Erie that overfished?"

"No, it's not that. People have been fishing these waters since before European settlers came. It's the pollution, the nitrogen runoff and the invasive species . . . Then the lake is gradually getting warmer, though this past winter you wouldn't have known it. It was unusually cold January through April, more like the old days.

"My daddy used to tell me how they'd drive their Ford Model Ts across the ice to Leamington for supplies in the winter. Even went over the ice to Ohio sometimes. Drove the truck right across, it was that thick. No fool would do that nowadays." (*Really,* I think. *I know at least two fools. Not mentioning names.*)

When I leave, Molly reassures me that it probably won't be hard to find another place to live on Seagull Island. "There's lots of empty houses in the winter. You'll find something. I'll keep an eye open and spread the word."

Back at my cottage, I open the windows to let in the air and sit on the sofa with my orange cat. Though I know Seagull Haven was never *my* house, it feels like my home and I can't imagine living on the island anywhere else. "Oh, what will we do, Tiger?" I ask, but my cat only licks my hand.

Folk Fest

Friday morning, the phone rings just as I get home from my swim. "Hello?" I answer, panting and shaking my short wet hair like a dog.

"Hey, Sara. It's Jed. I'm calling from Windsor. Had to come

over with a patient for tests. Did you remember the folk concert is this weekend?"

"Aaaah, no. I was going to help you, wasn't I?"

"Well, are you still up for it? We need to set up the emergency medical tent with cots and arrange our supplies this afternoon. Can I pick you up after I get back, so we can go out to the park?"

"It's tonight? What time does the music start and when does it end? I just got my bike fixed and I could ride out there."

"Starts at six, lasts until midnight, but you better let me drive. Most of the participants camp at the park, but some will stay at the B and Bs and rent cottages, then they'll hang out at the taverns until late. You don't want to be riding your bike after dark."

When Jed picks me up, his mood is somber. "You worried about the concert?" I ask him.

"Nah. Why?"

"You look a little under the weather."

"Too much to drink last night. Met some friends in Windsor."

BY SIX WE have our tent and supplies set up. Jed has bought a couple of red T-shirts with a big white cross on the front to indicate we're medics and I pull mine on over my other clothes. Not far away from our area, I catch a glimpse of Rainbow, Dian, Wade and the others from the commune at their booth where they're selling green smoothies.

Looking at the festival program, I realize how little I know about contemporary folk music, especially Canadian. First on the stage is Poor Angus and the crowd goes crazy when the all-male group opens with a wild Celtic number that includes a bagpipe and drums.

Fortunately the clinic has no patients, so I'm free to stand out front and listen to the music. Poor Angus is followed by Black-

wood Honeybees and then a country group called Doghouse
Rose. "Where do these people find their names?" I ask Jed, but
he's stretched out on a cot sleeping off his hangover.

About an hour into the music, Peter Dolman approaches the
tent, half carrying a very drunk teenage girl with purple hair. I
help her lie down just as she vomits all over my sandals and then
we get really busy.

Jed wakes up. A woman with facial piercings arrives hyper-
ventilating and we give her albuterol for her asthma. On the next
cot, a man wearing only cutoff jeans is disoriented and Jed shines
a penlight into his eyes. Then a mother brings in a little boy
who's cut his foot. It goes on like this until midnight.

The last group on stage is Poor Angus again, belting out a
crowd favorite, "Never Come Back." The fans seem to know the
lyrics and half the people sing along. A tin flute repeats the tune
and then everyone comes in with the chorus, even me.

*"And one more time, set it on fire and burn it all down, One
more night, let it all go, let it all out."* I look over at the New Day
commune and catch Rainbow's eye.

Torrington, West Virginia, seems very far away.

Let Me In!

The whole time I was at the folk festival, I kept expecting to
see Lenny. It seemed the sort of event he would show up for. (I
even shaved my legs, just in case.) Once I thought I spied his long
gold and silver ponytail during a lull in the music and my heart
sped up, but whoever it was moved away in the crowd.

On the way home, Jed is unusually quiet. He seems sad about
something, but maybe he's still hung over. Coming along Grays

Road through the woods, he swerves suddenly, stops the Jeep and jumps out.

"Did you see that?"

"What? Where?"

"Look!" He puts his arm around my shoulders and turns my head to the left. Just in front of the headlights, two eyes shine in the dark.

"Is it a cat?"

"No, a fox, maybe a *gray fox*. They're common in Ohio and Michigan, but are on the endangered species list in Canada. The only place they've been spotted before is on Pelee Island. The Nature Conservancy had scientists on Seagull, trying to find one. Thank God we didn't hit it."

When I get home, I put on my summer nightgown and stay up until two, thinking Lenny might still come after the taverns close, but then it starts to storm and it seems unlikely, so I go to bed.

THE SQUALL BEGINS with lightning and thunder so close it shakes the cottage. *Flash and boom. Flash. Flash and boom.* I'm in the middle of a war zone and wonder what primitive people in tents or grass huts would think. Do they assume God is angry? Do they fear for their lives?

The thunder is so loud that at first I don't hear the rap on the window. "Sara," a man's voice whispers from outside. "Sara, let me in! I know you're in there. It's Lenny. Let me in."

Shocked by his urgency, I turn on the bedside lamp, throw a flannel shirt over my thin summer nightgown and hurry to the door. "What's wrong? You're out of breath."

"You don't want to know. I just need to rest and think how to get out of here. They saw where my boat is docked. They know I'll be coming back for it."

"Do you think they might come here? Who are we talking about anyway?"

"You don't need to know. Just turn off the overheads and light some candles. I came down the beach and through the woods at the end of the point and they're in an SUV on the road. If someone didn't know you lived here, they'd drive right by."

I do what he says, turn off the lights, lock the door again, then take him by the arm . . . "Come into the bedroom and I'll dry you off. It's not the Nelson men, is it?"

"Jake and William? No. The Nelsons confine themselves to white-collar crime."

Lenny comes to the bedroom, lays a pistol that he pulls out of the back of his jeans on the dresser and drops onto the bed. My eyes get big. What kind of mess have I fallen into?

"How do you know the Nelsons anyway?" Lenny asks after I take off his wet clothes and cover him.

"Their parents used to own this cottage." I crawl in beside him. "The men and their sister were here the other day, and if they're looking for you and know we're involved, they may come back."

I stumble on the word *involved*. Are we *involved*? It seems presumptuous. For all I know Lenny has a honey in every port from Lorain, Ohio, to Paris.

"God no. They're little fish in a big pond."

"These other guys are *big* fish?"

"Yeah, big."

"You're mixed up in something, aren't you? Do you need help? I can call Sergeant Dolman. I have his number. He's a cop here, but not a bad cop. Maybe he can help."

"Pete? No. I just have to get off the island. . . ." He pauses in thought. "I'll get my brother-in-law at Red Hawk to fly in tomorrow morning and pick me up and then I'll leave the country for a while. Someone can come back for the boat next week."

"Shall I make you some coffee? A sandwich? I have some money. Do you need money?" (I feel like I'm in the middle of a TV cop show and I'm not sure whose side I'm on . . . the good guys or the bad.)

"No. Thank you anyway, Sara. You're a sweetheart. I just want to sleep until it starts to get light. And, Sara, you can't mention me to anyone. I don't want you mixed up in any of this!" He grips my hand and I nod soberly. "Now, can you rest with me?" he asks.

There is no lovemaking this time, just the comfort of each other's bodies. Lenny holds on to me as if I were a life preserver in the middle of Lake Erie and when his breathing slows I know he's asleep. Once in the night he kisses me on the back of my neck and I shiver. "I'll miss you," he whispers. "I'll miss you."

When I wake, Lenny is gone.

CHAPTER 34

Roadhouse

est pizza on the island," Jed tells me a few evenings later
after we've ordered a pepperoni and black olive to share. "Way
better than the Black Sheep." I invited him out because I still
owe him for helping me fix up the house and yard, but really
because I want to find out if anything strange happened after the
folk concert.

We're sitting in the Roadhouse at a table that looks out on the
marina. Ten sailboats are docked and their masts look like naked
black trees against the pale lilac sky. Each sailboat is doubled in the
calm water and the reflections shimmer when a trawler comes in.

I take in the Roadhouse. MUSIC, FRIENDS, FOOD the sign says
over the long oak bar. The large room with wooden tables and
red-and-white-checkered tablecloths is almost full, a good crowd
for a Wednesday and the guitarist is just tuning up. Jed waves
hello to a few of the locals.

"Do they have music here every night in the summer?" I ask.

"No, not usually, but the musician on stage was at the folk fest
last year and is now in love with Seagull Island. It happens a lot."
There's a pause as we listen to the first few lines of her song, a familiar tune. *There is a house in New Orleans they call the rising sun . . ."*

Jed stares out the window at a small white bird that's struggling in the wind. The bird takes a vertical plunge into the water headfirst. "What kind of a seagull is that?" I wonder out loud.

"It's not a gull. It's a tern. They're smaller with more pointy wings and they do that incredible dive when they see a fish."

"And it's been the ruin of many a poor girl, and me, oh God, I'm one . . ." We listen to the vocalist until she's done.

"Anything happen at any of the taverns, after you brought me home the other night?" I ask, trying to sound casual.

"You mean the fight? Peter tell you about it? It was kind of weird. A couple of gangbangers from Cleveland got into it with some dudes from Toronto. Knives were flashed, but no guns. Dolman and I broke it up. He thinks they were arguing about a drug deal.

"It could have been worse," he goes on. "Serena runs a tight ship." He nods toward a beautiful woman behind the bar with smooth olive skin, a long black ponytail and dangling turquoise earrings. "She even hired a bouncer for the festival. I left about 1:00 A.M. Everything had calmed down by then, but the joint was still rocking."

"So you didn't see what the fight was about? I didn't think there were drugs on Seagull." (I'm thinking that Lenny arrived at my house just after two.)

"You kidding?" Jed says. "There are drugs everywhere, sister. Oxycontin, morphine, speed, heroin. Everywhere."

COMMON TERN
Common on open water
Nests in large colonies on beaches
Range: US to Canada
Diet: Feeds on fish by diving headfirst into the water
Congregates in flocks for feeding frenzy
Voice: A descending *keeeeyur* also a high *kit*
Size: 12 inches
Wingspan: 30 inches

Secret

*T*his morning the sun rises into a clear blue sky and a tiny bird about the size of my thumb darts among the zinnias out by the picket fence. It has a long beak and tiny legs and zips around like a helicopter. It's the first hummingbird I've seen since I left West Virginia and I wish that I had a hummingbird feeder.

I'm mulling over how I could make one when Molly Lou pulls into my drive and gets out of her Subaru, carrying an old dented mailbox. "Thought you could use this. We got a new one and Eugene Burke says he'll deliver your mail if you put it on that old post by your driveway."

"Well, that was nice of you!" I greet her. "Come in and have some ice tea. Where's Little Chris?"

"He's with his daddy. I wanted to talk to you alone."

This gets my attention and I go very still. From my experience as a midwife, women don't start a conversation that way unless something's wrong. I wait, but she's not ready.

"Is this tea herbal?" she asks, tasting it.

"Yes, it's peppermint. I dried it myself from some mint plants I found on the side of the house. What's up, Molly Lou? You and Big Chris doing okay?"

It's then that the woman breaks down in tears and cries so hard and loud that even Tiger backs into a corner. "I'm so sorry!" she keeps saying as she takes another tissue and wipes her eyes. "I'm so sorry!"

"What is it, Molly?"

"*You can't tell anyone!* You swear?"

"I won't tell. You know I won't."

She takes a deep breath and blows it out, takes another one like she's getting ready to dive underwater and looks right at me.

"Last Christmas just before the final ferry of winter went out, I had an affair."

I wait, wondering how else she can surprise me, but when she doesn't go on, I ask the next question. "Does Chris know?"

"Chris can never know! The trouble is . . . Well, the trouble is I feel so guilty I can't look at him. I finally moved upstairs to the spare bedroom. We haven't made love in eight months."

"Were you a good couple before? I mean, were you close?"

"Yes. Well, yes and no. We had a big fight around Thanksgiving about finances. He wanted to buy another tractor and I put my foot down. That was the last time we made love and then this thing happened . . . You're going to think I'm terrible."

(*Lord,* I think, *maybe that floozy at the Roadhouse was right.* Seagull Island is a hotbed of infidelity.)

"Wait a minute, Molly. Doesn't Chris ask why you don't want to be with him?"

"I told him I'm going through premature menopause and I'm hot flashing so bad we can't sleep together. I told him that's why I can't make love. He doesn't know much about women."

"So was it a long affair? I mean, you don't have to say who the other man is, but do you still see him?"

"He's gone back to Mexico. It was one of the migrant laborers at the Cider Mill Farm, a boss of the crew who worked in the orchards. I met him at the country store. We were just flirting around. I never knew his full name. Then one night it happened. We were in the Subaru behind the Black Sheep Pub." Here she starts crying again.

I feel like saying, *Molly Lou! You have got to be kidding!* But I keep my face still. As a nurse and a midwife, I hear all kinds of stories and I never want to show that I'm shocked. "So what are you going to do?" I step into the bathroom for a tissue.

"I don't know. I'm afraid if I don't start making love with

Chris I'll lose him, but I feel so dirty . . . and I love him, Sara. I don't know what I was thinking. I guess I *wasn't* thinking . . . and there's something else. Ever since I was unfaithful . . ." (Here she looks away.) "I have a *smell*. Jed told me a long time ago that you know about women's things. What should I do?"

"Are you asking me what you should do about Chris and your marriage or the smelly discharge?"

Molly looks at me with her big blue eyes still full of tears. "Both. What should I do about the discharge? I think it's an infection but I can't tell Jed. And what should I do about Chris? I can't lose him." She says this last part again.

I pour us another cup of tea to give myself time to think. "Did you use a condom?"

Molly Lou shrugs meaning no and I can't help it, I roll my eyes, then I let out a long breath. "You could go to a physician in Windsor."

"But don't you see? It can't be anyone who would put it on my health record."

She begins to sob again until I move over to the sofa and hold her in my arms, absorbing her sorrow, accepting her imperfections, agreeing to help her find a clinic in Detroit.

"I'll have to be off the island all day," Molly thinks out loud. "If I take the 8:00 A.M. ferry to Leamington, I can drive to Windsor and then across the bridge to Detroit. I've never done this before by myself. Chris always drives. Maybe you could come with me . . ."

"Sorry, Molly. I can't go back to the States." (Here I bite my tongue, but Molly is too involved in her own crisis to think about what I've said and she doesn't ask why.)

"You must not tell *anyone*," Molly Lou warns me. "Chris is already hurt and angry. If he found out I was unfaithful and had a sexually transmitted disease it would be the end." Here she breaks down again. "I miss him so much. At night I hear him moving around in the bedroom below and I want to go down and snuggle up with him, but I can't."

She dries her eyes again and stands to wash her face. "I have to go home now and make Chris his lunch. You probably wonder why that's so important . . . always making him lunch. It's because I feel so guilty. I've been unfaithful and I'm no longer a real wife, but I can still feed him . . ."

RUBY-THROATED HUMMINGBIRD
A small gray and green bird
with a slender long downward-curved bill
Males have a metallic ruby throat
Flies fast but can stop on a dime
It can also hover and adjust its position up and down
Habitat: Lives in fields, yards and parks
in the eastern US and southern Canada
Winters in Central America
Loves sugar water feeders, but lives on nectar and bugs
Voice: a distinct high-pitched twitter

Midwives Help People Out

The first thing I do in the morning is bike to the ferry dock and do some research on my cell phone. Then I bike back to the cottage and call Molly Lou. "Can you talk?"

"Chris and Little Chris are out on the tractor."

"The way I see it, you have three problems. The first one is finding out if you have an STD. Hopefully, it's something that can be cured with antibiotics. Some viruses stay with you for life."

"I know about herpes, HIV and vaginal warts. I looked them up on the computer. You don't think I have them, do you?"

"I can't say if you've been exposed, but you haven't seen any lumps or bumps in your private area, have you?"

"No . . . nothing."

"Well, that's a good sign. I got you an appointment next Tuesday at a Planned Parenthood office near Wayne State University in Detroit. It will cost seventy-five dollars. They don't ask for ID or an address and you can call for the test results. I'll write it all down. Can you drive in the city?"

"I will. I have to."

"Once you come back and are treated, the next challenge will be learning to forgive yourself. You did something stupid. We all do stupid things now and then."

"But how will I ever get back with Chris?" She sniffles.

"I don't know, Molly. I'll think about it. Where there's love, there's a way."

"Thank you, Sara! I had no one else I could turn to." We hang up and I look over at Tiger.

"Pretty strange. I left my husband because he was unfaithful. Now here I am helping an unfaithful woman. The difference is Molly Lou had only one episode. She didn't do it over and over again and she's truly remorseful." My kitty comes over and licks my hand. I pet his head and he purrs. "What kind of craziness have we gotten ourselves into, Tiger?"

Then I remember that I'm a midwife and this is what midwives do. Like the medallion I still wear around my neck says, MIDWIVES HELP PEOPLE OUT.

CHAPTER 35

Threats

For five days the wind blows and big waves march across the cove with military precision. At night they roar and I leave the window open in my bedroom so I can hear them.

Molly's visit to Planned Parenthood goes well. She has chlamydia but not gonorrhea and if she takes all her antibiotics (and I'm sure she will), it will be gone. She has to wait another week to get the results of her blood tests for HIV, herpes and hepatitis, so we hope for the best and go on as before, while Chris, puzzled and angry, receives his lunch exactly at noon.

FOR TWO NIGHTS it rains and I try not to dwell on Molly Lou's situation. How ironic that I'm playing marriage counselor when I couldn't keep my own marriage together! Finally it clears, a beautiful day with whitecaps, blue sky and blue water.

It's time to visit Terry Jacob, the weaver. (I'm ashamed of myself really. Though I've called her four times, I've never been to her home.)

I'm just getting on my bike when I see in the distance the white convertible. *It's the Nelsons.* Damn! Maybe I should have told them in person about Lloyd's new will, but not wanting to get involved, I just gave the document to Peter and let him take care of it.

The BMW pulls up in a cloud of dust. "So what the hell were you trying to pull? Hiding that so-called handwritten will from us." The younger brother, Jake, jumps out of the vehicle with his hands balled in fists, but his sister pulls him back.

"Jake," Charlene shouts. "Calm down. Let's talk about this civilly."

"I don't know what there is to talk about," I defend myself. "I found Lloyd's will in the top of the closet. It looked legitimate, so I took it to Sergeant Dolman to get his opinion."

"Why didn't you notify *us*? Why Dolman? How do you think it made us feel, having to learn about this from our lawyer?" Jake towers over me and fires his questions like bullets from an automatic weapon.

"Can we come in?" Charlene asks. "Sit down and have a talk?"

"There's nothing to talk about. The will is legitimate or it's not. That's for the courts to decide. What do you want from me?"

Jake looks at Charlene. "Well, we have some questions. When did you find the handwritten will? Before or after Lloyd and Wanda died?"

"A couple of months ago. I probably should have given it to someone sooner, but I didn't know Lloyd was so close to death. I just didn't know who to give it to."

"How about giving it to the family?" Jake asks sarcastically. He pulls a silver flask out of his back pocket and takes a snort, then takes two more. "I think you had your own reasons for coming up with the will after you found out we were planning to tear the cottage down and build the hotel and casino. I think you wanted the house for yourself. If it goes to court, our lawyers will make you look like the scheming little bitch that you are!"

"No threats, Jake, but be realistic, Miss Livingston. We could have you evicted right now."

"How? Why?"

"Do you have a signed copy of your lease?" Charlene asks.

Here she's got me. I have no lease at all. I steel my jaw. "You'll have to do what you have to do. I can get a copy of the last check that I mailed to Wanda that she signed and deposited. I wrote 'Rent for Seagull Haven until end of November' on it. I have nothing else to say. Excuse me." I try to roll my bike past them, but Jake grabs my arm.

"Don't think you can get away with this! We know you hang around with those hippies and environmentalists. We'll sue you for conspiracy and throw so much shit on you at the trial that you'll look like a walking outhouse." I feel like laughing at his simile, but the laughter is false.

A minute ago, I just wanted to get away, now I stand my ground. If I leave, they may go into the house. Maybe they'll trash the place. The vein in Jake's forehead stands out like a rope.

"Take your hand off my arm, Mr. Nelson. You're hurting me. I don't think you want me to report you for assault." This is said with as much strength as I can muster, but my voice cracks at the end.

"Come on, Jake," Charlene says. "We're getting nowhere."

I watch as they turn their white convertible around and disappear behind a cloud of dust, then I put my visit to Terry on hold. *This is not good.*

"I GUESS I was naïve to think I could just give you Lloyd's hand-written will and that would be the end of it. You said there would be trouble. I just didn't know it would involve me."

Peter Dolman and I are in the cruiser with my bike in the trunk and he's driving me home.

"I was just getting ready to visit Terry Jacob when the Nelsons pulled up. As soon as they left, I counted to one hundred, then biked like hell to your office. I didn't know what else to do. These people scare me. It's like there's a screw loose or else they are so used to always getting what they want that they can't stand it when they don't.

"Jake was pretty liquored up and got mean, threatened to kick me out of the cottage right now and take me to court for conspiracy. I guess they think I'm in league with the Nature Conservancy."

Peter breaks my flow of words. "I thought you were friends with the Nelson family. How was it you never met the brothers and sister before?"

"I exaggerated my relationship with Lloyd and Wanda because I wanted people on the island to like me. I thought it made me seem more connected. Was that so bad?"

At the corner of Sunset and Middle Loop the cop stops and looks at me. "What the hell. Let's go see Terry anyway. She might cheer us up."

Terry

Ten minutes later we pull up next to a yellow one-story building with a small wooden sign over the door that says SEAGULL ISLAND FIBRE GUILD AND ART SHOPPE. Inside the sunny showroom, the woman sits in her wheelchair behind a big table sorting balls of colored yarn.

"How you doing?" she greets us. The weaver is not what I expected. At forty-four, she looks more like thirty-four with brown shiny shoulder-length hair and brown eyes. She's wearing a long skirt and a low-neck black cotton top and hoop earrings, a beautiful woman.

"What's up, Dolman? Making your rounds on your flock like a shepherd, protecting the weak and vulnerable? I told you last time—I'm fit as a fiddle." Her wide smile illuminates the room.

"I just can't stay away, Terry. You're so entertaining you could be a stand-up comedian."

"You mean a *sit-down* comedian!" The woman grabs his hand and pretends to arm wrestle. "I could take you down anytime, copper!" she says.

"This is Sara Livingston, RN. I don't think you've actually met."

"Oh, we're old telephone pals. Hi, Sara."

"It's nice to finally meet you," I respond. "Do you dye your own yarn?"

"Sure. We work as a collective when we do the colors. That way each fiber artist doesn't have to buy or make their own dye." She indicates a row of deep sinks and an electric stove in the back. (Every table, I notice, is made so a wheelchair fits under it.)

"Now the shop . . . we take turns behind the counter." She looks around at the shelves that hold knitted sweaters, caps, shawls and mittens in natural white, gray and tan wool and some that are brightly colored. There are also woven blankets, rugs, scarves, shawls and placemats.

"I'm amazed. All this time, I could have shopped here and I didn't know it. I want one of everything."

While Terry and Peter clown around, I peek into the studio. It's a large cozy space with three looms and an antique wooden spinning wheel. There's also a small flat-screen TV and a desk with a laptop computer. All over the walls are skeins of yarn: gray, white, purple, green, gold, red.

On a table, I notice a folder of drawings. "Gull Point Proposed

Hotel and Casino," it says on the cover. *Why does Terry have plans for the casino?* I decide to come right out and ask her.

"So, Terry . . . I noticed a folder on a table that said something about the casino on Gull Point. Is that something you're involved in? I was kind of surprised." Peter looks away, embarrassed at my snooping.

"Surprised? Why? I sit on the township council."

"So what do you think of it? The plans, I mean? The proposal."

"I'm trying to keep an open mind. We have until November to reject or require modification of the plan. The council is split down the middle."

"Well, we have to do *something*," Peter puts in. "The island is dying."

"I thought Jed said that the number of full-time residents went up for the first time in years," I offer.

"Yeah, but 304 isn't much. We don't have a big enough tax base to grade the roads, keep the water lines running and make repairs on the school. We have to do something," he says again.

"I agree," Terry concurs. "The question is what do we gain and what do we lose with this casino idea? It's tricky. You should come to the next township meeting, Sara. You might find it interesting." This raises my adrenaline.

"Did you hear about Lloyd Nelson's second will, Terry?" Peter asks.

"Yeah." She blows across her handmade pottery mug to cool her coffee. "Heard a simple written will surfaced that gave his land and cottage to the Nature Conservancy."

"Sara is the one who found it."

"Really?" The woman looks at me sideways, probably surprised and I squirm, wishing Peter hadn't divulged that information.

"Don't tell everyone, okay?" I ask.

"Why not?" Terry asks, turning to me. "You didn't do any-thing wrong, did you?"

"No," Pete defends me. "All she did was find the folder in the top of the Nelsons' closet and bring it to me. That was the right thing to do. Anyone asks, Terry, you tell them that."

Fall

CHAPTER 36

Vigil

When Jed calls me, it's already dark and I'm in my flannel nightgown, curled in front of the fire.

"Hey, sweetie. Could I get you to come down to Nita's and sit with me tonight? I need the company."

"What's up? Is it her hip? Or her lung problems?"

"Both, also her leg and her back hurt. She doesn't want to be alone."

When I get to Nita's house on my bike with a flashlight tied to the handlebars, the house is dark, except the front bedroom, the one that faces the lake. I don't knock but quietly open the door and step in.

I haven't spent as much time with Nita as I should have and her health has been poor, but she assured me, when I called last week, it was just some kind of bronchitis and she'd be better after she finished the antibiotics. Now Jed is acting like she's in a bad way.

"Hey," I say quietly, approaching the bed. "How're you doing?"

Jed turns and I see that his blue eyes are red. He swipes them with the back of his hand, embarrassed.

"Hi, Sara," Nita whispers. "It's the cancer. I've known for a month. I'd already decided two years ago that if it came back I wasn't going to fight it. My time is over." (She says it like that, just as simple as anything and reaches out for my hand.)

"Over?" I say, not wanting to understand, and I lower myself to the side of the bed.

Jed hands me a report from Windsor Regional Hospital, but my vision is blurred by a sudden burst of tears and all I can read is something about carcinoma of the breast and tumors in the left femur and the right lung base.

"It's okay," Nita says to me. Her brown skin is chalky and her face is too thin. "I'm ready to cross over. My husband, Lowell, is waiting."

I hear Jed let out a long breath. "Need some coffee?" he asks, nodding toward the hallway.

"Why didn't you tell me?" I hiss in the kitchen. "How long have you known?"

"Since before the folk fest when we flew to Windsor to have her last MRI. They found tumors all over. That's why I was so bummed and got drunk. We had a long talk when she went through chemo and radiation with her breast cancer a few years ago and now she has a 'do not resuscitate' form in her chart."

"How long does she have?"

"Hard to say. She's going downhill fast and she didn't want an IV, so I've been giving her morphine drops by mouth. Might be a couple of days. When she starts coughing she sounds like shit. I wanted to tell you weeks ago, but Nita said no. Tonight, I just couldn't stay awake again, so I told her I had to phone. I've been here since Wednesday and the clinic is closed."

"Damn!" is all I can think to say, although there's much more, like, "Nita, don't leave us!" Then the old lady begins to cough again and we run to her room.

To Suffer

*F*or two days I don't leave Nita's house except to run home and check on my cat. Finally I bring him over and let him bounce around Nita's bedroom. Tiger likes to sit on the bed where the old lady can lay her hand on his head.

Most of the time Nita is peaceful. She watches the cat play with some cat toys I brought over and that makes her laugh, then we listen to music or watch old movies on her DVD player: *The Manchurian Candidate* with Denzel Washington, *In the Heat of the Night* with Sidney Poitier, *Men in Black* with Will Smith. "I like to see their beautiful brown faces," she tells me without apology.

During the day, Jed decides to go back to the clinic. I change Nita's linens, wash her small body and braid her white hair. These are the things I used to do for women in labor and it gives us both comfort.

Jed brings us adult diapers from his office and meatloaf and mashed potatoes from the pub. Molly Lou stops by with a macaroni dish and a blueberry pie from the Baa Baa Bakery.

"How's she doing?" Molly asks in the kitchen.

"Not so good."

She tips her head to one side and smiles sadly, then pokes her head in the bedroom door to say hello, but the old lady sleeps. With Nita so sick I haven't had time to find out how the remaining STD tests came out, so before Molly leaves, I catch her and whisper, "Any lab results yet?"

She smiles and raises a thumb. "Except for the chlamydia, I dodged a bullet or God was looking after me."

ON THE THIRD afternoon, Jed tells me to go home and rest and get some clean clothes. "Hate to tell you, babe, but you stink."

Once back at the cottage I turn to the comfort of the lake and the sky. First I swim, letting the cold water wash away my exhaustion and then I walk, with Tiger on his leash, searching for pieces of smooth colored glass.

Looking down at the ripples in the sand, I spot a trail of small footprints leading back toward the cottage. I kneel down and study Tiger's prints, comparing one to the other. My cat's heel has three parts. The other heel has two and is slightly bigger. They both have four toes, but the wild animal has claw marks at the end of its toe pads. I'm no expert but I'd say the footprints in the sand were clearly made by a canine, perhaps a fox, but there's no way to tell if it's gray or red.

As I stroll past a patch of tall beach grass, I hear a clucking sound and Tiger goes on alert. In the shadows of the foliage, a strange brown bird stares back at me. He's as big as a chicken with a black fringe of feathers on his head that makes him look like a punk rocker on the city streets. Almost hitting me, the bird flies off in a rush and I watch as he skims the sand toward the point.

LEAST BITTERN
A small bittern with a black cap and brown body
a long yellow bill and white belly
Diet: Small fish, amphibians and insects
Found in wetlands among the reeds where it feeds and nests
Voice: *Cluck, cluck, cluck* with a twitter
Breeds in the central and eastern US and southern Canada
Winters in Central America and the West Indies
Wingspan: 18 inches

Alpha and Omega

O n seeing the strange bird, a great sadness washes over me. The world is so beautiful and it's so hard to see the old lady suffer, but maybe there's no way to get through this life without pain. I deceive myself if I think we can . . . We all suffer. We are born in suffering, and we die suffering, we leave loved ones behind to suffer, *but in between we fly.*

THINKING SUCH WEIGHTY thoughts as I walk, Nita's beautiful brown face comes back to me. She keeps talking about going to meet her husband, Lowell, and seems sure of her place with him. I envy that faith. I'd like to ask Nita what she thinks about death, but it doesn't seem appropriate to bring up the subject.

"Oh, by the way, I know you're going to die pretty soon, so what do you think happens next? Will your soul silently slip out of your body or does it explode into the heavens like fireworks? Or do you even believe in a soul, that unseen part of a person that has nothing to do with their flesh and bones?" No, these are the questions I must ask myself.

Then I see it . . .

Sticking up sideways is the largest green glass beach stone I've ever seen, the bottom of a beer bottle, I would bet. It's round and flat and fits in the palm of my hand, a perfect stone for skipping on water, but it is much too special for that.

Before Nita, I wouldn't have known what beautiful art objects could be made of such glass and this gives me an idea. The old lady sleeps most of the time and is too ill to go into her studio. What if I could bring the studio to her? I return to her house with a mission.

WHEN I GET back, I find Jed snoring softly in his chair next to Nita's bed with his chin on his chest. "Why don't you go home?" I ask him. "You need to lie down and get a good night's sleep." Nita's eyes are closed and the sun is just setting. I light some votive candles. Only once does she begin to cough, but she stops in two minutes.

Before he leaves, Jed shows me how many drops of morphine to give. The poor woman hasn't eaten for a week. She takes only sips of Gatorade and Jed is okay with that. "It's her time," he says. "She's in control." He seems so confident and sure, but that makes me wonder.

When women are in labor, some make good choices and some do not. Some walk and rock and shower and bathe and lean over the sink and roll their hips and hug the baby's father and slow dance in his arms, while others are so afraid they retreat behind anesthesia, crouch there, hiding, until the event is all over, more a victim than a participant.

So, I consider . . . if some women don't know how to give birth gracefully, some people probably don't know how to *die* gracefully, either. Maybe everyone needs a midwife to help them at both the beginning and the end, the alpha and the omega . . . the beginning and the end.

Kum Ba Yah

Around nine, after watching *Coming to America* with Eddie Murphy, I sing Nita to sleep with an old church camp song I used as a lullaby when Jessie was little.

"Kum ba yah, my Lord—Kum ba yah—Someone's singing, Lord—Kum ba yah."

"Do you know what that means?" Nita opens her eyes and asks so softly I have to lean over.

"Kum ba yah?" I shrug my shoulders, indicating that I don't.

"*Come by here, Lord. Come by here.* It's a spiritual from the Gullah people who live on the coast of South Carolina. The Gullah are the descendants of African slaves . . . I'm a descendant of African slaves. Don't you forget that! We are strong people. To have made it alive from Africa to America in those awful slave ships, we had to be strong people. Don't you forget."

Here she trails off as if telling the story has exhausted her. I squeeze her hand to give her strength, but she's on her own journey in a little white boat bobbing over the waves across Lake Erie. Then she opens her eyes and smiles.

"Are you happy, Nita?" I ask. "Have you had a happy life?"

"Don't you know that's not what it's about, Sara? There are *moments* of happiness, but life is not a fairy tale or an Eddie Murphy movie. It's not supposed to be." She stops and takes a couple deep breaths and coughs once. "Happiness is a necklace of colored glass beach stones and each stone is a *moment* of happiness. Right now is one."

Then the old lady fades back into that place between death and dreams, where she seems to sleep, but is maybe just gliding through the clouds with seagulls.

CHAPTER 37

The Temple

When Nita's breathing is regular and slow and I think she's going to be out for a while, I enter her studio as if it were a temple. Colored light streams through the sparkling sea glass made into sculptures, mobiles and jewelry; deep blue, turquoise, green, amber, brown, gold, even red.

Then I begin to decorate her bedroom with her glass-beach-stone creations. I hang the mobiles from the curtain rod in the big window and cover the window ledge with her small sculptures. The smooth beach stones gleam like gems in the candlelight.

"Kum ba yah," I sing, feeling stronger than I have for months, maybe years. *"Kum ba yah."* Strange to feel peace and content-ment at such a sad time, but I suppose it is because I'm doing something that I imagine will bring joy to another person.

That's something I've missed since I left my midwifery prac-tice and patients. Every time I went to work, I had the chance to make the day a little better for someone, to bring peace, to bring hope, to let them know that I cared. Sometimes it was as simple as telling the patient that she looked pretty today or that she made me laugh or that I was proud of her for keeping her chin up during such hard economic times. Sometimes it was just giving a hug.

THREE TIMES DURING the night Nita has a coughing spell and I must sit her up and pat her back. She's as light as a dried-up leaf. I wish we had oxygen or a suction machine to pull out the phlegm that's in her airway, but Jed says Nita doesn't want anything mechanical, not even for comfort and, anyway, if we had oxygen we couldn't have candles.

I reflect on the choices Nita's making and wonder if I'd make the same ones. If I had a child, I would fight to hold on. I think I would anyway, up to a point. If all I had left was pain and suffering, I might choose to die like Nita, but I'm not sure I could be as brave. (Maybe I'd just ask someone to give me a shot and get it over with.)

I do have a child, I remind myself, a grown child. As I sit at Nita's bedside, I let Jessie's face float into the candlelit room.

Jessie as a toddler comes first with her round innocent face and firm soft little body. She crawls into my lap as I stroke Nita's wrinkled brown hand.

Sitting with my dying friend, I watch my daughter grow taller. She's eleven and then twelve, still sweet and innocent. I close my eyes and wish I could hold on to those years, but they are long gone.

Then trouble starts. Jessie rolls her eyes as if everything I say is stupid and she's now a sassy little vixen. I blame myself. I was exhausted, in clinic all day, in the hospital every other night and running on empty, too tired to put my foot down. If she spoke back to me when I asked her to take out the trash, I'd ignore her and take out the trash myself; it wasn't worth the hassle.

Half the time, Richard was away in Alaska or at a conference, expounding on the effect of climate change on polar bears, and when he was home he was uninterested in discipline, preferring the fun part of parenting—movies, trips to the arcade, eating out, the occasional concert.

Our childbirth practice was growing and Linda and I were each delivering eight or ten babies a month. So I marched on as I lost control of my daughter, my marriage and eventually my life.

At dawn, as the sun rises, Nita wakes, her mind clear, almost like her old self. "Oh, look at the beautiful colored glass," she says, clapping her hands. "Am I in heaven?" (I can't tell if she's joking or maybe she believes she's at the pearly gates.)

"They're your creations," I tell her. "I hope you don't mind that I brought them in the bedroom. I figured if you couldn't go to your studio, I would bring the studio to you."

"I wish I could work. There's a big project I left half-done . . ." She starts a coughing spell again just as Jed pops his head through the doorway.

"You okay?"

"I'm fit as a fiddle," Nita says, catching her breath. "As good as a dying old lady could be surrounded by friends, a pussycat and colored glass. Can I have some peppermint tea? Just a sip?"

"I'll get us all some. Be right back. Want a piece of the Baa Baa Bakery's blueberry pie for breakfast, Sara? I'll warm it up."

"Sure," I answer on automatic, thinking . . . *Fit as a fiddle. As good as a dying old lady can be . . .*

"Nita, you make me happy," I say, lying down on the bed with her. "And I want to be like you when I grow up."

"Well, you better hurry," she says, "because you're going to have to take charge when I'm gone."

I blink in surprise. "What do you mean?"

"You know, you'll be the keeper of the green trees, the yellow sunflowers, the blue waters, the red fire, the white seagulls, the brown earth, the purple sky at sunset." I have no words, but I squeeze her hand as Jed comes back with a tray.

When I stand to look at the sunrise out the window, the large green glass beach stone falls out of my pocket and drops on the carpet with a clunk. "Oh, look, I have something for you! Something I found on the beach." I hold it out to show her.

"Have you ever seen a bigger glass beach stone than this?" Nita doesn't reach for it. Her arms are limp at her sides. "Nita?" I think maybe she can't hear me or maybe she's dead, and I lean over to take her pulse, but her hand opens and then closes again.

"I was just talking to my husband, Lowell." (Hallucinations are common when a patient's on morphine, but Nita hasn't had any medication in the last six hours.)

"What color is it?" she asks, her eyes still closed.

For a minute I don't know what she means and think she's confused, but she turns her hand over and opens it.

"What color is the glass?" she asks again.

"Green, a deep rich green. Look." Her breathing is shallower now. "Nita . . ."

From somewhere a breeze enters the room and curtains sway as if the pressure has changed, a door or a window opened.

"Give it here." That's Nita, lifting her hand, and I place the sanded flat green glass on her palm. She closes her fingers. "It's a beauty," she says, her eyes still closed. "Is it cold in here?" I tuck the covers around her, thinking I should check the windows in the other rooms.

"Can you lay down with me, honey? It keeps me warm."

I climb into bed and get under the covers, warming the woman with my bare arms, then Jed's at the door. "Blueberry pie, anyone?"

"Sure," I say softly, putting my hand around Nita's soft thin old lady's hand, which still holds the green glass beach stone. Jed takes the bedside chair and starts cutting pieces of pie. The warmed berries oozing out of the thin golden crust make my mouth water.

I move two of my fingers under the bedcovers to Nita's wrist and take her pulse. By the clock on the dresser it's very slow, but her respirations are regular and unlabored.

"Can I have some?" Nita surprises us with her request. She hasn't eaten a bite for days. "Can I have some pie?" I look at Jed. She's really his patient. He can decide.

"Just a little. But it's nice you feel up to eating." He takes a straw from her water glass and dips it into the berries, then touches it to her lips.

The tip of her pink tongue comes out and she licks the berries. Jed puts a little more on her tongue and she makes a small smacking sound.

Then Nita dies.

Amazing Grace

On Sunday, we have our first hard frost. The lawn is covered with white so thick you'd think it was snow and every golden or red leaf is rimmed with lace. By noon, it's in the fifties and by three, when Molly Lou and Big Chris pick me up for Nita's funeral at the cemetery in the north end, it's warmed up.

Molly Lou is dressed in black slacks and a flowing black tunic, and Chris even wears a sports coat and tie. Myself, I'm just wearing my black knit pants, a turquoise long-sleeved T-shirt, the rainbow scarf and the heavy sweater I got at the yard sale. (Maybe I should have dressed nicer, but the fact is, this is all I've got.)

It's five days after Nita's death because she had to be flown in a special plane to Windsor to be embalmed and then flown back. The casket was constructed by Dolman out of plain polished oak and Jed has placed a framed photo of Nita and Lowell on the top.

Reverend Easton, the part-time clergyman from Molly Lou's church, is officiating and he begins in that singsong way of a cleric. "Nita Adams has been part of the island community for years . . . She was a woman of faith and had no doubt that she would be with her husband, Lowell, and live in God's house when she crossed over . . ."

My mind wanders to the last funeral I went to. It was at the Lutheran Church in Torrington and I sat through the service dry-eyed, watching photos celebrating my friend's life flash on the big screen behind the podium. There was Karen, larger than life, as a baby, a young girl in a ballet tutu and then graduating from medical school. In every picture she had a big toothy grin. There was even a photo of Karen and me taken just a month before her death. We stood proudly holding twin infants we'd delivered together, both of us laughing.

That was the trouble. Whatever dark sorrow pursued her was a secret she kept from everyone. Even me. When she died, I was cut off at the knees and, I realize now, I'm still walking around on the stumps.

The reverend's voice brings me back to Nita's service . . . "Shall we pray . . ." I bow my head but then take a peek to see who's got their eyes closed. Some people are dabbing their faces with tissues. Some clasp their hands. Officer Dolman, like me, is surveying the crowd and he catches my eye, but I look away.

Finally the casket is lowered by ropes into the grave and we all walk slowly past. I take a handful of sandy dirt and sprinkle it on the coffin. "Goodbye, dear friend. If I had a grandmother, I would want her to be you."

Then from out of the trees, at the edge of the cemetery, comes the shepherd Austin Aubrey, dressed in a bright red-and-green plaid kilt and playing a bagpipe. *Amazing Grace, how sweet the sound, That saved a wretch like me . . .*

The lump in my throat is as big as the green glass beach stone that Nita held in her hand as she died. I bite my lips to keep from crying but the tears come anyway. I'm crying not just for the loss of Nita or Karen or Robyn Layton. I am crying for the whole messed-up beautiful dance we call life.

CHAPTER 38

Township Meeting

What possessed me to go, I don't know, but the township meeting made me question democracy!

"The island needs something big." Chris explains his point of view as we drive north on Sunset toward the Black Sheep Pub. "If there aren't more opportunities, Little Chris, like the rest of the kids, will leave when he grows up." It's getting dark early now and only a few red clouds linger on the horizon. "When I went to high school here we had six boys my age, enough for a basketball team. Now there's just ten kids in the whole school from five to seventeen."

"But aren't you worried about the environment? A casino is a big operation . . . all those people coming down Grays Road?"

"Nothing ventured, nothing gained." He barks a short laugh.

When we get to the pub, half the tables are full of people I don't know. Dolman is there and Terry Jacob and Helen Burke and her husband, Eugene. Earl Prentiss, a slim man with salt and pepper hair, who's the manager of the Cider Mill Farm, sits on the aisle and Austin Aubrey, the shepherd, and his wife, Elsa, sit up front. Jed is hunkered down in the back with his knit cap almost over his eyes. I sit with Molly and Chris.

The session began with a prayer, which surprised me. (I don't know what the laws are in Canada about such things, but in the US anything religious at a government meeting wouldn't fly.)

Eugene from the store stands and asks us to bow our heads. "Oh God of all, bless this community as it seeks to move forward. Help us listen to each other with respect and an open mind. In the name of all that is holy. Amen."

"Amen," the group repeats.

After that, it's all downhill, beginning with Mayor Nell Ambroy, a petite dark-haired woman wearing a black jacket with a pair of wings embroidered on the left breast. She's the pilot that Rainbow told me about and she reminds me of a few female surgeons I've met, small and determined.

"I want, at the very beginning of this gathering, to clear up some false rumors that are going around. Someone is saying that I get a kickback from any development on the island. Someone is saying that I'm going to financially benefit from the casino at the Gull Point, but it's not true, so you can go to hell, Earl Prentiss!"

"Gosh," I whisper to Molly. "That was personal!"

"It's just getting started," she whispers back. "Nell's a pistol."

"While you're on the subject, I've got some questions," someone pipes up.

"Point of order," the mayor yells, and the man sits back down.

THE MEETING GOES on like this for an hour, a creek running wild and I think of leaving, but it's dark and cold out tonight and I'd have to walk home. Finally we break for coffee and I slink to the back to sit next to Jed. "I can see why some people wouldn't come to these things," I whisper. "Are all these folks residents?"

"No. About half are summer people. The summer people and retirees always have a lot to say and some of it's worth listening to, but locals don't want to hear it.

"The way I see it is," Jed goes on in a low voice, "the rich folk from Toronto, Michigan and Ohio can go home to their good jobs, their nice schools and their paved highways whenever they want. The rest of us need jobs *here,* a good school *here* and the roads graded and plowed. You know what conditions were like here last winter. It was like living in the Yukon in the 1920s."

"I kind of liked it."

"You would. This is a vacation for you."

"Come on, Jed. I'm kidding." I give him a nudge with my elbow and he nudges me back, all forgiven.

After cookies and coffee, the residents sit down to sling mud at each other again. The owner of the Old Oak Bed and Breakfast complains that a hotel and casino on Gull Point won't help her small business any. She barely gets by as it is.

Earl Prentiss of the Cider Mill, representing the Nature Conservancy, points out that there have been sightings of the endangered gray fox on Gull Point and if that can be validated, Environment Canada won't allow the casino to be built, but he's shouted down.

"Screw Environment Canada," someone mutters and someone else yells, "That's right. Screw 'em!"

"I have some questions," says a tall man in a blue V-neck cashmere sweater and khakis. He stands and waits until the room quiets.

"We rent our four cottages now, mostly to people who come here as ecotourists, or people into biking, the arts or meditation. Every year we get more requests and I think the island should market itself that way. People in the cities are hungry to get away to a quiet, beautiful place like this."

"People who live here year-round are just plain hungry," a smart aleck comments, loud enough for everyone to hear.

"So what's your *question,* Dr. Marco?" The mayor is edgy.

"Well, has the township thought about marketing to people interested in the arts and as an ecotourism destination?"

"I'll give you a copy of our 'Ten-Year Development Plan' after the meeting," Ms. Ambroy cuts him off rudely. "I don't want to go over all that again. Tonight we're focusing on the casino.

"Charlene and Jake Nelson submitted their architectural plans a month ago and hope to break ground next spring," the mayor continues. "But again, the plans have to be approved by the council and an environmental audit must be conducted. There's also been some opposition. A woman, an outsider, who's against the casino, has threatened to take the Nelsons to court."

A ripple goes through the room. "Who?" "What?" "I hadn't heard."

Are they referring to me? I shrink down in my chair. Talk about false rumors! I'm not taking anyone to court! *I'm trying to stay out of court.*

Finally someone respected by the community rises and the room goes quiet.

"Who's that?" I whisper.

"You know," Jed whispers back. "It's Austin Aubrey, big sheep man on the island, also the head of the Sheepdog Association of Essex County. That's how we end up getting the sheepdog trials here every year."

(I remember him now. He's the shepherd who blocked the road with his sheep and also the fellow who played the bagpipes in his kilt for Nita's service. He's not wearing a kilt now, just a worn blue plaid flannel shirt and old jeans.)

"I think we all have to calm down." Mr. Aubrey holds out his hands as if gathering us in. "Everyone here, sheep farmers, fishermen, bed-and-breakfast owners, cottagers and fruit growers . . . we all want the same things: peace, happiness and success.

"A great deal has been said tonight and a lot of points made, but there's nothing else to do but wait for the environmental report. There may be something lost from development, but a lot can be gained. We just have to make sure things are done right. So now let's go home, take off our boots and open a beer . . . I mean a bottle of hard cider." He grins and nods to Earl Prentiss because that's a new product the Cider Mill is marketing, Seagull Island Hard Cider.

"Hear! Hear!" a few people shout.

The mayor doesn't ask for a motion to adjourn. She just uses her gavel and raps three times.

After Death

*A*ll the way back to Gull Point, I worry about the story that some woman is suing the Nelsons to block their casino. Who could have started it? The Nelsons? But what would that gain them?

"Thank you for bringing me home," I tell Peter Dolman as we pull in my drive. "It really wasn't necessary. Chris and Molly had room in their Subaru."

"I wanted to talk to you about the rumor that someone is taking the Nelsons to court. I feel responsible somehow because I gave the original will to a lawyer in Windsor, but word must have gotten out and someone misunderstood."

"Are the meetings always that awful?" I ask.

Dolman laughs, surprising me. "That was one of the better ones!"

"Mint tea?" I ask. Then, still wearing our jackets, we sit on the side porch.

"Smell the air. It's the dead leaves, the smell of fall . . . Your yard looks nice," Peter observes. It's odd, I think, to be sitting here with the cop like we're friends. I forget he's someone who could put me in jail, have me deported and sent back to Torrington. I must remember to be careful.

The porch light streams out across the newly cut grass and pale purple asters and goldenrod, just inside the picket fence, circle the clearing.

"I hadn't even noticed the lawn. Jed must have mowed again."

"That's how it is after a death, even when the death is expected like Nita's. You don't see what's in front of you. You're walking around in shock and you have to reorient yourself."

"Is that social-work talk or from personal experience? You sound like you know a lot about it."

"Remember I told you I was married?"

"Yeah, but I thought your wife left you after the shooting. Did you get back together?"

"It was ovarian cancer. Six months after the divorce, she went for her yearly pap test and something was wrong. Surgery two weeks later confirmed the gynecologist's suspicion. It was a big tumor, already stage four. Cancer all through the pelvis. A bad way to go . . . She was the one that wanted out, but I moved back in before she had chemo, and I remarried her in a simple ceremony down in Santa Fe. We went through the death together." He says all this looking out at the lake. I reach over and take his hand because it seems like the right thing to do.

"Is that when you got your ring?" I ask, touching the silver piece of Navaho jewelry he always wears.

"No, I'd been to New Mexico years before, back in college. I just always loved the desert."

Staring down, I notice a thin white scar that runs from his ring finger down to his wrist. *Knife fight,* it comes to me, but I don't ask.

CHAPTER 39

Window

In the days following Nita's death I miss her more than I could have imagined. I only knew her for a few months, but going through a death with someone, like going through a birth with someone, brings you close.

Since Nita has no immediate family, I go back to her house to do a good cleaning.

Everything looks as it did before, only my friend isn't there and she's never coming back. It's here in the bedroom that Nita died and all her artwork is hanging. When I walk into her bedroom, tears come to my eyes, but I don't start bawling.

Grief is like that. It washes in and washes out, at first a tsunami, but as time goes on the waves get smaller, then, just when you aren't looking, a big wave of sadness will catch you again and knock you off your feet.

As I wander the kitchen-studio, one of Nita's unfinished projects catches my eye, a *rainbow window*. Curved rows of different colored beach stones are fixed to the glass of an old wooden window. Purple. Blue. Green, yellow, orange and red. This must be the project she wished she could work on. A bowl of blue and green stones sits on the table nearby.

Pulling the cord on the light above her creation, I sit on Nita's stool and stare down. Then, using a tube of Gorilla Glue that I find on the table, I begin to arrange the colored beach stones on the glass. One by one, like a string of prayers, I press them down. Yellow for Nita. Blue for Jessie. Red for Robyn. Orange for Karen. Purple for the woman who needs it most . . . me.

Expecting

*W*hen I get home, because I'm so low, I decide to call Terry. She's usually upbeat. "Hi," I begin. "What are you up to?"

"Weaving. What did ya think? That's what I do most of the time."

"Weaving, yeah, but *what* are you weaving?"

"A shawl. You should come over. I'd love to show it to you."

"I've been meaning to and I will the next time Sergeant Dolman is making his rounds."

"Why wait for him? You know where I live."

An hour later, I'm biking up the east side of the island and, as I pass the marina and the Seagull Island Sailboat Club, I notice Molly Lou's Subaru next to a row of tables with a sign that says CHRISTIAN CHAPEL FLEA MARKET, so I stop to look around. It's a beautiful fall day with a blue sky and a blue lake with whitecaps. Only three sailboats are still tied at the docks.

"How are you doing?" I ask Molly when the other customers leave.

"Okay," Molly Lou says. "The church decided to have their fall fundraiser down here near the Roadhouse so we can pick up the last of the tourists. Do you think I could come over and talk someday?"

For the last few weeks, all my thoughts have been on Nita. Now I'm back to Molly, but will I know what to say? Maybe it isn't my place to say anything, just to listen. "Anytime. Call first to be sure I'm not out on the beach."

"I feel so much better since I got the test results back and got the medication for the infection," she whispers. "I'm even nicer to Chris." Then another vehicle pulls up so we cut the conversation short. It's Rainbow in the New Day truck.

"Howdy, girls," she says, sliding out from behind the steering wheel.

"Rainbow!" Molly calls and goes over and hugs her. (Molly Lou hugging a hippie? What's that about?)

I move around the table to greet her, my arms open too, and as we collide I feel an unmistakable hard round bump under her flowing Indian-print jumper. "Rainbow. You're pregnant!" Molly Lou doesn't even look surprised.

"I know!" she giggles. "And not just a little bit. I came to look for some baby clothes."

I follow her around the tables while Molly Lou looks through some boxes.

"So how far along are you?" I ask. She turns to the side, smiling, and smoothes her skirt across her abdomen that's about the size of a basketball.

"Eight months," Rainbow says.

Laying my hand on her, I feel what I'd hoped for, a strong baby kick, and this brings tears to my eyes. *It's been so long.*

"I conceived sometime in late January," she confides. "And probably was already pregnant when I met you, but I didn't know. My periods have always been irregular. I went five months without one and didn't think much of it this time, thought I was just eating too much homemade bread and honey and then one night I felt the baby move." She stops to look at a hand-knit white baby sweater and hands it to Molly to put aside.

"For as long as we could, Wade and I kept it a secret, even from our friends at New Day . . . We'd been trying to have a baby for years and I've had three miscarriages. So we were afraid if we told anyone, we'd jinx ourselves." Here her face gets pensive and she puts her hand on her abdomen as if protecting the life inside her.

"So, how did you and Molly Lou get to be friends?" I can't help myself; I have to ask.

"We started going to services at her church last summer, John and Jed too. We enjoy the music and have formed a little choir with Molly and Chris and Helen and Eugene.

"I'm going to be Seagull Island's primary teacher this year, did you hear? Is that great or what? That's why I've been away so much this summer, taking required courses in Windsor. The province is even paying for them."

"That's wonderful. Who set that up?"

"Molly Lou! She approached me at church." Molly smiles and puts the sweater in a paper bag along with a pair of tiny beaded moccasins. "The four kids from New Day will come with me."

"So do you get your prenatal care in Windsor? Will you go to a midwife there for the delivery?"

"No, I wanted a midwife and a home birth too, but because of my age and having lost three other pregnancies, they want me to deliver at the hospital. I have a doula who's going to be with us, though."

"I'm so happy for you!" This is true. Rainbow is a beautiful, kind woman and I hope the best for her, but there's part of me that's jealous. Why didn't she tell me? She told Molly Lou. I'm a midwife, for God's sake . . . but she doesn't know that.

Walking Wounded

I leave the two women, but not before I purchase a few things for winter—a heavy green hooded sweatshirt, a red V-neck sweater and some silk thermal underwear (top and bottom).

As I bike along, I try to shift my mood. It hurt me that Rainbow didn't tell me she was expecting, but why not be happy for her, instead of sad? It's a beautiful day and Molly Lou and Rainbow are both my friends. I also have Jed and Terry. Once I knew no one on the island. I was totally alone with the ice and the snow. I didn't even have Tiger.

At the Fibre Guild and Art Shoppe, I find Terry at her handloom, throwing the shuttle back and forth. The shawl is made of fine yarn in browns, blues and greens and is about half-done. "Beautiful," I say. "I love the colors."

"Want a turkey sandwich? I need a break." Terry swivels away from the loom and rolls into the kitchen.

While she prepares lunch, I stroll around the shop, admiring the fiber art, tables full of woven tapestries and racks of knit goods, even some silver jewelry and some carved wooden boxes. Maybe I'll come back and shop here for Christmas, now that I have a few people on my list.

"This pumpernickel bread is from the Baa Baa Bakery," Terry explains when she returns with a tray balanced on the arms of her wheelchair. I pull up a stool and sit down beside her. "You ever go there? Some of the women from the Weavers' Guild own it."

"I'd like to, but the north end is out of the way for me." I take a deep breath, letting out my sadness. "Nita Adams died with the taste of their blueberry pie on her tongue. Not a bad way to go."

"Not a bad way at all! I'll tell the women at the bakery.

They'll love it," Terry says. "Maybe they could use the idea for marketing. *Pies you could die for!*" This cracks us up and I laugh so hard I almost pee.

"You have a boyfriend, Terry?" I ask when I get control. (I'm thinking maybe she and Peter Dolman have something going. They seem to enjoy each other.)

"You mean *man friend*?" She grins her wide grin.

"I mean, do you date?"

"I have lots of male friends, but no one special. I was married for seven years, but he left me after the boating accident. Said he couldn't adjust to my *new body image*." She waits for my reaction, but I just sit there thinking, *What a jerk!*

"Have *you* ever been married?" Terry breaks the silence.

Oh no! Here it comes again. I try the old line. "Yeah. He died in Iraq. I don't like to talk about it." It rolls off my tongue with ease now and I try to look the part of a grieving widow.

"That's fine. I don't like to talk about my accident either." She pulls her brown hair back from her beautiful face. "We do okay, a couple of gals like us. The walking wounded."

Five

*F*acing into the setting sun, I bicycle home, wearing my new green sweatshirt, feeling happy that I took the time to visit Terry. Despite her injury, she's one of the most positive people I know and she always gives me a lift.

Fall is coming. You can tell. Pale purple asters line the road along with yellow wild sunflowers. The tips of the sumac are turning red. One last mosquito whines around my head and I brush him away.

Halfway home, I smell smoke and at first think maybe Big Chris is burning brush, then I think of my cottage. *Holy shit! I left Tiger locked in the bathroom.*

I push down hard on the pedals, then I push even harder. Despite the chill, sweat is dripping into my eyes. Twice I almost fall but keep going.

"Fire!" I yell as I pass the Ericksons'. I don't even stop. "Fire! I've got to save Tiger!" The closer I get, the thicker the smoke is, until I'm half-blind.

It isn't until I make the turn that I see the van, dirty, dark gray with tinted windows, speeding toward me and I have to jump off the trail to avoid being sideswiped. Riding on, I see flames, but it is not my house that's burning. Not yet. It's the woods all along the point. *What the hell?* Though I'm relieved it's not the cottage and I'm able to retrieve Tiger, we aren't out of danger yet.

Before I have time to call 911, I hear a long wail rising and falling from the direction of the village. Though no one has said anything about it, I recognize the sound as a community distress signal. Molly Lou or Chris must have smelled the smoke or heard my cries as I passed and reported it to Jed or Dolman.

With help on the way, I look around for anything else I should try to save. The first thing I think of is my money. The briefcase is stuffed way up on top of the closet and I'm just able to reach for the handle. Then I grab my purse with my fake ID and my bank card. I stuff it all in my backpack and, at the last minute, toss in some of the Nelsons' best seagull carvings and the green beach stone I gave Nita when she died.

By the time I'm out of the house and down on the road with Tiger in the bike basket, the volunteer fire squad is already ar-riving. First to show up are Chris and Molly Lou. Then Dolman arrives with his siren wailing. "Are you okay?" he asks.

I nod yes, but hold tight to my bike to keep my hands from

shaking. Next comes the cook from the Black Sheep Pub, driving the volunteer fire truck, *again siren wailing,* followed by Jed in the island ambulance *with its siren wailing.* More folks arrive and finally the pickup from New Day. Four hippies leap out of the back and Wade and John jump out of the cab.

"Let's get out of here, while Jed and Dolman organize the crew," Molly Lou says. "We're only in the way. They'll stop the fire; don't worry. The truck has a pump with long hoses that can reach to the lake. We should go up to my house and make coffee and sandwiches."

Looking over my shoulder at the fire as it leaps from tree to bush, I struggle to lift my bike and backpack into the bed of Chris's truck and place Tiger with me up front. I'm still trembling, but Molly takes charge and I think she's right. With the number of men and women heading toward the fire, the cottage will be saved. It isn't until we're safely in the Ericksons' house that I start to cry. Molly washes my face like I am a child and gives me a glass of cold milk.

Finally, I'm down to sniffles. "Molly, what was that? *What* could have started the fire? Or *who*? A dark van came out of the smoke when I was pedaling like hell to get to Tiger. It almost ran over me."

"I don't know. You better stay with us tonight. I can lend you a nightgown and a toothbrush and tomorrow we can go over and see how bad it is. Hard to tell which way the wind was blowing." She leads me upstairs to a spare room where I can lie down and we put out milk for my cat.

Refugee

*T*hree hours later, the fire crew arrives at Molly Lou's house. They've saved the cottage and are in high spirits. Chris gets out a six-pack of beer and a couple of bottles of Gull Apple Wine and Jed starts singing an old summer camp song. *"Late one night, when we were all in bed, Old Mother Leary left a lantern in the shed. There'll be a hot time in the old town, tonight!"* I can't help smiling . . . all the firefighters are so jolly, hippies and islanders together.

While we eat and sing, I watch Molly Lou and Chris, wondering if they've patched things up and if they're sharing a bed together. It's hard to tell. Twice I see Molly Lou touch Chris on the shoulder, but he's not touching her back.

It isn't until almost everyone leaves that Dolman motions me out on the porch. I'm surprised that I can no longer smell smoke. The west wind has blown it out to sea and, from the looks of the clouds, rain will soon dampen the blackened woods.

"Molly Lou told me about the van. Did you see who was driving?" Dolman asks.

"No. The smoke was so thick. If I couldn't see them, it's possible they couldn't see me. They had their foot on the pedal though. I had to jump off my bike to keep from getting hit."

"I'll come over tomorrow first thing and look around. If it's arson and the van is still on the island, I'll find them."

"And if the van's not here?"

"Well, the ferry left for the mainland about an hour ago. They could be gone."

I frown, thinking of the Nelsons, but not wanting to accuse anyone. Could they be that desperate?

"You going to stay here tonight?" Dolman asks.

"I guess. To be honest, I would rather go home with Tiger, but Molly insists."

"I agree with her. Until we find the dark van, it may not be safe."

For two nights I sleep at Molly's but it's getting hard. For one thing, Tiger's a pain in the butt. He's restless, scratches at the door and meows to get out. For another, the tension between Molly and Chris is as tight as a banjo string.

There's another heavy frost again the first night I'm there, but the next few days are warm and each afternoon I take Tiger back to the cottage to let him play and run where he won't bother anyone. I walk along the beach to see how close the fire got.

Around the house it's still green, but further south the tall grass and bushes are gone. I think of the least bittern that hid in the reeds, the bird with the Mohawk hairstyle. The reeds are now gone. The woods are blackened and only the larger old-growth trees are left standing.

Secrets

On Thursday, Molly comes with me to the cottage where we can have some privacy to talk. She cuts the brownies she brought in a pan while I make some tea and build a fire.

"So," Molly says, "I'm now STD-free. You don't know how ridiculous that sounds. I've only made love with two men in my life. Big Chris and Antonio.

"It's just so weird with Chris. The other day, for a change, I was kind of friendly and he wanted me to come back to our bed and sleep with him."

"So what happened?"

"I said I wasn't ready, that the hot flashes had stopped, but my period had come back.

"He freaked out and said I always had some excuse. 'What is it, Molly Lou?' he yelled at me. 'You getting something on the side?' *He actually said that* and my face got so red, I ran upstairs before he could see the guilt written over it. Do you think I'll ever be able to look him in the eye and love him like before?"

I mull this over and decide to think positive.

"Yes," I say. "True love can repair what is broken. I think you always loved Chris, you just got carried away with the excitement of someone new liking you." Molly looks at me gratefully and nods her head. "The thing is," I continue, "you have to forgive yourself."

"How do I do that?"

I take a big breath and let it out slowly. "That's a good question . . ."

Then we sit for a while and watch the flames while we drink our tea.

When Molly Lou leaves, I go back to the living room and pull the rocker up to the window. "It's so good to be home, Tiger. Isn't it good?"

At the top of the tallest cottonwood tree, something catches my eye. A black-and-white bird with a bright red head is pecking at the bark of a dead branch and I don't even have to go to my bird book to look up the name. I can see the chips fly.

RED-HEADED WOODPECKER
All red head, black body & wings with a white tail,
white belly and white under the wings.
Habitat: Lives in open woodlands.
Diet: Feeds on insects, which it pecks out of bark
or catches with open mouth as it flies.
Range: Year-round in the eastern and Midwestern
United States
Summers in the upper Midwest and Canada
Voice: Queerp queerp
Size: 9 inches
Wingspan: 12 inches

CHAPTER 40

Barroom Brawl

It's the first week of October and each day it's colder. Winter may be a couple of months off, but I can feel it coming. When the sun breaks through the haze in the afternoon, I bundle up and ride my bike down to the village to see if Jed has heard anything more about the plans for the casino.

As I pass the orchards at the Cider Mill Farm, I see that the harvest is in full force. About twenty people are picking, mostly the men from Mexico, but I see a few hippies that I recognize and a few island teenagers. Wooden crates and ladders are everywhere and big green trucks stand waiting to carry the apples to the warehouses or ship them to the mainland on the ferry.

"Hey," Jed says when I get to the clinic. "Want to go over to the pub?"

"That's a nice offer." As we walk along the road with our arms around each other, I study the big waves that splash up on the breakwall.

"Wind coming in from the west tonight," Jed announces. "It'll be cold and clear. Almost a full moon too." He opens the door to the pub and we find an empty table. It isn't until we're seated that we realize they're setting up for another township meeting.

"Damn!" curses Jed under his breath. "I forgot about this."

"Yeah," I respond. "We'll have to sit through another exercise in democracy. It would look really weird if we walked out now . . ."

I SCAN THE room. Helen and Eugene Burke are here with many of the others that were at the last meeting. Peter Dolman is here, along with Big Chris and Molly Lou, who are sitting two rows apart. The Nelson brothers and sister are up front, and I'm surprised to see a group of citizens along the back wearing green T-shirts that say SAVE OUR WILDLIFE. I assume they're with the Nature Conservancy, but they may be a separate group.

Mayor Nell Ambroy, the pilot, starts the meeting with a no-nonsense bang of the gavel. "We're here tonight to consider the Gull Point Casino and Hotel. Drawings and architectural plans have been submitted to the township board, but the committee has decided that the developers ought to have an opportunity to speak to the community and answer questions too." There's a rumble from the back row.

"Does the opposition get to present their point of view?" Earl Prentiss asks.

"There will be time for everyone," Mayor Ambroy cuts him off. "To begin, I'll turn the floor over to the Nelsons, longtime summer residents and supporters of Seagull Island." Jake stands up, steps to the podium and takes the microphone.

"I'd like to take a moment to explain that we're collaborating with a Toronto investor, Mr. Robert Burroughs. He too will be familiar to residents. Like us, his family has had a cottage on the island for decades."

A very tanned bald man, wearing a dark sports coat and a diamond stud in one ear, stands and turns toward the crowd. There's polite applause as if the locals especially respect him.

"Thank you," says Mr. Burroughs. "I'm looking forward to investing in the island and have found the Nelson team competent and sincere. I'm going to leave the presentation to them."

Here Jake stands again, glares at me defiantly and throws a white sheet off a large easel. On the easel are architectural plans for the proposed casino, complete with docks for individual boats and a swimming pool. Seagull Haven has been wiped off the map.

Charlene stands too and waves the pointer as if she's a good fairy creating a certain rosy future. "The Gull Point Casino and Hotel will be approached via a new paved two-lane road where Grays Road is now and the facility will cover the entire five acres bequeathed to my brothers and me by my late father, Lloyd Nelson. I'm sure he would approve of the development because he loved the island and understood the hardships faced by island residents who have to scrape to get by." She smiles like the Cheshire Cat in *Alice in Wonderland.*

"The casino and hotel will bring in jobs for local people in the construction phase and later we'll need employees to keep the property repaired, rented and cleaned," she explains. "The island will thrive. There will also be jobs for clerks, cooks, secretaries, lifeguards and hostesses."

There's a murmur of satisfaction from the crowd, but my heart drops like a stone in Lake Erie. "Hear. Hear!" someone up front says.

"Bullshit!" a redheaded nature girl in a green shirt yells. "What about the gray foxes that live on the point? What about the water fowl that nest in the cove? What about the light pollution from all the bright neon signs?"

The mayor bangs her gavel. "Quiet! I will not have swearing or any outbursts at this meeting. If this continues, the instigator will be removed."

"I have something to say." Earl Prentiss stands and the green shirts quiet down. "As president of the Seagull Island Nature Conservancy I must point out that there are a number of reasons that the casino and hotel plans need to be halted, at least temporarily. For one thing, a handwritten last will and testament by Lloyd Nelson has surfaced. It donates the five acres in question on Gull Point to the Nature Conservancy for a park. It is in the hands of our attorney in Toronto.

"For another thing, there's the gray fox question."

A few of the green shirts stand and quietly begin to pass out a three-page document entitled *Petition for the Protection of Seagull Island, Ontario.* There's a rumble of voices as people react. Skimming, I see that the manuscript is a request for further environmental study before things get out of control.

"Damn," Jed curses. I look at him, puzzled.

"What?"

"We were afraid of this."

"You mean protests, petitions? I'm glad I'm not the only one opposed."

"Well, you're in the minority." His voice has an edge I haven't heard before. "It's mostly the kooks who are making a fuss. Without some kind of change, this community is doomed. All the young people leave because there's no future."

"Thank you, Earl," the mayor says with sarcasm, banging her gavel. "Your petition will be considered in due time, but Charlene and Jake Nelson still have the floor."

Jake's face is as red as the day they found out I'd given Lloyd's handwritten will to Peter Dolman. "I'm sorry to hear of this opposition. We have lawyers in Toronto and Detroit, and I'm sure they will sort this out. Meanwhile, I want to reassure the public that all environmental issues have been addressed in our plans."

"Hogwash!" says another of the protestors. "What about the

wetlands? That's a delicate ecosystem and your road would cut right through it."

Charlene stands to respond, but the green shirts begin to chant, *"Save Seagull Island! Save Seagull Island! Save Seagull Island!"*

"Oh hell," Jed says, putting his head down on his arms as if hiding.

Jake grabs one of the young guys still handing out petitions and doubles his fist in the man's face. Mayor Ambroy bangs her gavel over and over. Chris Erickson pulls Jake away and a chair falls over. Charlene tries to help her brother and trips on the easel. *Bang* it crashes to the floor.

"Save Seagull Island! Save Seagull Island!" the protestors yell. Things are out of control and it looks like a real barroom brawl until Dolman blows a shrill whistle and all heads whip around.

"This meeting is adjourned," he says quietly into Ambroy's microphone. "I'll ask the Nature Conservancy people to be seated in the back while everyone else leaves. I don't want this to spill out into the parking lot. When the others are gone, the protestors can leave too."

It's not like he has a gun. It's probably locked in the glove compartment of his patrol car. His authority must be in the uniform because the green shirts sit down in the back along with Earl Prentiss, Terry and, of all people, Molly Lou and Chris. I guess, despite their marital problems, they agree on one thing. All the traffic going past their farm to the casino on a two-lane paved road would change their lives forever.

"Come on," Jed says to me in disgust, as the majority of the islanders leave. But though he's my friend, I can't go with him. I join the protestors who, arms crossed against their chests, sit in silence. I fold my arms too.

Moon Shadows

*J*ed was right. He said the moon would be full and it's now so bright I can see colors as I stand in my flannel nightgown up on the deck with the quilt wrapped around me. There's not a breath of wind and I've never seen anything so beautiful. The moon shadows of the trees spread black against the green lawn.

Still keyed up after the contentious meeting and unable to sleep, I sing the old Cat Stevens song . . . *"I'm bein' followed by a moon shadow. Moon shadow. Moon shadow."* I spin around with my quilt out like wings. *"Leapin' and hoppin' on a moon shadow . . ."*

And then I stop . . . a vehicle is rolling quietly down Grays Road! Quick as a rabbit, I kneel down behind one of the wooden deck chairs. Since the fire and the sighting of the van through the smoke, I'm paranoid about autos coming this way and I watch, holding my breath, as the headlights flicker through the trees.

The automobile slows at my drive as if someone is checking the mailbox and then moves on. I should run for the house and call Peter Dolman, but for all I know this is Dolman himself, cruising the island and checking on me.

Letting out my air, I watch as the taillights fade in the distance. Are they turning? *Yes.* Maybe it's just a tourist lost on this country road . . . but no, on the way back, they stop at my mailbox again.

Then *CRACK!* A blast comes from the driver's window and in the same instant a flash and the sound of glass shattering. *Goddamn!* They shot out my kitchen window!

"Goddamn!" I say again, under my breath, cowering behind the deck chair, watching the vehicle screech away.

Ten minutes later Peter Dolman is standing in my kitchen

picking up pieces of glass and looking for the bullet, which we find opposite the window in the wood trim of the arched doorframe to the living room. He puts the bullet in a plastic evidence bag and then goes to the shed and brings back a piece of plywood to nail over my window.

"I can't let you stay here anymore, Sara," Dolman says. "First the fire and now this." He's all cop tonight and his usually kind gray eyes are like steel.

I snort through my nose. "Like you're my boss?"

"You know what I mean. It's getting too dangerous."

"Well, I can't just leave. Where would I go?"

"You could stay with Molly Lou and Chris again. Or check in to a B and B. Hell, you could even stay in one of my empty bedrooms."

"Sorry, Officer Dolman. I know you're worried and I don't want you to have to keep running down here, but I can't leave."

"I can't order you to, Sara, but be realistic. Someone set a fire in the woods around here. And tonight someone shot at your house. Most women would be terrified."

"You be realistic, Peter. If they'd wanted to kill me, they would have walked up to the porch, broken down the door and fired a bullet into my forehead. This is just their way of trying to scare me off. Who knows what they'd do to the cottage if I left."

"Fuck it," he says and slams out the door.

IN THE MORNING Peter's squad car is still parked in the drive where he left it last night and when I look out the front door, I see him pouring some kind of plaster on the ground, making casts of the van's tire tread in the sand like a crime-scene investigator.

"Do you want some coffee?" I call out, but he ignores me, still pissed, I guess. *Oh well, if he wants to sleep all night in the cruiser, it's up to him.*

THE TRUTH IS, I was lying. I'm scared to death. There's nothing I'd rather do than check in to a B and B with some warm grandmotherly type to take care of me, but I feel responsible for the cottage.

No, I must stay here, scared or not, but Peter Dolman needs to believe I'm fearless. I think of brave women throughout history—Alice Paul who was jailed for fighting for a woman's right to vote; Harriet Tubman, an escaped slave who went back into the south time and time again and risked her life to bring other slaves out; Mother Teresa . . . Rosa Parks . . .

What I'm doing isn't nearly as heroic, but I will not be moved!

CHAPTER 41

Keep Calm and Call the Midwife

Dolman and I aren't speaking, but he continues to show up every night and sleep in my driveway. It's making me crazy.

On the third night, it rains and Dolman goes home. I fall asleep at about ten but wake to the sound of the phone ringing. When I lift the receiver, it's Molly Lou.

"I'm coming over," she says. I look at the time on my wind-up alarm clock. "Now? It's past midnight. It's raining."

"I have to," she says. "Chris is having a fit and I'm afraid he'll get physical if I stay here tonight."

"Molly, should I call Officer Dolman?"

"No. It's okay. I'm coming."

God, what next? I think to myself as I turn on one lamp, quickly get dressed, grab the old red umbrella that Wanda Nelson left and hurry out into the dark and the rain. Just as I close the door, Tiger slips out. "Kitty, Kitty!" I call, but he doesn't come back.

Flashlight pointed at my feet, I walk quickly, trying to avoid the puddles and wondering what's been going on at the Ericksons'. Now and then, I direct the beam down the road, hoping to see Molly, but I don't catch sight of her until I take the bend. She's marching toward me, wearing an old yellow parka over a long nightgown and untied running shoes, her mouth tight and her eyes fixed on the blackness in front of her.

It isn't until I actually see her standing there in the pounding rain that I realize how hard this last year has been for her. She hears me sloshing along and looks over. "You didn't have to come out!"

"It's okay. I know you're upset." In ten minutes, we're at the steps to my porch. I'd left the light on but now regret it. Ever since the fire and the shooting, I've been feeling I'm being watched. Now Dolman is no longer on guard, but Tiger is.

Fist through the Wall

*O*nce inside, the first thing I do is turn off all the lights, lock the doors, light some candles and get Molly settled down.

"So what the hell's going on?"

The disheveled woman paces the living room floor. "I blame myself. It was awful. Such a mistake . . . I thought I was ready but when it happened . . . when it happened . . ." Here she chokes back her tears. "When it happened it was a disaster."

"What, Molly Lou? What are you telling me?"

"Well, I was feeling so much better, knowing that I didn't have an STD, that I kind of started flirting with Chris and I let caution fly.

"I put on my sexiest nightgown and . . . well, you know . . . seduced him. It wasn't hard. He was ready in five minutes. We tore off our clothes. He threw me in bed and that's when I saw myself in the mirror. I'm not that kind of woman, Sara. I'm shy, really. The only time I've been wild was with Antonio in the back of the Subaru. Chris was just coming into me when I threw him off.

"'I can't do this. I can't do this,' I said, and then I started to vomit. That broke the mood.

"'What is it?' Chris roared. 'Is there another man? Or are you just a prick tease?' I jerked away from him, but he grabbed me.

"'Little Chris!' I managed to hiss and he let go, but then he slammed his fist through the wall. Punched right through the drywall. He had trouble getting his hand out. I think maybe he broke some bones and that's when I ran. I didn't have time to get the car keys, but my cell phone was in my parka pocket." She takes a long breath and falls onto the sofa.

"Oh, Molly Lou, I'm so sorry." My friend doesn't say anything. She just sits there and cries. "Should I call Peter Dolman?" I ask her again. "He told me he sometimes deals with domestic disputes."

"No. I don't want Chris to get in trouble. It's my fault. He's never been bad to me before. Not in fifteen years. Never touched me."

This time it's my turn to wash Molly Lou like she washed me after the fire. I get a clean warm wet cloth from the bathroom and wipe her face and her hands and her neck. Then I give her my flannel nightgown and tuck her into my bed. Outside rain slashes against the side of the house and waves crash on the breakwall. I go to the door to call for Tiger and finally he comes in looking like a drowned rat.

I HAVE COUNSELED the victims of domestic violence before, but I was sitting on my rolling stool in the clinic exam room. This is different. This is just down the road. The right thing to do would be to call Officer Dolman, but Molly Lou begged me not to and really, though she did the right thing to get out of there, Chris didn't actually hurt a hair on her head.

When I was on the board of the Rape and Domestic Violence Center in Torrington, I thought that all domestic violence was perpetrated by domineering men who needed to beat on defenseless women to release their pent-up rage. Later I realized it's more complicated than that.

Sometimes it's the woman who's the aggressor. Sometimes she hits or spits or scratches first. Sometimes she just gets in a man's face so viciously, he loses it . . . a sad thing and even worse when children are involved.

The wood in the fire crackles and pops as I make my bed on the sofa. Molly Lou and Chris are in trouble and I don't know what to do. How did I get involved in this anyway?

Oh yeah, I remember. Like my medallion says, MIDWIVES HELP PEOPLE OUT . . .

Finally, I fall into a troubled sleep and dream I'm walking along the beach during the storm. The surf rolls up and out again. Sometimes I have to jump back to keep my shoes from getting wet. Something is out in the bay, a log, I think, or maybe a barrel. The dark shape floats closer with each surge of waves and then, with one big breaker, the body of the dead man rolls up at my feet. This time I can see his face. It's Chris Erickson. His big hand grabs my ankle and holds on! I wake, frantically kicking the dead man away. In the firelight I can see Tiger staring at the door. His ears twitch as if he hears something.

Someone or something is outside in the dark.

Night Visitors

Sara! Open up." It's a man banging on the door.

"Who's there?" I call while reaching for Lloyd's old walking stick and moving close to the landline phone in case I have to call Dolman.

Molly peeks out of the bedroom. "Is it Chris? Oh God, has he been drinking?"

"It's Wade and Rainbow," the voice answers. "Can you help us?"

I open the door just a crack, keeping my foot jammed at the bottom in case it's a trick, but of course it's not. Standing on the porch are not only Wade and Rainbow, but Peter Dolman. The squad car sits in the drive, red lights still flashing.

"What's going on?" I inquire, but really I don't need to ask. Rainbow is holding on to the porch rail and panting, her mouth grim and tight. "Come in. Come in! Get out of the weather."

Outside, rain gusts in sheets across the yard and small branches fly. All three of the night visitors are soaked, Rainbow worst of all.

"Come in. Come in. It looks like you're in labor. I thought you were going to Windsor Regional to have the baby."

"We were," Wade answers. "We planned to but wanted to spend one more weekend on the farm, helping with the harvest. When Rainbow started having contractions, Greg drove us to the marina and we got in Lenny's boat. We were a few miles from the island when I realized the waves were too big and I couldn't make it. We had to return, but by this time Greg had gone home.

"Standing in the rain, we tried to call the farm, but we had no cell reception. Peter found us walking along Sunset Road. Can you help us, Sara? You're a nurse."

"What about Jed? He's a nurse too."

"He's stuck in Leamington," Peter chimes in. "The ferry doesn't run until tomorrow morning and maybe not even then because of the breakers. The winds are twenty-five knots with gusts over thirty and there's no way to get a helicopter here either."

"Please, Sara," Rainbow says. "You can do it. I trust you.

Even if you've never delivered a baby, you can do it. I brought my copy of *The Emergency Childbirth*." Molly drifts into the living room, already dressed.

I shake my head, smiling. These people don't know that I'm a midwife and I can't tell them the truth. "Come on, let's get you dry. I don't have any men's clothes for you, Wade or Peter, but there's a dryer and, while you wait for your things, you can wrap up in quilts and sit by the fire. Can you organize that, Molly Lou?"

"That's okay!" Peter says, blushing. "I think I've done my part. Call me if you need anything." And he slips out the door.

Back in the bedroom, I dry Rainbow and now give *her* my flannel nightgown. I braid her long hair, something I used to do often for women in labor. While I get her comfortable, I ask the usual questions. Molly slips out with a quilt and back with Wade's clothes, which she throws in the dryer.

"When did the contractions begin?"

"Four hours ago. That's when we started trying to get off the island. We were counting on Lenny's boat, it's been such a nice fall . . ." She twists away from me and takes a big breath then begins to pant, while I think about Lenny. I'd forgotten that Lenny and Wade were old friends. That's who Lenny left his speedboat with.

The Big Ben alarm clock on the dresser says it's now two-fifteen. Placing my hand on her abdomen, I feel the strength of the contraction. It's firm, but not woody hard. When it's over, Rainbow takes a long trembling breath and smiles. The contraction was forty-five seconds.

"Any leaking of fluid or bloody show?"

"Not yet. But I think this is the real thing, don't you?"

"Are the contractions getting stronger?"

"Yes. Yes. Much stronger."

"Then I imagine it's real. I need to consider what supplies we need and where to find them. . . . Molly, can you walk Rainbow around the house while I get organized? Labor is easier if you stay on your feet. I'm going into the bathroom where I can think."

SITTING ON THE john, I rip a piece of lined paper out of my journal. A baby can be delivered in an elevator with nothing but a pair of hands, but I do have that box of old medical supplies that I took from Nita's house.

I open the cupboard under the sink to see what we've got and in the carton find two pairs of sterile gloves, an unopened roll of two-inch sterile gauze, some adult diapers, Betadine and a bottle of baby oil the old lady must have used for her skin. The rest of the stuff has to do with her diabetes.

For a midwife who's delivered over a thousand babies, I find myself surprisingly rattled. What else do I need? I write it all down as if I'm a first-year midwifery student.

Warm sterile water
Sterile scissors
A bowl for the placenta
A saucer for the baby oil
I can use the sterile gauze to tie off the umbilical cord
We have clean sheets and the adult diapers can be cut up
     for sanitary pads
Dish towels for baby diapers
A warmed bath towel for a baby blanket

I take a deep breath. . . . Now what should I do next?
Oh yeah. Examine the patient.

Drill Sergeant

Only three centimeters!" Molly wails.

"There's no way to hurry this, Rainbow. The baby is head down, low in the pelvis and the cervix is completely thinned out. Just take one contraction at a time. You're healthy and strong. Your body knows what it's doing. Let's get you back out of bed again."

The clock ticks. There's rain on the tin roof. Wade finds some music on his cell phone, a James Taylor song. *There is a young cowboy, he lives on the range. His horse and his cattle are his only companions.* I throw a log on the fire and the flames shoot up. We are slipping into the timeless waters of childbirth, where there are waves and then rest. Waves and then rest.

AROUND FOUR-THIRTY, I notice that Rainbow is sweating. "Damn!" she says. "I can't do this much longer. My back hurts so bad! Rub harder, Wade!"

This gets my attention. When a laboring woman begins to swear, the delivery is getting close. Even very proper women have been known to curse at nine centimeters. "Would you like to get in the shower? Let the warm water massage your back?"

"No!" Rainbow says as if that's the dumbest idea she's ever heard. For the last half hour, she hasn't moved. She's been kneeling next to the sofa, gripping one of the cushions as if it was a life preserver out in the lake. "If I move it will hurt more. Oh, I wish this was over!" Wade looks at me with big eyes, helpless in front of this force of nature.

"Come on. Give the shower a chance," I implore. "I really think it will help you."

THERE ARE TWO midwife voices . . . one *soft and reassuring* and the other a *no-nonsense drill sergeant.* I'm forced to use the second one now . . . "Enough of this! Up you go!" I walk her into the bathroom by holding her under the arms, then I turn on the water.

"Could I get down in it?" Rainbow asks meekly.

"Sure. Take off your gown while I put in the plug. Then get in and stand and let the spray beat on your back while the tub fills." I assist the big woman over the high side of the old claw-foot bathtub.

"Mmmmmm," she says. "Can you make it a little hotter?"

"Just a bit." It's halfway full when Rainbow slides down into the water.

"Ahhhhhhh!" she says with a sigh. The puffing and blowing, moaning and whining stop as suddenly as if Black Sabbath had been playing on the radio and someone changed the station to Brahms.

I go to the living room for a candle and notice that Tiger is wary again. "Wade and Molly, can you go in and keep Rainbow company?" The cat's ears flick back and forth, then he goes and lies down. A few minutes later he jumps on the back of the sofa and meows, then under the roar of the wind and the rain, I hear the sound of a vehicle.

Is it the Nelsons, looking for trouble? As before, the headlights flicker through the trees getting closer, only this time the vehicle isn't creeping, it's moving fast, and I jerk back from the window when it pulls into the drive.

CHAPTER 42

Cleansing Breath

Who is it?" Molly Lou whispers, coming out of the bathroom. "The Nelsons?" She knows of the trouble I've been having with them.

"It looks like Chris getting out of his truck." I take a big breath and let it out. How can this night get any crazier?

The big man, dressed in a red poncho and tall rubber boots, slams the door to his truck and stomps through the wet grass and up on the porch.

"Is Molly in there? Is she okay?" he asks when I poke my head out the door. I was expecting him to be full of rage, but instead he appears sick with worry. "I saw Dolman come up and down the road a few times with his red lights flashing. Has something happened? Can I talk to her?"

"Yes, she's here, Chris, and she's okay. I don't know if she wants to see you though. I'll ask." I shut and lock the door again. Molly is right behind me and she grabs my arm.

"What did he say? Is he still acting crazy?"

"He's worried about you. Do you want to see him?"

"Maybe I could talk to him just for a minute."

"Sure. But just in the kitchen. We can't have any disruption. I'll tell him what's going on." I go back on the porch.

"It's okay, Chris. You can come in *for a minute,* but I have to tell you, Rainbow from New Day Farm is in labor. Because of the storm they can't get to the hospital, so we're having the baby here. It's very important that the cottage remain calm and the energy positive, and I need Molly Lou's help with the birth, so don't upset her."

"Sure," he says, stepping out of his boots. "Sure. I'll just be a minute."

I go back into the living room to give the two couples some privacy and take a minute to lie down on the couch. Wade's cell phone now plays a new folk song. James Taylor again. *Well the sun is surely sinking down, But the moon is slowly rising, And this old world must still be spinning 'round, And I still love you.*

FIFTEEN MINUTES LATER, Rainbow lets out a moan. "Mmmmm!"

"You feeling pressure?" I stick my head into the steaming bathroom.

"Just a little."

Wade, still wearing his boxers, is now in the tub too, sitting behind his wife, holding her around her waist and caressing her breasts and big belly.

"I've got the bed already fixed up, Rainbow. So if you feel like pushing, we're going to move to the bedroom."

"Oh, can't I stay here? I read that some women have water births."

"Let me think about it."

I've delivered babies in the water before, but Rainbow is considered high risk and her amniotic sac hasn't even broken. How do I know the fluid is clear? How do I know the baby is okay? I have no way to listen to the fetal heartbeat. On the other hand, even if I had a Doppler and heard a deceleration, what could I do? We are just going on faith here.

Rainbow and Wade are watching me. Waiting for an answer.

In Pastures Green

*F*ive minutes later, Rainbow is on her hands and knees in the tub rocking back and forth. When a contraction hits, she strains toward Wade and Wade seems to know what she wants. He puts both his big hands out so she can press her butt against them.

"Mmmmm," Rainbow moans. "I felt my water break."

Molly Lou slips back in the bathroom. "Everything okay with Chris?" I whisper. She nods but doesn't smile, so I doubt that *everything* is okay.

"Is there anything I can do?" she asks.

"Yes, check the water on the stove. Bring the pan in and pre-pare some warm compresses. We'll need the supplies I laid out on the dresser moved in here. It looks like we are going to have a water birth. . . . Her amniotic fluid is clear.

"You're doing great," I say to Rainbow as she begins to push. These are the familiar words I've said to women a thousand times. "You're doing great." "Keep it up!" "You can do it." "You are powerful and strong." "Push for your baby!"

An hour later, the laboring mother begins to lose it. "This is really hard," she whispers. "Oh no! Here comes another one." And she strains. She growls.

"Slow it down, Rainbow. Give me a minute. If you get an-other urge to push, try blowing . . . Molly Lou, can you open a pack of sterile gloves?"

"Oh my God, I saw it!" Wade cheers. "I saw the top of the head."

Rainbow catches her breath and bears down, pushing harder, and I see that the man is correct; there's a little dark hair showing at the opening. It peeps out and retreats.

Wade's face is shining with joy and he breaks out into a sort of singing prayer. *"The Lord's my Shepherd, I'll not want. He makes me lie down, In pastures green . . ."*

"Slow it down, Rainbow. Blow like this. Whoooo! Whoooo! Whoooo!

"Molly, get down there and breathe with her. Wade give me some room." The father climbs out and drips all over me, but the water is warm and I could care less.

Kneeling on the bath mat, I lean into the tub to hold on to Rainbow's perineum. There's no need for warm compresses to help the skin stretch. I swipe a little baby oil around the opening. "Push a little! Blow a little! Push a little! Blow a little!" I command. "When it stings, stop pushing and blow."

"Yea, though I walk through shadowed vale, Yet will I fear no ill," Wade sings, kneeling with me.

"Ughhhhhhhhhhhh!" grunts Rainbow.

"Stop, don't push. The head is out. I want to check for a cord!" But there's no stopping Rainbow. She bears down another time and a very blue baby squirts into my hands.

"Is it alive?" Wade asks.

The baby boy opens his eyes and looks around. I hand him to his mother.

"I did it!" she says, and she holds him in the warm water, just up to his chin. "Oh my God! *We* did it. Oh, Wade, I love you! I love you! Molly Lou, Sara, I love you. It's our baby. It's Zachary!"

Wade is silent, tears running down his face, and I think that he's praying.

Finally Molly asks, "Why isn't the baby crying?"

"It's the warm water. He hasn't gasped from the cold air hitting his body yet and the cord is still pulsing, so he's getting oxygen . . . Talk to your baby, Rainbow and Wade. Rub his back. Make him talk back to you." Rainbow does what I say.

"Come on, buddy. Let's hear you sing. Sing with your daddy."

"Goodness and mercy all my life shall surely follow me, And in my Father's house, My dwelling place shall be," Wade sings. Zachary opens his mouth and howls.

Then we all cry.

Storks

At dawn, I am shocked to find, when I put Tiger out, that Peter Dolman's squad car is parked in the drive. I stretch my tired body. I'd fallen asleep in the rocking chair, staring at the fire, and now only a few coals glimmer in the grate. Banging around a little more than I need to, I put on more logs.

Molly Lou is the first to awaken. "I'm starved. Do you have any eggs? I'll make breakfast. Then I have to get home to get Little Chris to school."

"Don't worry about it," Wade says, coming out of the bathroom. "I'll cook. You go ask Dolman if he wants some grub."

Twenty minutes later, we're all sitting around the table eating eggs, juice and toast except Rainbow. We took her breakfast to the bedroom so she could rest.

"How come you slept in the driveway again?" I ask Peter.

"I tried to go home but couldn't sleep, so I came back with my sleeping bag. Even then, I felt like an expectant father in the waiting room. I even got out a few times and paced back and forth."

"Did you hear anything?" Molly Lou asks. "We were pretty noisy. There was a lot going on."

"I heard voices and singing and then the baby cry, so I knew the stork had come."

After Rainbow nurses one more time, we gather their things, wrap the baby up and assist her out to the cruiser. The sun has come out and the water has calmed.

"Thank you," Rainbow says. "Thank you, Sara. You were a wonderful midwife. Maybe you should do it full-time." This is said as a joke, but she doesn't know how funny it is.

"And thank you too, Molly Lou. I'll always remember your support." We give hugs all around, then Dolman takes the new family back to the commune.

As I walk Molly Lou home along the muddy road, we are both tired but happy. Birth is like that. No matter how exhausted you are, a new life gives you energy, brings you joy.

"You sure you'll be okay? I mean with Chris. What did he say last night?"

"That he loved me and that he was sorry if he hurt me."

"Take it slow, Molly Lou," I advise her. "Don't push it. Chris has waited for you for almost a year. He can wait a little longer. Just don't get yourself in a position like you did last night."

"I know that now. You're right. I'm not ready. No fooling around, if you get my meaning. Maybe in a month, we'll start sleeping together again. I miss the big lug."

As we approach her drive, we see Chris standing at the kitchen door. "I made breakfast," he calls out. "You must be hungry. Is the baby okay? I saw Wade and Rainbow go by with Peter."

"I'm starved," Molly says, though she just ate a whole omelet.

On the way home I see three white egrets, like storks, flying over the cottage.

GREAT WHITE EGRET
A large slender white heron with a yellow bill
Diet: Eats fish by standing still in shallow water
and spearing them with its beak
Voice: A hoarse croak
Habitat: Marshes and shores, often found in colonies
Range: From the US and southern Canada to South America
Size: 38 inches with a wingspan of five feet!
(Was hunted for its feathers, almost to extinction, in the 1900s.)

CHAPTER 43

Thanksgiving

*T*hanksgiving in Canada, I'm surprised to learn, is the second Monday in October, but the feast can happen on any day that weekend and I have two invitations. The first celebration is on Sunday at the Black Sheep Pub, the Community Harvest Dinner, open to everyone.

Jed and I arrive a little late and the place is already hopping. Most of the tables are full and most of the islanders are here, except the New Day folk. Maybe they have their own Thanksgiving. Kristie, the waitress, seats us with Peter Dolman and Terry who are already eating.

For a change, the tables are covered with white tablecloths and each one has a centerpiece created by a child from the island school, turkeys made with paper cups and multicolored feathers of construction paper.

"Sorry we started without you," Terry says, all smiles. "It smelled so good we couldn't help it."

"I don't blame you," Jed comments. "You ready?" he says to me, and we rise to take our place in the buffet line.

"I'm sorry about our conflict over the casino," he whispers. "I just feel so strongly that something has to change on the island if we're to survive."

"It's okay. Friends can differ."

"I guess the home birth went okay? God, that was quite a night! I felt bad not being able to get back to the island, but I wouldn't have been much help anyway."

"It went fine. It took me a while to get organized. At first I was concerned that I didn't have a stethoscope and blood-pressure cuff, a fetal monitor of some sort and all that, but later I thought, what good would they do? If there were complications, we still couldn't get to the hospital.

"Basically Rainbow was healthy, with all the organic food and heavy physical farm work, and she had a good attitude about pain. She was only high risk because of her age and having had miscarriages before. This pregnancy and delivery were entirely normal."

Besides the usual fare there's another whole table of desserts, pumpkin pie, apple pie and blueberry pie from the Baa Baa Bakery. I take some of everything, except the yams. I've never been a big fan of yams.

"I saw Baby Zach at the clinic," Jed tells me. "Healthy little guy. Six pounds but I figure he'd probably lost a few ounces."

In the kitchen, country-western music plays softly on the stereo, a Willie Nelson song. *And today, you know, that's good enough for me, Breathing in and out's a blessing, can't you see?* I look around the room at these familiar faces, some of them now friends, and take a big breath, thinking . . . *Yes, this is also good enough for me.*

"Heard you went to Windsor the other day, Pete," Jed begins when we get settled at the table.

"Another missing-person report came in from Detroit," Peter shares between mouthfuls. "A gang member involved in drugs. They thought he might have recently been on the island and the Mounties are sending someone over to investigate. That's probably already more than I should say."

The turkey in my mouth has gone suddenly tasteless, but I force myself to swallow. All the rest of the meal, I'm thinking of Lenny and the night he came to me at the cottage.

Game Day

On Monday afternoon when I bike up to Molly and Chris's for my second Thanksgiving, I'm surprised to discover four other vehicles already there. The hostess welcomes me with a warm hug.

It turns out the gathering is not really another big dinner as I anticipated, but a tailgate party for the Canadian Football League Thanksgiving Doubleheader. Chris stands up to get the remote for the big-screen TV, and when he sits down, Molly Lou kisses him on the back of the neck. The poor guy must be confused. After almost a year of the cold shoulder, his wife is coming on strong.

"You doing okay?" I ask under my breath when she's back in the kitchen.

"Sure, I'm great."

"Really?"

Molly takes my chin in her hand, stares into my eyes and answers firmly, "Don't ask me that again. I'm fine!" And I have to believe her.

To break the mood, I bring up another subject. "You know I'm not going to be your neighbor for much longer. Nothing has come through from Environment Canada about endangered species and Lloyd's will is still up in the air, so I guess I have to move. The Nelsons gave me until the end of November. I've been procrastinating, but I'll have to face it sooner or later and find a new place to live."

Molly's getting more hard cider out of the fridge. "What about Nita's old place? Jed or Peter could ask the probate lawyer. He's checking to see if there are any distant relatives."

"I thought of that . . . The trouble is I don't want to move. I know that's why I'm putting it off. I love the cottage . . ."

The fans are cheering about something, so we carry more refreshments back to the living room. Finally the last game is over and it's time to go home. Since it's already dark, Chris offers to drive me, but I have to wait until the rest of the guests leave. Then Molly hands me a bag with another dozen hot wings. "I'm glad you came," she says.

"It was fun!" I answer, though the truth is *one* football game would have been sufficient.

A few minutes later, we pull into my drive. Chris hauls my bike out of the pickup and walks me up to the porch.

"Thanks," I tell him as I unlock the door, but he doesn't leave. He puts his hands on the rail and looks out across the lawn. Little waves hiss in and out at the bottom of the breakwall and the air smells of snow, though it's not falling yet.

"I know you think I'm an asshole," he says.

"What do mean? I never said that."

"Molly Lou ran to your house that night. You heard what happened between us."

I'm unsure what to say, so I don't say anything. "Just tell me the truth, Sara. Is she having an affair?"

What to say now? I can continue to insult him by trying to fake it or I can be honest, but being honest means breaking Molly's trust.

"She loves you, Chris. She loves you so much. She made a

mistake. It was only one time and she wants to be with you. She can never know I told you."

"I was so scared, Sara. I don't want her to leave. I can't lose her."

"She loves you. She's not thinking of leaving."

Then the big man drops to his knees on the dark porch and I hold him while he cries.

He cries a long time.

CHAPTER 44

Sheepdog Trials

In the last few weeks, Rainbow has come to the cottage for two postpartum visits and all goes well. Her nipples were sore for a few days, but for comfort she's used cabbage leaf compresses. Life is almost back to normal for me, or what you call normal if you're a runaway fugitive, thief and soon-to-be-homeless person living under an assumed name without a passport in Canada.

The day of the sheepdog trials dawns sunny and cold, but by the time I arrive at the fairground on my bike, it's starting to warm up. I put the Raleigh in a bike rack at the entrance to the park and try to get my bearings. A fence that wasn't there before has been placed around the perimeter of the big field. In the center are two wooden gates and a circle drawn on the ground with white chalk (the kind used to mark the lines on a baseball field). There's also a square pen the size of my kitchen.

Three big tents are arranged along the north edge of the field and sitting in the wooden bleachers and leaning against the vehicles drawn up to the fence are around three hundred onlookers and a few dozen dogs.

From things I'd heard, I'd anticipated that the crowd would be rowdy. Instead, they are as quiet as spectators at a Florida golf tournament. A man on a microphone in a soothing voice announces the name of the next contestant, George Hope of London, Ontario, and his dog, Patch. I work my way up to the front where I can see.

The shepherd and his animal walk onto the green and stand at the post. At the far end of the field four sheep graze, unaware that they are about to be part of the show. Patch, a black-and-white border collie with a circle of black around his left eye like a pirate, waits on alert for a sign from his master. The shepherd whistles and the dog races toward the flock.

"That's a great *outrun!* . . . Watch him now; he's fast!" says a man behind me.

The trainer whistles twice more. "Come by," he says, and the dog begins a long curve around the sheep to get behind them.

"Nice move," says the voice, and when I turn around, I see Austin Aubrey, bagpipe player, shepherd and president of the sheepdog association.

"Hi, Mr. Aubrey. It's Sara Livingston. Do you mind explaining the game to me?"

"The sheepdog *trial* you mean?"

"Yes, *trial.*"

"First time here?" Mr. Aubrey asks, apparently forgiving me for calling the serious event a *game.* I nod and he begins an explanation.

"The border collie was bred to gather, not drive the sheep, so he works without barking or nipping. All it takes is his gaze and he wills the sheep to obey. These animals are working dogs, not show dogs, and they follow the handler's commands—a whistle, a few words or the move of a staff." Clearly the man is an expert on the subject and he's in his element. The whole time he's talking he's not looking at me, but the action on the field.

"Does it take years of training?"

"Yep, but all border collies are natural herders. Patch out there is smart as hell, a two-time Essex County champion."

"Stand," says the master out in the field. He whistles again. "Walk on." There are murmurs of appreciation from the crowd.

Patch crouches low in the grass and sneaks forward like a wolf stalking his prey, but there's no malice in his movements. He's just waiting the four sheep out, staring them down. His master whistles twice and Patch moves slowly forward again. In only minutes, he gets the four ewes into the pen where the shepherd stands with his crook waiting.

The crowd doesn't exactly go wild, but the quiet clapping makes it clear that Patch is one of the favorites.

"That will do, dog," the master says with a smile. "That will do."

"What an amazing dog! Thanks for explaining everything to me."

"Patch was my dog a few years ago," Mr. Aubrey informs me. "I raised him from a pup. Sold him in 2012. Amber, here, is his sister." He indicates another border collie standing next to him on his right.

Amber looks up when she hears her name. She's all white with one tan ear, so different from the other border collies that are almost uniformly black and white. Not only that . . . the one ear droops down, which gives her a comical look.

"Is Amber the dog I've seen with you out herding the sheep? Is she going to be in the trials?"

"Yes, she's my regular sheepdog, but she's not going to be in the trials this time. She just had foot surgery. The vet said not to run her for six weeks. I'd better go. I have another younger dog in my truck and it's almost our turn . . . Come," he says quietly, and he and Amber move off in the crowd.

Circus

*W*hile there's a break, I head for the tents to see what's going on. The first is for food—hot chili and corn bread prepared by the Seagull Island Women's Association. The second houses vendors who sell all kinds of sheepdog supplies, books and dog-training videos. The third is a big yellow structure that I've seen before belonging to the Fibre Guild.

The minute I enter the yellow tent, I am soothed. As before, all around the walls are shelves that support the colorful shawls, blankets, rugs, scarves, table linens, sweaters and mittens that the artists make. Music is coming from a guitarist in the corner. Terry is there, holding court. "Hiya!" she says, waving me over, but I stop to catch excited words coming out of the speaker out on the field.

"Look at this, ladies and gentlemen!" the announcer shouts through the sound system. "We have an interloper . . . A gold-and-white border collie streaking across the field . . . It's Amber of Seagull Island!"

Terry leads the way in her electric wheelchair as we all hurry outside. There's a shrill whistle from Mr. Aubrey back in the stands, but Amber doesn't return to him. Aubrey whistles again. "Stand. Stand down!" he yells firmly, but the white-and-gold dog doesn't respond.

She's headed straight toward four sheep that are huddled in a corner afraid of a large growling black sheepdog, about the size of a small black bear we'd see in West Virginia. Everyone in the audience is on alert. Are the dogs going to fight? Will the sheep scatter in every direction?

Mr. Aubrey whistles again. "Come by, girl! Come by!" But Amber still doesn't stop.

"This is a real circus," a familiar voice behind me says. It's Peter Dolman and it's the first time we've talked since Rainbow's delivery. "The dogs are usually very obedient. I wonder what's gotten into Amber."

"Mr. Aubrey told me she had surgery on her foot last week. She wasn't allowed in the trials. Maybe she just wants to have fun . . ."

But no! Amber isn't just running for the fun of it; she has other ideas. Without so much as a pause, she circles the four sheep, guides them away from the big black dog and brings them down the hill.

Aubrey has given up whistling. He stands for a moment scratching his head, then smiles and walks into the field. Amber doesn't hesitate. She brings the sheep down, directs them through the two gates and heads for the square pen completely in control. Her master is now laughing, along with the rest of the crowd. Sore foot or not, Amber is the unofficial winner.

As the shepherd closes the gate, his gold-and-white border collie looks up at him for approval. "That will do, dog," Mr. Aubrey says and pats her head. "That will do."

CHAPTER 45

Bad Weather

By late afternoon, a sharp wind has come up and I'm thankful that Peter Dolman has offered me a ride home. We wrestle my bike into the trunk of his cruiser and move along slowly in the long line of cars. All over the island, leaves fly, red and yellow. Some of the trees are already bare. Red sumac bushes are on fire.

As we near the Roadhouse and the marina, I can't help but ask, "Any more news about the missing person?"

The cop shrugs and shakes his head. "No."

Observing his profile, it's hard to believe. I smile to myself. Probably he just can't talk about it because it's "still an ongoing investigation." Dolman must have caught me smiling, because he smiles too.

"What?" he asks.

"Nothing," I answer, and then to divert him I say, "I was just thinking you aren't a bad guy. I appreciate the ride." This seems to embarrass him.

"Did you think all cops were jerks or something? Hey, want to get dinner?" Before I can answer, he pulls into the nearly full Roadhouse parking lot. Now *I'm* embarrassed. I don't really want to hang out with him, but I can't come up with an excuse to say no.

Before we get inside, I hear familiar music—bagpipe, flute and guitars. "Poor Angus is playing tonight," Peter announces. "Have you heard them before?" My attitude about going into the tavern with Dolman suddenly changes.

"Just once, at the folk fest. They were one of my favorites."

"Me too."

As the township police officer, Peter apparently has pull because we don't have to stand in line for a table. "Dolman. Party of two. Peter Dolman. Party of two!" Serena, the pretty owner of the bar calls out, laughing. Then she takes us to an empty table near a window that looks out at the wide expanse of blue, the ever-present Lake Erie. Today, there's not a boat in sight, just water and sky with white clouds marching along the horizon.

"You going to the next township meeting?" Peter asks after we've both ordered Reuben sandwiches and a bottle of hard cider.

"Are you kidding? The last one was torture. You think I should go?"

"Well, yeah. You've heard the old saying, 'If you aren't sitting at the table, you'll be on the menu.'"

"Is that an old saying?"

"Well, something like that . . ."

I mull his words over while listening to Poor Angus's music. *Give up on fear . . . Give up a war you aren't ready to fight . . .*

"Is there still a lot of bickering about the casino?" I ask when the song is over.

Peter shrugs. "Yeah, there's still a lot of controversy, but mostly it's between the environmentalists and those who want to see progress at any cost. Some people don't look very far into the future. Some people don't look into the past." He takes a sip from his bottle and goes on.

"Half the plans that get cooked up for the island by outsiders never get finished or even started . . ." he goes on. "It would be better if we thought about what people *here* could do instead of depending on outside investors."

"You put it so well. Are you going to say that at the meeting?"

Dolman grins. "I will if you come to support me. I don't want to get booed off the stage."

Jed has come in, as always wearing his navy knit cap. Apparently, he's forgiven me for taking the side of the folks who oppose the Gull Point Casino because he gives us an easy smile. "You sleep in that thing?" I tease, and he takes his hat off, shakes his long hair and pulls a chair over.

"Can I buy you both another cider?" he asks as he waves over a waitress.

Then we listen as Poor Angus fills the room with their voices. They've changed the mood from pensive to fun, singing about a bunch of fishermen who get drunk on the beach, and the music is so spirited I can't stop tapping my toes. Peter notices and nods toward the dance floor where people are putting on quite a show, clogging and stomping.

"Want to join them?" he asks.

"Not me!" I laugh. "I can barely slow dance." (This isn't true. I love to dance, just not in public.)

Serena, with the long dark hair and dangling earrings, comes up behind Peter and taps him on the shoulder. "Come on, Pete!" she says, smiling. "Give me a whirl." And she takes his hand.

In a way, I'm jealous. Not of Peter Dolman and the woman, but their freedom to dance with abandon, to not worry if they're doing it right or look funny.

By the time we turn onto Grays Road it's dark and has started to rain. Peter jerks to a stop just before my driveway. "What the hell?" he curses.

In the headlights, we can see two huge pieces of machinery

parked on the side of the road. When I roll down my window, I don't say a thing. The wind has been knocked out of me. While we were out, the Nelsons have moved in rented demolition equipment. The crane and bulldozer loom over my little cottage like dinosaurs from a *Jurassic Park* movie.

Prayer

It's a cool evening and I can smell the oil from the machinery and winter coming, but I'm bundled up, sitting on the upper deck with Tiger. The trees are all leafless now. Only one seagull circles the bay, my guardian.

Suddenly into the silence comes an *Eeeeeek! Eeeeeek! Eeeeeek!* and a rowdy bunch of blue jays lands in the bare cottonwoods. I haven't even thought about jays, a common bird back in West Virginia. I assumed they didn't live this far north, but here they are, hopping from branch to branch like small clowns. There are six of them. *Eeeeeek! Eeeeeek!*

As I watch, the clouds turn red and tumble across the sky like waves of fire. Then one by one the stars come out. I think about Lenny, wondering where he is and if he ever mailed my letter to Jessie. Did he make it safely to Europe or Mexico? Will he ever be back? So many people I've cared about have left me. Karen and Robyn and Lenny . . . On the other hand, I have left people too, Jessie and Richard and Linda, my midwife partner.

I think of my daughter, a little speck of light like a star and just as far away, a trillion light years. The pain of leaving her is still there, but since I sent the note, it's grown dimmer. If I only knew she'd received it and she was alright, I could lay one of my burdens down.

Tonight, under the stars, I get down on my knees. The deck boards are already covered with frost. Like a Catholic sister in a cold chapel, I begin.

"Hail Mary, full of grace, the Lord is with thee. Blessed art thou among women . . .

"Holy Mary . . . All I ask is that my daughter be safe and be happy. That's all any mother wants in the end."

Then I remember another prayer to Mary, a song by the Beatles, and that brings me comfort too. *When I find myself in times of trouble, Mother Mary comes to me, Speaking words of wisdom, let it be.* Let it be.

BLUE JAY
A medium-sized noisy bird
Bright blue with gray underparts and a black necklace
Range: Lives east of the Rockies as far north as southern Canada
Habitat: Prefers forests and fields
Diet: Omnivorous, eats seeds, small caterpillars, insects, loves acorns
Call: a high-pitched *jeeeer jeeeer*

Winter Again

CHAPTER 46

Discovery

I wake at sunrise, hearing geese bark, and run out on the deck to see three huge flocks in long Vs flying south against wave after wave of pink clouds. How do they know that it's time? How do they know where to go?

Snow is falling, big flakes like feathers, the first of the season, and I open my mouth to catch some. What a wonderful world we live in, I think. How could anyone not believe in God if they saw this? (Richard didn't believe, I remember, and he loved the earth as much as I do.)

All along the edge of the lake, ice is forming. "Am I crazy to live here?" I ask Tiger when I come back inside. "Last winter when I arrived, my life was falling apart, but this year, I'm choosing to stay on the island . . . Am I crazy?" I ask again. He just licks his paw.

Around four, I get out a broom and mop to begin a *serious cleanup.* I've been so worried about the imminent destruction of Seagull Haven that I've let the place go. I start in the kitchen scrubbing everything down, including the floors. I move on to the bathroom and then the living room, spending twenty minutes dusting Lloyd and Wanda's seagulls. As I'm sweeping the bedroom, I see something shiny between two of the floorboards and when I kneel down, I realize that it's a thin metal chain.

What's this? I think, as I try to work the chain out of the crack with a safety pin. Gently tugging this way and that, I finally hold in my palm a delicate silver bracelet with a small sailboat charm.

"What do you think?" I ask Tiger, dangling it in front of him. "A new toy?" He gives it a swat. Maybe it was Wanda's or maybe Charlene's. That's when I notice there's a name on the boat. I hold it up to the light and go as cold as the ice along the shore of Lake Erie. The name engraved there is *Charity*.

Shocked, I sit down on the bed. *Charity was once in this cottage . . .* Then a disturbing thought comes to me. The girl was raped and found tied in the woods on the other side of Gull Point. Could the Nelson brothers have been involved? Instinctively, I know that they were . . . but she *said* her attackers were hippies.

I stare at the bracelet, wondering what I should do with it. Give it to Charity's mother, Helen? That would only cause the family more pain. Give it to Officer Dolman? The rape case was never solved.

I pace the house until it's nearly dark, mulling things over, jiggling the bracelet in my hand. "Meooowww!" cries Tiger, alerting me that something is wrong and I pick up my head. Is that a vehicle coming? A white BMW pulls into the drive.

Mistake

*C*harlene Nelson and her brother Jake get out of the white convertible, both looking like jewel thieves, black pants and black knit caps pulled over their hair. The wind has come up and they pull their coats close.

What the hell do they want? Peter told me to call him if they came back, but before I can lock the door or get to the phone, the two are up on the porch. Quickly I open a kitchen cupboard and drop the bracelet in a teacup. The Nelsons knock once and let themselves in.

"Excuse me!" I say. "This is still my home. You can't just walk in here whenever you like!"

"We knocked." That's Charlene. "We're still your landlords, remember. Do you have something to hide?"

"No, but I'd appreciate it if you gave me a chance to come to the door. How did you even know I was dressed?"

"We didn't," Jake says with a leer. "That's what makes it interesting."

"Listen, Sara," Charlene says, taking off her cap, shaking out her dark thick hair and ignoring her brother. "We don't know what you're up to, getting involved with the law and siding with the environmentalists against us, but it won't work."

Jake takes a chair at the kitchen table and leans back against the wall. "Yeah. We've tried to be nice, but we're about out of patience. We want to give you one more chance to tell us what you want. If it's money, name your price."

I turn to him, not believing I heard right. "Money? You think I'm opposing the casino for the money? I told you, I found Lloyd's handwritten will. I turned it in to Sergeant Dolman, and that was the end of my involvement. You're correct that I think a four-story hotel and casino on this beautiful spot is a bad idea, but that's just my opinion and I don't carry a lot of weight on the island."

"Sara, I think you misunderstood Jake," Charlene interrupts in a voice as sweet as cotton candy. "We're not offering a bribe. We're just asking what you need for relocation. We own some reasonable condos in Sandusky on the US side of Lake Erie. In fact, if you wanted to move this week, I could give you the keys to a nice one-bedroom tomorrow. I'd sign the deed over to you just to get you out of our hair. I'd hate to have to evict you or take other action. I don't think you'd like that either."

"That's a very generous offer, but I'm not interested. The island is my home now. What *I'd like* is for you to get out of here."

Jake stands up and leans over me. "I guess we will when we're done, but I really don't think you want to cross us. You're very isolated out here, Miss Livingston."

"And what? What? You'll beat me up and rape me like you did Charity?" As soon as the words are out of my mouth, I know it's a mistake and I want to suck them back, but it's too late.

"You bitch!" Jake grabs my wrist and pulls me toward him so that I can smell the alcohol on his breath.

This time Charlene doesn't intervene. She just stands there with a strange smile on her face, as if she's enjoying it. "I think you're getting the idea now," she snarls, and then she pulls her knit cap back over her hair. "Come on, Jake, let's go. We're leaving, but we'll be back."

The bully twists my wrist a little further until he brings me to tears, then pushes me away so hard I drop to the floor and am still sitting there crying when their BMW roars out of the drive.

Night Ride

I sit on the floor in the middle of the kitchen, stunned. What to do now? The Nelsons don't know I have the bracelet, but they said they'd be back. It's not safe to stay here and I have to get the bracelet to Dolman. I try to call, but he doesn't pick up, so I leave a message.

"It's Sara. The Nelsons were here again and I've done something stupid. It's too dangerous for me to stay at the cottage, so I'm biking toward your office. Please come."

Before I leave, I put Tiger in the bathroom, but then change my mind. If the Nelsons return, they're crazy enough to burn the house down. "Okay, Tiger, we're going for a ride in the dark, so don't give me any trouble." I grab the bracelet, tie my cat with his leash into the padded basket, and then strap a flashlight to the handlebars.

It's a bitterly cold night and the sky's spitting snow, but I lower my head into the wind and push on. I pass Molly Lou's but the lights are off so they must be at church. I pedal by the Cider Mill, but they're closed for the season. No lights at Jed's clinic either and the pub has a sign that says SEE YOU NEXT SPRING. The village is deserted.

"It's okay, Tiger. It's okay," I say to reassure myself. Even the ferry terminal is dark.

A few hundred yards from the cop shop, I see headlights coming my way. Could that be the Nelsons returning to Gull Point? I use my last bit of energy, push harder on the pedals and just make it to the cop shop, intending to hide around back, but I'm not quick enough. The beams flicker over me. Did they see? Tiger meows, protesting the rough treatment. "Hush. Shush!" I shrink into the shadows on the side of the building, not moving a hair, willing myself to be invisible.

False Witness

"Take a deep breath," Dolman says, getting out of the squad car and unlocking the door to his office. I do what he says, breathe in through my nose and out through my mouth like a cleansing breath in hard labor. I do it again and wipe my nose with the back of my hand.

"I'll put on some hot water," he says. "Big storm's coming in tonight; Arctic air mass moving south. I got your message and came as fast I could. I was up on the north end. So what's happening?" Dolman asks, getting out tea bags.

I take another deep breath. "As I said on the phone, the Nelsons came to my cottage again." His face doesn't change. His head doesn't move.

"And . . . ?" he asks. Outside, the surf pounds against the ferry dock. *Boom. Boom.*

"And . . . they tried to bribe me. Offered to move me into a condo in Sandusky and give me the deed." Peter smiles. "That doesn't sound so bad." I tell him the rest of the story and end with Jake grabbing me and pushing me down.

"And it gets worse. I think I did something stupid." Here I reach in my jeans pocket and hold out the delicate silver bracelet. Dolman takes it and lets it dangle between his fingers.

"I found this between the floorboards in the bedroom this afternoon. Read the inscription."

The cop squints, then puts on his glasses and finally understands. "*Charity* . . . Charity was once at Seagull Haven. . . . I distinctly remember interviewing the Nelson men during the investigation and they denied knowing her . . . Did you tell them you found this? If you did you're in more danger than before."

"No, I didn't mention the bracelet, but I did throw Charity's name at them. 'What are you going to do?' I said to Jake as he held on to me. 'What are you going to do, beat me up and rape me like you did Charity?'"

"And their reaction?"

"Jake was pissed, but he didn't deny it. Then he called me a bitch and threw me to the floor. Charlene looked like she was enjoying it and said they'd be back."

Peter runs his hands through his short hair. "You know where they found her, don't you? Charity? Not far from your cottage in the woods on the other side of Gull Point. But why did she say her assailants were hippies? Why did she bear false witness?"

"I thought the same thing. Maybe she was afraid. Maybe they threatened to kill her."

Dolman's phone whistles and he looks at his text. "It's Jed, at the marina," he says. "Shit. What jerk would go out on the water on a night like this? I gotta go over there."

He pulls his coat back on. "You stay here, Sara. They won't look for you here. I'll be back as soon as I can. Lock the door and turn out the lights. Pull all the shades."

CHAPTER 47

Courage

As I push the door closed, I hear the island emergency siren go off on the tower behind the clinic, a long wail rising in pitch and repeating three times over, communicating the need for the island volunteer emergency squad to check their phones and follow the instructions texted to them by Jed or Dolman. The siren wails again. I pull down the blinds, turn out the lights and lock the door, then sit down with Tiger in my lap.

A few minutes later, I hear a rattle on the window and peek out to see water running down the glass. A huge wave has made it over the breakwall and across the narrow road.

Thinking that the Nelsons are not likely to come here with the weather so bad, I pull on my parka and grab my flashlight. When I step out . . . I almost fall on my butt again. The wave that made it over is already freezing and there's a thin sheet of ice over everything . . .

I can't help myself. I have to see what's happening on the lake, so holding on to the side of the building, I creep up to the road. *Splash,* the spray hits me. *Splash . . . Slosh . . . Splash . . . Splash.*

The lake is in chaos. There's no organization to the surf. Huge whitecaps race the wind, pushing chunks of ice in front of

them. *Boom. Boom.* The little ferry, lashed to the dock, is rocking and rolling. It's exhilarating and frightening at the same
time. I want to howl with the wind and I do! "Ahhhooooo!
Ahhhhooooo!"

Then I see a sight I could never have imagined. Four-inch ice
needles begin to form on the rocks and as they grow they fall
over and tinkle like a thousand tiny silver bells. I stand watching
with my mouth open. When I reach down to touch them, I pull
my hand away. The crystals are too cold! Too strange!

Crash! Another big wave leaps the breakwall, almost pushing
me over. I'd better go back inside before my wet clothes freeze. I
shine my light across the silver ice-covered road and creep back
inside.

Inside Dolman's office, I shake my wet parka, turn up the
thermostat and sit down in the dark again, wondering what to
do now. Peter said to *stay put* and there's no way I want to ride
my bike home in this weather, so using my flashlight I explore his
books. Here's one that looks interesting, *The Last Policeman.* I'm
deep into the first chapter when the phone rings.

Pretending I'm a cop, I pick up the receiver. "Seagull Island
OPP."

"Hey," a familiar voice responds. "It's Jed. Quit kidding
around. We have a potential disaster over here. I'm not sure how
many people are on the loose sailboat, but the lake is so rough
I'm afraid it will go down. Molly Lou is on her way up to the village to get you. I need you to set up a triage station in the tavern.
Tell her the roads are a sheet of ice, take the turns slow or she'll
end up in a ditch."

Twenty minutes later, Molly honks outside Dolman's office
and, leaving Tiger to guard the place, I carefully walk out to her
Subaru and get in. "Jed says there may be injured at the marina.
I wonder what's happening."

"I don't know," Molly says, leaning forward and gripping the steering wheel as we slide at the turn onto Middle Loop. "But I can't stay. I left Little Chris home in bed. Big Chris took the pickup when the siren went off. I hate it when someone does something stupid and other people have to risk their lives saving them."

"Is there a Coast Guard station here with a rescue service?"

"No, that's the trouble. In the summer we have a Coast Guard boat, but it's docked in Kingsville on the Canadian side now. Everyone on the island who owns a watercraft has already pulled his or hers out for the winter. All we have are two motorized inflatable Zodiacs the Coast Guard left, safe enough in the summer but not with the lake like this." You can tell that she's worried.

When we get to the marina, I hurry through the now flying snow toward the ambulance. It's parked close to the docks with its lights still flashing, red . . . blue . . . red . . . blue. Jed stands in a yellow slicker with the hood up, a cell phone at his ear. Out at the end of the pier, the waves look like they are topping ten feet.

A searchlight is pointed at Wade, Peter Dolman, Big Chris, Earl Prentiss and the mayor of the township, Nell Ambroy, as they climb into a bucking red rubber rescue boat with a gas motor on the back. John from New Day and Austin Aubrey hold the rope and I watch them struggle with the uncontrolled watercraft.

What courage it takes to jump into a flimsy Zodiac and face waves ten feet high, I think. *It's not some macho thing; it's true guts.*

Red . . . blue . . . red . . . blue, a strobe-light effect. "It's too rough over here to fly a helicopter," Jed yells into his cell phone. "Don't even try. You could send the forty-seven-foot boat, but that would take two or three hours and we can't wait. I'll call you back if our rescue operation is successful. If we aren't, you'll be searching for bodies in the morning."

When Jed sticks his cell back in his pocket, I ask him what's happening out on the water. "It's a sailboat tipped on its side, bobbing around out there like a cork in a washer. Serena saw the fore lights when she was closing the Roadhouse, so we know there are people on the vessel, but now the lights are off, so they must have lost power. You probably heard me talking to the Coast Guard. It's too dangerous for a helicopter to make it with the weather like this, so we're on our own."

He pauses to throw back his hood and glares at the breakers. "When the rescuers got close last time, they could see the boat has three masts and is tilted to the side, probably taking in water, but the waves keep dragging our dinghies back to shore, so they can't get out far enough. Lake Erie has turned into a raging animal and this ice doesn't help. Chris Erickson already slipped once and I almost fell. If they can't get ropes on the sailboat and pull it in, it'll go down and the passengers with it."

"So no one knows how many people are out there."

"There's no way to tell. We have nine of our own in the two Zodiacs and who knows how many on the sailboat. I've tried to look with my binoculars, but with the snow, I can't see a damn thing. We called out to them on a shortwave radio and a bull-horn but there's no answer. It's a hell of a night to be out on the water and I can't even fathom why someone would try."

Five minutes later, when we enter the Roadhouse, I see that Serena is way ahead of us. The heater is cranked up and she's back in the kitchen making coffee. She's also got bread out for sandwiches.

While Jed goes back to wait on the docks, I set up a triage

area by pushing tables together for beds, laying out the blankets that he's already brought in and organizing IV sets. Then I go out to bring in the orange lockbox of meds.

The wind is so strong and cold, I have to crouch low and lean into it to get to the ambulance. If someone falls in the water, I know that their heart rate will plummet and within minutes they'll lose muscle coordination and be unable to swim.

At the last moment, I grab some gauze and Ace bandages just in case someone has some other injury. When I'm done setting up my makeshift ER, I call out to Serena. "Anything I can do to help?"

"Sure," she says. "Spread mayo and mustard on every slice of bread. I'll layer on the pastrami." She puts some reggae music on the stereo and I've almost forgotten that we aren't getting ready for a party when the door bursts open.

Rescue

*H*ypothermia!" Jed yells as he and John wheel in an ambulance stretcher with a body wrapped in an army blanket. "The men in the first Zodiac pulled the victim out of the water about twenty meters from the end of the dock," John yells.

They place the body on a table and run back outside. I have no idea what I'm supposed to do, so I pull the blanket off the victim, expecting to see a stranger and discover it's Charlene Nelson. Her face is white, blue around the lips, and her breathing is slow and shallow. "Jakey," she mumbles. "Save Jakey!"

"Get her clothes off," Serena tells me. "Warm her trunk first then her hands and feet. You'd better start an IV. I'll do the rest."

"Thanks. I know about hypothermia from the textbooks, but I've never actually seen a case of it."

With competent gentle hands, Serena peels off Charlene's wet black jeans, black jacket and black knit cap. It takes me a few minutes, but after three shaky tries I find a good vein and insert an IV catheter in her forearm, then run in normal saline at 125 drops a minute.

"Mama!" Charlene calls. "I'm sorry! I'm sorry, Mama." The woman is clearly delirious. I quickly wrap her up again with the warm dry army blankets and then I get the patient's vital signs. Her pulse is slow, forty beats per minute, and her temperature, taken under the arm with Jed's thermometer, is thirty-five degrees Celsius. "Do you know how much that is in Fahrenheit?" I ask Serena.

"I'm not sure, but it's way too low."

"Can you bring some warm towels from the kitchen? Turn on the oven and put a stack on the door." Within minutes Serena's back with a pile of warm dish towels and a white mug of warm tea with sugar and a spoon. "That was fast," I commend her.

"I microwaved them," she says with a grin. Quickly we layer the patient's body with the warm towels then tuck the blankets back around her again.

"Charlene. Can you hear me? It's Sara Livingston. You're safe now. We want you to sip a little tea."

I don't get to serve tea. I leave that to Serena, because two minutes later the door bursts open again. It's John, from New Day, wheeling in Mr. Aubrey on the ambulance cart. John's face tells me something is very wrong.

"What happened?"

"He slipped on the icy dock helping the men tie up the Zodiac. Hit his head really hard on a metal dock cleat."

We get Austin on a table, wrap him up and then turn him on his side, so I can see the back of his head.

He's bleeding of course, but he's also unconscious and this worries me more. Though he hasn't gone for a dunk in the freezing waves, he's wet just from freezing spray so again we go through the steps of undressing him, warming him and starting an IV. Luckily, the man has good veins and I get the needle in with one try.

Once more the door blows opens, only this time it's Jed by himself. "They've got lines on the sailboat and almost have it in," he says, looking tired. John brings him tea, helps him get out of the wet rain gear and puts a blanket around his shoulders.

"Want a sandwich?" offers Serena, setting up a buffet with the coffee.

Jed waves her away with a quiet "No thanks." You can tell he's exhausted, but he still makes rounds on our patients. First he checks Aubrey's pupils. They're equal and reactive, which is a good thing. Temp 36. Pulse 60. Respirations 14. Blood pressure 94/50. He gently shakes him but the shepherd doesn't respond.

"How's Charlene Nelson?" Jed asks me, and I take her temp again.

"Temp's up to 35.5."

"I've already called the emergency team in Windsor and they expect the storm to wear out in a few hours," the nurse practitioner says. "I think both Charlene and Aubrey need to go to Regional. Can you call Aubrey's wife, Serena? She might want to fly over with him. I don't know who to call about Charlene."

"I've got that." It's Peter Dolman coming in the door with the men and Nell from the rescue boats. They're all wet and cold and Nell Ambroy begins to pass out blankets, but there aren't enough to go around so the strongest give them to those that are most worn out.

Jake Nelson shuffles in with the others, wet and reeking of booze, but apparently unharmed. He pulls over a chair and sits next to Charlene, taking her hand. "Is she going to be alright, Doc?" he asks the nurse practitioner.

"Yes, I think so. Thanks to Sara," Jed says. Jake holds my eyes, glaring as if his sister's having hypothermia was my fault.

Peter Dolman is at the buffet getting coffee and looks over, then he approaches Jake. "Care to tell me what you were doing out on the water on a night like this?" he asks.

"Hell if I know," Jake growls. "I thought I could make it home to Sandusky. I guess I had too much to drink."

CHAPTER 48

Dead in the Water

"So I had to arrest Jake Nelson," Dolman informs me when he drops in a few days after the boating accident. The sun has come out and the surface ice has melted, but there's still snow in patches. Nature is like that, a raging beast one day and a kitten the next.

"Took him in for reckless endangerment," the cop goes on. "Driving a boat under the influence . . . and everything else I could think of. Someone could have been killed that night. We were lucky that more people weren't hurt because of his stupidity."

"How's Charlene?"

"They stabilized her in Windsor and flew her back to a hospital in Detroit. Hope she has good health insurance. It will cost about $10,000 US for her hospitalization in Michigan."

"How about Aubrey? He worried me more."

"He's weak but okay. Coming home on the late flight this afternoon. His wife, Elsa, called and asked if I could meet her at the airport in case she needs help getting him off the plane and into their vehicle. He'll have to take it easy for a few months. Bad concussion.

"It was a hell of a night . . . I took Jake into the cop shop, but we don't have a jail on the island, so I handcuffed him to a chair and let him sleep it off. He's home now too. His brother, William, bailed him out. I don't think they'll come back. The casino and hotel are dead in the water."

"Wait! Will you say that last part again?"

"Which part?" he asks, sipping his coffee and smiling.

"The Nelsons won't be back and the casino and hotel are dead in the water!"

"Well, Jake would have to face charges for operating a boat under the influence if he returns to Canada."

"Like that's gonna stop his big plans for the development! A drunken escapade. His siblings will keep at it."

"Not just that. I showed Jake and William Charity's charm bracelet and explained where it came from. With both of them lying ten years ago about not knowing her and with the bracelet as evidence that she was once in the cottage, I made sure they understood that I could have the cold case reopened and they would be my prime suspects. There's no statute of limitation on rape in Canada."

"Is the evidence strong enough to convict them? Would Charity come back and testify?"

Dolman smiles. "I didn't say I had enough to *convict them,* not without Charity's identification, just enough to *reinvestigate* and possibly arrest them for suspicion. The newspapers in Ontario, Michigan and Ohio would do the rest, pick up the story and drag the two of them through the mud for months. It would be a big scandal: PROMINENT DEVELOPERS ARRESTED FOR RAPE. They'd never be welcome on the island again and in the end their names would be ruined in the States too . . .

"Helen and Eugene say Charity is doing so well in Montreal," he adds. "They just came back from a visit. Charity is married with two kids. The assault was twelve years ago and it probably wouldn't help her to relive that horrible night in front of a court-room."

"So the Nelsons won't try to get the permit to build the casino? You have it in writing?"

He pulls his keys out of his pocket and holds them out. The thin silver chain is double looped through a Swiss Army key ring. "Nope. I have the bracelet."

Light through the Window

Molly Lou and I are on our way to the country store when we see a small animal standing on a snowbank at the edge of road about halfway between her house and mine. I'm not a natu-ralist, but it looks like a gray fox to me. Gray body, red around the face with red ears; tail as long as the animal is long, with an orange fringe. Before we can roll down the window to get a better look, it darts into the trees.

When we get to Burke's Country Store, the parking lot is almost full and the building has been decorated for the holidays with blinking red-and-green Christmas lights.

I check out the vehicles to see who I know. There's Peter Dol-man's squad car and the Nature Conservancy van, Jed's yellow Jeep, plus eight autos with a variety of license plates, none from West Virginia, thank goodness!

"Funny there are so many cars and trucks here from Ohio, Michigan and Indiana," I comment. "It's almost like tourist season."

"They belong to the families who own cottages and come back for the holidays. Those Ontario plates are cottagers too, but they're from the mainland. You're coming to the Christmas Eve party at the Black Sheep Pub, aren't you?"

"I haven't heard about it. Does everyone go?"

"Yeah, pretty much everyone. I don't know about the people from New Day. I guess they'd be welcome. We could ask them."

"I thought the pub was closed."

"It is until spring, but they open for events like this."

Inside, the store is as full as I've ever seen it, with cottagers and even a few migrant workers picking up special treats before they go back to Mexico.

I wander the aisles with my shopping list but see Pete Dolman sitting at the counter and walk up behind him. "Want half a sandwich?" he asks, turning on his stool, and I sit down for the company and the free lunch.

When Molly is done with her shopping, she wants to go home right away so Peter offers to drive me. (Neither the cop nor I mention the silver bracelet. It is our secret and apparently will remain so.)

While I eat, Helen makes me a cup of coffee then sits down to show us the photos she took while visiting Charity in Montreal.

"I'm so proud of her." She holds out picture after picture on her cell phone of Charity and her husband and two little boys who are blond like their mother. "She left the island under terrible circumstances, but she's thrived. She learned French, got her degree and works in a high school as a counselor. She could never have done that here.

"The months after her assault were the darkest days of our lives. I didn't know what to do, how to help her and then she tried to cut her wrists and had to be hospitalized for a year. I thought the sun would never shine again, but look, it does! Charity and the kids are coming to the island for Christmas!" She nods toward the windows at the front of the store, where patches of light stream in, reflecting the ice and the blue water beyond.

The sun will shine again, I think. She's right. *No matter how dark the night, if we wait, the sun returns.*

I take a last sip of my coffee, thinking about Charity. Maybe if the Nelsons were arrested and convicted of rape, it would bring Charity and her family peace or maybe it would just rip open old wounds. Peter seems to think it's better to be silent and let the healing continue.

I shake my head, realizing I don't know the answers. I barely know the questions.

Give up on Fear

*E*very morning, first thing, I look out the kitchen window and see the demolition equipment with KINGSVILLE DEMOLITION stenciled on the side. What did I think? The machines were just going to have a change of their mechanical hearts and slink away in the night?

"Tiger," I say to my cat who rubs his furry body against my ankles, waiting for his breakfast. "It's already early December, the November deadline has come and gone and I still haven't found a place to live. What are we going to do? I know this isn't my home; it belongs to the Nature Conservancy or it probably will belong to them after the courts sort everything out. Peter feels sure the Nelsons aren't going to build a casino, but that doesn't mean they won't tear down the house just out of spite, if they get the chance." I glance out the window again. It's raining cold tears.

At a quarter to seven in the evening, Peter Dolman picks me up to go to the third township meeting. "Give up on fear," the folksingers said, so I get in his car and prepare myself for another shouting match.

I know why I hate such meetings. Since I was a child, I've never done well with conflict. The sounds of people arguing remind me of my parents' fights when I was little. *Posttraumatic stress,* a therapist once told me.

The minute we enter the pub, I wish like anything I could duck out. This time every chair is full, but there is no easel with plans. I sit with Dolman and hope for the best. If the Nelsons give up the casino, there's no point in argument.

Mayor Ambroy calls us to order. No prayers tonight. This woman means business and I have the feeling she's not in a very good mood.

"The first thing I want to announce is that the Nelsons have backed out of the casino and hotel project. Those who opposed it, I hope you're satisfied."

The room erupts with hot lava. "What?" "Why?" "God-damn!" "Was it the gray fox?" "Was it the environmental audit?" Even people like Molly Lou, Chris and Terry look concerned. Now what?

Ambroy pounds her gavel. "Settle down!" The room goes quiet. "I can't tell you much more. I received an email this afternoon from Charlene. I'm sure they were concerned about the audit and the Nature Conservancy, but she said they also felt unwelcome. They're giving up on the island, selling all their real estate here and taking their project somewhere else." I look at Dolman, but there's no smile, no sign that he isn't as amazed as everyone else.

The room explodes again and there are so many voices it's

hard to sort out who's happy the casino has been scrapped and who's disappointed. Then Kristie the waitress jumps up, almost spilling her coffee. "You mean we aren't going to do *anything*? Just turn every opportunity for growth away?

"What about young people like me? I work two jobs just to survive and even with that, I'll never be able to buy my own place. I love this island and I want to stay here, maybe even have kids here someday. What about the other investor?" She's almost crying and you can tell by the murmurs that the crowd sympathizes.

"Can I speak?" It's Bob Burroughs, the man from Toronto. "I wanted to do something to help the island, but I'm not one to push my way around. Apparently this is not the time to invest in a hotel and casino and I can take my money elsewhere." There's a low buzz in the crowd like someone hit a beehive with a stick.

"Nah, Burroughs. You're takin' us wrong." Big Chris stands up, lightening the mood. *"We want your money!"* Everyone laughs, even the investor. "We just weren't sure about the casino . . ." He sits down quickly with a red face, almost tipping his chair over and Molly Lou puts her arm through his proudly. I look over at Dolman and raise my eyebrows. People are surprisingly thoughtful tonight.

"We're not saying that we aren't going to do *anything,* just that we have to be careful," Austin Aubrey answers Kristie. "We need to figure out how to develop in a way that doesn't change the fundamental character of our home."

"I have an idea I'd like to share." It's Wade from the New Day Farm and people shift in their chairs. *Who's this new voice and how dare he intrude?*

"I've been thinking about this quite a lot." The hippie man

walks confidently toward the front. He's wearing a button-up shirt with clean khaki slacks and has his long hair tied back in a ponytail.

"I can see the island needs *something,* but my friends and I moved here for the peace and quiet, the clean environment and the chance to raise children where they won't be afraid. What if, instead of a casino, we ask Mr. Burroughs to build a health spa and resort, a really nice place with healing pools, massages and a high-end restaurant with locally grown organic veggies and meat as well as fresh fish from the lake? The commune owns ten acres in the north end that we could donate.

"We could have classes on health or stargazing or weaving or painting. We could have art shows and concerts. In the long run, even the B and Bs and the cottages would thrive. People would come for the healing and then bring their families for vacations . . ."

No one says a word for a moment and I'm not sure if what Wade said makes sense to people or if they think he's a starry-eyed fool.

"I know I'm an outsider, but I've lived here two years now and I love it," Wade goes on. "The idea of a place of peace where people could come and relax and connect with nature is what the world needs. And those qualities are moneymakers too. What do you think, Mr. Burroughs? You're the potential financial backer. Would a health spa and resort interest you at all?"

All eyes go back to the front and when the investor stands again you can hear a pin drop. "It's definitely something to consider," he says. There's a positive noise from the crowd and it's not just the Nature Conservancy people either. "Maybe you could get up a committee and we could discuss it sometime."

More murmurs of approval from the crowd. This is something that feels good. Feels right. It's doesn't matter if the idea came from a hippie . . .

"So," I say to Dolman as we pass the wrecking machines and bump into my drive, "that was a surprise. When we walked in, I was expecting the worst, more bad-mouthing and shouting each other down.

"You want to come in for a cup of tea?" I ask Peter, just to be friendly, though in truth, I'm exhausted. Crowds tire me out.

"Nah, I gotta get an early flight to Windsor in the morning."

As I stand on the porch, watching the taillights of the squad car blink out, I feel hopeful. I might not be able to live in the cottage, but the beach will probably still be available for people like me to walk on, and the bay will be here for the geese and the ducks and the seagulls.

OoOoOoOoooooo. OoOoOoOoooooo, an owl calls in a quivery voice from out by the cottonwoods and I smile. It's the first one I've heard since I came to Seagull Island.

EASTERN SCREECH OWL
A brown spotted night bird with pointy ears
Common over much of eastern North America
Spends the day roosting in holes
Becomes active at dusk
Brown and white with a pale green beak
Diet: Small mammals
Voice: A quivery trill
Habitat: Woods, farm groves, shade trees
Size: 7–10 inches
Wingspan: 18–24 inches

The Past Is Past

*F*or two days it snows and I wander the house wondering what now? The Nelsons have withdrawn, which is welcome news, but someone must own Seagull Haven and it isn't me. I should get serious about finding another place to live. "Could I really just move into Nita's?" I ask myself. "What do you think, Tiger? Are we two lost souls or just two travelers on the edge of an adventure?"

Tiger, I'm sure, knows the answer but doesn't get a chance to tell me because the phone rings and when I run in to answer it, it's Peter.

"Hey, want to go over to visit Terry? I need to see how she fared in the last storm. Someone told me her house had some damage."

"Sure, I was just feeling restless. I need to get out."

THIS TIME WHEN Dolman and I visit the Fibre Guild's shop, Terry's leading a knitting class. I've always wanted to learn to knit and now I have time. Maybe I could ask for a private lesson. Helen is sitting in the circle of participants along with a blond woman in her thirties who must be her daughter. I watch as they lean their heads together, laughing at each other's ragged first attempts at knitting.

Terry nods and raises her hand to indicate she'll only be a few more minutes, so while Peter goes out to look at the ice that was rammed against the house on the night of the storm, I look around. Maybe it's time to do a little Christmas shopping.

Everything in the store is pricey, but I have a bank card and plenty of green hidden in my briefcase, so I try not to concern myself and just buy what I like. After all, the money goes back to Terry and the other artists. Might as well share the wealth!

That's when I notice a basket with three skeins of thick home-spun red yarn and a knitting book. *Ten Patterns for a Beginner,* the cover says. That would be me! There's a red bow on the handle, as if it's meant to be a gift . . . a gift to myself, I decide. Maybe I don't need a class.

Terry takes the money for my purchases and then I sit down on a flowered sofa under the window to wait for Peter while she takes care of the last few customers. I'm surprised when Charity sits down beside me.

"So you're Sara, the midwife," she says.

The hair on the back of my neck goes up. "No, just a nurse."

"Oh, I thought you were a midwife. My cousin, Molly Lou, told me you delivered a hippie woman's baby at the old Nelson place." I watch her face when she speaks of Seagull Haven. No frown or darkening of the eye.

"Molly Lou said it was awesome. The coolest thing. I had a midwife for my babies too in Montreal."

"I used to be a mother-baby nurse in the hospital a long time ago. It was a pretty straightforward delivery . . . It's nice to see you on the island. I've heard a lot about you. I know your parents are thrilled. Helen was showing everyone pictures."

"That's Mom for you." She laughs and runs her hand through her short blond hair and that's when I see it, a silver bracelet with a heart-shaped charm engraved with one word. *Charity.*

"That's a pretty chain," I say, taking her hand.

"My husband got it for me."

I take a big breath. There's no time to think whether this is the right thing to do. Nita would say, *Just do it.* "I found a brace-let almost like that between the floorboards of the bedroom in

Seagull Haven the other day, only the charm was a sailboat. It said *Charity* too. Maybe it was yours?"

"Nope. Must be another Charity." We stare at each other, my blue eyes into her green ones.

"You were never in the cottage?" I asked. "You never knew the Nelson brothers or their sister, Charlene? Maybe you dropped it there."

"No," she says again, more firmly. I'm still holding her wrist and I run my finger gently along the silver chain. "You should be a midwife," she says, changing the subject.

I let go. "Yeah? Why?"

"You have a way about you. You're a person who could deal with a woman's secrets, if she had secrets . . . you wouldn't be shocked . . . and your hands are warm." She stands up and pulls on her parka. "I'm happy in Montreal, Sara. The past is past." Helen waves to her from across the store. "Got to go. It was nice meeting you."

The past is past, I think. *My past and Charity's.* The past is past.

The door blows open as Dolman comes in, stomping snow off his boots.

"So, what do you think about the chunks of ice behind the house?" Terry asks. "Some of them are half the size of a bathtub and right up against the foundation. Except for Christmas, the store doesn't bring in much this time of year . . . Just give me a ballpark figure, Pete. What do you think it would cost to have someone come in and remove them?"

"Couple of hundred," Peter answers her.

"Whew!" Terry says. "I'll think about it. Maybe I'll be lucky and we'll get a few warm days and they'll melt."

"You might," Peter agrees. "Or another storm might come in and slam the ice into your house and crush the foundation."

"Thanks! I really feel better now!" Terry gives him a little shove and he grabs the back of her wheelchair and spins her around.

CHAPTER 49

Lighthouse

Returning home from Terry's, Dolman turns north instead of south when we hit Sunset Road. At first, I think maybe he's dropping by the Estates for some reason.

"Where are we going?" I ask, still thinking about Charity.

"I want to show you something. It will put what we did the night of the rescue in perspective."

"Sure . . . I guess."

Twenty minutes later, we pull into a parking lot surrounded by an orange snow fence. A sign pointing to the beach says, LIGHT HOUSE NATURE PARK. DANGEROUS CURRENTS.

"I met Charity at the weavers' shop," I say before Peter has a chance to turn off the engine.

"I saw her there with Helen. Seems like she's doing great," Peter responds, looking out the window at the ice sculptures along the shore. "I was wondering how it would be for her to come back."

"She was wearing a silver bracelet almost like the one I found. It had a heart on it that says *Charity*. I asked her about it and told her I found one like it at the cottage."

"And?"

"She denied ever being in the cottage." Peter lifts his eyebrows as if he doesn't believe it.

"She said something else. 'The past is past.'"

"What do you make of that?" he asks as he turns off the engine, takes his keys and we get out of the cruiser.

"Maybe it's like you said—she doesn't want to think about what happened so long ago . . . or maybe she's forgiven them."

Peter doesn't say anything at first. "Well, without her willingness to testify, there's no point reopening the case. Let sleeping dogs lie, I guess. The Nelsons won't be back." Then we walk in silence until we get to the lighthouse.

THE BIG STONE structure, about sixty feet tall, towers over us. It's clear it hasn't been used as a lighthouse for years. There's no glass in the windows and the openings, like eyes, stare out at the water.

"It was built in 1830, the first of its kind in Ontario," Dolman tells me. "Pelee Island got a similar one in 1833. The province paid for materials, but the homesteaders built it themselves . . . probably because they were tired of risking their lives to save the crews and passengers of ships that came too close to the shoals. Scores of boats have sunk here."

"Molly Lou has a map that shows where ships went down." Touching the rocks, thinking about the people who lived on the island when the lighthouse was built, I walk around the building.

"I always imagine a rough sea," Peter explains, looking out at the water. "Waves ten feet tall, like the other night, a wooden passenger vessel powered by steam is on its way from Detroit to Buffalo. It grounds on the shallows about a hundred meters out. The boat breaks apart. Island men must brave the rough water to save the drowning victims. Some don't make it . . ."

"You're right. It puts things in perspective. I don't know if I have enough courage to do what you guys did the other night . . . or what the old timers did with only wooden rowboats, no gas motors, no safety equipment. Probably not even a life preserver."

HIKING BACK TO the cruiser, I notice the sun is close to the horizon and a wind has picked up. *Time to get home and build a nice fire.*

Now and then we come to chunks of ice, big thick slabs like the kind that were thrown into Terry's backyard, and we have to walk around them. Out of habit I look down for colored beach stones and that's when I see it . . . a Timberland boot.

Dolman stops. It's not the boot, it's the leg connected to it that brings him to a halt. Strangely there's no smell, probably because the corpse is frozen again. The body I discovered last spring, still clothed in torn jeans and a ripped black jacket, may have been sucked twenty miles off shore, but the recent gale has brought it back again.

The cop squats next to the man and with a stick carefully pulls away the sand and ice. "Don't look if you've got a sensitive stomach," he tells me.

"I'm a nurse," I say but turn away when he gets to the victim's face. "Peter, I have to tell you . . . that boot is familiar. Last March I saw it on Gull Point."

"Timberland is a popular brand . . ." Dolman pulls out his cell. "I have to call the division chief in Windsor. Since we're so close to the States, this may be an international issue and they'll get the Mounties and the FBI involved."

"No, what I meant is . . . I didn't just see *a Timberland boot*. I saw the body too. On Gull Point . . ." I wait for his reaction.

"So you saw *this body* on the beach . . . ?" he asks in his cop voice, lifting his sunglasses, his gray eyes like steel. "When was this exactly?"

"Just before the blizzard, in March, maybe April." I sit down on a nearby log that's been worn smooth by the waves.

"I'm sorry. I realized I should contact the authorities, but I had no phone and didn't know anyone. I was afraid Customs would discover that I was here without a passport. I didn't want to be sent back to the US or thrown in jail." I begin to cry softly. Peter holds up his hand.

"Slow down."

"*The guy was already dead!* I wasn't thinking clearly. I didn't consider he could be someone's father or someone's son or even a drug dealer. I just wanted him to go away. There was a dead swan too, lying next to him . . . I was scared . . ." The sobs are harder now.

Peter Dolman, social-worker-cop, throws the stick he was using to uncover the body out past the lake's white collar of ice.

"You aren't who you pretend to be, are you, Sara? Let's go back to your house. . . . You're going to tell me everything." We move toward the squad car, but I stop to look at the dead man one more time. "Can we say a prayer first?"

CHAPTER 50

Confession

*S*o," Dolman begins, sitting in the rocking chair with his little cop notebook on one knee. "What were you afraid of?"

I begin my story with coming to Canada without a passport and the snowmobile ride across the ice, but have to backtrack to the Mountain State Federal Bank and stealing all of my husband's money, then go further back to Richard's most recent affair, losing my connection with my daughter, my feeling of failure as a mother, the home-birth death of Robyn and the suicide of my friend Karen that so affected me.

Peter stops taking notes about halfway through and just listens. When I start to cry again, he goes to the bathroom for tissues.

"Let me see if I've got this straight. Your friend kills herself, your OB patient dies, you're in this big mess and want to run away. You take all the money in your joint bank account . . . You leave without telling your almost-grown daughter where you're going, but she hasn't been communicating anyway, and you abandon your asshole of a husband. That doesn't sound so horrible . . . I still don't understand why you were so afraid you couldn't notify someone about a dead body."

"*Well, I didn't have a passport.* Don't you get it?" I stare into his eyes. "I never came through Customs. I came in the night illegally on a snowmobile. If I reported the dead guy, someone like you might start wondering about me and I didn't want to be sent back. I still don't know what's going to happen if I'm returned to the States." I lick my dry lips.

"Also you have to understand, I'm not talking about a little money! There was over thirty thousand in the bank, mostly my husband's, and Richard takes his money very seriously . . . Also, I stole a woman's ID. And I'm wanted for manslaughter, did I mention that? So, I'm a liar, a robber, an identity thief, on the run from the law and an illegal immigrant besides." Dolman closes his notebook.

"Are you going to arrest me tonight? I have to find someone to take care of Tiger."

"Settle down, Sara. I'm not arresting you tonight. I have to think . . . I wish you hadn't told me you saw that body last spring . . . but then you wouldn't have told me the rest of your story.

"I knew something was off when I kept hearing different versions about your dead husband. First he died in Iraq. The next time Afghanistan. I did a background check on Sara Livingston three months ago. There are hundreds of Sara Livingstons in the US and Canada. Not one driver's license photo looked like you."

"I know you have to do what's right, Peter, but please don't send me back. I'd rather go to jail in Canada."

IT'S NOT A good night for me. You'd think I'd be relieved after finally telling someone my secrets, but now I have to worry about what Dolman will do . . .

For a long time, I sit in front of the fire watching the flames with Tiger in my lap. I'm a dead woman washed up on the shores of Seagull Island.

CHAPTER 51

Attack

Three mornings later, I awake with bright light shining in the window. New snow covers everything—the deck, the breakwall, the roof of the gazebo, but not my misdeeds. They are exposed.

Then, *CRASH*. There's the sound of metal on metal. *BOOM, BANG*. More metal and then a deep voice and the roar of an engine.

What the hell? I open the door and am surprised to see two men in bright yellow vests working on the machines that have been parked on the side of my road for weeks.

I used to imagine that I would tie myself to the front porch of Seagull Haven if they tried to bulldoze the cottage down. I would put my life on the line, like those people who chain themselves to redwood trees, but I knew I wouldn't really do it. I'm not that brave.

What if the Nelson siblings forgot to tell the workers that the plans for the casino were scrapped and the men are here to tear down the cottage? Or what if Jake and his siblings are just destroying it out of spite?

I should call Peter Dolman or the Nature Conservancy people. The big demolition machines are moving. I can tell by the sound they're getting closer, ready to attack. I hang up the phone without dialing and run out on the porch in my night-gown. "Wait! Wait! There's been a mistake."

The crane, with its wrecking ball dangling, turns like a bron-tosaurus and the bulldozer, a triceratops, lumbers forward. The bulldozer coughs, stalls and roars up again.

Shit! What else can I do? I run in bare feet out across the snow-covered lawn, waving my arms to stop them before they crash through the picket fence. "Wait! Stop!" I trip, fall and get snow in my mouth, but I push myself up and keep going . . . "Wait. Stop!" I race clear out to the mailbox, where I find . . . that . . .

The men are turning their machines around in Grays Road. They're leaving! The gears of the crane grind, the bulldozer picks up speed; the drivers wave and move off . . . to catch the next ferry to Kingsville.

The Letter

The last few days have been so tumultuous and my anxiety so great about what Dolman will do that I haven't bothered to look in the mailbox, and it's only the honk of the letter carrier as he turns around in the road that reminds me.

Frowning, I trudge out to the drive where Eugene Burke holds something for me. "Do you ever check your mail?" he asks. "I can't get any more in the box and this is a big envelope. Something from Portugal or France. It's got a foreign stamp on it. Might be important." I take what he hands me, thinking it's probably just junk like the rest of it.

"Thanks."

Helen is with him. "Did you hear? A body was found on the

beach on the east side! All decomposed and naked. Gruesome! No one knows who it was. Dolman discovered it while walking the other morning."

"Really . . . Oh my gosh!" I make the right noises even though I know much more about the corpse than she does (and the man wasn't naked!). Back in the house, I dump the pile of mail on the kitchen table and pull out the big envelope that Eugene mentioned. The stamp is from Spain and the address, written in cursive, says only, *Sara, Seagull Haven, Seagull Island, Ontario, Canada.*

At first I'm excited and think it's from Lenny, but there's something about the writing that looks distinctly feminine. With foreboding, I put it aside and go through the rest of the pile.

As I predicted, it's mostly fire starters. Only a few items need to be saved. One is a handmade watercolor invitation from New Day Farm to their "Welcome Winter Party." The second is a postcard from Molly Lou's church, announcing a Christmas service. And the last is a phone bill, overdue tomorrow.

Finally, I get up my courage. You wouldn't think a woman who was fearless enough to charge a bulldozer would be so nervous about opening an envelope, but that's how I am. What I fear is that some stranger is writing to tell me that Lenny was tracked down by whoever he ran from and is dead. With shaking hands I tear back the flap. Inside is a cardboard folder with a note taped to it.

Dear Miss Sara,

Your boyfriend, Mark, say do not worry. He took your letter to Australia and he will now climb the Alps, sail around the Horn of Africa and walk the Great Wall of China. "You should let yourself fly." He tell me to write that. (I think he breaking up with you in a nice way.) He also ask that I post this small card and gift.

Yours Truly,
Señora Campo

Walking to the front window with the note and the cardboard folder held close to my chest, I look out at the drift-covered breakwall. The sky today is as white as the snow. White. White.

Mark is really Lenny; I have no doubt. The man is as clever as a fox and probably enjoys his crazy life. Running from danger. Rescuing distressed maidens who can't get into Canada and hand-carrying mothers' messages to Australia. But where is he now? And will I ever see him again?

Maybe he's working with the British Secret Intelligence Service. Maybe he's a tourist guide in Bulgaria. Maybe he really will climb the Alps. I should be sadder and yet I'm so glad that Lenny's alive that I laugh.

Quickly, I peel back the tape that holds the cardboard folder together but when I see what's inside I drop onto the sofa. It's another note; this one in Jessie's familiar round print and there's a small gift wrapped in white tissue paper. I read the note first.

Mom, I met your friend Lenny. Thank you for reaching out. I know you've been so unhappy since Karen died and since Daddy started screwing around. (Yes, don't look so surprised. How dumb do you think I am? ☺)

Dad told me about the home-birth death. I know how much you love your patients. Don't be scared. It will all be okay.

I also know that you love me and I love you too.

Next spring, I'll be back at the university. You can find me there. Meanwhile, be good to yourself and wear my love close to your heart. Jessie xoxoxooooxoxoxoxo!!

I wipe my tears and read both letters again and then unfold the tissue paper. Inside is a silver chain with a seagull pendant carved out of white shell, the work so delicate you can see each feather and feel the love in the carver's hands.

This is Jonathan Livingston Seagull, I decide, with his wings wide, soaring in and out of the clouds. I don't know if the gift is from Jessie or Lenny but I touch the gull to my lips, kissing them both, first my daughter and then Lenny. Carved on the back of the seagull is one word. *Fly.*

CHAPTER 52

Christmas Bush

I open my eyes to the same white ceiling I've looked at for nearly a year and peek out the window. It's been five days since my confession and there's still no word from Peter Dolman. He's a kind man and he'll do the best he can for me, but he can't control the Ontario Provincial Police or the Canadian Mounties, let alone the FBI. To work off my worries, I get dressed, go outside and saw up the wood that Jed brought me in the fall. If I'm sent back to the US, I can get Chris to haul it to his house.

Back inside, I stare at the invitation to the Welcome Winter Party that still lies on the kitchen table and I don't know what to do about. Ordinarily, I would enjoy going to New Day to see Rainbow and the baby, but I just feel so anxious.

"I'm Queen Anne Boleyn looking down from the Tower of London at the gallows below as she waits to be beheaded," I say to Tiger, referring to the second wife of King Henry the Eighth, but he doesn't get the reference.

Looking out the new kitchen window that Jed generously installed, I stare at the pines covered in light snow. "I know. I'll put up a Christmas tree. That should cheer us up!"

I don't really want to chop down an actual evergreen, but I go out in the yard and cut a few low branches from the big pines with my crosscut saw. When I'm done, I carry them into the living room and stick them in a bucket of water in front of the picture window.

"Not bad," I say to my cat, who's watching me from the top of the sofa. "We used to pay seventy dollars for a spruce off the Christmas tree lot in Torrington."

Soon the branches are decorated with paper chains and the smallest of Wanda and Lowell's seagulls from the mantel. My few packages are wrapped in the only thing I could come up with, the colorful Sunday funny papers from a pile I found in the shed. "That looks quite cheery," I say to my cat. He licks his paws. Just as I'm placing my wrapped gifts under the tree, the phone rings. It's Rainbow.

"Wade's on the way to pick you up for our Welcome Winter Party," she announces as if this has all been arranged. "Dress warm."

There's no way to say no.

Winter Solstice

The bonfire at New Day is not on the beach this time, but in the sheltered farmyard between the main house and outbuildings where there's less wind. Rainbow, dressed in jeans, heavy boots and a long brown wool cloak, hands me her spirit drum and pulls me down on a homemade bench. In a circle, all around the fire pit, are similar benches and there's a view of the lake where the sun will go down.

My friend gives me a one-armed hug and opens her cloak to show me her sleeping baby, wrapped in a sling and held against her body. He's beautiful, with long dark hair and a mouth like cupid.

"He's really growing," she tells me, then stares at me like a cop or a social worker. "You doing okay?"

"Sure," I say, not meaning it. "I'm good as gold."

I'm saved from more questions by the bass drum John holds between his legs. He lets his stick come down hard. *BOOM.* Jed is there too, sitting next to him and he throws me a kiss and I throw it back. *BOOM,* the big drum says again.

Boom. Boom. Boomity, boom boom, answer the smaller percussion instruments. Louder and louder the drums sing . . . louder and faster, until there's a crescendo; then as the sun finally drops into the lake and the last rays turn the clouds red, the drums get quieter and then slower . . . then we stop as if someone with a baton was directing us.

When we enter the kitchen, I see a stack of pottery bowls and a big pot on the stove that smells of garlic and onions, but people aren't sitting down to eat, they're taking off their winter gear and heading for a room at the end of a hall, a carpeted space of about twenty by thirty feet, furnished only with big pillows, no decorations on the walls, no TV or sofa or chairs. There's a fire in the fireplace and votive candles flickering on the mantel. There's also a metal washtub in the center, tipped over to make a table and covered with a red cloth. On it are more candles, the homemade tapered kind, and it occurs to me that the room is more like a temple than a living room.

At last, someone turns off the electric lights and Dian holds up a little brass bell and rings it once. No one says a word, except a three-year-old sitting in his father's lap. "Pretty!" He points to the gleaming multicolored votives on the mantel. When the twenty or so of us are seated, Wade speaks.

"On this winter night, the earth is sleeping under the snow. Our work in the fields is done and we take this time to reflect on our blessings and our hopes for the coming year.

"When the bell comes to you, please ring it once and say your prayer. Then pass it on. If you have nothing to say, just ring the bell and hand it to the next person. We'll continue until there is only ringing, no words." Dian takes her turn first. "Thank you for these friends and the love that surrounds us."

I calculate that there are eight people before me and wonder what I'll say. *What do I have to be thankful for? I'm about to be deported from Canada or jailed for being an illegal immigrant. Alternatively, I might be extradited to West Virginia and arrested for stealing my husband's money and most likely for manslaughter . . . then there's the identity-theft issue, I wonder how many years I could get for that . . .*

"I'm grateful for the trees," says a man wearing coveralls. *Ting* goes the bell.

"I'm grateful for the earth that gives us life," says Wade. *Ting* goes the bell.

"I'm grateful for our new baby," says Rainbow. *Ting.*

"I pray for soldiers everywhere, to heal their broken bodies and souls," says John. *Ting* goes the bell.

"My turn. My turn," says the three-year-old as he grabs the bell from John and rings it over and over, grinning gleefully. *Ting, Ting, Ting. Ting* . . . Finally his father gets it out of his hand. He whispers something in his son's ear and the child wipes the grin off his face. "I'm *tankful* for my toys," he says in his little-boy voice and no one laughs.

I still haven't a clue what I'm going to say and there's only one more person before me, a woman with dyed bright red hair and a nose ring "I am grateful for the sun that gives us life and warmth," she says in a low voice. *Ting.*

She hands me the bell, which is now warm from the many hands that have held it and words come out of me that I had not planned. "I pray for a young woman who lives far away. Bring her peace. Help her be strong." Silence. Then I shake the bell. *Ting.*

Four times the brass bell goes around as both adults and children say thanks for everything from cows to having a bed to sleep in at night and we send blessings to the homeless, to those in jail, to the lonely and forgotten. I pray out loud on my turns for Nita, that she found Lowell in the other world, and for Karen, that whatever wounds she endured have healed. On the final round, I ask for peace for Robyn Layton's family . . .

At last, the bell makes the circle with no prayers, just *Ting— Ting—Ting* . . . Dian stands like a priestess and we all hold hands.

"For the beauty of the earth, for the beauty of the sky." We sing a song that I learned from the nuns at the Little Sisters of the Cross Convent. *"For the love that from our birth, over and around us lies. Spirit of all . . . to thee we raise, this our hymn of grateful praise."*

After the service we eat our simple meal of bean soup and corn bread, then bundle up and go back outside to the bonfire. Jed comes over and gives me a hug. "Glad you came, Sara," he says, and warmth floods through my body.

Wade and John throw more logs on the blaze and the sparks rise into the dark. *Boom,* the drums start again. *Boom. Boomity. Boom.* This time I'm not embarrassed to dance. I dance in the snow in my funny snowmobile suit until I'm out of breath and the spirit of the fire dances with me.

CHAPTER 53

Offering

*E*very day I think of calling Peter Dolman. (*Officer* Dolman, I remind myself. I've put him between a rock and a hard place and we're probably not friends anymore . . .)

How can he proceed with the investigation and leave out the information that the victim has been dead since last April, maybe longer? Once it's revealed that I discovered the body and didn't report it, everything will come out . . . I picture myself in an orange jumpsuit. Maybe I'd better get a tattoo.

When Molly Lou calls to tell me she's going up to the country store to pick up a few things for Christmas and wants to know if I'd like to come, I jump at the chance to get away from my worries.

A few hours later, standing at the checkout, Helen reminds us that there are only two more days until the last ferry of the winter comes in. "Here's a special order form from Foodland in Leamington. Put down anything you'd like for winter and I'll fax it over. You know, stuff you can freeze or keep in your pantry. We'll still be open three days a week and we'll have fresh milk, produce and eggs, but when the ferry stops running we can't afford to fly in canned goods and such from Windsor."

Molly Lou knows the ropes and she's got her list ready. I glance toward the coffee bar, half expecting to see Dolman there and afraid of what he'll say . . . but he's not in the store, so I sit down to make out my list. What should I get? Where will I be this winter? I haven't a clue.

I decide to order canned fruit, canned vegetables, dried beans, oatmeal, oil, flour, sugar and cereal. Nothing frozen. If I'm arrested, I can give the food to Molly Lou.

"Hey," Jed says, strolling through the bread aisle to give me a hug.

"How you doing? Got a minute?"

I look over and see that Molly is still gossiping with Helen. No need to hurry, she doesn't need to get home for an hour.

"Sure."

Jed holds out a flat packet that he's wrapped with red Christmas paper and his blue eyes are as shiny and round as a kid's.

"What is it? A book?"

"You'll never guess."

"Can I open it now?"

"Hmmmmm . . ." He looks at me sideways as if he's going to say no, but I can tell he's excited. "Okay! Sure. I want to see your reaction."

I rip the tissue paper back and discover a book of poetry. *"Light,"* it says on the pale blue cover, "by Jed Williams."

"I only had a hundred copies made for the first run. They'll sell online in Canada, the US and Great Britain. An outfit out of Toronto published it. I wanted you to have one of the first editions. It's signed, in case I ever get famous." He grins.

"Oh, Jed! I'm so happy for you and I can't wait to get home to read it."

"There's more. Look in the back."

Here I find a plain white envelope, no stamp. No address. "What's this?"

"Open it!"

I pull out a copy of an official-looking letter from the Ministry of Health and Long-Term Care and read the first paragraph. "Request for supplemental staff at the Seagull Island Medical Clinic APPROVED. Starting March 1, you are funded for a part-time nursing assistant budgeted at $25,000 per year."

"I don't get it. This letter is addressed to you." I look up at him.

"It's a job offer! I'm offering you a job as an office assistant! I know the money isn't what you're used to as a traveling RN, but you could be my nursing assistant and help me with the women patients. We could be partners. I need you. I really need you, especially for the ladies!"

"Oh, Jed!" I say, trying to look enthusiastic. "I'd be delighted!"

He picks me up, laughing, and swings me around as if it's all been decided.

And I would be delighted if I wasn't pretty sure I'll be behind bars by then.

All Ye Faithful

At one in the afternoon, just as I'm getting my knitting book out, Molly Lou calls. "Hi, Sara. I just wanted to remind you . . . tonight is the Christmas service at the church. We'll be down to get you at six. Little Chris is playing one of the wise men in the pageant and he really wants you to see him."

THE SEAGULL ISLAND Chapel, on the north end of the island between the country store and the cemetery, is an old white wooden building with a little steeple, probably built in the 1920s. There are four stained-glass windows on each side, two rows of gleaming oak pews and a simple oak cross at the front. On the dais is a manger scene complete with straw, a bed for Baby Jesus and farm animals the children have constructed out of cardboard boxes. I sit with Molly and Chris who are all dressed up in church clothes, but I'm just wearing my black knit pants and the red sweater I got at the fall yard sale.

Reverend Easton, the part-time clergyman who was at Nita's funeral, begins with a simple invocation that we read aloud from the program.

> *"God, help us remember that the birth*
> *of Jesus Christ is the birth of hope.*
> *Let us sing with the angels, worship with the shepherds*
> *And give love to each other as if we*
> *were the three wise men.*
> *Amen."*

"There will be no sermon this evening," the pastor says, "because tonight is about the children." Then we open our hymnals to begin the first carol. *"Oh come, all ye faithful. Joyful and triumphant . . ."*

I look around as we sing. There's Terry in her wheelchair up front with Austin Aubrey and his wife, Elsa. There's Helen Burke with her husband, Eugene, and Nell Ambroy, the pilot/ mayor who I've now come to admire after seeing her in action on the night of the boating accident. Across the aisle are the New Day folk, easy to spot with their unique and colorful outfits. Jed is sitting with John just in front of us and there are thirty or so others who I recognize, but don't know by name.

Next, the pianist begins "What Child Is This?" one of my favorites and a little choir steps forward. It's Rainbow, Wade and Dian; John, Jed, Elsa and Aubrey; Molly Lou and Chris. *"What child is this, who, laid to rest On Mary's lap is sleeping?"* they sing, and I get tears in my eyes.

All heads turn as the children march in, led by Little Chris, wearing his homemade king's outfit (a bathrobe and a paper crown he made himself). He's carrying a chest of frankincense, clearly constructed out of two egg cartons and sprayed gold, and he grins as he passes.

The preacher reads the familiar words from the bible, while the children act out the scene.

"And it came to pass in those days, that there went out a decree from Caesar Augustus that all the world should be taxed . . ."

Halfway through the reading, I feel my neck burn and am certain that Peter Dolman is somewhere in back, but I can't turn around.

Then the service ends with the lighting of candles, done by two little girls dressed as angels, while Jed plays his guitar and the children sing, *"This little light of mine. I'm gonna let it shine. This little light of mine, I'm gonna let it shine!"* I think of Nita and her colorful beach glass decorations with the sunlight shining through. How she would love this!

It's snowing outside as we leave, big soft flakes that coat our clothes and tickle our noses and once again I scan the crowd. No Dolman.

CHAPTER 54

Night Call

*O*nce home, I pull on my flannel nightgown, light some candles and look at the gifts under my decorated pine bush. I wish I had some Christmas lights, but there's no way to get them.

Under the branches are the presents I bought at the Fibre Guild for Molly Lou, Rainbow, Jed and John. I even got a pair of mittens for Dolman, but I never thought of Big Chris and Little Chris and there's no way to go back to the shop now.

After going to church, I felt inspired. Little Chris was so cute in his king costume. I bought mittens for Peter, but I've put him between a rock and a hard place, so we probably aren't friends anymore. I could change things around, give the mittens I purchased for Dolman to Big Chris, but what would I have for a seven-year-old boy?

I walk from room to room, looking for ideas and stop in the kitchen where I discover a big unopened bag of M&M's I bought for myself at Burke's Country Store. A kid would like that! Just then, I hear an auto about a mile away. Funny, how sensitive I've become to that low-pitched hum, especially at night.

Though supposedly the Nelsons are no longer a threat, out of habit I run from room to room switching off lights. The sound of the motor gets louder. Already, from the kitchen window, I can see headlights between the bare trees. *Who would be coming down the road at this time of night?*

Just in case I have to escape, I step into my boots and put my parka on over my flannel nightgown. Then I continue my vigil at the window. I have no doubt the driver knows where he's going. When the headlights turn into my drive, I jump back. The doors! Because the Nelsons seemed out of the picture, I've let my guard down and haven't locked up!

Quickly I turn the latch on the front door, then run to the back and lock that one too. As I return to the kitchen, I seize Lloyd's heavy walking stick. Then from the counter, I grab a butcher knife and crouch in the corner next to the fridge. There are heavy footsteps on the front porch.

"Sara!" a man's voice calls. "Sara! I know you're in there."

Conundrum

I let out my air. It's Dolman. Though I'm apprehensive about talking to the cop, it's not like he's going to assault me . . . *(just ruin my life).*

"Coming!" I put the knife away, feeling foolish, turn the kitchen overhead back on and open the door. Dolman stands in his winter cop parka, snow on his hair, holding a two-inch-thick folder. He also has a bottle of apple wine under his arm, probably to sweeten the bad news.

"Going somewhere?" He grins, indicating my outfit, and I realize how silly I must look holding a walking stick like a club and wearing a white flannel nightgown, a parka and untied hiking boots.

"I heard the car. I was scared. I thought I might have to run for it."

Dolman raises his eyebrows, probably imagining me running like a fox through the snowy woods to Molly Lou's house.

"Sorry. I probably should have called." He peels off his coat and hat, throws them on a kitchen chair, then gets out two wineglasses. (He's only been in my kitchen twice, but he moves around as if he knows the place.)

"Can we talk?" he asks.

I stare at the file folder. "Is that all about me or about the dead man?"

"Both."

I take off my coat and wrap up in the flying-goose quilt. "I've been waiting to hear what you'd have to say. Dreading it, really. Let's sit by the fire."

Might as well take this like a grown-up, I think. *Face the firing squad.* While Peter pours us each a glass of wine, I throw a log in the fire and stir up the coals. *I just hope I don't start crying again.*

"Sorry this took so long. I had a lot to think about and research to do, and then I had to deal with the provincial police and the Mounties. Let's start with the dead guy.

"When I left you, I felt that discovering who the man on the beach was would hinge on *when* he had died. He could have been a fisherman in a boating accident from anywhere on the lake or a victim of homicide. I felt that his body appearing on Gull Point *last April* would be critical for solving the puzzle, but how could I put that in my report without involving you?

"Unsure what to do, I gave myself until the next morning to figure that out. Around three I woke up and it came to me that *where* and *when* the victim was found on Seagull Island weren't as important as I first thought. The approximate date of the man's death could actually be determined by the forensic examination. And the *place* he was found wasn't that significant either . . . He could have died on either side of Lake Erie. Most likely he didn't die on Seagull Island or I would have heard gossip about a missing person, a fight . . . or something. Word gets around."

I look down at my clenched white hands and open and close them.

"So, with an almost clear conscience, I wrote up my report and called Windsor to tell them I'd just found a dead man, while walking *solo* on the beach that morning."

"Oh, Peter! Thank you." I jump up to give him a hug but stop myself. "I hope you don't get in trouble. I'd feel terrible . . ."

He brushes my concerns aside. "So that's where we stand with the dead man. An autopsy is scheduled and, after we find out *when he died and what he died from,* the Mounties will run an international computer search to see if we can find out *who he is and where he came from* . . .

"Now about you . . ." He opens the manila file and the light in my heart grows dim.

Good News or Bad

"Do you want the good news first, or the bad?"

"The good, I guess. *Is* there some good news?"

"Well, I spent a lot of time at a library in Windsor that has a database of all the newspapers in English and also did some research on the computer at the office. Here's what I found, working from Lorain, Ohio, back to Torrington, West Virginia." He opens the file.

"First of all, the real Sara Livingston never reported her driver's license as stolen. Seems crazy, but she just said she lost it and applied for a new one." He hands me a copy of an Ohio DMV application dated March 1 . . . "There's also no alert about a stolen nursing license on the Ohio Board of Nursing website. It's like the theft never happened."

"Most nurses don't carry their licenses on them," I interrupt. "Maybe she didn't notice it was gone. To be honest, I don't even know where mine is or my social security card either."

"So, back to your other legal problems. I checked the Torrington paper online and Clara Perry, certified nurse-midwife, was reported missing back in February. There was a ten-thousand-dollar reward for information leading to her return put up by Richard Perry, PhD. That your husband?" (I nod, wondering where Richard would get that kind of money since I thought I cleaned him out . . . He must have had a secret stash at another bank. The rat!)

"You were in the headlines for quite a while and so was the death of the woman at the home birth. Of course you were implicated and the hospital made a strong statement that you'd been instructed not to go to home births and that you were immediately dismissed pending your trial."

"My trial?"

"Yeah, you were right about that." He looks straight at me. "You were charged with manslaughter for leaving the delivery, but that charge has been dropped."

Here he spreads out a series of articles from the *Torrington Times,* all from last spring and summer. There's a photo of me that was used on our practice's brochure. LOCAL MIDWIFE CHARGED WITH MANSLAUGHTER AND MEDICAL NEGLIGENCE, the headline screams.

"You had long dark hair then, but I'd still recognize you."

"There's nothing about the missing money?" I ask. "Richard didn't report it? That's not like him."

"I couldn't find anything. Maybe his lawyer advised him to publicly ignore it, so it didn't seem like he was more worried about the cash than getting his wife back."

"The manslaughter charge was dropped?"

"Yeah, look here . . ." He leans down and digs in the folder for copies of another two articles, headlined HOME-BIRTH MOTHER DIES OF RARE OB COMPLICATION and MIDWIFE CLEARED OF MANSLAUGHTER CHARGES.

"Can I read these? It will take a minute." Peter Dolman sits next to me so we can read together and I feel his warmth where our shoulders touch. He's wearing a green V-neck sweater with no T-shirt underneath, hasn't shaved for two days and smells like a guy who's been working in the sun . . . but not in a bad way.

I scan the articles and then read them again. *Robyn Layton died of an amniotic fluid embolism as I suspected . . .* The medical examiner concluded his report with . . . "The patient could have died from this unpredictable OB complication just as well in the hospital. Survival is rare, and if women do survive, most of the time they are brain damaged. The death was an unfortunate tragedy and not medical negligence."

I sit back, stunned. "So, I'm in the clear? I could go back to West Virginia if I wanted to?"

"Do you want to? Do you want to go home?" Peter surprises me by taking my hand and looking into my eyes for so long I have to look away. I take a deep breath, trying to picture my return to Torrington.

Even though I've been exonerated, the hospital will refuse to take me back and probably no one else will hire me after being in the headlines for the home-birth death. . . . Here on Seagull

Island there is deep snow and peace, a lonely peace maybe, but clean and sweet.

"No . . . I don't want to go back. West Virginia isn't home. Clara Perry doesn't exist anymore and also I'd have to go through a bitter divorce."

"Oh yeah," Peter says, digging around in the file again and pulling out a few announcements in the classifieds. "You won't have to mess around with that. Apparently, in the US, there's something called a three-step divorce, a procedure for filing with the courts if your spouse goes missing. You just list all that you've done to find him or her, like hire a private detective and advertise in the newspaper with a special code. You wait a few months and if there's no response, the state declares you're divorced. Richard Perry officially divorced you months ago. I found the court record. You're a free woman."

A free woman. We drink another glass of wine and slip lower on the sofa, our sock feet on top of the coffee table. Dolman surprises me by patting my knee through my flannel nightgown and I don't move away.

"So this is the *good news,* right?" I question. "What's the bad news?"

"Well, you're still in Canada under a false name and you don't have a passport. You're here illegally, a woman without a country."

"Oh . . . that!" I laugh.

CHAPTER 55

Armor

*M*aybe it's the wine. Alcohol has always had a strong effect on me, but I slip lower until my head is on Peter's lap and he's touching my hair. That's when I come undone. I'm like Tiger, I love to be petted and it's so long since anyone has petted me.

With his tenderness, Peter removes the armor I've been wearing for almost a year, for more than that really. Then he removes my flannel nightgown and takes off his own things. We are standing naked in front of the fire, except for his turquoise eagle ring and my necklace. I kiss his ring. He kisses my carved seagull.

"It's from Lenny Knight," I say. "He had it sent from overseas." (I don't say from where and I don't mention my daughter.)

"I'm glad he got out of the country. He'd been working with the Mounties for years, trying to untangle how heroin is getting into Ontario. He's one of the good guys." That's all we say about Lenny. *Lenny is one of the good guys and he's still alive, maybe in Switzerland, climbing the Alps.*

Peter shifts the coffee table across the room and spreads the green-and-white quilt on the rug.

Like animals meeting in the woods, we greet each other's naked bodies. We curl and uncurl around each other. We smell each other and lick each other. We warm each other in the fire-light and when it is over, we lie quiet and sweating.

"You know," I think out loud. "I grew up in a time when women were supposed to be the hero of their own story, but I'm not a hero. Running away was the act of a coward." Peter doesn't comment, but rolls over and wraps us in the quilt, face-to-face, as if we were in a big burrito, and I snuggle up against him.

"Sometimes letting someone help you can be a gift to both," he says, looking in my eyes.

We lie there like that, quiet for a long time, listening to the wind outside and the crackling of the logs on the fire. I can feel both of our hearts beating and Peter's hand between my legs again.

Mirror, Mirror

In the stillest part of the deep night, Peter's cell whistles once and he reaches over to the sofa, finds it and looks at a text. "Gotta go," he whispers, getting off the floor and tucking the quilt back around me. "Some fool is stuck in the snow out at Light House Park. Now why would you go out there this time of night?" He stirs up the fire and pulls on his sweater and pants.

"I hope I didn't take advantage of you."

"Maybe I took advantage of you!" I respond.

IN THE MORNING, I stare at myself in the bathroom mirror, splash cold water on my face and can't decide if I look beautiful or a mess. My short hair is sticking up and my cheeks are pink from rubbing against Peter's two-day-old beard.

Clara Perry has been cleared of the manslaughter charges, I think, looking at my reflection, but I'm not Clara Perry anymore.

If I ever become a Canadian, I'll change my name. I want to be *Sara Livingston. I like being Sara Livingston.* Peter said he found hundreds of females with that name in the US and Canada. One more won't matter.

"Okay, that's settled," I tell Tiger who is meowing around my feet for his breakfast. Then I dress, fill his bowl, place the coffee table back where it goes and hide the incriminating file about me in a dresser drawer.

"Might as well get back to reality," I say out loud to my cat, who has spent the whole night shut up in the bedroom.

The rumpled green-and-white flying-goose quilt is still on the floor. I pick it up, shake out the wrinkles then press the cool cloth to my face. Peter is gone but his smell is still here.

All day it snows and I work on my knitting. It's easy, I find, to make a scarf even if you don't know what you're doing. I have thick homespun yarn and big needles. Following the directions, I repeat the same stitch over and over—twelve stitches across, then twelve back. It's called the popcorn stitch and the scarf is already a foot long. I'm making it for Peter.

Knitting the scarf makes me feel close to him and I keep rubbing my face in the softness, the way I rub my face in Tiger's fur. I can't believe I'm dating a cop! Are we dating? Or was last night just a fling, something to be forgotten, locked in a dark closet and never mentioned again?

Outside the picture window the gentle snow has turned harsh. Big wet flakes are now blowing hard and I can hear waves crashing up against the breakwall. The fire crackles. The clock on the mantel ticks.

ALL THE NEXT day it snows, and I wonder about my relationship with Peter. Is it odd he hasn't called? Does he regret getting involved with a crazy woman? Or is he just busy pulling people out of the snow?

To keep from thinking about it, I knit and knit until the scarf is four feet long. But that's not long enough. Outside the world whirls in white, and when I go out on the porch for more wood, I see a large white owl sitting on a low branch of the cottonwood tree. It stares at me with round golden eyes. I stare back.

I remember that even though snowy owls are Arctic birds, the last few years, people have seen them as far south as West Virginia. Richard said it has something to do with climate change and not enough food, or maybe it's too much food, I forget.

"You look kind of hungry, bud. I'd like to feed you, but I don't know what snowy owls eat, probably mice and lemmings, but there are no lemmings here. I wonder if you'd like some salami? Worth a try!"

Back in the cottage, I dump my load of wood near the fireplace, return through the kitchen and slip out on the porch silently with three pieces of lunchmeat. I brush the snow away and lay the circles of salami on the porch rail, an offering to one of Richard's Arctic kin. "Let's see if you like that!" I say to the owl. "If you don't, I'm sure Tiger will."

Happy to have done a good deed, I retreat to the bathroom where I can watch through the window. At first nothing happens, but then the owl swivels his head and looks around.

With two flaps of his huge white wings he floats to the rail. With three bites, the salami is gone. He sits for a minute, enjoying his meal, swivels his head again, looking right at me through the window glass and silently flaps away.

Stunned, I sit down on the toilet. I was five feet from a snowy owl in broad daylight! A rare visitor from the north . . .

SNOWY OWL
One of the largest owls
Almost all white, usually nocturnal
Range: Rare in the US, lives mostly in northern Canada
and the Arctic
Diet: Small mammals
Voice: A deep muffled hooooo
Size: 23 inches
Wingspan: 4 feet 4 inches!

Keeper of Colors

"You coming to the Christmas party?" Molly asks on the phone without even saying hello.

"Tonight? I forgot about it."

"*You forgot it's Christmas Eve?*" she says with scorn. "How does that happen?"

"Molly," I say as gently as I can. "When a person has no family, holidays don't mean that much."

"Sorry," she says by way of apology. "Anyway, you have us. We'll pick you up at six."

Five minutes later the phone rings again and I lay down my knitting . . . "Just wanted to apologize if I was insensitive about Christmas," she starts out where we left off. "You'll come over on Christmas Day tomorrow and eat with us, won't you?"

"Sure. I guess. Thanks a lot." We hang up.

Another five minutes and she's on the line again. "The last ferry comes in with our winter supplies about seven tonight, Chris will be on the ferry and pick yours up along with ours. And wear something nice. People dress up for this party."

"Yes, Molly. Now I have to get back to work."

Work? I think. *What work? I'm not a writer. I'm not a midwife. What am I?* I stare out the window. Outside the water is blue, but all along the shore whitecaps slash the beach and all along the beach ice is piled up like a wall. Another storm is coming in, that's for sure.

"What am I?" I ask myself again.

Keeper of the Colors, I think. Nita told me I would be the keeper of the green trees, the yellow sunflowers, the blue waters, the red fire, the white seagulls, the brown earth, the purple sky at sunset.

AN HOUR LATER, the scarf is five feet long, but still not long enough. Peter must be six feet or taller. Tiger bats the ball of yarn on the floor below the rocking chair, and I know what he's thinking. *Oh, that looks fun!* He'd like to pounce on the ball and tangle it up. "No you don't!" I put the red yarn in the basket, before he gets his claws into it.

The wool scarf is soft, and though the stitches are uneven, each one is made with love. *Love,* I think. This surprises me. Do I *love* Peter Dolman?

Do I even know what love means? I love my daughter . . . in my secret mother heart, but the love and the pain are locked away together . . . I used to love Richard, but that's gone with the wind.

I remember how I felt when wrapped in the quilt with Peter, how our hearts beat together, and I press my cheek to the unfinished scarf.

At five-thirty, I realize the scarf still isn't quite finished, but unless things are really awkward with him at the party, I'll at least show it to him . . . I put it back in the basket with the red bow on the handle and cover it with one of Mrs. Nelson's clean white dish towels. Then I take my presents from under my Christmas bush, put them in a plastic garbage bag along with my flats and try to think what I can wear for the party. Something warm, for sure, but Molly Lou said to dress up! What do I have?

Finally, I remember the long white skirt with the ruffle I bought at the yard sale months ago. It's just homespun cotton, but I can wear it with the white silk thermal long johns underneath and the white silk thermal V-neck on top. When I'm dressed, I drop Lenny's necklace back over my head, giving the seagull a kiss, and look in the mirror. *Perfect,* says a voice in my head. It's Karen.

Ten minutes later, Molly honks out front and I pull on my boots and my parka (completely ruining the effect of my elegant ensemble!). Then I grab my bag of gifts and head for the car. Stepping outside in the gale, my skirt lifts up like a parachute.

"Hi, Santa," Molly greets me, indicating my big sack of gifts.

"Where's Chris?" I ask.

"I'm here!" says the little boy from the back.

"I meant Big Chris." I throw him a smile.

"I'm big!"

"Quiet, honey," says Molly. "Remember? Chris went over on the ferry with most of the men to bring back the winter supplies. It's kind of a tradition. Earl Prentiss at the Cider Mill provides the hard cider. It's the only time the captain allows liquor onboard."

We both look at the waves splashing over Sunrise Road as we drive slowly over the frozen spray. It's almost as rough as the night of the sailboat rescue.

"The weather's turning bad." Molly passes the pub and goes down to the ferry dock. She peers at the slabs of white that are churning around in the water and states the obvious. "Ice."

"You think they'll really come?" I ask. "The breakers look bad, almost ten feet again."

"Yeah, they'll come. It's Christmas and the captain of the ferry is an island man. They'll come." The surf and ice crash against the cement piers, sounding like drums. *Boom . . . Boom . . . Boom.*

I squeeze Molly's arm. I can see why she's anxious. She lost both her dad and her brother to the dark inland sea.

CHAPTER 56

Big Waves and Wind

A few minutes later when we enter the Black Sheep Pub, I see that they've set up an eight-foot lighted Christmas tree next to the piano and there are already presents on the red felt skirt below. Since I don't know the customs, I leave my gifts against the wall in my St. Nicholas bag.

Music's playing on the stereo—*Hark the herald angels sing, Glory to the newborn king*—and the room smells of roast lamb and biscuits, baked apples and pumpkin pie. Always the life of the party, Terry is reading the story *How the Grinch Stole Christmas* to the children and Little Chris runs right over to join them.

Without hesitation, Molly Lou puts on an apron and hurries through the wide doors that lead to the kitchen. I stop to take off my coat and boots and slip into my flats. There are mostly just women present, with the exception of a few of the older men and kids. Lots of kids . . .

Helen's cell phone rings and she waves for everyone in the kitchen to be quiet. I watch her face. She's biting her upper lip, not a good sign. When she gets off, she tries to sound cheerful, but fear shows in her eyes.

All the good-natured joking stops and Helen says in a low voice, "That was Dolman. The men on the ferry will be a little late. They're hitting some weather." *Hitting some weather* is clearly an island euphemism for *big waves and wind* . . .

I picture the little white ferry loaded heavy with the island men and their winter supplies, tossed up and down by the huge dark water and battered by ice floes, and I remember what Molly Lou said about shipwrecks. Lake Erie is shallower than the other Great Lakes . . . There are more hidden reefs . . . And the waves get as big as those on the ocean.

To busy myself, I take out my knitting. Terry rolls over in her electric chair, wearing a long black velvet dress. She brings me a glass of cold cider. "Nice outfit," she says, indicating the white skirt, white V-neck tee and the white seagull pendant. "You look like a snowflake." She moves closer and inspects my unfinished scarf.

"Thanks for sending Big Chris over with his front-end loader to get rid of the ice behind my house. That was a welcome surprise."

"It was nothing." I drop a stitch and have to go back. (It's a lot harder to knit when someone's talking to you.)

"Yeah, but he said you insisted on paying him," Terry says, and I finally put down my needles.

"I was happy to do it. Consider it a Christmas present or you can give me free knitting lessons." (This is said lightly, but how do I know I'll even be living in Canada for another season? I may still be deported. Dolman can't fix everything.)

At that moment, there are footsteps on the porch and everyone looks toward the door, hoping it's the men from the ferry, but it's the women and the kids from the commune, carrying hot dishes and plates. Rainbow waves and sends me a flying kiss as she takes off her long woolen cloak and unwraps her baby, but when she hears from the women in the kitchen that the boat is in trouble her expression changes. Like the other women, she listens to the wind, imagines the huge waves battering the little white ferry and says a silent prayer.

"Say, where's Austin Aubrey?" one of the cottagers asks in a voice that bounces around the quiet pub like a ping-pong ball. He apparently doesn't know about the little ferry out on the raging water. "Where's the cop? Are they boycotting this shindig?"

"No," Nell Ambroy explains. "The island men went on the boat to bring back our winter supplies. They'll be here." I look at my watch. It's already eight.

Finally, I can stand it no longer. No one is eating. No one's talking or opening presents. I put the unfinished scarf back in my basket and, before I lose my nerve, start tapping on my cider glass as if I have an important announcement.

Next, I jump up and yell into the crowd. "Okay, everyone! Let's get this party rolling! The island men are probably having a blast out on the lake, drinking hard cider and telling stories of worse storms than this. We don't want them to come in and find us sitting around like we're at a wake.

"Come here, Little Chris." I lift him up on a chair. "You can help me lead some songs. Let's start with 'This Little Light of Mine' . . . I bet everyone knows it!"

"This little light of mine!" the seven-year-old begins bravely in his high angelic voice. *"I'm gonna let it shine . . ."*

At first the voices are tentative, but as Elsa and Rainbow join me everyone comes in. I walk around the room waving my arms like the director of a high school choir. (I'm a midwife for God's sake, good at sitting on my hands, but also good at ordering people around when the going gets rough.)

We follow "This Little Light of Mine" with "Jingle Bells." (Anything to drive the worry away.)

"How about 'It Came Upon a Midnight Clear'?" Elsa suggests, but this is a mistake. When the voices get softer, we can hear the surf and chunks of ice pounding the breakwall.

"Mother of God!" someone says, imagining the little ferry out on the water . . . and the singing stops.

It's then that we notice, under the wind, what sounds like someone crying. Molly Lou grabs her coat and runs outside, followed by everyone who can squeeze through the door.

Standing on the porch, we can hear the wail clearly now, but it's not someone sobbing. It's the sound of a bagpipe as the bellows fill. A quarter mile away on the icy road, lanterns and flashlights are coming this way, and in the distance there's the shadow of the ferry, already secured to the dock.

As the parade of men get closer, they break out in a familiar Scottish marching song. *"Hark when the night is falling. Hear! Hear! The pipes are calling!"* Austin Aubrey is leading the group, playing his bagpipe, but there's a second bagpipe too. With surprise, I recognize three of the musicians from Poor Angus. One plays the flute. One plays the other bagpipe. One carries a guitar case. Wade and John are beating the New Day drums. *"Hear! Hear! The pipes are calling!"*

When the men get to the steps, we all back away to let them into the warmth. Molly throws her arms around Big Chris. Elsa helps Aubrey off with his coat. John and Wade and all the other fellows from the commune are loud and jolly.

Peter Dolman enters last, his face serious and red from the cold, the flaps on his cop hat fastened under his chin. *The shepherd bringing his flock home,* I think, and I catch his eye, but there are a dozen people between us.

Gift

*H*aving done my part to jolly things up, I retire to the corner as far away from the commotion as I can get and watch as the band sets up by the piano and everyone is served their hot food.

The musicians tune their instruments and soon music floats over the crowd of happy faces. Quickly the women clear the plates and wash the dishes and then the men push back the tables.

Before the dancing begins, I hurry around the room, handing out my few gifts. Jed and John put on their matching knit beanies from the Fibre Guild's shop. Then they give each other a big smooch right in front of everyone.

Big Chris unwraps his mittens, holds up his hands and makes them dance like puppets. Molly loves her new shawl. Little Chris laughs with joy when he sees his big bag of M&M's and Rainbow, with a smile that illuminates the room, wraps up her baby in her soft handwoven blue wool baby blanket.

"Thank you," she whispers, looking into my eyes. "Thank you." And I know she means more than thanks for the blanket.

"Happy Christmas, Sara!" "Merry Christmas, Sara!" Everyone greets me with hugs as I move around the room.

Then the music starts up. It's a waltz with musicians from Poor Angus on the piano and fiddle, so sweet and pure that tears come to my eyes and no wonder! I'm on an emotional ledge. What a night! The storm, the worry about the men on the ferry . . .

I stare across the room. Molly and Big Chris are waltzing like two dancing bears. Elsa and Austin are swooping around as gracefully as if they've taken ballroom dancing lessons and Kristie, the cute waitress, is with Santiago, the young nephew from Mexico. Then a hand touches my back.

"Dance?" asks Dolman.

When the tune ends, I tell Peter I have a present for him. "I have a gift for you too. Let's go in the back." He leads me into a dim pantry.

First I give him his gift. "I've been working on it for a couple of days," I say as I place the unfinished red scarf around his neck.

"I didn't know you could knit."

"Well, I just learned. But there's probably a lot you don't know about me!"

"I know more than I did a week ago . . . I have a present for you too." He pulls out a white envelope and a small carved wooden box that he must have made in his woodshop.

"Which one first?"

"The card, I guess."

When I open the Christmas card, it says only *Happy Holidays, from Peter,* but I also discover two official-looking Canadian immigration forms and a copy of Clara Perry's birth certificate tucked inside. I look at the official certificate first. "How did you get this?"

"Cops have their ways. You'll need it to get a new passport and real ID."

Then I turn to the forms. One is an application for a visa if you're employed in Canada. The other is about becoming a citizen by marrying a Canadian.

"Is this for the job with Jed at the clinic?" I ask, holding up the first form. "Does Jed know about everything?"

"Not everything. Just that you're here without a passport and you might want to stay. He got the funding for a nursing assistant before he even knew about your problem."

I go back to the second form, the one about marriage, not sure what it means, but afraid to ask.

"Open the other present now," Peter orders.

"Okay." I admire the delicate carving of a perfect snowflake on the lid of the little wooden box and smile. "You made this for me?"

Peter nods. "Go ahead."

The box is sealed with Scotch tape and it takes me a minute to peel it off. "Go ahead," he says again, impatiently.

"Okay. Okay." I remove the top of the box, which is perfectly fitted, and find Dolman's silver-and-turquoise ring. When I look at him, the smile is gone. He takes my left hand and slips the ring onto my index finger, the only one it will stay on.

"Two possible solutions to your remaining on Seagull Island," Peter explains, kissing my palm and then my wrist. "You're a free woman. Will you stay with me, Sara?" I let go and kiss his face and his mouth and his eyes.

"Yes!" I laugh. (It's been that kind of crazy night. Why not throw caution to the wind?)

We stand in the dark pantry holding each other. Outside the snow is still blowing. There will be no incoming ferry for five months and no airplanes until the storm wears itself out and the runway is cleared. Seagull Island is cut off from everything.

The musicians start a new song, one I've heard before. I put the little box and the envelope in the pocket of my long white skirt, precious gifts, but continue to wear the ring. Out on the dance floor with Peter again, I no longer think about my feet.

RICHARD AND I never danced. He wasn't much for social engagements unless they had something to do with the biology department or saving the planet, but Richard is gone. I don't even need to make fun of him anymore or refer to him with bitterness. *Someone has to save the polar bears!* And that thought makes me laugh. *Let him be.*

The same with my good friend Karen and my patient Robyn . . . Their deaths weren't my fault. I don't have to be weighed down with them anymore. The two are at peace in the place where dreams live. *Let them be.*

Outside the wind screams, but it cannot get us. Our hearts are fiercer and we are together in this big warm room. The music rises . . . All around people are dancing, even Terry in her electric chair, spinning with Little Chris in her lap.

My feet hardly touch the floor and I throw my head back, understanding for the first time the folksinger's words. *Lead me to the waterside, Lead me to the morning light, Fill me with a sun so bright, It kills away the darkness of my night.*

As we circle the room, it's not Peter's lead that I follow, but my own. The chains that have bound me to fear and grief fall away . . . and like a white swan, I soar.

The Beginning